The Last Dance of Low Seward

Vagrant Mystery Book 2

Brad Grusnick

Strange Scribe

Book Cover Design by Melissa Williams Design

KDP PRINT ISBN-13: 978-0692406366
INGRAM ISBN-13: 978-1732601802

Watch for more at strangescribe.com

For my parents. Sorry it's so gross.

1

Cold January rain spit into Ray's straining face. A mix of sweat and dirt dripped from his greasy hair. Polluted water filled the deep lines in his weathered skin as he cursed into the offending sky. It trickled out of the gloom in a misting stream, as though the clouds were trying to pass a kidney stone and piss was spraying out around the obstruction.

Soaked through, wishing to pass into the hereafter, the details of Ray's diet from the past day ran through his head. A tight fist squeezed his intestines as potential culinary culprits flashed across his memory.

He was usually careful about his pickings before he indulged in a meal. Fast food was the choice of most homeless people. The constant piles of garbage and open dumpsters made it a simple solution for a grumbling stomach. But Ray couldn't eat that crap anymore.

A couple of years ago, he'd opened a door to a world he shouldn't have and got a bullet in his guts for the trouble. He thought having his digestive system blown to bits would've kept him from living a normal life, but his scar tissue had healed enough he didn't even limp when he walked. The biggest challenge became what he ate. Processed junk didn't agree with him and he couldn't exactly do his shopping in the organic section of Whole Foods. Good thing Ray Cobb was a resourceful guy.

The restaurants of celebrity chefs had grown in number as more cooking challenge shows were splayed across the cable networks. A couple choice visits to the public library showed him who the best restaurateurs were; who used the best ingredients, who didn't favor art over portion size, and most important, which chefs were perfectionists. High-end restaurants focused on small, flavorful portions, leaving the dumpsters filled with nothing more than carrot peelings and shrimp husks. However, perfectionist chefs would rather have their eyelids branded shut than serve anything that didn't meet their exacting standards. The result was a lot of dumped plates of great food. Delicious to the palates of the unrefined, garbage to the chef who detected a dash too much fennel.

These goodies were kept under tight security, the dumpsters locked to prevent wandering street scroungers from digging through the upscale leavings. Another short visit to the library taught Ray how to make a simple locksmith's bump key. A less intelligent guy would take this information and delve straight into a life of crime, then earn a stint in county lockup after a botched attempt at breaking and entering, but Ray had spent enough time in holding cells to know he didn't want to upgrade to an orange jumpsuit.

As far as he knew, there wasn't a garbage theft division of the LAPD. There were plenty of people arrested for trying to break into scrap yards, but not too many people busted for breaking the lock off a dumpster. Besides, Ray never damaged the lock. He just opened it, took what he needed, and sealed it back up, allowing him multiple hits on the same location with no one the wiser. Unfortunately, Ray must have made the mistake of digging up the wrong plate of grilled quail with plum char-siu.

And the problems kept piling on. Aside from the pissing rain and the knots in his stomach, Kelvin the Chatter had latched onto him.

Fucking Kelvin.

Plenty of homeless wandered the streets talking to themselves, having conversations with no one. Angry rants, hair pulling, heads beaten raw against brick walls—these were the people who scared the normal citizenry, prompting city council meetings about cleaning up the streets. But as long as ranters were engaged in an uninterrupted debate with an imaginary friend, they were content in their own little worlds.

Chatters were a different breed. They lacked the common courtesy to keep their conversations private. Lampreys of the homeless world.

"So you see, that's why... that's why, man, you gotta avoid anybody with contact lenses. That's where they put the cameras. Get off the grid to avoid them man, cuz—"

"Get the fuck away from me," Ray strained.

Ray had screamed, thrown stones, and even beaten Kelvin with a fallen branch. Every attempt to get rid of the dirty son of a bitch had failed. When he thought Kelvin was gone for good, a needle of pain would stab at him and he'd have to stop. And when he stopped, it was always long enough for Kelvin to either build up enough courage to approach him again, or forget Ray was the man who'd beat him with sticks.

Another powerful ripple sent an aftershock through his abdomen and Ray doubled over.

"No, you gotta listen, man, this shit here is important, lemme tell you—"

Ray sprang from his squat, rage taking over. He pressed his elbow down onto The Chatter's sternum, hoping he could snap one of his ribs and puncture one of his lungs, silencing the stream of bullshit. The Chatter flailed beneath him, eyes bulged, face red.

"Shut. The. Fuck. U—"

Ray's bowels trumpeted, filling his pants with warm wet-ness.

"Ah, fuck me," Ray cursed to himself.

He let go of The Chatter's neck and rolled off of him. Shit-ting his pants had sobered Ray out of his fury and relieved much of the tension in his GI tract.

He sat in his own filth and smiled with strange gratitude as he looked at the limp body beside him. He checked Kelvin's pulse and sighed in relief when he found a heartbeat, shallow but present. Ray had killed before, but had never murdered anybody. He wasn't about to start a life of homicide because some asshole wouldn't shut up.

Ray kicked his shoes off, along with his soiled pants and underwear, using the cleanest parts to wipe away the residue dripping into his socks. He tossed his dungarees into the bushes and yanked off Kelvin's pants from the ankles. Stealing a man's pants went against Ray's code of ethics, but the chatty fuck had caused him to lose control of his temper and his sphincter. Ray considered it a win he hadn't choked the life out of the talkative bastard.

He slipped on his victim's pants and found them too tight to button. He didn't mind. His gut needed as much room as he could give it.

The Chatter was beginning to groan back to life as Ray made his way down the hill through the trees. He transferred his small collection of possessions into his pockets and found five bucks in the jeans. It was the first good thing to happen to him in the last twenty-four hours.

The pharmacy on Hill Street was still open, one of the few glowing lights in Chinatown. As Ray stepped through the automatic doors, he passed by another skinny homeless man writing on a stolen sales flyer with a broken pencil, the paper close to his face.

"Hey, Notebook," Ray said. Garrett "Notebook" Wilson, didn't bother to grunt in reply.

"Fourteen different kinds of gum, nine types of mints, one cunt-sucking prick face," Notebook said to himself. He walked through the parking lot up toward the highway.

"Good to see you too, Notebook," Ray called to the skinny man's back, not expecting an answer.

He took a glance down the aisles, looking for a restroom sign. Nothing.

"You got a bathroom in here?" he asked the clerk running the only open register.

"You guys part of a club or something? Employees only."

"Make an exception?"

He presented his newly acquired five bucks.

The clerk gave him a look before sighing into, "You gonna buy something?"

Ray figured the clerk must have been the "cunt-sucking prick face" Notebook cataloged. He shoved the worn bill back into his pocket and headed into the store, tempted to drop his pants in the aisle next to the Ruffles and Oreos, leaving the smug dickhead behind the counter to clean up after him.

He grabbed a Snickers and shook it in the security mirror the clerk was using to keep an eye on him. Another lap of the store brought him to the stomach aides and he was able to swipe a box of chewable Pepto-Bismol off the shelf and shove it into his pocket when the clerk decided to answer an incoming text message.

Ray plunked the candy bar and a bottle of water down on the counter and flicked the crumpled five-dollar bill at the clerk.

"Now can I use your toilet?"

"Employees only," the clerk said.

Ray's anger bubbled just below the surface, but he'd already expended enough adrenaline taking out Kelvin.

"Keep the change," Ray grumbled.

The clerk scoffed at him, picked the cash up off the floor, and shoved it into the register. He made a point to squeeze out a handful of anti-bacterial gel. As the doors slid open, Ray heard the clerk mumble under his breath, "Fuck you, you filthy hobo." It gave him pause, but Ray decided it wasn't worth getting into another scrum. He stepped back into the rain.

With half the box of Pepto chewed and washed down, even the waft of pink wintergreen wasn't strong enough to get the residual smell of his accident out of his nose.

He sighed and rubbed the familiar scars under his shirt. The cramps were still present, but dulled. He'd feel better once he had a chance to lie down.

The neon lights of the Foo-Chow Restaurant were a beacon in the distance. Home sweet home.

While most of the city was trying to decide whether it was worth their rental dollars to get a one bedroom with a bigger living room in exchange for access to a washer and dryer, Ray had a smaller list of amenity requests. Warm and dry were at the top of the list. It was also nice to find a place where he wouldn't be ass-raped by a broken bottle in his sleep. If Ray managed to find a special corner of Los Angeles he could make his own, soon there was going to be somebody ready to fight him for it. He tended to avoid altercations, but it was part of life on the streets. He'd won just as many fights as he'd lost, and found even when he'd won a claim, it never seemed worth the cracked tooth or bruised ribs.

The 1974 Chevy Impala abandoned in the Foo-Chow parking lot looked like it had been sitting there for decades. The hood was almost completely rusted through. Small patches of dull yellow paint along the door panels were the only things betraying the car's original color. The tires had probably been flat when the car was left for dead, all of them rotted off the frames, strings of rubber melted into the pavement, the rims scraping the blacktop. Most of the interior had been chewed through, tufts of soiled cotton-poly filling spilling out among the rusty springs and rat droppings. Some other resident had layered the inside in newspaper, old enough to be cracking with age. When Ray found it, there didn't appear to be anyone living in it. His claim to the warm place to sleep had gone unchallenged for a week. Ever since his bowels had rebelled, he'd dreamt of curling up in a fetal position in the back seat.

The Foo-Chow valet lit a cigarette in the doorway of the restaurant and headed down the street, popping the collar of his windbreaker against the damp. The cherry of his cigarette struggled to glow in the rain. Based on the Impala's fixture in the lot, Ray doubted the valet gave a shit whether or not anybody lived in it, but with his intestinal difficulties, he didn't want to run the risk of being found out. He waited until the lights inside the restaurant went dark, leaving only the humming glow of neon.

His hand was on the door handle before he saw the form of a body in the backseat through the dust-layered window.

"Are you fucking kidding me?"

Ray was in no physical condition to get into another fight. Even if he got a drop on the car's new resident, there was no guarantee he would have the upper hand.

Ready to put a fist through the window, Ray took a deep breath and two steps back. Remembering the candy bar he'd bought, he unwrapped it with shaking hands and dug into it, the first food he'd had since that morning. It wasn't going to be good for his sensitive stomach, but he hoped the sugar rush would provide him with enough energy to send the squatter packing. He was so pissed off, he needed to find comfort in anything that might turn the day in his favor.

He sucked at the caramel stuck to his teeth as he made his way into the alley behind the restaurant. The residents of the surrounding apartments treated the alley like they'd never left the Shanghai slums. There was rotting detritus strewn about everywhere. Stained clothes and stinking trash overflowed in small narrows where garbage trucks didn't fit and sanitation workers didn't investigate. Ray pried an old two-by-four off the pile of a half-built shed, complete with a snarl of rusty nails. If he couldn't best his new nemesis, at least he could give the fucker tetanus.

Ray whipped open the door of the Impala, the two-by-four raised over his head.

"Hey, fuckface. Find some other place to sleep."

The figure didn't stir.

"Hey!" He kicked the sole of the man's dirty bare foot.

Nothing.

Ray smiled. The drunk asshole fell asleep in the wrong spot, now he would wake up on the wet pavement.

He placed the two-by-four at his feet, careful to keep it within range if the guy came to, grabbed the drunk's ankles, and yanked. The weight didn't move easily and a load of old newspaper came along with him out onto the blacktop. The drunk's bare feet slammed into the pavement with a force Ray was sure would rouse him awake, but no dice. Wanting to get more leverage, he grabbed the guy by the collar of his jacket and pulled, hoping to get him as far away from the car as possible. After a couple steps, his feet slipped from underneath him and he fell on his ass, the drunk's head resting in his lap. It wasn't until that moment that Ray noticed how loose the drunk's neck was.

The blinking neon sign highlighted the man's face with a glow of pink and green. It didn't matter how blitzed Ray got, he never passed out with his eyes open. And the red lines ringing the man's throat were a sure sign he hadn't died of natural causes.

"Fuck."

Eyewitnesses tended to misremember things, but if he was lucky enough to get someone who saw him drag the body out of the car instead of being the one who put it there, there'd be a reason his fingerprints were all over the victim's jacket.

He pushed the body off his lap and got back to his feet. He looked around to see if there was anyone in the area. The street was empty.

If he left the body out in the rain, it would be discovered right away. If not that night, then first thing in the morning. By that time, the rain would've washed away most of the evidence of Ray's tampering, but it would also wash away any evidence of whoever had actually killed the guy.

He decided his best bet would be to get the body back into the car, preserving anything that hadn't already been washed away, then he'd call it in. He'd spent enough time trying to avoid police interference to know calling them wasn't always the best course of action. Then again, he was more likely to get a fair shake if he called in the body. The murderer only called the police in the plots of those cheap novels shelved across from the toilet paper in the supermarket.

Ray put his hands under the man's armpits. He noticed the suit coat was well-tailored, raindrops beading on the shiny wool. If the guy had been breathing, Ray might've thought to take it as a toll for occupying his squat, a warm coat to match his new pants. The sleeves bunched up as he dragged the heavy corpse and he caught the faint outline of a tattoo on the dead man's forearm. Whoever this guy was, he wasn't in Ray's social circle.

A flash of rotating red and blue halted his movement. He dropped the body and placed his hands over his head.

There was a new sinking feeling in his stomach and it had nothing to do with what he'd eaten.

2

Bzzzt. Bzzzt. Bzzzt.

Detective Nick Archer didn't feel the vibrations in his pocket until after the empty Kleenex box had hit him in the head.

"Hmph... the fuck?" Nick mumbled, coming out of his deep sleep. His body barely had time to register the corner of the tissue box hitting him before the rest of the pain receptors in his body sent their alert messages to his brain.

"Language," Janice Archer said. His mother was sitting up in her bed, her eyes transfixed on the silence of the television bolted into the wall over Nick's head. The fluorescent light above her created an odd shadow, darkening her face and reflecting off the bare parts of her skull where bits of hair had fallen out.

"Sorry, Ma," Nick said, stretching his back from the cramped position in the pink pleather easy chair.

"Are you going to answer that?"

By the time he'd found the phone, it had gone to voicemail. The glow of the screen stung his eyes and he blinked away the phantom square dancing in his vision in the dim light of the hospice room.

His new partner calling. They must've caught a body.

The second thing his brain was able to compute was the time illuminated at the top of the screen. *5:12 a.m.*

"Why're you awake?" Nick yawned. He stood up and rubbed his palm along the prickles of his short hair. There was less and less of it by the day and he'd taken to having the barber buzz it close to the scalp to avoid looking like he was trying too hard to cling to his disappearing youth.

"I don't sleep anymore, you know this," his mother said, followed by a fit of coughing.

In a movement that had become instinct, he poured her a glass of water from the large plastic pitcher at her bedside.

"And why am I still here?" he asked, scratching his belly under the untucked white button down.

His mother took small sips of water, the coughing fit subsiding. The tremor in her hand as she raised the glass to her lips had become pronounced instead of merely noticeable.

"You fell asleep. What was I going to do? Wake you up and tell you to go home?"

"That's exactly what you should've done. I've gotta work in the morning."

Bzzzt. Bzzzt. Bzzzt.

His pocket vibrated again. He made a mental note to add impatience to the things he was learning about his new partner every day.

"I take that back. I've gotta work right now."

He hit the "Accept" button on the touchscreen.

"Yeah... okay... text me the address... I'll be there in ten," he said into the phone.

As he tried to uncrumple his suit coat from between the cushion and arm of the easy chair, he heard the ping of rain on the window and sighed. It was bad enough he had to wear a suit in the heat of summer, but on the rainy winter days, he felt like he was wrapped in a wet sheep.

It was his own damn fault. The more cases he solved, the more people he had to interview. He got no respect when he showed up to a deposition wearing jeans and a short-sleeved plaid shirt. The first time he came into the station wearing a tie and clean shirt without being asked, he thought his boss, Lieutenant Jenkins, was going to have another heart attack.

"I'll come back tonight." He kissed his mother on the forehead and stepped out into the hallway before waiting for her to respond.

The Garden Commons Assisted Living Facility in Echo Park was an eerie cacophony of noise in the wee hours of the morning. Machines whirred and clicked from open doors; some monitoring heartbeats, others keeping people breathing. Whistling snores mixed with the sound of televisions at low volume, late night infomercials competing for the residents' attention.

Nick wished he could've chosen a different place for his mother. One of those homes with brochures featuring old folks smiling as they played tennis or one that sent them on field trips to the Morongo Casino. Something that looked more like a resort than a place where people went to die. But he needed a place in the city, so he didn't have to drive all the way to Altadena when something went wrong or he wanted to visit her. It also had to have close access to a hospital, in case the medical facilities of the home couldn't handle severe complications. It wasn't the best place in the world and it wasn't the worst. It was a compromise.

Janice Archer had been living with emphysema and cancer when a crazy homeless man broke into her house and stabbed her several times. Because of the advanced state of her diseases and the severity of the injuries, Nick figured that was the end of it. His mother was dead. But the old bird just kept on going. He started to think she would live forever. But after the attack, she wasn't the same. He'd moved back home when she was diagnosed with cancer so he could take care of her, but the attack had pushed her afflictions too far. She needed around-the-clock care. It didn't matter how much she protested or refused, there was no way he could afford a full-time nurse and the repairs to the house her attacker had almost burnt down.

After he'd gotten over the near loss of his mother, he took the loss of the house pretty hard. Insurance would've covered a portion, but by the time someone came in and took a look at the damage, the old Craftsman was a blight of building code violations. Nick had to put it on the market. His girlfriend at the time, Penny, helped him get a good deal from a house-flipping vulture. Most of the money from the sale went toward his mother's new lodgings. He was stuck renting a condo in North Hollywood and visiting his ailing mother nightly. Eventually, Penny couldn't take Nick's lifestyle anymore.

His whirlwind romance with a murder suspect had soured much quicker than he'd expected. Penny Searle entered his life during a routine questioning on a bullshit case and became his impromptu partner in the case that made his career. At first, Penny was intrigued by his work, found what he did to be endlessly exciting, but when he had started to come home later and later, the novelty wore off. It would've been easy for him to blame the souring of their relationship on how much he'd put the job before her, but he couldn't. It was his mother.

She found his relationship with his sick mother endearing at first. Then she realized she took third billing in Nick's life after Janice and the job. He didn't see how unhappy she was toward the end. His interactions with her had dissolved into early goodbyes and late hellos. Weekends were filled with projects or birthday parties for their friend's kids, neither of which involved a great deal of deep conversation.

He'd never had a connection with anyone the way he had with Penny, but he did nothing to cultivate that comfort and it faded. What they had together never felt like work, but maybe that was the problem. He knew with a good relationship you had to put in the effort to keep it alive. And he didn't. So, she left.

The drive to Skid Row didn't take as long as he thought it would. With a gaggle of official vehicles already double-parked, he had to circle the block to find a spot. By the time he got into the building, his suit coat was wrinkled and wet.

One step through the open front door and a wave of nastiness hovering in the air smacked him across the face like a jilted lover.

"Please tell me the smell gets better at the top of the stairs."

Nick pulled a handkerchief out of his back pocket and held it to his nose as he squeezed past a couple of uniformed officers making their way back down to the street.

"What dream world you living in?" the uniform at the top of the stairs said to him as he passed.

"How much time do we have before the shit show starts?" Nick asked.

"We're not at his primary residence and black and whites don't draw much attention in this part of town. But given the retirement plan TMZ seems to be supplying to half the department, I'd give us ten minutes before we're mobbed. Fifteen, if we're lucky."

"Great," Nick said, snatching a paper mask out of the uniform's outstretched hand and putting paper booties over his wet shoes.

The main room of the apartment looked like it had been designed by an art department on acid. The furniture was ragged and had been dragged off the street. A leather lounge chair and a brand new curved flat screen television, covered in what appeared to be mustard, stuck out amongst the threadbare wreckage. It was as though a rich cousin had come to stay with his poor kin and wanted a bit of finery speckled throughout the disaster area. The crime scene photographer was snapping away, getting the living room from every angle. The photo prints would make for an interesting art installation at one of the galleries a few blocks away in the thriving Arts District.

"Can we open these? It smells like an elephant gave birth in here," he asked, looking at the row of closed windows.

Willie poked her head out the bedroom door, "You wanna quit your bitching and come in here and take a look at this?"

Nick had only been partnered up with Willie Grant for a couple months. Budget cuts pulled him off of the cold case desk where he'd comfortably sat for the past few years. He'd known it was only a matter of time before he was back out on the streets with the rest of the Robbery-Homicide Division catching fresh bodies, but the thing that worried him most was getting stuck with a partner he didn't get along with. The last partner he'd liked was when he was cruising in a squad wearing a starched black button down, but his good buddy Hank Drees refused to take the detective test.

Willie and Nick were still figuring each other out. The one thing that made the transition easier was that she loved to bullshit as much as he did. The problem was, neither of them knew when to turn it off. They hadn't developed the ability to let the conversation wane naturally. When the two of them got together, it annoyed everybody else in the room.

"Is the smell getting to you? We've got a standing bet to see who pukes first. You want in for ten bucks?" she asked him, her face buried in her notebook, writing down every detail that caught her fancy.

"I don't find being accustomed to the smell of shit and garbage to be a redeeming quality."

The floor had the tacky feel of a dirty movie theater and he had to peel his shoes from the wood with every step.

"Don't forget semen," she said, waving her pen at the foot of the bed.

"Is that what that is?" Nick asked, cringing.

There was a milky-yellow residue lining the floor around the bed. Nick picked his feet up, trying not to step in any more of it.

A tittering giggle came from behind the bedroom door. Nick looked over to where the noise was coming from and back at Willie, his brow contorted in confusion.

"What the hell was that?"

"Oh yeah, forgot to mention that," Willie said, bringing her face up from her notebook just long enough to give him a smile.

Nick moved the warped bedroom door. He cocked his head slightly and turned back to his partner.

"Dare I ask?"

Behind the door were two Filipino women, no older than twenty-two years apiece, with tiny, tight, perfect bodies. Nick knew this because they were both completely naked.

If this weren't an odd enough sight, they were playing poker with tarot cards, using dominoes as chips. The dominoes kept falling through the holes in the milk crate they'd flipped over and were using as a table, but it didn't seem to bother them. The one on the left placed the King of Cups over her opponent's Death card and they both giggled with glee. A small part of Nick wanted to keep watching, not just because of the enticement of the young and naked, but he also wanted to figure out the rules of their game.

"A new guildmaster has arrived," the one closest to the door said.

"Will he try to burn us like the rest?" the other asked, more out of curiosity than fear.

"I know I'm going to regret asking this," Nick said over his shoulder to Willie, "But what *exactly* is happening right now?"

"As you can tell, the Tagalog Twins over here are a bit out of it. Attempting to interview them has been... I'll just say it...

fucking hilarious. I'm pissed I can't post it to YouTube. Some of the shit that came out of these chick's mouths, Hunter S. Thompson on an ether binge couldn't come up with."

Nick knew his new partner was a competent cop; brilliant at controlling a crime scene, and not flippant when it came to investigations. Her behavior was so out of character, he was certain there had to be a catch.

"Can I ask a follow-up?"

"They're superglued to the floor," Willie said, opening one of the dresser drawers.

"No shit," Nick said, peering down to where they were sitting.

Sure enough, the skin of both the girls' buttocks and legs were affixed to the scratched hardwood floor.

Just as he was internally scolding himself for lingering too close to the wonderful canvases of light brown skin, one of the girls started rubbing his freshly cropped head.

"Mr. Cream Cake Maker... where do you find such wonderful pieces of death flakes?"

He stood up, trying to play it cool.

"Don't pretend like you weren't admiring the view, Mr. Cream Cake Maker," Willie said.

Flustered, Nick tried to play it off, "I get why we aren't turpentining the floor, but you couldn't be bothered to give them windbreakers or blankets or something?"

"They freak out when we try to cover them up. Scream their goddamn heads off. And we can't sedate them until we've figured out what the hell else they've got pumping through their veins. So, for now, just treat them like evidence. They're not bothering anybody as long as we let them play cards."

"One more thing—"

"The Fool appears to be the best card in the deck. Swords and Wands beat Coins and Cups," she said, "Kinda like War."

Satisfied, he shrugged and went around to the other side of the bed.

"It'll definitely be in my top five weirdest things at a crime scene," he said.

"Though not on mine," she said.

"I find that hard to believe."

"One of the first calls I caught as a rookie before going back to school, saw a baby and a dog stapled butthole to butthole," Willie said, "And they kept yanking at the staples. Both of them."

He cringed as he pictured it, "I can't unthink that."

"Whatever their abuser was trying to accomplish... it didn't work. Shit was coming out of the crevasses like marshmallow coming out of a s'more someone pushed down too hard. There's not enough scotch in the world to forget that one."

"Please stop talking about all the things you are talking about please," Nick spit out fast, swallowing to keep down the nugget creeping up his throat. He did a full body shudder and peered out through the only open window. The slick street was becoming visible in the low light bursting through the gray film covering the sky.

"I can't believe we found this dude on a rainy day. How fucking cliché."

"I don't think we'd have fewer murders if people were only killed on the sunny days," she said.

Below them, an entertainment news van streaked around the corner of 7th Street and a handful of camera-wielding parasites got out, pressing against the police barrier.

"How the fuck do the photographers always get here before forensics?" Nick asked no one in particular.

He turned back to the bed, exhaling hard as he looked at the disturbing corpse before him.

"What did you do to deserve this, Mr. Seward?"

Lowell Seward had recently become a box office cash cow. After clinging too long to the action stars of old, casting directors realized audiences were no longer buying sixty-five-year-old men fighting terrorists. They'd been trying for years to find someone to replace them, scouring the casts of the latest YA book adaptations and the Disney Channel, but the audiences never took to anyone for more than a film or two.

Enter Low Seward.

Soon everybody wanted to "Get Low" and his quote shot through the roof. Not bad for a kid from St. Louis whose only previous job had been as Researcher #2 in a commercial for cheese crackers.

Nick looked at the stained wall over the mattress. Why would someone with a multi-million-dollar mansion in Hancock Park be bedding down in a Skid Row walk-up in the middle of the week? The answer probably had something to do with how much of his head was plastered into the cracking paint. There was so little left of Lowell Seward's face when the first responders arrived, it was a wonder the deceased hadn't been passed off as someone else. One of the first officers on scene had noticed the tattoo of a whale on the dead man's hand.

It was his signature, much like the sombrero woman on the chest of Danny Trejo. Seward had yet to star in a movie where he let the tattoo be covered up. It became an interesting challenge for screenwriters, finding a way to justify why each one of Seward's characters had that particular trait. There were whole blogs dedicated to The Whale; something his character got while they were in juvvie, a remembrance of the character's dead mother, or an addition to a plethora of other tattoos labored over by a makeup artist. Lowell Seward never revealed what the tattoo meant.

The speculation would be tenfold now that he was gone, though Nick didn't expect Seward's fan base to mourn him long after his death. It wasn't the time of icons whose legend would live on through the ages. Stars who died young got their tribute during the Oscars and the SAG Awards, then disappeared into the ether, replaced by the next person in line for stardom.

Nick would've rather handed this one over to the detectives in the Central Division, but the body was identified early so no one else had been assigned the case. Robbery-Homicide Division was tasked with handling all cases of multiple murder, serial killers, and high profile victims. Movie star dead in a crack house fit the bill of high profile.

"Looks like they stuck his toe into the shotgun trigger housing to make it look like a suicide," Nick said, crouching next to the bed. He looked for familiar grease on the barrel and didn't see any. "It's wiped, though we might find a partial print. No powder burns on his foot."

"Yeah, I saw that too," Willie said, "Think we can just call it a suicide and be done with it?"

"It'd help our clearance rate if we never put it on the board. But why fake a suicide, then leave two witnesses?" Nick said.

"Maybe our unsub figures those girls are too far gone to register reality."

"Even if we've got somebody doing a hasty job, they aren't going to take that chance. Even an idiot criminal knows that's way too big of a loose end."

Willie crouched under the bed and slipped the end of her pen into a spent shotgun casing.

"With the rest of the sloppy job here, there's gotta be a print on that," Nick said, producing a plastic evidence bag.

"Look at the ropes," Nick said, "the ligature on his wrists is minimal. He was tied up voluntarily."

"No doubt to enjoy a romp with the twins," she said.

"But he was tied up and they were glued down. There had to be a third-party to mediate between them."

"You have any dominatrixes on speed dial that would be into this sort of thing?" Willie asked.

"My usual girl is on vacation," Nick smiled.

He looked down at the body, one tanned leg sticking out from under the bedding.

"Where are his pants?"

"Strange. When I got here I asked, 'Where's his penis?'" Willie said.

Nick flipped back the sheet covering Lowell Seward's crotch, revealing an empty hole spattered with dried blood and skin.

"What the fuck, Will?" Nick said, dropping the sheet back down, "That's not something you just spring on someone."

"Was trying to think of the best way to ease into it," she said.

"You did a shit job."

"Was hoping it would put you over the edge for the puke pool."

Once the initial shock of the horror show had passed, the wheels in Nick's head started turning.

"So, why the hack and grab? Crazy fan with a souvenir?"

"I'm sure stranger things have been sold on eBay," Willie said, "We haven't even started to go through the clutter in this place. I'm sure we'll find his pants in one pile or another. As well as the penis."

Nick looked under the rotting pizza boxes, hoping he was the one to find the pants and not the severed penis.

Willie put her notebook down on the dresser and started scouring the apartment for any sign of discarded men's pants. For all of the crap strewn about, the place was devoid of clothing. She did come up with both of the girl's dresses, short and shiny. The girls had either been out clubbing or were professionals. She had one or two of the same dresses in her own closet that could've gone either way. She set them aside to be tested for DNA and flipped over the living room rug, discovering several transparent worms hidden there.

"Anything?" Nick asked from the kitchen.

"Six... yeah, six used condoms," Willie said, "And I'm leaving them for you to bag."

"Be sure to put numbers down so I don't step on 'em," Nick said, finding another condom hanging from the exhaust over the stove.

"If all these are his, he's got a lot of stamina," she said, finding a treasure trove of sex toys in a chest in the closet, "Or he did before the grand severing."

They found lots of ungodly things that would have to be entered into evidence, but no pants and no penis.

Nick stepped back into the bedroom and went over to the twins. The smaller girl had just won whatever game they were playing and was swatting her bare breasts in celebration.

"Hey, Dum and Dee," he said, crouching to meet their faces, "Pants?"

"Bluebirds gotta fly," the tiny one hummed.

"Mr. Cream Cake Maker doesn't make the cream in the open air," the other said, biting her lower lip. Nick was pretty sure she would've lunged for him if she hadn't been glued to the floor.

"And they just continue to be helpful," Willie said, looking out the open window down to the throng of tabloid reporters growing on the sidewalk.

The glued down girl on the left lifted the milk crate. Tarot cards went everywhere, but she'd revealed some evidence. A dick covered in dominoes.

"Welp, we can stop looking for the penis," he said, pushing the milk crate back on top of it. Now that he'd found it, it was forensics' problem.

When he turned around, he saw Willie was examining the sash of the window.

"Should we close that? The rain's coming in," Nick said.

"It was open when we got here. Thought it might be an escape route for our killer, but..." Willie stopped mid-sentence and stuck her head out of the window, the drizzle forming a beaded layer on her tightly pulled back hair.

She stepped out onto the fire escape and beckoned to him, "Archer."

He followed her out onto the wet black metal and they looked over the edge of the balcony. Hanging precariously, a few floors down, was a pair of waterlogged blue jeans, about Seward's size.

"Pretend like we're just casually looking around," Willie said, "One of those vultures catches wind we're going after those pants, they'll form a human ladder to grab 'em and we'll never see 'em again."

"Good point," Nick whispered, peering around the exposed brick wall like someone scanning a vista with no particular focal point. When he made his way down the stairs, it was in a casual gait, but that didn't stop the herd of reporters below from noticing the badge on his belt.

"Detective," a small blonde woman in a trench coat yelled up to him, "Can you comment on whether this is an investigation of the death of Lowell Seward?"

He recognized her from one of the many red carpet shows during awards season. Carly Wentworth. A teleprompter-reading pretty face. She also had a gossip blog not-so-cleverly named, *For What It's Worth*. Not the type he expected to be doing investigative journalism at 6 a.m., but she was the first one on scene.

"No," he said, reaching the balcony where the pants flopped in the wind. He put his hand over them, as though he hadn't noticed they were there and called back down to her, "But I really like that coat. What is that? Burberry?"

"Sources tell us Seward committed suicide in that apartment," Wentworth replied, ignoring his glib answer.

"And what source would that be? I'd love to talk to them about interfering with an open investigation. Maybe give them an executive tour of the police station."

"C'mon, Detective, you gotta gimme something," she said, smiling up at him through the rain. She was pretty and she knew it, but Nick had passed the stage in his life where he was easily influenced by a pretty face.

"No, I don't," he said.

The cameras flashed below him. He pulled out his cell phone and pointed it down at them.

"Smile," he said, clicking a picture of the pants into evidence before turning around and taking them with him. Questions yelled from below bled into each other as he ducked back into the apartment. No one seemed to notice he'd taken the pants, but it would be the focus of media scrutiny as soon as they got back into their vans and reviewed the tape.

Nick shook off the damp and started poking through the pockets of the jeans.

"Cell phone?" Nick asked.

"Already bagged. Last call was to Shane Davidson, his agent, a few hours ago. Don't know what sort of business they were discussing at 3 a.m., but it must have been important. They talked for about twenty minutes."

"Sounds like that's the first man we visit once the sun comes up. Did we log the wallet and keys yet?" Nick asked.

"Nope," Willie said. She turned to the closest uniform. "Make sure to check out any homeless in the area when you're canvassing. If they fell out of the jeans somebody could've picked them up off the street and kept walking. And start doing a scan for his vehicle. If it's not parked nearby somebody could've picked up the keys and gone for a chop ride. Put it out on the wire."

The uniform got on the radio and headed down the stairs, certainly glad to have a task to get him out of the stink of the apartment.

Nick felt a small bump in the useless watch pocket and dug two fingers in. Between his index and middle finger, he held a small baggie filled with a bright purple powder. It looked like somebody had emptied out a couple of grape-flavored Pixie Stix.

"Jackpot," Nick said, shaking the bag.

"If that turns out to be novelty sand, I'll be pissed," Willie said.

"You and me both."

The cell phone in his coat pocket buzzed. He answered it, handing the baggie over to Willie to log into evidence.

"Archer."

"There's a confidential informant in Central Division got picked up last night on a homicide. Won't stop dropping your name," Lieutenant Jenkins said. It sounded like he was polishing off his typical breakfast of half a dozen donuts and two breakfast sandwiches.

"I don't have a registered CI," Nick said, searching the catalog in his mind.

"Looked him up. Hasn't collected a check in years, but he's yours. The name Ray Cobb ring a bell?"

Nick hadn't heard that name in a long time. After the Keller & Hoff investigation, Nick had dropped Ray off on the curb on Beverly Boulevard and he hadn't seen or heard from him again. That was a little over two years ago.

"What'd they pick him up for?" Nick asked.

"Caught with a body in Chinatown. I'm not gonna give you the whole play by play on the phone. You wanna claim him or do we put him through processing?"

Nick looked at the apartment. The photographer was finishing up with his pictures and the forensic team was starting to pry the twins from the floor. One of them used a pair of tongs to bag the severed penis and Nick gave him an enthusiastic thumbs-up.

"Gimme a couple hours."

3

"What do you got him on?" Nick asked.

"Right now we're holding him as a witness, but the 911 call said they saw him moving the body," Detective Oscar Jimenez said, "Of course, the call was anonymous, so who knows? Might have trouble making anything stick. Because of his lack of permanent address, we've kept him around so he doesn't disappear."

Nick nodded at the image of Ray Cobb on the video feed coming from the interrogation room. Ray had aged a lot since Nick last saw him, every year rougher without a roof over his head and proper nourishment.

"Who's the stiff?" Nick asked.

"John Doe," Jimenez said, "No I.D., no prints in the database."

"How'd he go?"

"Windpipe was crushed. Garroted, like something out of a spy thriller," Jimenez said.

"Sounds planned. Street murders have a different kind of urgency to them. Choking someone off with a wire... I don't know. If Ray had done it, he'd have used a broken piece of glass or a rusty knife he found somewhere."

"Well, your homeless here is our only suspect, no matter how loose the charge. After the boys got a closer look at the scene and the body, looked like the vic had been dead less than an hour," Jimenez scratched the acne scars on his chin, "Says he was moving the guy out of his squat, didn't realize he was dead. Fits the story, but it's not unlikely for the killer to get second thoughts and try to move the body after the deed."

"Was the guy done inside the car?" Nick asked.

"Moved there after the fact," Jimenez said, looking at the notes he had yet to put into an official report, "Problem with that timeline is the restaurant was open at the estimated time of death. So, Cobb, or whoever else killed Doe, moved him there during business hours."

"You call in possible witnesses?"

"Valet didn't see anything. Gonna take us a while longer to gather a customer list for questioning. Seems like everyone on the block got sick of paying for their security cameras at the same time."

"That doesn't sound suspicious at all," Nick said, raising an eyebrow at Jimenez.

"Bunch of cheapo chinks if you ask me," Jimenez said, "But can't exactly write that in my report."

Nick hoped to get this over with as soon as possible. Jimenez wasn't on a list of his favorite people. On top of the rampant racism, he also wore too much cologne.

"Can I take those? Just want to have something to reference if he starts talking." Nick reached his hand out for the notes and Jimenez handed them over.

"Don't think you'll be able to read my chicken scratch."

He couldn't. Jimenez had the handwriting of an epileptic fourth grader.

"One more thing," Nick said, "How long did it take him to drop my name? Did he give it to the arresting officer or wait until you had him in that room?"

"Wasn't until we threatened charges," Jimenez shrugged, "Which I don't get. Either he should've said something right away or not at all. The charges wouldn't have stuck and he would've gotten a couple meals and a night or two out of the rain. What do you figure?"

"Ray Cobb is an odd case," Nick said.

While Ray was recovering from a gunshot wound to the belly, a gunshot he sustained saving Nick's life, he was cagey with the details of how he'd ended up homeless. But Nick was good at reading people. Even if he couldn't wheedle the details of Ray's life out of him over a couple of games of cards, he knew plenty about Ray Cobb. Ray did things for a reason. He'd only dropped Nick's name because he had to. He must have felt like he was being driven into a corner with no other escape. Now Nick had to figure out why.

When he opened the door to the interview room, the smell hit him right away. Body odor and feces. A common stench among the homeless, but one he hadn't associated with Ray. When he'd picked him up all those years ago and shoved him into the back of his car, Ray had only been without a shower for a few days. Ray had told him he'd gotten into a shelter somewhere and cleaned up, though when Nick checked the area, none of them had a record of his registry. Nick chose to let it go.

In the short time he'd known Ray, the vagrant seemed like an outsider. Someone with a deft awareness. Someone who didn't seem to belong on the streets. Not everyone on the sidewalk was mentally ill or an addict, but Ray held himself with a certain dignity. It was hard for Nick to describe when talking about the Keller & Hoff case. A mysterious homeless man solved it about the same time as a trained detective. Maybe all those weeks in the hospital had pulled the wool over Nick's eyes. He'd never pictured Ray as homeless, had never seen him in his natural element outside of a couple of pictures snapped before he was tossed in the drunk tank. But it was different now. Real. The Ray Cobb before him might as well have been another person. And Nick was going to operate under the assumption he was.

"Long time no see," Nick said, sitting down in the chair across from Ray. He tried to keep cool, but the smell was getting to him.

"Trust me, I'd prefer to talk in a better ventilated room too, but what're you gonna do?" Ray said. He must've noticed Nick had stopped breathing in through his nose.

"Thought you were dead for a while there," Nick said, "Almost went looking for you after those first few weeks and your CI check hadn't been cashed."

"I was between banks at the time. Didn't like getting hit with all the hidden fees," Ray said.

This was the guy Nick remembered. Always ready with a line before giving a straight answer. Playing out the situation to get a bunch of information before he had to reveal anything himself.

"It's too early, Ray," Nick said, exhaling the breath he'd been holding, "I don't have time for the banter. Why'd you drop my name on the detectives?"

"Sorry, didn't realize you had to get home to the wife. What was her name again? Polly?"

"Penny. And we're not together anymore,"

"Sorry to hear it. My fault for not keeping up with current events. Remind me to leave you a forwarding address so you can send me your Christmas letter."

"Ray," Nick said. The look he shot across the table told Ray to quit fucking around.

"Aren't you gonna ask me if I killed the guy?"

"Pretty sure you didn't, so why waste our time?" Nick said.

"That's why I dropped your name," Ray said, leaning forward, "You and I both know I have a low opinion of most of the other shits in this department, but on look one, that other asshole should've seen I'm no good for this. I should've been interviewed and kicked to the curb."

"Maybe he wanted to keep you out of the rain," Nick said.

"Don't give me that bullshit. You guys aren't running a shelter."

"You've avoided tapping me this long. Why now? No fucking around."

"I thought a guy was sleeping in my house. That's it. I pull him out, he's dead. I try to do the right thing. Even put him back. All the sudden I got cop cars all over me. Out of the blue."

"Never pegged you for a conspiracy theorist, Ray. You think maybe someone saw you dragging that body and dropped a 911 call?"

"The LAPD response time sucks a dick. You know it and I know it. I wasn't out there more than three minutes. Less. Check your logs, Archer. I bet you don't find call one. Or if you do, it was well before I even showed up," Ray said.

"You're still tossing a bunch of horse shit in the way of answering my question. Why'd you drop my name and why'd it take you so long?"

Ray glanced up at the camera in the corner of the room.

"I'm not saying your boy in there is involved. But he knows he's got nothing to hold me. Starts tossing out obstruction of justice charges."

"You disturbed a crime scene."

"Unknowingly."

"Still—"

"I saw the marks on the dude's neck. He was dropped there on purpose. I'd only been living in that car for a few days, week at most."

Ray took in a deep breath, looked down at the table, then back up at Nick. His tone changed.

"You wanna know why I dropped your name? Because I can't get stuck in another one of these. Last time I decided to take the law into my own hands I found out a whole bunch of shit I didn't want to. Instead of keeping my head down and disappearing, I watched the bodies pile up. You can clear me. You can get me out of this early, before I get woven into whatever shit that what's-his-name, Jimenez, is trying to bury me in. You haven't heard from me in years for a reason. I played private eye once and lost a lot. Not ready to do that again. Even if it means clearing my name."

Nick was prepared for a couple more minutes of banter. Ray was sincere. He had nothing to do with this thing. Wrong place, wrong time. Problem was, it wasn't enough reason to cut him loose and he knew it. That's why he'd dropped Nick's name. He figured it was a get-out-of-jail-free card once he'd exhausted his other options.

"Here's what I can do," Nick said, pausing to think about what angle to play, "I can get you out of here and can keep them from charging you with anything, but you aren't out of this."

"Great, let's go," Ray said, holding up his cuffed hands.

"This isn't my jurisdiction and you're still Jimenez's only witness. It's Central Division's case. He's not going to let you disappear."

"So switch with him or some shit. I'm sure you got something you can toss him."

"It doesn't work that way. We work in different worlds."

"So what do you suggest?"

"You called me out as your supervisor at CI status, so that's what you get," Nick said, "You're back on paper, whether you like it or not. That's the compromise. You'll go back to drawing checks, which you'll cash, so there's a paper trail. What you do with the money, I couldn't give a shit, but we need a tag on you until this case is closed."

"Fair," Ray said.

He'd agreed to the deal too quick. Both of them knew it.

"And I'll set you up with a bed at a shelter. You'll have to check in every night."

Ray cringed at the thought.

"I think I'd rather take my chances getting booked through the system."

The homeless shelters in L.A. offered decent basic services, but security wasn't one of them. The staff were either minimum wage workers or former homeless trying to get a fresh start. More people were raped and beaten inside those places than out.

"That's not on the table anymore. Shelter or a Low-Jack. Your choice," Nick said, knowing he'd only given Ray one option. Cobb would gnaw his foot off at the ankle before he agreed to wear a bracelet.

"There won't be any beds available. It's been raining all week. Every place will be full up," Ray said.

"Well, you're not staying at my house," Nick said.

"Why not? I'm sure your mom wouldn't mind the house guest."

"Now that I think of it, I could use a night nurse. How do you feel about being constantly berated for being single?"

Ray snorted out a small laugh. The joke broke the tension in the room.

"I've got a connection over at Dawkins," Nick said, "That all right with you?"

The Dawkins House was one of the better shelters in town. The director had been homeless years ago and took the time to understand what the people who came through his doors were going through. Ray stared across the table at Nick, as though he was waiting for the rest of the deal. It didn't come. He'd gotten all the compromise Nick was going to give him. He just had to say yes.

"Nightly check-ins. Got it. Anything else?"

Nick stood up and went for the door.

"I have to make some calls and I'll get Jimenez to process your release," Nick said, "Glad to see you're still alive, Ray. Was worried about you for a while there."

"Then you forgot about me," Ray said, "Like you were supposed to."

"Guess I did," Nick said with a sad smile. He opened the door to go, but paused and looked back in. "Hey, since I've got you back on my payroll, maybe you can earn your money. Nothing active, just keep your eyes peeled for me. Lost something in Skid Row last night."

"And what am I looking for if I see it?"

"A movie star's wallet."

Nick closed the door behind him, not waiting for Ray's curious response.

Jimenez was at his throat when he met him in the monitoring room.

"What the fuck are you doing, Archer? Offering to release my only witness? No way."

"You're gonna have to cut him loose in forty-eight hours anyway. After that you'll lose him," Nick said, undercutting Jimenez by not matching his volume.

"So instead I lose him right now? Good plan."

"He's not good for this body. You implied that yourself. You're not gonna learn anything by keeping him here."

"We're not done questioning him."

"Yeah, you are," Nick said. He could see Jimenez's rant brewing underneath the surface. A diatribe about Robbery-Homicide Division coming in and screwing up local investigations.

"Did you check the time on the 911 call?" Nick asked.

"One of the first things we did," Jimenez said.

"And?"

"Timeline is tight, but not impossible. There were already units in the area so the response time was quick. It won't hold water as an alibi," Jimenez said, "You going to question my whole investigation from start to finish?"

"Look, I'm not trying to fuck up your case. I'm trying to help," Nick said.

He pointed at the monitor where Ray seemed to be staring at the wall, pondering life.

"That homeless guy in there is smart. But he's got a weakness. He doesn't have a problem breaking the law, or doing things you and I might be uncomfortable with, but if he does something, he owns up to it. He's got this weird sense of honor. That guy doesn't like being called guilty of something he didn't do."

"Don't see how this helps me," Jimenez said. He leaned against the table, pissed, but listening.

"He lied to me in there. If he didn't give a shit, he'd take the two days shelter and walk out of here, looking for a new place to sleep. But he thinks someone tried to frame him for that murder. Which means he's going to start doing some investigating of his own."

"So you're saying forgo real police work and leave the fate of my case in the hands of some guy who stinks like shit."

"Put a tail on him. You may not get your guy right away, but you'll get a lot closer than what you've got on that body right now."

"Or he could leave here, go on a bender, and forget the whole thing," Jimenez said.

"Not if I know Ray Cobb."

4

Edgar Parrish pressed the last of the bright pink flowers into the fragrant layer of mulch in his front yard. Sweat pooled in the armpits of his faded Texas A&M t-shirt, a leftover from a relationship that had ended long ago. He vaguely remembered Jeremy rooting for the Aggies on Saturday mornings when Edgar was out in the yard. It would make sense the t-shirt was his, as they had always been roughly the same size. Edgar had been using the shirt for gardening so long that any olfactory remnants of his former lover were gone, replaced with the smells of perspiration, grass, and fertilizer.

He strained up from his right knee to his feet. Just beyond the mid-point of his forties, he wondered when it became such a chore to sit and stand. He wasn't a gym rat, but he kept fit, enough to keep his loose belly from bending over his belt. If he'd dedicated part of his garden to growing vegetables, he would eat healthier, but he never had luck with so much as a tomato plant. There was a diffcrence between fostering the growth of flowers and the growth of food. For one thing, there were the pests. Every sort of insect imaginable seemed to be drawn to small herb gardens, but a sprouting bed of gardenias only feared the weeds Edgar removed as soon as they poked through the fertile earth.

Edgar also thought gardens of food were unsightly. There were so many contraptions needed—fencing, stakes, trellises—it was an aesthetic nightmare. Flowers needed their own kind of care, but the beauty they offered in return was well worth the work. If Edgar did everything right in the planting phase, they developed an ecosystem all their own, the bees and other insects pollinating, the soil balancing its own pH to keep the flowers thriving.

He took off his wire-rimmed glasses and pulled the end of the t-shirt up to wipe the sweat from his brow. Even after days of cold rain, the sun was starting to win out through the cloud cover and bore familiar heat down onto the suburban landscape. The sweat soaked the tail of the shirt, creating a Rorschach blot over his stomach.

Suddenly remembering something, he made his way to the side of the house.

The green garden hose was almost fully uncoiled when he heard a, "Yoo-Hoo!" coming from the front yard. Edgar let out a heavy sigh, twisted the water on, and pulled the hose with him.

Adelaide Morehouse was bent over his flowerbed as far as the scoliosis in her spine would let her go. She was trying to inhale every fragrance the flowers had to offer, but Edgar doubted she was getting even the faintest of smells at that distance. He figured she was more likely to suck a bumblebee into her nose than get the full effect of the garden.

"I swear your thumb grows greener every year," she smiled at him. The gold crowns of her front teeth glinted in the sunshine, dental work last replaced in the early 1970s. She smoothed her blouse over her round belly, stretching her polyester pants to give her what another of Edgar's former boyfriends used to call a "Front Butt."

"I can't take all the credit," Edgar said. He twisted the hose head to a spray and doused the petals with a light dew. "Once I put them in the ground, the flowers do most of the work."

"Don't sell yourself short, dear. Your lawn is the highlight of my morning walk. You should submit this to one of those gardening magazine contests. I'm sure you could win something. Or at least get your picture in one of their spreads," Adelaide glowed.

"I appreciate the compliment, Mrs. Morehouse, but I doubt I would even score in the top hundred flowerbeds in the city. Pasadena is known for its roses, after all," he said, forcing a smile.

He waved the hose in her direction, giving her the hint that if she didn't make her way back to the sidewalk, she would get a face full of water. She stepped back at the last possible second and watched him wave the spray over the flowers.

"My, how I love those big blue ones. They are almost perfect pentagons. And with that bit of yellow pollen smack in the middle, I feel like they are eyes watching me. The bright blue eyes of newborn babes," she smiled, pulling the straw hat hanging at her back over her reddening face.

"The Heavenly Blues are my favorite as well," he said.

"Heavenly Blues! Ah, what a wonderful name. What sort of flower is that?"

"Morning glory."

"I'll have to remember to write that down," she said.

They stood in silence, Edgar watering the flowers without looking up, Adelaide fanning herself with her chubby fingers. It took her longer than it should've to realize he wasn't going to re-engage in the conversation.

"Well, I best be on my way. I have knitting club this afternoon and so much to do beforehand. One of these days, you'll have to give me some tips on how to get my garden looking this good. Perhaps why you'd water the flowers after three days of rain? I'd think they'd be waterlogged by now," she said, the smile not leaving her face.

Edgar's eyes flicked at her and he tried not to let the smile evolve into a scowl.

"Well," he started, trying to come up with a rational answer, "There is so much toxicity in the atmosphere, I'm more washing them than watering them. You and I can stand the small bit of acids in the rainwater, but to such delicate petals, it could be as hazardous as an aphid infestation."

"See, I never would have thought. We get the rain so rarely out here, and you don't hear that acid rain nonsense on the news. Out of sight, out of mind, I guess," Adelaide shrugged, "Enjoy the sunshine while it lasts. See you tomorrow."

She waved at him and lumbered down the sidewalk, then stopped to bother another one of his neighbors a few houses down. Edgar wiped the sweat from his brow again, this time more from nerves than heat, and grumbled to himself as he dragged the hose back around the side of the house. He took one more glance over his shoulder as he unlocked the padlock on the tall, heavy wooden gate.

The sweet, earthy smell of the compost heap tickled his nose as he walked past the small greenhouse. It was better than having to buy chemical fertilizer, but the grass clippings were starting to emit a putrid stench. The rain had let in too much moisture. He made a mental note to gather some leaves and cardboard to add to the pile.

Edgar dropped the hose into the grass and bent down in front of the compost heap. Lifting with both legs, he felt the familiar strain in his knees and propped the wooden ledge up on a small brick.

The protein bars in his back pocket were melted and smashed. He tossed them down into the space below and grabbed the hose out of the manicured grass.

"Eat and drink slowly," Edgar said down into the darkness of the hole.

Clothes ripped, head swollen from the beating she'd taken, a small, frightened woman scurried over to the trough at her feet. She cupped her bound hands to the cold water and gulped at it, dehydrated though she had been surrounded by damp for the past few hours. There was a cut above her eye and her dirty blonde hair clung to her moist forehead. Her eyes darted around the dank oubliette, refusing to dilate in the sliver of sunshine coming through the gap in the ceiling. She sniffed at the air around her and her movements were stilted like a chipmunk caught in a trap. Edgar figured she still had a few hours before the fog cleared her brain and reality came rushing back. Then he'd know what sort of prisoner he was dealing with.

He pulled out the brick and lowered the wood of the compost pile back onto its moorings. As he stood back up, he rubbed his right knee, making another mental note to take an anti-inflammatory with his lunch.

5

Nick rode shotgun after Willie picked him up at the Central Division. He'd dropped twenty bucks into Ray's pocket and wished him luck. There were no guarantees Cobb would take the money now that Nick had him back on paper, but if he didn't check in at Dawkins every night, Nick couldn't protect him anymore. Innocent or not, he was the only lead in a murder investigation, in a division where closing cases was nearly impossible. No matter how hard the cops in Central Division worked, they were up against it, their jurisdiction covering Skid Row, downtown, and many neighborhoods chiseled out into warring gang territories. If an easy closure was handed to them, they took advantage of it. Ray was smart to invoke Archer's name. It was unlikely anything would be done to find another suspect. It made Nick hope his hunch about Ray's need for justice was correct.

The whole process took much longer than he would've liked. She didn't say anything, but he could see Willie wasn't pleased he'd left her to clean up the rest of the Seward scene.

They sat at a light on Beverly Boulevard, packed with the remnants of morning rush hour. Nick was lost in thought.

"You want to clue me in as to where your brain is?" Willie asked.

"Hmm? Oh, uh, that CI in there was the one who saved my life."

"The homeless guy?"

"The same," Nick said, rolling down the window to take in the cool breeze. The smells of Hancock Park flower beds wafted into the car. The rain had broken briefly, but there was another brooding gang of dark clouds creeping over the mountains in the distance.

The light changed and they inched forward.

"Jesus," Willie said, "Did you guys have a heartfelt reunion?"

"He was caught with a body this morning."

"Did he do it?"

"Not the type. Though he did kill a man in my house, so he's capable of it," Nick said. He was ninety-nine percent sure Ray Cobb was innocent, but his time as a detective had taught him to never count out any possibility.

"Who caught the body in Central?" Willie asked.

"Jimenez."

"I hate that prick. Can always feel his eyes on my ass when I'm in that division."

"And when you leave the room, he describes it in full detail. Wish that guy applied his ability to memorize the female anatomy to his ability to remember details about cases. It would make him a much better cop."

"Good thing he wasn't the primary on those Asian twins we found this morning or there would've been no way to pry the case out of his grubby little fingers."

When she turned the car off of Rossmore, they could see the mass of reporters had spread their frenzy away from the madhouse in Skid Row. It was the kind of activity Hancock Park residents paid high property taxes to avoid, but it wasn't every day the biggest star in the world was found with a shotgun blast to the head and his genitals mutilated, though the respectable news stations would leave the second part off of their reports.

Willie pulled the car into the driveway and Nick flashed his badge at the uniform in drying rain gear, standing watch at the vacant house.

Seward lived alone in the cavernous mansion, but based on his reputation, he wasn't ever without company. If he wasn't attached to the starlet of the week, he was getting sucked off in a gas station bathroom by whomever he happened to pick up at a party the night before.

"Jesus," Nick said, stepping into the large marble foyer. He wiped his feet on the Oriental rug. Willie swatted him on the shoulder.

"What?" he said.

"Have you, maybe, considered not tainting the area with your gross?" she asked.

"One, I taint every area with my gross no matter what, and two, were you planning on having somebody come in here to analyze the dirt particles that were left in the rug? You've been watching way too much CSI."

"How do you wanna do this?" she asked, ignoring him.

"You take the bedroom. I'll take the office. Figure you'll be the envy of your girlfriends being able to paw through Seward's underthings before anybody else."

"Even if I were attracted to him before this, after seeing his bits chopped off, it would be gone. And women don't have the same relationship to men's underwear as men do to women's underwear."

"You don't want to sniff the crotch and roll around in piles of it?"

She rolled her eyes at him and headed up the huge staircase.

"I'm coming up in five minutes to check on you," Nick called up to her. He was met with nothing but her middle finger.

Nick shrugged and headed for the back of the house, in awe of the 72-inch widescreen on the wall. He stepped down into the recessed living room and sat on the white leather couch, melting into it.

"Dear God, is this thing made of the skin of unicorns?" he said to himself, digging his hands into the cushions. He came up with nothing. The cleaning lady must have been good at her job.

In the large drawer of the oversized coffee table he found what he'd expected; a small pipe and a couple ounces of weed. Nothing out of place in any home in Los Angeles. He replaced the drawer and put the weed in an evidence bag. Before leaving the room, he grabbed the high-tech universal remote and pointed it at the television. Thinking the "On" button would just turn on the TV, he was met with a wall of sound. The speakers came to life and panels beneath the TV opened to reveal a set of all the newest gaming consoles. He shut it off before it could get a minute to calibrate.

The kitchen was spotless. The fridge stocked. Examination of the meals sealed in Tupperware showed Nick that Seward's diet was carefully controlled. Quinoa, kale, jicama, wheat grass — an encyclopedia of buzzword foods meant to keep him action lean and romance fit. If Nick's eating habits had been so meticulously monitored, he would have a secret apartment in Skid Row too, but it would be full of In-N-Out wrappers and chocolate stains instead of a severed penis and Asian adhesives.

The walls of the office were covered in more bookshelves than Nick expected Seward to have. On closer examination, most of the books were plays or acting guides. There was an entire section of sci-fi. Some obscure stuff. First editions of *Fahrenheit 451* and *2001: A Space Odyssey* were wrapped in plastic, displayed nicely among the rest of the ragged books on the shelf. Not that Nick paid attention to celebrity news, but he never picked up a nerd vibe from Lowell Seward. He probably would've supported the crap movies Seward made if he'd known he was a secret dork.

Nick looked up at the painting above Seward's oak desk. After seeing the scene of devastation at the Skid Row flophouse, he expected it to be some Scarface-emulating nude or an indulgent Lichtenstein. Instead, it was a simple blue canvas with the number "42" in large white letters. Based on the color scheme, Nick assumed that Seward was a huge Jackie Robinson fan, but aside from the painting, there was nothing that would indicate he was either a follower of the Brooklyn Dodgers or the Negro Leagues. The bookshelves held no copies of *Sandlot Seasons* or *Baseball's Great Experiment*. The only book about sports he found was a copy of *Quidditch Through the Ages*. Low Seward really was a nerd.

He flipped open the MacBook on the desk and turned it on. The familiar startup sound echoed in the otherwise silent house. There was no password protection on it, so he went for the address book. It was unused. Like most folks, Seward probably stored everything in his phone, but didn't bother to sync it with his desktop. When he opened Gmail, the password hadn't been stored in the system. Nick tried the typical "password" and "12345", even "Jackie Robinson," but none of them worked. He pulled open all of the desk drawers, thinking maybe Seward created such a complicated password he had written it down for easy access, but didn't find anything other than a few office supplies, abandoned scripts, and another stash of medical marijuana. He popped the prescription bottle into another evidence bag. If they got some unusual results back from Seward's toxicology report, looking into his dispensary might provide some answers. Weed was so common in Los Angeles he didn't expect it to be anything more than part of Seward's daily cocktail.

He felt like an idiot doing it, but he checked behind the painting for a wall safe. Nothing there. He stared at the "42" for a bit, then turned back to Seward's bookshelf.

Scanning the sci-fi novels, he came across what he was looking for. Each book in the series of Douglas Adams's *Hitchhiker's Guide to the Galaxy* was bent and well worn, the spines creased from heavy reading. Old scotch tape repaired a couple of the paperbacks and *The Restaurant at the End of the Universe* was in such bad shape, it had a twin copy that was equally abused. The thing that caught his eye was a black leather-bound collection of the *Hitchhiker's* books. All of the books in the series were collected in one tome, gold inlay on the spine making it look like a treasured bible. But it was new. Unlike the well-read paperbacks, the spine was intact and the leather shined without wear.

Nick had read the books in high school and remembered enjoying them, but hadn't gone back to them since. Most of the details he recollected from the series were manifestations of the movie made in the early 2000s. But he did remember one thing. According to Adams, the answer to Life, The Universe, and Everything, was the enigmatic, "42." On first read, it seemed like a joke, a mathematical output to a philosophical question, but it was the perfect answer. It said the question itself was ridiculous. Perhaps having the answer is only the beginning to finding what the right questions are.

He picked up the leather tome and flipped it open.

Jackpot.

A wood box was set in the cut-out text. It seemed a strange thing to have a fan abuse these words, but because of Seward's rabid consumption of the individual books, it was likely a gift given to him by someone who knew he was a fan. Someone in his inner circle who knew the real Low Seward. Someone who knew to come to his house before the police did and clean out his secret stash.

Nick brought the book over to the light of the window and could see there were streaks of fingers in the fine purple dust that had collected in the corners of the box. He couldn't see the grease of a fingerprint, but that's what technology was for. He shut the book, put it on the laptop, and took both of them out of the office with him.

"Hey."

Willie jumped at the sound of his voice, turning on him in anger. She happened to be going through Seward's underwear drawer and was gripping different colored boxer briefs in each hand.

"Busted," Nick said, smiling.

She flung the underwear back into the drawer and scowled at him. Any attempt at trying to explain what she was doing would be met with sarcasm and further teasing.

"Find anything?" she asked, appearing to move on to the other drawers, even though Nick could see by her sloppy replacement of the shirts she'd already gone through them.

"Nope," he said, "But someone else did."

She looked at him, expecting him to finish the thought.

"Whatever other drugs, contact info, or anything else incriminating has been lifted already," he said, shaking the bagged book in her direction.

"Could it have been the cleaning woman?" she asked.

"Her schedule was tacked to the fridge, along with the gardener and masseuse," Nick said, "None of them have been by in the last few days."

"Which means Seward hasn't been here either," Willie said.

"How do you figure?" Nick asked.

"Bachelor living alone with a proclivity for adolescent behavior?" Willie said, "Within a few hours without someone cleaning up after him, this place would've been a disaster area. Guarantee Seward hasn't been here since the maid last came."

"Three days ago," Nick said more to the air than Willie.

"I'll get a team down here to scrub the place. Check all the places we haven't," Willie said.

"Pretty sure anything we'd be looking for is already gone," Nick said, "You wanna grab some breakfast?"

"The Griddle. Your treat," Willie said, pushing past him.

She was halfway down the hallway before he called after her, "So do his Underoos smell like heaven?"

"Shut up," she said, her voice echoing up the stairs.

He chuckled to himself and followed.

6

Ray figured Nick wouldn't let him walk out the door without supervision, but didn't think he would load him into the back of a squad to check him into The Dawkins House. When the cruiser pulled up to the front of the shelter, Ray leaned into the cage, talking through the racked shotguns to the driver and his partner.

"Cuff me before you take me in there," Ray said.

The uniform driving the car turned around in his seat. Ray noticed Nick had pulled this guy aside and asked that he take care of the matter. Releasing a witness out into the wild, especially one with no permanent address, was tricky business.

"You walked out of that station a free man, now you want us to treat you like a criminal?" the uniform asked.

"You seem to have a good relationship with Detective Archer. You remember what he went through a couple years back, the real estate thing? I'm the one who got him into that fiasco," Ray said.

The uniform and his younger partner exchanged a look. The elder passed his cuffs through the gate.

"How long did it take you to convince folks you weren't a snitch?" the younger uniform asked.

"Still retain that reputation, depending on who you ask," Ray said.

He brushed his long hair forward with his hand until it hung over his forehead and eyes, then he snapped the cuffs on behind his back.

The sun had shooed away most of the clouds and the only testament to the days of rain was the damp garbage and rows of waterlogged tents on the sidewalk. The breakfast line outside of Dawkins was bustling.

As he was led past the queue, Ray kept his eyes to the concrete. The last thing he needed was to make eye contact with a familiar face waiting to get a free helping of powdered eggs.

The officers held him lightly at the elbows and walked him into the hallway outside the registration cage. The bored volunteer behind the counter flipped through an old copy of *The New Yorker*, not bothering to look up.

"Check-ins aren't until 9 p.m."

"Special circumstance," the elder uniform said, "Your supervisor is expecting us."

The volunteer flopped the magazine down and grabbed a Post-it note off the clipboard in front of him.

"Cobb, right?"

Ray didn't answer, just nodded.

"He's not dangerous, is he?" the volunteer asked, noticing the cuffs.

"No more than anybody else you've got staying here," the younger officer said. When Ray was uncuffed, his arms just dropped to his sides, no sigh of relief or wrists rubbed for emphasis.

The volunteer pulled out a registration card and handed it to Ray to fill out. Ray still hadn't said a word, his eyes to the ground. With a few quick scribbles, he filled out the card in illegible handwriting, then passed it back over the counter.

"Detective Archer will be checking in to make sure this one is signed in nightly, so be sure to keep that card handy," the elder uniform said.

"Didn't realize we'd become babysitters."

"Just keep an eye on him. He's an important witness," the younger uniform said.

The radio on his shoulder squawked.

"This is 49. Show us responding," he said into the talk box, nodding to his partner. They left Ray standing in front of the volunteer without a goodbye.

Once the officers were gone, the volunteer's tone softened. His contempt was clearly directed at the LAPD and not toward the homeless he served on a daily basis.

"We'll have a bed all set for you tonight. Lucky break considering the rain. Don't think we've seen the last of it this week," he said, trying to get Ray to raise his eyes from the floor. Ray didn't oblige him.

"Also we can wash those clothes for you and give you something to sleep in. You can either have these back or we can give you a new set."

Ray nodded to the volunteer to show he understood. The gesture had enough movement in it to evoke the pity Ray was hoping for. He wanted to give the impression he was a stray dog who had been kicked one too many times. It was working.

"Breakfast line has been cut off already, but you don't have to get in line," the volunteer said, "I'd slide you in early, but if you were sitting in the cafeteria with your tray full of pancakes when the first of the others came through the door... not good. Some of those guys were out there before the rain stopped. They see you in here, you may have a rough first night."

Ray nodded again. The volunteer actually gave a shit about him. He regretted in advance that his actions were probably going to get the kid in trouble.

The doors opened. Employees in reflective vests wrangled the breakfast line into the facility, a stream of destitution flowing through the lobby and into the cafeteria.

"Guillermo," the volunteer said to the short Guatemalan man holding the door. The volunteer gestured in reference to Ray and Guillermo nodded him over with his chin.

Ray raised a hand in thanks to the volunteer, keeping silent, and walked over to Guillermo. He stopped Ray with a hand to his chest, a gentle gesture telling him to wait until the next group was let into the cafeteria. At the head of the next group, Guillermo let Ray step into the line.

"Let this guy through fellas, he had to use the facilities," Guillermo said.

"Smells like he didn't make it in time," the toothless woman standing behind Ray said, cackling behind her rotting gums.

"You ain't one to talk, Lucille," a tall man in a ragged jacket said, "I can smell your rotten snatch from here."

The remark caused a ruckus in the line, a combination of laughter and anger, but Ray kept his head down, choosing not to react.

Guillermo doused the growing fire with a wry comment, "All right, we all stink a little this morning, keep moving."

"Even you, Guillermo," the tall man said, "What the hell you wearin' this mornin'? Eau de beaver?"

The men standing behind him let out hardy chuckles.

"My wife got this for me for our anniversary," Guillermo said.

"She ought to have her nose checked," the tall man said as he moved through the line, "And if she married you, her eyes too."

The final comment elicited an elaborate handshake from his compadre.

"Better watch yourself, or I'll replace her cooking with your eggs this morning, then you'll really be in trouble," Guillermo called after him as the line kept moving.

Ray could see these people were good at their jobs. But he also knew light-hearted quips diffusing a tense situation in the breakfast line would be worthless in the dormitory. Quiet and invisible was the way he wanted to stay and he hoped to sustain it through breakfast.

He made his way through the line, his tray loaded with pancakes, scrambled eggs, and breakfast sausage and sat down at the closest table to the door. He shoveled the food down as fast as he could, not only because he was hungry, but also because he needed to get out before anybody engaged him in conversation. His stomach had settled enough he was confident he could keep it in, but it would be at least half a day before all the Pepto was out of his system. He didn't want to push it just in case his gastrointestinal troubles came back.

Rolling up the last pancake and eating it like a burrito, Ray got up, his seat filled as soon as he stood. He bussed his tray and headed out into the yard with the rest of those who had gotten in and polished off their breakfasts early.

The early comers were pulling out cigarettes, chatting, rubbing their full bellies. He smoothed his hair down over his eyes, glancing up from the ground through the greasy strands, hoping he would hit pay dirt before the place got too crowded.

The chain link fence strung between the walls of concrete made him think it was more of a prison yard than a shelter. Citizens imagined places like The Dawkins House were the solution to the homeless problem, but they didn't know a lot of people were on the streets because they didn't like being cooped up. Ray knew lots of folks who wouldn't trade the freedom of their tent for a Section 8 apartment. Most of the people at Dawkins were just looking for a meal. They would be gone as soon as their food had a chance to digest.

The yard was filling up and he knew he couldn't linger much longer. Then he saw her.

The edge of his mouth went up in a smile as he squeezed through the crowd. Slipping between people and trying not to disturb their conversations, he settled where Mama Nomad was arranging her bags in the corner.

Mama only brought her most important things inside the shelter; various pictures cut out of magazines, chipped teacups she'd found in the garbage, an abandoned kite in the shape of a dragon with so many holes it would never fly again. Most of her gear consisted of the cherished pieces of clothing she didn't want to risk having someone pick through when she came in for breakfast.

Everybody had to leave their carts outside the walls, and though there was an unspoken understanding that people didn't touch what wasn't theirs, there was a contingent of thieves who didn't give a fuck about unwritten rules. Sometimes a group of bold teenagers would come through and see how many carts they could steal and ride down 4th Street to dump off the bridge into the concrete river below.

Mama Nomad was a favorite among the homeless. She always flashed a smile in someone's direction, whether they returned it or not, her teeth yellowed from tobacco and coffee, hanging loose in her graying gums. Crevasses ran along her motherly jowls and split her forehead into several sections every time she laughed. The dark skin on her hands was dry and chapped, but when she took Ray's hand in hers and asked him to sit down next to her, he didn't want to let go.

"Why, I tell you what," Mama said, adjusting the clear brown rims of her thick glasses and pushing a strand of crinkled gray hair behind her ear, "If'ns you don't just look like a man I had a love affair, wonderful love, lovely affair, with when I made my home on Hispaniola."

"Amos you said his name was," Ray said, speaking for the first time since he'd reached the shelter, keeping his voice low.

"Oh, we've met before. That sure is nice. I meet so many of these lovely peoples, the peoples just blend together in my mind," she smiled.

"I don't mind. Good to see you, Mama," Ray said with a smile.

"Child, I tell you what, though. You wouldn'ta been able to resist sitting so close to me back then. No sir-ee. Well, what I sure didn't have, I tell you for sure, was this belly made wide with baby making and I did have me some dancer's legs that the Governor of Tennessee his own self wanted to fly me across the pond to have these things bonded and certificated by the London Lloyds. For the God's honest," Mama said, gesturing to herself in pride. She smiled up at the parting clouds as she reminisced.

What Mama Nomad said she had done in her former life changed every time Ray saw her. Sometimes she told tales of her four kids, who now lived in Tallahassee with a man who took them away from her when she owned a restaurant voted "Best Grits in Florida." Other times she was a dancer from the Dominican Republic who'd had an affair with a high government official and had gotten in a bad car wreck with him. He died and she fled the country on two broken legs to avoid scandal. The latest tale involved a stint in the Ivory Coast as a clandestine entertainer for roving bands of poachers who she could tame like cobras in a basket with her singing voice. There was always enough detail in her stories to make the listeners wonder how much of it was real. If it all was true, then Mama had lived the ultimate nomadic life, but her advanced alcoholism made everyone wonder how she got where she was if a fraction of the stories could be verified. Her sweet demeanor and welcoming smile never made anyone want to doubt her.

Once a person took to living on the streets, it was their choice to offer up information on the life they'd had before. Most people chose to say nothing at all and that was respected. When someone was forthcoming about life before the fall, willing to reveal details, people knew better than to challenge their veracity. Even if something was complete and utter fiction, who was anyone to take that fantasy away? For Mama, her stories were probably the only thing keeping her from dying at the bottom of a bottle every evening.

"It's nice to see you, Mama," Ray clutched her hand tighter, "You come here for breakfast most days, is that right?"

"If'ns I can wake up that early," she cackled, "Sometimes, though, I get too deep into a gibber-jabber with a heap of sleepytime juice and can't manage to rouse myself 'fore noon. But if I can't find a pint, or let's be honest, a man with a pint who will warm me more than the booze, you find me here, for sure enough."

"Good to know," Ray said, "It's always good to see a familiar face. I'll be sure to visit with you each time I see you, that all right with you?"

"Conversing with folks is what drives me through my day, honey," Mama said, "When I was one of them elephant wranglers for a circus that was based in Reno, I had hardly no one to talk to excepting them pachyderms. Thought I'd go mad from not having a human ear to bend, but as you know the clowns were a sad folk and those tent boys wouldn't listen for more than five seconds without a lecherous bit o' nonsense flowing from their flappin' tongues. Not that I didn't get so lonely I didn't ignore their dirty dog ways every once and a bit, but sometimes a woman just has to make her standards, then forget them when it suits her, but look at me go on."

"I promise next time I see you to not flap my tongue at all. Just listen." Ray stood, letting go of her sandpaper hands. "I've got to head out for the day. Maybe you can tell me more about it tomorrow or the next day."

"Honey, if'ns you can listen to it, I can talk 'til suppertime. And I'll surely remember you when you come by. What was your name again?"

"If anyone asks, it's Ray Cobb. Just keep on remembering me as the fella who looks like Amos. And that I listen more than I talk."

"You sure is a good listener, for certainly sure. And that bit about you and Amos? That be one thing I surely will not forget," she adjusted the glasses on her face again, "No matter how much these old eyeballs wish to betray my own knowing." Mama waved goodbye, then dug into one of her bags, arranging and rearranging her worthless goods.

When Ray reached the gate, he looked back at her. It was as though he had ceased to exist. She was smiling at every man who passed, maybe hoping they would see a glimmer of the dancer from Santo Domingo, or the waitress from Florida, and give a formerly pretty face a cigarette.

Ray slipped through the open gate and headed for the red line. He had his witness, now he needed a decoy. Nick wouldn't check in on him until later, but he needed to get everything in place so he could figure out his next move.

He'd only made it about half a block before the Crown Vic started creeping after him. The tail was going to make his job much harder, but not impossible.

When he was riding in the backseat of the black and white, he'd caught a glimpse of the other car in the rearview mirror. He'd thought it was just another unmarked car heading out for the day, but it stayed on them the whole time, parking half a block down from Dawkins when they stopped. When Ray asked the uniform to hand him the cuffs, he was able to turn around and get a good look at the tail.

The detective, Jimenez, wouldn't want to waste all of his energy on one unlikely witness, but Ray knew Jimenez wasn't confident in Nick Archer's ability to keep his CI under wraps. Nick had been too trusting. Ray's plan was to disappear all along. But now that he had a tail, he needed the cop in the Crown Vic to follow him so he could dodge him properly. He didn't want to be looking over his shoulder for the rest of the day.

Ray circled the block around the Pershing Square Metro Station a couple of times, cutting through a small alley, seeing how willing the tail was to follow him. The unmarked car was having some trouble maneuvering around traffic and the tangle of one-way streets. Ray found himself stopping and begging for change a couple of times, waiting for the cop to catch up with him. When the car pulled into a legal parking space, Ray trotted down the steps into the subway.

He went over to the TAP kiosks and bought a card with the money Nick had slipped him. The tail raced down the stairs, thinking he would have to catch Ray before he got on the train, but had to pull to an awkward stop when he saw Ray buying a fare. The Crown Vic's driver was thin with a basketball player's frame. Ray wouldn't have trouble picking his fresh-shorn brown head out of a crowd.

Since the Metro changed their fares, there was no one at the turnstiles for Crown Vic to flash a badge at. Unless he wanted to deal with a swarm of transit cops, he would have to buy a TAP card like everybody else.

There was a train in the station, but Ray didn't want to get on before the cop had a chance to see which way he'd gone. Leading a tail around wasn't going to be as easy as he'd thought.

The doors closed and the train pulled away. Crown Vic ran down the marble stairs and jumped to the bottom. He smacked the passing train with an open palm as it flew past.

Ray peeked out from behind the other stairwell and watched him scan the platform, thinking he'd lost his man.

If Ray just stepped out onto the platform, casually waiting for the next train, Crown Vic would wonder why he didn't get on the last one and would probably figure out Ray knew he was being followed. He had to figure out a way to let Crown Vic know he was still there, but look like he'd missed the train accidentally.

Behind Ray, a teenager started tapping on a couple of empty buckets. He had been there all along, entertaining subway patrons for change, but had halted his playing as the train passed, not wanting to waste the energy of having his drums drowned out by the noise of the cars thundering down the rails. Ray wandered over to the bucket boy and started grooving to his sound.

"Was wonderin' why you quit playin', man!" Ray said, overloud. There was a waver in his voice, a tone he put on to make Crown Vic think in his bobbing and weaving around 7th Street, he'd scored a packet of meth and put it up his nose. He shook in front of the bucket boy, his body moving in no way connected to the music, playing the part of a homeless meth-head in his own little world.

"Give this man some of your dollars, people," Ray said, swinging his head around. Crown Vic pretended to read the rail line map while he occasionally glanced over at Ray grooving to the bucket boy's jam.

The thunder of another train soon echoed down the rails and the bucket boy finished up his song in an epic climax. Ray let loose a drunk's guffaw and held out his hand for a slap. The bucket boy obliged and Ray became his own personal carnival barker for another moment, calling for other patrons waiting for the train to load the kid's hat with dollars and cents. But soon the rush of the train drowned out his voice. He slapped the kid's hand one more time before stepping onto the northbound train. Crown Vic hopped onto another car. The ploy had worked, but Ray was going to have to play his meth high all the way to Hollywood.

He stayed standing, continuing to dance to the beat the bucket boy was no longer there to provide. Crown Vic was smart enough not to draw attention to himself by moving into Ray's car, but he kept close to the window, peering in every few seconds to make sure Ray wasn't moving, ready to follow him the moment he got off the train.

When the doors opened at Hollywood and Highland, Ray bounded up the stairs, focused on finding No-Tongue Duggan. He didn't check to make sure Crown Vic was behind him. If the cop was good on his feet, he would have eyes on Ray the whole time.

Popping up underneath the Dolby Theater, Ray dodged between the kiosks selling phone cases and random tourist crap. He needed to keep Crown Vic's eyes on him as long as he could, but make sure the cop didn't put his eyes on Duggan in the process.

He hit the flashing "Don't Walk" light on Hollywood Boulevard just in time and bobbed between the straggling flurry of tourists trying to make it across before the light changed. Crown Vic couldn't follow him across the street without stopping traffic and had to hover with the rest of the rubes, waiting for the honking to stop so he could continue following Ray.

Ignoring the change of lights, Ray wandered across Highland, weaving between stopped cars. He made sure the cop got a glimpse of him passing by the cheap Marilyn Monroe statue positioned outside the old Max Factor building before ducking into the parking lot of Mel's Diner. When he was out of Crown Vic's eye line, he ran down the alley, hoping No-Tongue hadn't chosen that moment to go take a piss. The signal would have to be quick and Ray didn't have the time to make another pass.

Billy "No-Tongue" Duggan was in his usual spot. A small lean-to next to the dumpster behind Mel's Diner had become his semi-permanent home. It was hidden from the Highland side of the street so the only people who ever saw him there were garbage men and Mel's kitchen staff, who knew he was both harmless and mute. He must have had a good metabolism because with the amount of junk he consumed—burgers, fries, milkshakes—he should've been huge. But he was thin and muscular, an identical build to Ray. The way his greasy hair shagged into his face and the red whorls in his beard showed beneath the increasing gray, Ray Cobb and Billy Duggan could have been brothers. The way Ray had brushed his hair forward and puffed out his beard in The Dawkins House, the two men could be mistaken for each other. That is, unless someone was paying close attention. One of the benefits of being homeless was nobody paid that close attention. They all might as well have been invisible.

Ray crumpled up a ten-dollar bill and threw it at No-Tongue's head. It bounced off the bridge of his nose and he looked up to see his old friend.

"Parking Structure. Take McCadden," Ray said, "Wait until I pass the corner to move."

No-Tongue smiled a wide smile that revealed brown teeth and the scarred stub that earned him his namesake.

Ray dug in the dumpster. He grabbed the first thing he could find, a quarter of a hamburger chewed to shit and cooked well done. When Ray closed the lid and made his way back the way he came, Crown Vic was standing in front of the diner. He'd pulled out his phone and was pretending to send a text message.

Ray stepped into traffic, causing a black Range Rover to screech to a halt, guaranteeing the cop's eyes would be on him.

In the alley, No-Tongue got up from his squat and headed in the opposite direction toward McCadden Place.

Ray took a bite of the old burger and tossed it in the middle of Highland Avenue, spitting out what he'd put in his mouth. No more taking chances with food.

His fish on the hook, Ray wandered up past the Lucky Strike Bowling Alley, through the mall, and down the escalator into the parking structure. On the bottom floor, he found No-Tongue waiting for him under the last small set of stairs. No-Tongue had already started to undress.

"Need you to spend a couple nights at Dawkins for me. Guaranteed bed, shower, clean clothes," Ray said, emptying the pockets of his coat onto the ground before handing it over to No-Tongue. Standing there in his stained boxers, No-Tongue made a slice across his neck gesture.

"Heard about that already, huh?" Ray said, adjusting No-Tongue's hair to look like his. There wasn't much time to get him back into sight and catch the tail.

"Anyone gets a bead on you, spend some time with Mama Nomad and disappear. She'll confirm she'd seen you that day," Ray said.

No-Tongue tried to hand Ray the ten-dollar bill back. He'd been stubborn since the moment Ray had met him.

A couple of months after Ray burned the last vestiges of Ernie Politics, he was panhandling outside of LACMA and a tourist berated him for asking for change twice. He had no clue what the guy was talking about until he saw No-Tongue across the street by the imported section of the Berlin Wall.

Ray was ready to get into a territorial dispute with the copycat asshole, but then he saw the mutilated stub through No-Tongue's smile. They decided to take advantage of the resemblance. If there was a situation where Ray could talk No-Tongue out of a jam or where No-Tongue's speech imped-iment made it so Ray wouldn't be saying anything to anyone, they switched. When the threat had passed, they switched back.

Asking No-Tongue to impersonate him to avoid the police was more than either of them had ever requested of the other. There was more risk involved in this venture than their twin-switch game had ever toyed with, but No-Tongue was loyal to a fault. Ray didn't have much time to think about the position he was putting his friend in. He needed to disappear.

"You gotta keep a tail on you. Get on the red line this afternoon, half that tenner's for the fare. The other half's for lunch. A cop gave it to me, gotta look like I'm spending it," Ray said, walking up the next flight of stairs. No-Tongue turned his hands into makeshift goggles and put them to his face.

"He's black. Bald. Wearing a gray suit, yellow tie. Has the look of PD all over him. He should've followed us in here. Get him back on you, but don't let him get too close. Pretend you're napping on the subway and cover up good," Ray said.

No-Tongue patted Ray on the shoulder, gesturing that he could use his bed behind Mel's if he needed it.

"Until I find a way to get clear of this thing, I'm not gonna do much sleeping. But if I'm not clear by pickup day, I'll be sure to move it for you so it doesn't get scattered by the truck," Ray said.

Three fingers were shoved in his face.

"Yeah. I know. Wednesday morning. If I'm not out of this by then, I may not be around to clear your bunk," Ray said, "Get going."

No-Tongue made his way up the stairs and out into the first floor of the parking structure. Ray waited behind for a bit, fixed his hair in a different way and adjusted his newly acquired clothes. They didn't stink as much as the ones he'd given away, but weren't far off. It was always worse when he had to breathe in someone else's B.O.

Once enough time had passed where No-Tongue could've gotten the cop on the hook, Ray went back up to the surface. He snuck around the side of the display windows of The Gap and saw the back of Crown Vic's shiny head bobbing down Hollywood Boulevard, following No-Tongue as he walked toward the Chinese Theater.

7

Willie turned the car onto the Avenue of the Stars and pulled into the parking garage of The Voight Agency. The booth security guards looked like they didn't bother spending a portion of their minimum wage on dry cleaning.

"Open your trunk please," one guard said.

Willie flashed her badge at him and he let them pass into the depths of the parking garage without checking the trunk.

"Now I know which building I'm going to blow up when I finally snap," Nick said, waving to the other sweetly retarded guard.

"Did you really want him digging around in our trunk? There's a loaded shotgun back there," Willie said.

"Point taken."

"I hope they validate. Parking here costs twenty bucks an hour."

"Is that your subtle way of telling me not to make our interviewee hostile so he'll volunteer validation tickets?" Nick asked.

The tires screeched on the painted asphalt as the car turned each of the corners down deep below Olympic Boulevard. Willie pulled the car into a space across from the escalator.

"You don't seem to have a lot of finesse if there isn't a pretty girl involved," Willie said.

"I've got plenty of finesse, even if there are ugly girls involved."

"Yeah? Do you remember the incident at the Drexel Corporate Headquarters?" she asked, heading up the escalator.

"I'll admit, that was handled poorly. But he looked like he was about to hit me with a golf club."

"He was practicing his putting."

"He was also guilty," Nick said, "What floor is this place on?"

"The first. And he almost got the case thrown out on a police brutality charge."

"Good thing I accidentally hit my head on his desk when I took him down," Nick looked around at the walls, trying to figure out where he was, "How have we not passed the first floor? We've gone up like four floors already."

Willie rolled her eyes at him, "Parking, then level A, B, and C."

"Why am I the weirdo for thinking that's misleading?"

She didn't answer him as the escalator let them out into a vast lobby of clean white marble, one wall a spectacle of glass.

"Finally," he said, going over to the security desk.

"Which way to The Voight Agency?" Willie asked. She opened her badge to the security guard with a practiced flip of the wrist.

"Up the stairs and to the left," the security guard said.

"This isn't the first floor?" Nick asked, Willie already on her way up the stairs.

"This is the mezzanine, sir."

"Archer!" Willie called down to him before he had a chance to get into it with the security guard. He bounded up the stairs behind her, glancing at a stainless-steel sign for The Voight Agency.

Through the double doors at the top of the stairs, there was another security desk. It was starting to get ridiculous. Nick had been in airports with fewer guards. He ignored the desk and hit the elevator button.

"May we help you?" one of the guards asked. A tight blue blazer stretched across his barbarian girth, the buttons straining to hold in his chest. An icy stare told Nick and Willie they'd be in trouble if he had to come out from behind the desk.

"LAPD here to see Shane Davidson," Willie said before Nick could speak.

A pudgy, slightly effeminate Hispanic man in an argyle sweater and button-down shirt looked up from his phone. The dark circles under his eyes testified to a lack of sleep, but his perky demeanor was fueled by a full morning of espressos.

"Oh, yes, we've been expecting you," the young man said, "I'm Bernard, Mr. Davidson's assistant, I'll take you up."

Bernard didn't wait for them to introduce themselves. He hit the same button to call the elevator Nick had pressed, swiping a plastic badge to light it up.

"Did our office call ahead, Bernard?" Nick asked, trying not to put a sarcastic twinge in his pronunciation of the assistant's affected name.

"Mr. Davidson texted me last night to open up a space in his schedule today for LAPD detectives. Figured you would be here around 10 a.m. You're late," Bernard said, a smile added to his last statement.

"There was traffic," Nick said, flat, "What time did he text you last night?"

Bernard's face was buried in his phone. He scrolled through an endless litany of text messages. Apparently, The Voight Agency did more business before noon than the New York Stock Exchange.

"3:34 in the morning," Bernard said, holding up his phone to show them the time of the text. It read: *LAPD, tmrw, 10a.* Satisfied they'd had enough time to read it, his gaze returned to the small device. The touchscreen made small clicking noises with every finger tap. It was an extension of his hand.

"What're you looking at there?" Nick asked.

"*Perez Hilton. Deadline. For What It's Worth.* Have to keep up with what's happening out there to get ahead," Bernard said.

The elevator opened on what appeared to be another lobby. Nick wondered if the entire agency was just lobbies and the assistants were stored in pods somewhere. The average age of the employees was about twenty-three years old and everyone was attractive. Nick felt like an old troll. He could see the place even made Willie self-conscious and she was a good-looking woman.

They passed by a custom coffee bar, through a gathering of couches, before Bernard stopped at a curved wall. He pulled a small handle, revealing a circular conference room. The table in the center matched the white marble surrounding the rest of the offices. Against the back wall, there was a flat screen television and a bar stocked with ice water, coffee, tea, and tiny cans of soda.

"Mr. Davidson will be with you shortly. Help yourself to whatever, it's all there for you. Anything else you'd like?" Bernard asked, smiling and eager.

"You don't happen to have an omelet chef back there, do you?" Nick said.

"I'll have some pastries sent up," Bernard said.

"He's kidding," Willie said, "We're fine."

"It's really no trouble," Bernard said.

"Go get your boss," Nick said. With that, the assistant was gone.

"You just had a gigantic stack of pancakes," Willie said.

"Walking up all those levels to the *first floor* made me work up an appetite."

Willie shot him an annoyed look, one he realized she was giving him more and more often. He went to the small bar and opened a soda.

"What're you doing?" she asked.

"He said they were for us."

The curved door of the conference room opened and Shane Davidson stepped through, talking on his phone via his headphones. He was wearing a slim-tailored blue suit and his dark hair was graying at the temples. From the way he'd refused to acknowledge the detectives, without a passing glance, Nick was already starting to form an opinion of the man. It wasn't a good one.

"TNT is playing *Darkness at the Edge of Nowhere* tonight. Make sure we get a tribute promo in there around the first commercial break. I don't care who you have to bump."

He ended the call.

"Sorry about that, the first twenty-four hours after a celebrity dies aren't just for mourning, they're also for leverage. Need to make sure the next of kin keep getting those residuals," Davidson said, extending his hand.

Willie shook it, and so did Nick, but not without adding a comment.

"Keep that ten percent commission going as long as possible, eh?" Nick said.

Willie gave him another of her signature looks, but Davidson laughed.

"That's right, Detective..."

"Archer. This is Detective Grant."

"Don't get me wrong, I'm sad Low is gone, but I can't say I'm surprised. He's been on a downward spiral for a long time coming."

The three of them sat around the table, Davidson alone on one side, addressing the two detectives on the other end.

"I'm going to cut through the idle chit-chat before my partner gets a chance to," Willie said, "We talked to your assistant, Bernard. He said you were expecting us?"

"You found Low's phone and saw he called me late last night," Davidson said.

"You were the last person he called," Nick said, "Did he give you any insight as to what was happening in the apartment that would cause you to schedule an appointment with us instead of calling 911?"

"If you want to know where I was around the time of his murder, my wife will confirm I was sleeping next to her. If that's not enough, I'm sure we could get you my security footage, though you may see some things we did before going to sleep you might not want to."

"We didn't ask you for an alibi," Nick said.

"But you'd eventually need one, right?"

"I suppose. But I'm curious why you seem to have everything scripted out in your head?" Nick leaned in. He avoided Willie's eyes telling him to back off.

Davidson let out a sigh and checked his platinum Rolex. Nick watched him fidget. It wasn't nervousness, per se, more impatience. As though he was less concerned his number one client had just died and was more aggravated that the detectives' presence was keeping him from discovering the next up-and-comer in an unheralded web series.

"Low discovered something on the set of his last movie. A new drug given to him by one of his co-stars."

The information was blunt. Prepared. Davidson knew what they were going to ask and chose to go on the offensive. Nick and Willie knew better than to take the bait and play defense.

"Meth?" Willie asked.

"I wish," Davidson said, "I know how to deal with meth addicts. This new thing makes me long for the days of cocaine. At least on that people were productive."

"Purple powder?" Nick asked.

Davidson nodded, "They would go on benders they called Shadow Dancing. Him and Rory."

Neither of the detectives had to ask who Rory was. Rory Knapp played sidekick to Lowell Seward's hero in a trio of action flicks set in the Middle East. Their faces were plastered on posters at every bus stop in town.

"Most nights he would get to calling me, blathering about the next stage of his transcendence," Davidson continued, "The next day he would forget we ever talked. At the end of every trip, he would end up in police custody, or whoever he was with the night before would report him missing. And I would end up with one of you detectives sitting where you are now," Davidson said.

An incoming text message interrupted him. The three sat in silence as he tapped out a response. Finished, he looked back up.

"I figured he'd end up in the hospital or arrested for assault. Instead of trying to fit the familiar LAPD visit into my schedule, I thought I should plan for it. Never expected him to turn up dead."

"What did you talk about when he called you?" Nick asked.

"I honestly have no idea. He was blathering. One minute he claimed to have climbed the mountain and seen the other side, the next he told me he was cumming—," he glanced at Willie and stopped himself, "—sorry, *ejaculating* on the chests of a couple of mermaids."

Nick thought of the twins and their slim brown legs. They would never be mistaken for fins.

"Nothing about his attackers? Or if he was in trouble?" Willie asked.

Davidson squinted at her in confusion. She didn't understand the look.

"What do you know about Shadow Dance?" Davidson asked.

"Had never heard of it until you mentioned it," Nick said.

"Hmmm... that would make sense," Davidson contemplated, "My guess is you're going to hear a lot more about it in the near future."

Willie looked over at Nick, who made a gesture to let him talk.

"It has a few names right now, nothing has really stuck; Shadow Dance, Flying Saucer, Picotee, and my personal favorite, Grandpa," Davidson said.

"Grandpa? Doesn't have the same ring as crack, does it?" Nick said.

"It's a psychedelic. A designer drug circling through the big earners in the entertainment business. It's only a matter of time before it trickles down."

"Going to preface this by saying, we aren't Narco, not looking to find anything but the murderer," Willie said, "You ever done this stuff?"

"Sober fifteen years. My poison was pills," Davidson said.

Nick watched Davidson's eyes before asking another question. There wasn't a shake to his voice or a glimmer of doubt. Davidson was either a man happy to tell the truth or confident enough to believe his own lies. Nick could see he got a charge from being the smartest guy in the room and right now he was the foremost authority on Shadow Dancing. Content to let him talk, Nick hoped the hubris would deliver a piece of information Davidson didn't intend to reveal.

"How long has this drug been around?" Willie asked.

"It appeared on my radar a few months ago. Access to it is akin to being part of a secret society. Nobody talks about it at parties. It's not passed around like ecstasy or blow."

"Seems strange this is the first we're hearing of it," Nick said, curious about this man's deep knowledge of something that hadn't shown up in any Narco cases. Davidson kept fingering the headset attached to his phone. Not enough it could be mistaken for anything other than him being worried about his business, but enough that Nick could tell it was a comforting gesture.

"You probably wouldn't. Nobody is getting in their cars and driving through a preschool or wandering the streets on this stuff," he switched his tone, "Low described Shadow Dancing as a waking dream, everything blending together. Life became a series of jump cuts, fantasy sequences interspersed with glimpses of reality. And Low said the quality of the high never dwindled. These junkies who get loaded on heroin, crack, they need more and more product to get the same high, but Shadow Dance gave him the same powerful jolt every time. Shadow Dance dealers are running a concierge service, which is why it's only known to a certain echelon."

"You know a lot about this stuff," Nick said, amused more than accusatory.

"Low changed overnight. I pressed him for what was going on. Threatened to drop him as a client. He told me all about it. I tried to get him to stop. A drugged-out client runs out of goodwill in this town fast."

"Would we find the number of his dealer in his phone?" Willie asked.

"He may have been a psychedelic freak, but he wasn't stupid," Davidson said, "You need to talk to Rory Knapp, he was the one who introduced Low to it while they were shooting *Blade of the False King*. And if Low's death is related to whoever is dealing Shadow Dance, they might go after Rory next."

"Any idea where we can find him?" Willie asked.

"He didn't show up on set this morning. I'm playing it off as grief, telling the director he needs a day to process the information about Low, but the movie is already behind schedule. I want to talk to him as much as you do, but he's not answering his phone. Figured I'd send someone to check on him at home, but since you're here it'll save me an assistant," Davidson said, checking his phone again.

He stood up, replying to another text message.

"I'm sorry, but between Rory's disappearing act and dealing with the fallout from Low, I'm going to have a hell of a day."

"We appreciate you being so forthcoming," Willie said, "We'll probably need some more information, so stay close to the phone."

"Always am," he said, shaking his phone at them before leaving.

They followed him out of the conference room.

"What do you think?" Willie asked when Davidson was out of earshot.

Nick looked over at the espresso bar.

"I think I'm going to get a coffee for the road. You want one?"

"Archer..."

"And then we can talk in the car," he said, raising an eyebrow. She understood.

"Americano. Double," she said.

8

Ray flicked at the Metro TAP card in his pocket. He would've handed it over to No-Tongue with the rest of his stuff, but was certain he'd have to hop on public transport at least one more time and didn't want to buy another one. Between the four dollars it had cost him to get up to Hollywood and the ten dollars he'd given to No-Tongue to get back downtown, he didn't have much capital left.

It was no coincidence the cops were on top of him as soon as he'd arrived at the Impala and pulled the body out. Someone was waiting for him to get back to the rusted car. If their intention wasn't to pin the murder on Ray, then it was to shift the focus to him so the trail would grow cold on the real culprit.

Ray couldn't think of anyone he'd pissed off lately. Sure, there had been small disagreements, but nothing so severe as to frame him for murder. He knew he'd have to come up with some answers quick. His decoy would only last so long.

No-Tongue knew the drill. He would wander around Holly-wood for a bit, dig in some garbage cans, beg for some change outside the Crossroads of the World, try to get someone around the Arclight to give him any leftover soda or popcorn, then he would head into the Metro tunnel and go back to Dawkins. The volunteers from the morning would've placed a description on his sign-in card and he would identify himself as Ray Cobb. Those who saw him would remember the shaggy hair and silence, let him register for his designated bed and give him priority in the dinner line. While this charade was happening, Ray couldn't risk being seen in two places at once. He had to change his look.

The best place for him to do some grooming would've been the public library on Ivar, but there was always someone washing up in one of the sinks and Keith D. was there from open 'til close brushing his teeth. Ray had watched him brush until his gums bled, but he just kept loading that brush up with baking soda and going at himself. Ray only wanted a select group of people to know he'd changed his appearance and word would get around if he was seen at the library. His usual haunts wouldn't work.

The racks on the Melrose sidewalk in front of the ram-shackle used bookstore boasted clearance books for a dollar. He wouldn't be able to finagle a bathroom stop by spending a buck, so he grabbed two paperbacks off the rack and opened the door to the darkened shop.

The aura of dust in the place was stifling. The bookstore was what Ray imagined the inside of a mad man's brain looked like. Aside from the hodgepodge of books covering floor to ceiling shelves, there were disorganized piles on the floor. Cardboard boxes lined the walls, stacked three high. Hundreds of books no one would ever buy; computer instruction manuals for obsolete software, atlases containing maps of non-existent countries, magazines no one read when they were on newsstands.

The proprietor's skin was as paper-thin as the pages of the Gideon bibles in the religion section. He was reading a worn Ross MacDonald novel, *The Instant Enemy*. The yellowed paper crinkled beneath his brittle fingers as he turned the pages, each whetted by saliva from his white tongue. Ray could see his dark blue veins crisscrossing between the liver spots and patches of pink discoloration. His crisp button-down shirt hung on his slight frame and the glasses perched on the edge of his nose were slung by a rope around his neck. He put the book down as Ray approached the counter, stretching over the wall of boxes to set the two paperbacks down in front of him.

"That be all today?" the old man said, examining the covers of the books, then reading the blurbs on the backs, as though he would refuse to sell them if the summaries sounded interesting. There didn't appear to be any judgment on the old man's face, he was just pleased to have a customer.

"Yep," Ray said, trying to be pleasant.

The old man flipped open the inside cover of both of the books, looking at the prices written there in pencil.

"Two dollars even," he said, "Need a bag?"

Ray handed over a couple of crumpled bills from his diminished bankroll.

"Nope, I'm good," Ray said. He picked up the paperbacks from the counter.

"Have a good one. Oh, and if you like that one on the bottom there," he said, referencing the biography of JFK Ray had chosen at random, "I've got a copy of that book by what's-his-name, the fella that did the movie, you know, was based on... uh... the author's name was Jim... Morrison," the old man said.

"Garrison," Ray corrected.

"Oh yeah," the old man said, laughing, "Two very different guys."

"You got that right," Ray turned to leave, "Enjoy the rest of your day."

"You, too. Let's hang on to this sunshine a couple more days."

Ray put his hand on the door, then turned back to the old man who had already re-immersed himself in the MacDonald paperback.

"I hate to ask, but do you have a restroom I could use?" Ray asked, knowing the answer.

The old man paused, letting out a long, deep breath.

"It's employees only, but since you paid for your books and aren't one of those loitering types who do a bunch of reading then don't bother to take what they got four chapters into, I suppose it's all right," the old man said, his humanity getting the better of him, not judging a book by its cover.

"Thank you. That hot wings place next door did something terrible to me. I'll be sure to clean up after myself," Ray said.

"All the way back to the left," the old man said, "And I understand about that place. Have had to close down for a full afternoon myself on account of a poor choice of lunch venue."

Pushing into the tiny bathroom, Ray realized the smell of musty books permeated the entire place. He locked the door behind him and looked into the mirror, pushing his long hair out of his eyes. He took off his coat and shirt, his pale torso looking back at him. The crisscross of scar tissue shined along his belly where the bullet had gone in. It had been his reminder for the past few years to stay out of affairs that didn't concern him. He'd lost too much getting involved in matters he didn't need to. But this time was different. It was his own skin he was saving.

Or was it just random? Did he happen to be the guy sleeping in the car that week, and therefore the unlucky recipient of a murder charge? Was he being paranoid?

The plastic bag from the 99-cent store crinkled as he pulled out the cheap scissors and disposable razor. Poorly constructed and already falling apart, the small scissors had trouble with his greasy, stubborn hair, but his new look didn't have to be perfect, it just had to be different. When the hack job was finished, his red-tinted brown hair cropped close to his head, he put all of the discarded hair into the empty plastic bag. The old man was nice enough to let him use the bathroom, even after he had falsely admitted he was going to use it to take a messy shit, he didn't want to clog up the ancient pipes with clumps of dirty hair.

Ray lathered up his face with hand soap and put the pink plastic razor to his cheek. He couldn't remember the last time he'd shaved. Trimmed his beard, sure, to avoid it growing into his food and becoming uncontrollable, but his bare face hadn't seen air in almost a decade. The first drag of the razor along the wiry hair snagged on his skin, slicing a small line into his jaw.

By the time he was done, his face was in good shape, though the razor had done a hell of a job on his neck. He wiped the bloody spots clean and dabbed bits of toilet paper on each of the cuts to stop the bleeding. He slipped No-Tongue's t-shirt over his head, catching a glimpse of himself in the mirror. He'd been so focused on getting the job done, he hadn't paused to see the result. It was a face he hadn't seen in a long time.

Lines ran deep along his nose, framing his mouth. The skin was red and pale from being long buried under a beard. A small scar he'd almost forgotten about curved over the dimple in his chin and his jawline was strong and sharp. Age branded his face, but without the gray tangle of beard, he looked like a much younger man, shedding at least a half a decade. If the haircut hadn't been done so hastily, he would've fit right in with the hipsters in Silverlake, the ones who spent hours trying to get the same rumpled look with dollops of expensive styling product. A set of black-rimmed glasses, an ironic t-shirt covered by a cashmere scarf, some skinny jeans, and Ray would've been one of the groovy cats who spent their weekends at Skylight Books, attending readings of essays by Chuck Klosterman.

"You die in there?" the old man asked through the door.

"Done," Ray said, "Just want to make it look better than I found it."

"Well, I appreciate the maid service, but I've gotta piss. Prostate is swollen to the size of a beach ball."

Ray did his best to clean out the sink of any stray hairs or soap suds. He tied the bag of hair together and dumped it into the garbage can in the corner.

When he stepped out into the bookstore, the old man took one look at him and his face went sour.

"Smelled so bad it burned all your hair off, eh?"

"Something like that," Ray said, pushing past.

"I don't appreciate people taking advantage of my hospitality," the old man said, peering into the bathroom, "Least you cleaned up after yourself."

"I'm sorry, I just—"

"Sign out front says bookstore, not barbershop," the old man said, "My son is up front managing the counter. Get outta here before I tell him what you pulled."

Ray hung his head, but made his way to the front of the store. It was rare someone offered unexpected kindness and he hated having taken advantage of the old man. It meant the next person who came to the store in need of something, the old man would think twice about helping. He hated having stolen that capacity for trust away from someone, even if for an instant.

Behind the counter at the front of the store, an overweight middle-aged man ate Thai food out of a Styrofoam container. Ray kept his eyes to the ground as he pushed open the glass door.

The heat of the sun hit the skin on his face for the first time in a long time. The exposure was uncomfortable.

9

Bernard had given them Rory Knapp's address in the Los Feliz Hills, though neither of them expected to find anyone home. Instead of making a run out of town, there was a chance Knapp decided to go on a solo Shadow Dance and deal with the death of his friend in a dream state.

"You going to talk to me about why you weren't your usual pain-in-the-ass self in there?" Willie asked.

"You haven't learned by now when I shut up, it's because I'm getting more out of listening?" Nick asked.

"Don't give me that master-sensei crap. I could tell he wasn't telling us the whole truth either, but didn't show my hand like you," Willie said.

"Agents are around to get actors jobs. That's about it. It isn't the crap you used to see on *Entourage*. Sometimes they have intimate knowledge of their personal lives, but really only when it's stuff that gets in the way of getting them work," Nick said.

"Which is the category this would fall into."

"For someone who claims to not be directly involved in selling Grandpa—"

"Don't call it that—"

"He knows an awful lot about it. How it works, how it gets delivered, what the trip is like. And he was nervous. Shane Davidson is high on my list of suspects."

"We find Knapp maybe he can tell us how they contacted this concierge service without using the phone. And my guess is with the NSA reading everybody's email, they weren't using an AOL chat room," she said.

"AOL chat room?"

"It was an example, dickhead."

"Though, it would be appropriate while we're looking for a drug called Grandpa."

"I'm going to call it Shadow Dance."

"Go ahead. It'll always be Grandpa to me," Nick said.

They sat in silence, driving up through Hollywood and turning on Sunset Boulevard heading east. Nick started to think about the logistics of something so exclusive it had to be delivered by hand. No texts, no emails, no phone calls. That meant either dead drop or use of a burner phone. Whoever was doing the deal probably had a small handful of trusted messengers. People they wouldn't have any trouble getting in and out of movie sets.

Movie sets.

Nick pulled out his phone and pulled up the browser.

"What was the name of the last movie Seward and Knapp worked on together? Can you beat Google?" Nick asked, typing into his browser.

"The movie Davidson talked about was *Blade of the False King*, but their last movie was *B*—"

"*Baghdad Shuffle*. Too slow Bobby Fischer," Nick said, holding the phone up to her.

"I don't understand that reference."

"Chess against a computer? You were a child of the eighties, right?"

"Pretty sure that was Gary Kasparov, not Bobby Fischer," she said.

"And *Baghdad Shuffle* was produced by... Regulation Pictures and Warner Bros.," Nick said.

"You want to let me in on what you're doing?" Willie asked.

Nick found the number of the production company and put the phone to his ear.

"Security on set is crazy tight. Anybody making a delivery would have to be on a list. They have to show their I.D. at the gate."

"Have you ever been on a studio lot?" Willie asked, "There's the illusion of security, but the guys working the gates aren't exactly a crack squad of investigators. I doubt they would spot a fake I.D."

"But they would notice if the same person came to the set often. We'll get a fake name, but the pictures still have to match. I'm not looking for—"

Someone on the other end of the phone picked up.

"Hi, this is Detective Nick Archer with the LAPD. I'm investigating the Lowell Seward case. I was wondering if I could speak with your production coordinator? Thanks."

If Nick could get the list of set visitors for *Baghdad Shuffle* and *Blade of the False King*, there would be a set of similar names on both lists. It would probably be someone using a fake name and a fake I.D., but they would have a much better idea of who they were looking for, maybe even a picture.

He got someone from production on the phone, and though it wasn't the production coordinator for either of those movies, they did have access to the files. He gave the person his email and hung up.

"It'll take them a bit to compile the lists. Let's hope the deliveries happened when they were on the lot. If they happened on location, it would be just as easy for Seward or Knapp to step off set and get what they needed. But both of those flicks were shot in Tunisia. I doubt the concierge service went that far," Nick said.

The sedan wound through the roads of the Los Feliz Hills, both of the detectives trying to get a bearing on where they were. Up where the money was, the roads had been designed to confuse anyone who might get curious. After the popularity of Star Maps sold in front of the Chinese Theater, many of the newer stars had migrated to places where it wasn't convenient for tourists to venture. It wasn't good business to take a group up to the tangle of roads in Los Feliz or Silverlake just to find one or two houses.

When Davidson had dropped Rory Knapp's name, Nick tried to hide his surprise. Often a person's public and private personality differed, but Rory Knapp was a consummate character actor. The only time anybody saw him in the press was when he was promoting a movie. He'd garnered a little more attention working with Lowell Seward. Their Baghdad trilogy was a thinly veiled remake of the 'Road To' movies Bob Hope and Bing Crosby had done in the '30s and '40s, albeit with a lot more violence and explosions. Regulation Pictures tried to do with Knapp and Seward what *Ishtar* had failed to do in the '70s. Now that Seward was dead, there would be a lot of money in the third unreleased Baghdad movie.

The facade of Knapp's house was modest. It had a flat-roofed Frank Lloyd Wright style and the yard was a series of well-manicured plants, but it wasn't overdone. The walk was polished flagstones and a serenity fountain bubbled on the front porch. It didn't look like much, but both of them had seen places like it before. The rest of the house had been built into the hill, stretching out and down; gorgeous views, exposed pool, windows open to the world.

Nick rang the doorbell. A small dog barked from behind the frosted glass, but there was no response. He knocked hard on the door, angering the dog even more.

"Think we can get a search warrant run up here?" Nick asked.

"It would take most of the afternoon. We'd be better off leaving and coming back," Willie said.

Nick stepped around into the yard, trying to get a glimpse in one of the windows, but he couldn't get a good view.

"Well, it was worth a—"

A scream from the back of the house made both of them alert.

"Aye! Mister! No!" a foreign-accented woman yelled out.

They both pulled their guns. Nick gestured for Willie to go around the side of the house. He tried the front door. It was locked. He kicked the jamb a couple times and the wood burst in.

A terrier leapt for him, biting down on this pant leg. The tiny dog didn't do any damage, so he ignored it, dragging it with him as he did a scan of the living room. He saw Willie pass by a window at the side of the house before he turned the corner into the kitchen. The dog clung tight to the fabric of his trousers, whipping around with each of Nick's movements. With his first glimpse of the balcony, large enough to hold a pool and cabana, Nick knew Willie wouldn't be able to cover the rear. She would have to double back and come through the front of the house.

Rory Knapp stood on the railing, teetering over the deep canyon below. There was a wild electricity in his eyes and he looked like he had been wearing the same set of clothes for a few days. A Hispanic housekeeper was on her knees on the other side of the pool, begging him in broken English not to jump.

His eyes went wide as soon as he saw Nick's gun and he tipped his body over the edge before Nick could yell, "Freeze!"

Nick ran through the open sliding glass door, the change in speed releasing the terrier's grip from his leg, sending the dog flying under the low couch. Knapp's body fell from sight in slow motion.

Finally arriving at the edge, he looked down and saw Knapp's twisted body among the brush about fifty feet down. He put his head on the railing and smacked it with his hand. Willie had entered the house behind him and was comforting the housekeeper.

"He just... just climb up when he hear the knock," she said, crying, "I just get here... didn't know he home..."

"You got her?" Nick said, watching Willie rub the woman's back.

"Yeah. I'll stay here. Go call it in."

Nick took two steps toward the house when another sound stopped him. An anguished whimpering from below.

He peered over the ledge and could see Rory Knapp, his head cracked open on a rock, reaching for his twisted legs, moaning in pain. He looked back to Willie, but she had already bolted for the car to call for an ambulance, the small dog nipping at her heels as she ran.

10

Notebook Wilson shuffled down Cahuenga Boulevard. His scraggly gray beard clung to his sunken cheeks and sweat-stains highlighted the pits of his navy-blue t-shirt. Olive cargo pants hung off his thin waist, weighed down by the hundreds of scraps of paper bursting from his pockets.

Notebook was a record keeper, a walking almanac of happenings on the street. He wrote down everything he saw, from the poignant to the mundane. Whenever his pockets became too full, he would unload his archive somewhere in Griffith Park, a meaningless Library of Alexandria that was blown into the woods as soon as Notebook walked away. Not that it mattered. Notebook never went back and looked at any of those notes after writing them down. The process of recording seemed to be his real compulsion, the thing that kept him breathing.

When Ray caught up to him, he was stopped in front of a boutique sauna across the street from the CNN building. It was an indulgent business, catering to women with perfect bodies and disposable incomes working to maintain their perfection. Gourmet sweating. Notebook stared through the window, pulled a folded spiral notebook out of his back pocket, and wrote down every detail.

"What do you see, Notebook?" Ray asked, unconsciously rubbing his short hair and smooth face.

"Nine perfect asses. One good ass. Six pairs of black yoga pants. Two pairs of shorts. One unidentified leg covering. Average bust size 34B. Average song length three point seven minutes. Smells like cedar and assholes," Notebook said, his eyes dodging between the paper and the rich beauties behind the glass.

"You dump your records from yesterday, yet?" Ray asked.

"Tuesday morning gone. Tuesday night left cargo pocket. Wednesday morning right cargo pocket. Wednesday night left pants pocket. Thursday in progress. Seven incoming phone calls," he said, writing it all down.

"Any chance I can get a glimpse at Wednesday's records?"

Notebook turned, not looking at Ray, and shuffled north up Cahuenga. He stopped outside the tavern that rotated owners every six months. At the time, it was a hip Mexican cantina. Notebook took record of the twenty-two televisions and then started to transcribe the conversation of the couple sitting next to the open windows. The guy was trying to impress his lunch date with some quote or another by Hemingway. It was incorrect and Notebook knew it.

"All you do is sit down at a typewriter and bleed!" Notebook yelled at the man, "BLEED!"

Ray grabbed him by the collar and pulled him down the street before the manager could call the cops.

"Take it easy, Notebook."

"If you use the... words of one of our greatest literary... minds, you should... you should use the correct words," Notebook said, his speech spit out at a punctuated clip, the anger bringing a stutter to the surface. His attention was suddenly diverted by an American Apparel billboard above them with a half-naked girl in a fair-trade bodysuit, reprinted in triplicate.

"I'm going to masturbate to that later. Twice," Notebook said, then wrote down that exact thing. The page of his notebook was full, so he tore it out, crumpled it up and shoved it into his right pants pocket. The Thursday archive in progress.

"I need to know if you saw anything weird in Chinatown. Over by the Foo-Chow Restaurant parking lot."

"I don't know. Pink paper would know," Notebook said.

"Can I see it?"

"Gimme a dollar."

Ray reached into his coat pocket. With the tax added at the 99-cent store, he only had a dollar and change left to his name. He held the wrinkled bill between his middle and pointer finger. Notebook snatched it from him and put it in the waistband of his stained underwear. He pulled wads of pink, white, and yellow paper from his cargo pants. Some of the scraps were notes jotted down, others were found pieces he had collected in the streets; receipts left at gas pumps, candy wrappers with a game code on the inside smeared by melted chocolate, and discarded flyers for Hollywood happy hours.

Ray sat down on the sidewalk, going through each of the pieces of the paper.

6 Pictures taken with Bruce Lee Statue between 7p.m. and 11 p.m.

13 Reese's Peanut Butter cups for sale at the gas station.

38 cars in the Foo-Chow parking lot at 7 p.m.

Black girl in truck sang the lyrics to "Maneater" by Hall and Oates. The correct words are "chew you up" dumb bitch.

19 cars in the Foo-Chow parking lot at 9:13 p.m. Black van has not left. Parked in spot 21. Next to other car occupying spot all the time.

Szechwan Beef. 39% chance of upset stomach.

Small, unclean bathroom. Not given access.

Parking five dollars.

"What do else do you have about the black van?" Ray asked.

Notebook was picking up the scraps of paper and shoving them back into his pockets as soon as Ray had finished with them. Ray dug through the remaining papers, looking for another reference to the black van.

581 cars enter 110 freeway off Hill Street.
17 of them need brakes replaced.
4 of them need taillights replaced.
6 of the cars are stupid.
4 cars parked in Foo-Chow parking lot at 11:46 p.m. Black van drives across street.
Walter Stinky Walter tries to take my pen. Stab him with it. Three drops of blood get on the sidewalk.
14 different kinds of gum, 9 types of mints.
One cunt-sucking prick face.
20 small red baskets.

Ray crumpled up the rest of the papers and handed them back to Notebook, who shoved them back into his pocket and shuffled down Selma toward Big Wang's sports bar. Ray didn't follow him.

The black van parked next to his car had to be how they unloaded the body without being seen.

"Why wouldn't it drive away? Why would it go across the street?" Ray asked himself, aloud.

He walked over to the nearest garbage can and dug out the cleanest cup he could find. At the corner of Cahuenga and Hollywood, he started to panhandle for change, emptying the coins from his pocket into the cup to create a familiar jingle. He needed to get back to Chinatown.

Clouds were starting to encroach on Hollywood again and Ray could smell another round of drizzle in the air. Once the sky opened up, it was going to take him all afternoon to scrounge together a couple bucks.

11

Edgar stared out at the parking lot of the Norton Simon Museum. The wipers swished across the windshield of his SUV, clearing the rain that had crept back into the Pasadena sky. He felt bad driving such a large car for a single man with no kids, horrified about his carbon footprint, but it was the easiest way for him to transport flowers to shows without having to drive a conspicuous white van or dirty pickup truck around town.

He stared out at the few deciduous trees around the parking lot. They had dropped their yellow leaves into the green bushes, a few still clinging to the bare branches. Because winter never really came to Southern California, it wasn't long after the last leaves dropped from the trees that they started to produce new buds again. It made him miss the autumn colors of his youth.

He got out of the car, braced himself for the wet and cold, and trotted up the short steps to the entrance into the warmth of the lobby.

Through the large glass wall to the Norton Simon Gardens, he watched the light rain sprinkle the pond fashioned after Monet's water lilies. Modern sculptures surrounded it like stoic sentries in the mist.

Edgar stopped to look at some of Degas' ballet dancers and waited for some of the patrons to clear the room at the end of the far gallery.

When he sat down on the square bench, he sat facing the same way as the man he was meeting. He was close enough they could whisper, two individuals discussing the works of art, but not so close it would look like they were together.

They sat staring at the painting in front of them for a few moments before speaking.

A vagrant man with torn dungarees and a walking stick stared out from the canvas into the gallery. His worn black hat hid the tufts of white hair growing into a tangled beard around his neck. His white shirt was ripped along the sides and the soles of his shoes hung from the leather. Hands, crusty with dirt, clutched a soiled sack flung over his shoulder. The background was a void of hued grays and dark browns, the only thing indicating he existed in realistic space was a small pile of garbage strewn in the foreground. Manet's *The Ragpicker*.

"Funny how beauty can be found anywhere, even in filth," Malkin said, not looking away from the painting. The sharp shards of his Slavic accent sliced into the silence of the room and even at a whisper filled the space. Edgar could smell hints of wood and citrus in Malkin's aftershave, but it wasn't hiding the fragrance of sleep sweat coating his skin.

"The homeless were as familiar a sight in the late 1800s as they are today, perhaps even more so," Edgar said, as though he was giving a lecture in modern art to a small group of tourists, "Whereas our vagrants pick bottles and cans to be recycled for change, ragpickers would collect discarded rags to be sold to paper manufacturers."

The two men had had the same conversation dozens of times. Given the scarcity of patrons, Edgar hardly thought it was necessary, but followed the script nonetheless.

"There will always be rich and poor, this is a universal truth. Even before there was money, it was who had the meat and who did not. Commerce of humanity."

"They were romanticized by the wealthy. People who could live their life on their own terms, outside of expectations," Edgar said.

Malkin nodded. They hadn't been compromised, despite Edgar's frantic call for an unscheduled rendezvous.

"Let us see if the rain has let up."

Buttoning his black coat over the white button down open at the collar, Malkin stood and walked out of the gallery at a leisurely pace, taking note of a Picasso or Van Gogh as he passed. The crown of his head shined through his thin blonde hair, reflecting the overhead lights. He stopped at the glass doors to look out at the garden, his hands knotted behind his back. Edgar followed and joined him there.

"Still a bit of a drizzle," Edgar said, his tone the same as when they were sitting. Two men making conversation, nothing more than that.

"I think we can risk it," Malkin said, opening the door and stepping out into the rain. He took several steps out onto the slick concrete and looked over to the small cafe that sold snacks and coffees. A girl about nineteen years old sat on a stool in a black Norton Simon windbreaker, highlighting a Biochemistry textbook.

"Would you like something to warm yourself?" Malkin asked.

"I'm fine," Edgar said, trying not to sound impatient, his hair getting sprinkled with mist.

"My treat," he said. The girl put down her textbook, ready to take the order. Edgar could see the ghost of the man standing before her made her uncomfortable with his penetrating stare.

He shook his head and Malkin ordered a black coffee, the steam rising out of the small hole in the travel mug cover. They walked past the umbrella-covered tables, watching the rain dimple the pond between the water lilies. Malkin paused at one of the many Henry Moore sculptures.

"I do not understand this. I have never liked art that does not look like anything. Rothko and Pollack. These are but squares and sprinkles to me."

"We could discuss art history all afternoon. Are you going to tell me what's going on?" Edgar asked, his calm finally breaking.

Malkin didn't meet his emotional pitch, "Delivery should proceed as planned. We need another shipment by the end of the week. Is this possible?"

"I'm talking about the girl," Edgar said.

"What about her?"

"Why do I have her?" Edgar hissed.

"Because if she were with me, she would be dead," he took a sip of coffee, "Surprisingly good."

He looked at Edgar, seeing the panic in his eyes.

"This is something you are used to, yes? Housing abductees. Making them trust you? Making them work? How is this different?"

"I didn't pick her."

"Our employer, he is... honoring a request. This is all you must know."

"She can't be placed with the others. She'll give away that she's not like them. What am I supposed to do about that?"

"When have any of your laborers ever been a problem?"

"I want her out of my house. She's a hostage. People are going to come looking for her. I'm very careful about the selections I make," Edgar said, angry.

"You will keep her until we say otherwise. She is a liability that must be managed," he said, his tone doing the job of getting Edgar to lower his voice.

"Why did you bring her to me? Why not just kill her?"

"Is this what I am to you?" he asked, offended, "A murderer of innocent girls? I thought we had developed a mutual respect. You don't see me calling you a slave trader, do you?"

"No, that's not what I—," Edgar stopped, collecting his thoughts, "This is uncharted territory. I'm just now adjusting to manufacturing new product. Throwing this girl at me makes me nervous."

Malkin took another sip of coffee. He stared out at the pond, thinking.

"We expect you to train her like the others. If she does not comply, keep her Dancing. If she does not take to your coddling, she will find the masters in Kiev do not give second chances."

"But—"

"The less you know of her the better. Complications have been piling up this week. Do not make me add you to that list. Focus on delivery. We are low on inventory and have lost a set of key customers."

Malkin drank the rest of the hot coffee in a couple of heavy gulps and tossed it into the garbage can.

"Keep the girl alive. Do not ask why," Malkin said, "And in the future, think twice before beckoning me here. The drive is long and becoming more difficult with the changing weather."

He left Edgar alone in the garden.

12

Nick grabbed his order through the window of the food truck parked outside Hollywood Presbyterian Medical Center. He stuffed a couple of bucks into the tip jar and wandered back into the emergency room lobby. Willie was talking with the attending physician about Rory Knapp's status. He found a couple of chairs away from the bleeding people and started chowing down on one of the Arroy truck's pork belly sliders.

Willie finished her hushed conversation and sat down next to him. He handed over her food.

"How long is the surgery supposed to take?" Nick asked.

"Couple of hours, the guy broke both of his femurs. And that was a nasty head wound. Who knows if he'll wake up when they bring him out of anesthesia," Willie said.

"I called Good Samaritan about the girls, you know, the ones with the boobs," Nick said, specifying for no reason, "They're still coming down. The doctor is supposed to call me when they're lucid. But if they were left in that room, they won't have much for us."

"Looks like we're going to spend the rest of our day driving between hospitals," Willie said, forking into some garlic fries.

Nick put the rest of his slider back into the bag and stood up.

"Let's walk and talk. If he's not waking up any time soon, I'd rather not waste the afternoon catching something in here."

With a mouthful of food, Willie gave him a frustrated look, but followed him out onto Fountain Avenue.

The rain had reduced to a light mist and they picked up their pace to get into their dry car.

"You mind if I recap this out loud? Figure out our next step? I fucking hate running into dead ends," Nick said.

They got into the car and unwrapped their food.

"Be my guest," Willie said, taking a bite of brisket. Some coleslaw fell into her lap and she wiped it onto the floor, checking her pants for a stain.

"Okay," Nick said, "So we have this movie star. He's found with his head blown off and his dick chopped off in a place that isn't his primary residence."

"And a place that isn't under his name. Rented week to week with cash under an alias," Willie said.

"Right, but we don't know if it's his alias or someone else's," Nick said, "Can you make a list of unknowns as we go through this? I feel like we could go down some rabbit holes if we don't cross out what doesn't matter."

"Can I finish this first?" she said with her mouth full.

They finished the rest of their meal in silence. The windows of the car were fogging up from the cool of the rain outside and the heat of the food inside. Anyone passing by might have thought the two of them were parked for some afternoon delight.

Willie wiped her mouth and pulled out her notebook.

"Go ahead," she said.

"The killer wanted it to look like a suicide, but did a sloppy job of it. Either it was someone who was new to this kind of work, or they were trying to send some sort of strange message. I'll go with the latter, because if it was a rookie murderer, they would've taken out the Asian twins as part of the gig, made it look like a murder-suicide thing," Nick said.

"That's the thing I keep coming back to," Willie said, "Why leave the witnesses?"

"And why would the killer glue them to the floor?" Nick asked, more to the air than Willie.

"Based on what Davidson told us, I think Seward glued them to the floor."

"That doesn't make sense."

"How much of the contents of that apartment made sense? It was probably part of whatever crazy bacchanal ritual they were doing in there," Willie said.

"No," Nick said, "I mean, if he brought them there to, you know, before his dingus went bye-bye, then logistically he'd get splinters on the underside of his junk when he—"

"Wow. Stop. Off track."

"Just saying, the floor needed refinishing."

He got the look again and chuckled. He enjoyed pressing her buttons, but thought it was best to get back to the relevant details before she delivered a fist to his jaw.

"Let's assume our suspect left them alive. Maybe because they were so whacked out on Grandpa—"

"—Shadow—"

"—Whatever—that they wouldn't have been able to identify the killer. Or were they left there as witnesses to send a message?"

"Seems to be a lot of message sending in your scenario," Willie said.

"And we don't trust the agent, Davidson. He knows way too much about this drug to be an innocent observer, so we have to take what he says with a grain of salt."

"He did lead us to Knapp, though, and just in time," Willie said.

"Or us knocking on Knapp's door drove him to suicide. Either Knapp was the one who murdered Seward and couldn't take the guilt, or he thought we might be the people who killed Seward coming after him. Maybe he thought he was next on the list and didn't want to get his dick cut off," Nick said.

"Could be Seward just happened to die with drugs on him and the murder is unrelated. The mutilated genitalia could point to a jilted lover."

"Based on what the tabloids say, that could be half the women in Los Angeles."

"I'll find out if there's anyone he'd been seen with recently," Willie said.

"You have a subscription to US Weekly?"

"We all have our connections."

"That angle, plus our list from the studio, should narrow down what direction we're going in. But so we don't stretch our limited resources too thin, let's assume we're looking at a drug-related hit. Perpetrated by a network of dealers who work in a small capacity. With a small client list, it could be easy to find folks who have gotten high on Grandpa," Nick said.

"I think we have to keep an eye on the agent. He's got a hand in this somewhere. I don't know what it is, but it's something. He could be our middleman. We should get the rest of his client list, see if any other red flags pop up there," Willie said.

"Good idea. Put that on our list of assets to acquire. Call Bernard directly. He'll have no reason not to supply us with that information. With the step-to attitude he had this morning, he'll think he's doing his boss a favor," Nick said.

"But he'll tell Davidson right away, so any one of those celebs we get in contact with will have a head start on us."

"We're also still missing Seward's wallet and keys. We found the phone, why not that stuff? His credit cards haven't been used. The car was nowhere to be found."

"Maybe the murderer took the car, chopped it, and sold it to recoup some of the cash. Job like that would only take a couple of hours. If it was out on a joyride, we would've picked up something on it by now."

Nick thought about the car. Why hadn't it turned up? It was this year's Audi coupe. It would've stuck out like a sore thumb down in Skid Row. Someone would've noticed a car like that.

No. Everyone would've noticed a car like that.

"We've got some homeless to interview. Anybody who was awake at that hour saw that car," Nick said, "Which means they saw who took it."

13

By the time Ray got enough change together to hop on the train back downtown, the sun could no longer fend off the storm clouds. Cold wind stung Ray's bare face on the walk from Chinatown Station up College Street. No-Tongue's clothes weren't thick and he made a mental note to look for another coat somewhere.

Headlights illuminated the length of Hill Street. The lunchtime commuters all thought they had a special shortcut to get onto the 110 to head to important meetings in other parts of town, but their hive mind caused a traffic jam. The rain stopped cars in Los Angeles like they were driving through a hurricane. At least the line of headlights gave him plenty of illumination as he returned to the scene of the crime.

His yellow car, covered in patches of rust, registration dated March 1981, was gone. It had been towed away by the city. For them, it was just another festering boil on the landscape. Pictures had been taken, samples analyzed. The car was probably sitting in a police impound somewhere, marked as evidence. As soon as the case was closed, it would be turned into a cube of worthless metal. If Ray couldn't find out who'd placed the body there for him to find, the only thing to prove his innocence would be compacted and melted down to nothing before his public defender had a chance to appeal the case. Remnants of the car remained; rotten bits of rubber, tufts of upholstery, and an oil stain that ran the length of the Chevrolet's body. The grave was marked by yellow police tape, but that didn't keep the valet from filling every other available space.

Ray looked up at the surrounding apartments. Old possessions were stacked in alleyways, faded children's drawings pasted to the windows, and air conditioning units nailed into the frames. Storage units built from old lumber and tin could serve as a blind for anyone who needed to keep an eye on the car. Ray wondered why anyone with such skill with a wire, such a clean and professional kill, why they would perch in a filthy alleyway just to make sure someone would come across the body that night.

Across the street, where Notebook said the van had gone after Ray left, was the Bamboo Plaza. It looked like a corporate office building, a large red marble facade, gold letters in both English and Chinese, but it housed the same cheap stores as its touristy counterpart just a block down. To its immediate left, there was a shop whose first floor was filled with stone statues, knock-offs of those found in Tibetan temples. In a single floor above the store was an empty office, the blinds drawn. A "For Lease" sign in the window had been there a while, faded from its time in the sun. It was a good place for a lookout to set up shop, but the white blinds on the white facade would give away someone peering through the slats. Ray knew where he needed to go.

He went around the back of the Bamboo Plaza to the parking garage entrance and walked up the wet stairs. When he reached the roof, he went to the concrete edge and peered over the side. It was the perfect vantage point. No matter where the van would've been parked, there was a good line of sight to Ray's car.

Parking garages were kept cleaner than the streets, owned by private companies that wanted to justify the twenty dollars per day they charged people to park there, but it didn't mean they were perfect. With the last few days of rain, sending a crew up to clean the area would've been pointless. As Ray walked along the edge of the wall, looking for anything that might tip him off, he noticed something in the garbage runoff lodged against the concrete wall. He bent over to get a closer look, making sure it wasn't the rain in his eyes deceiving him.

Despite quitting long ago, his brush with death made him take up smoking again. At first, it was something to calm his nerves, then it became habit, then routine. Picking through cigarette butts discarded in the street became a science, reading a tossed butt like tea leaves to understand who had been smoking it before it had been thrown away. A cigarette with thick lipstick on it down on the Sunset Strip was usually a woman coming out of a club to get a quick puff before tossing an almost full stick into the gutter. On Santa Monica and Highland, lipstick-lined cigarettes were probably the leftovers of some tranny hooker, putting out her butt as the 5-0 rolled by on a bust. Putting something between his lips that had spent time both in a stranger's mouth and in the dirty street took some risk-taking, but there was a difference between taking a risk and being stupid.

Among the usual discards, filters Ray could identify on sight—Camel, Marlboro, Winston—there was a variety of Chinese cigarettes, death sticks so potent only the bravest of men went near them. And then there was a brand of a different kind. Ray picked up a couple of them to compare. All of them had been burned down to the filter, which was dark gray instead of the traditional light brown. The feel of the cigarette was also different. Most of the American butts were soaked through, worthless wet caterpillars, spilling their remaining tobacco out onto the concrete. These butts remained firm, as if they were made of cardboard. There were no other distinctive markings on them. It was a long shot, but this was something he hadn't seen when picking through butts on the street before.

Ray brushed his hand through the trash, looking for one butt that hadn't been smoked all the way down, something else that might give him a clue as to the origin of the cigarettes.

There was a thin piece of plastic in the refuse, fluttering in the breeze. It was a familiar sight, the strip torn off the top of a pack, the first thing tossed to the ground instead of a garbage can. Even conscientious smokers, who took care to put their cigarettes out on the heel of their shoes, walking to find a garbage can rather than flick their butt into the streets, would peel this small piece of plastic off the top of the pack and toss it into the wind without a second thought.

He pulled the transparent strip from under a crackling leaf and squinted at it in the overcast light.

Written across the gold lining in tiny letters: Беломорканал.

"Fuck," Ray said to himself, "Fucking Russians."

Ray put the plastic and discarded butts into his inside coat pocket and zipped it up to his chin. When it came to sneaky Russians, there was only one man Ray could talk to.

Problem was, Ray didn't know if he would talk back.

14

For as bad as people along Wall Street smelled, they could still catch the whiff of police from a mile away. Nick and Willie couldn't get anyone to say anything to them. The sandwiches they'd bought as bribes where almost gone and they had nothing to show for it. Even cash wasn't enough to get the indigent masses to talk. If anyone saw something, took notice of a white Audi coupe, or had any knowledge about who they'd seen get into it, they weren't saying a word. There were enough people in broken down wheelchairs, crutches, and dirty bandages. Snitches get stitches.

Parked on the corner of 6th and San Pedro, the detectives watched the teeming community around them. If everyone had been dressed better, the scene might've been mistaken for a street festival or farmer's market in the more affluent parts of town. Instead, it was a parade of sadness, a group of people thrown together in collective misery.

It was an area that had always been a gathering place for the displaced of the city of Los Angeles. Once the end of the line for the railroad, it was where transients would disembark from a long cross-country trek. They came from every part of the country to ride the rails, getting off at each stop along the way to look for food or work, then getting back on another train headed west when there was nothing to be found. The bonds formed between the tramps and hobos on the trains continued when they reached the end of the line. Shanty communities were set up where everyone let off and it was where philanthropists built shelters. It was a perpetuating cycle. The highest concentration of shelters drew in the majority of vagrants and derelicts, and because of the growing population of homeless in the area, more shelters were needed.

If the city ever had any hope of gentrifying the Skid Row area, as it had the Arts District only a few blocks away, it would have to shut down the shelters or move them. Wherever the new shelters were, the homeless would congregate. It was a problem with no single solution. No matter how many food banks or housing programs were available, there would always be people who wanted nothing to do with it; the mentally ill, addicts, people who didn't qualify for Section 8 housing or were kicked out for showing compassion and letting a friend stay with them.

"Wasn't as easy as you would've thought, huh?" Willie said.

People peered into their windows occasionally, then shuffled away. Nick felt like they were on a guided safari, the animals surrounding the vehicle as they watched from relative comfort. When the thought passed into his head, the image of homeless as nothing more than animals, he felt sick to his stomach.

Willie rolled down her window and handed the last sandwich to a skinny girl unconsciously scratching at open sores on her forearm. The girl took the sandwich with minimum thanks and hurried away. As they watched her go, he wondered if the girl would eat the sandwich or try to trade it for whatever had her jonesing. For a junkie, a fix is always more important than staying alive.

"I once interviewed a recovering crack addict, asking her to describe how long a high lasted. The answer shocked the hell out of me," Willie said, "Ten seconds. Everything thrown away—family, health, wealth, all of it—for ten good seconds."

"I used to volunteer down here. After all the business with the real estate scam," Nick said, "Thought I could do my part, make a difference."

"Why'd you stop?" she asked. Both of them were still looking out at the sea of people, contemplating their own lives. Neither of them would say it, but they were both thinking the same thing: *How far am I from being one of these people? Could this have been me if a couple of things hadn't gone right in my life?*

"It was a combination of things. I got busy, or at least I told myself I did. Skipped a day here and there. Working late or had plans with friends. Soon I skipped weeks at a time, then stopped altogether. I don't know if I ever made the conscious decision to quit going, but there was always something in the back of my mind that knew I couldn't do it forever. It felt good to be helping people, but the cycle never stopped, you know? I mean, look at this. It's not getting better. I started to feel like being there to hand out meals or blankets or whatever, was a short-term solution. Yeah, it made someone's day a bit better, but did it really help them in the long run? I worked with volunteers who had been former homeless, recovering addicts. Then one day they'd be gone. Weeks later I'd see them in the food line, back on the streets. It's fucked up out here. The futility of it all really got to me. Dealing with murders all day and watching people on the edge of death all night... call it selfish, but I couldn't take it," Nick said.

"I'm sure you helped a lot of people in the time you did it. Most people can't even say they did that. They just wander through life worried about their own shit. We're all guilty of it."

"Yeah, well, sitting here talking about these people isn't going to get us any eyewitnesses," Nick said, getting out of the car.

"We've already tried the interview tactic, Archer. We do any more, we'll be wasting our time. There has to be some traffic or security camera footage we can get."

"Not in this neighborhood. If the car was parked out in front of that apartment building it would've been a target. It was around, but had to be somewhere Seward would've considered safe, even if it was only the illusion of safety," Nick said, "There are at least a hundred people out here, who knows if any of them were paying attention that night. We need to do some more focused canvassing."

He trotted across the street to the entrance of The Dawkins House. Willie followed.

Nick flashed his badge at the volunteer behind the check-in desk.

"My, we're popular with LAPD today," the volunteer said.

"Same issue," Nick said. He assumed the volunteer had been at the desk most of the day. "Looking for a guy a couple of officers dropped off this morning. Ray Cobb."

"Yeah, I remember. Quiet guy, beard, stringy hair," the volunteer said, pulling out the card Ray had marked earlier.

"Quiet?" Nick asked. In the time he'd known Ray Cobb, he wasn't a man who responded to a new situation with silence. He was always ready with a sarcastic comment, getting a laugh or a scowl from anyone in the immediate vicinity.

"I'm not going to judge, I don't know if that was how he got to you, but he was like an abused puppy. Wouldn't lift his eyes from the ground. Didn't say word one, even when they uncuffed him."

"He was cuffed when they brought him in?" Nick said.

He looked to Willie, confused. Not knowing the context of his look, she shrugged back.

"I need to talk to him, find out what's going on. He was supposed to be staying here as a favor, he's not dangerous."

"You can look around, but we're not a prison. He can walk out those gates whenever he wants. I know the officers said he needs to check in every night, but we don't open the doors for beds until nine. Can't be certain he's coming back, if he's gone, until after that."

"Thanks," Nick said. The card looked like it had been filled out in Ray's handwriting, but it was a hasty scribble, illegible, could've been anyone's signature. He'd seen Ray sign plenty of paperwork, both to get out of holding and years ago when he was signing paperwork at the hospital. The name he'd put down was clear as day, even too nice for someone who'd spent as much time as Ray had on the streets. Something was off.

Nick dialed his phone, the other end picked up.

"Homicide. Jimenez."

"Jimenez, it's Archer. Can you email me the mug shot of Ray Cobb you guys took last night?"

"Why?" Jimenez asked. Nick could hear the suspicion in his voice.

"I'm down at Dawkins and the volunteer who checked him in is about to go off shift," Nick lied, "I want to have something to show the next guy so they can make sure he stays put when they do bed checks later."

"What're you doing there?" Jimenez asked, "This is my case, Archer. Don't try to pull any of your sneaky RHD seniority shit on me."

"Just helping you out. We were in the neighborhood looking into another case, the Seward thing we caught in Central. We were here, figured I'd save you a trip." Nick wanted to fire back at Jimenez for the shit he'd given him, but he needed Ray's picture more than he needed to be right.

"Sorry. Just had one too many taken away from me by your department when I was right on the verge of putting someone away. You guys forget it ain't just about closing, those are my bonuses. Sending it now," Jimenez said. Nick could hear the keystrokes on the other end of the line. "You get it?"

Nick pulled the phone from his ear and refreshed his email.

"Got it, thanks," Nick said.

"Hey, hold up," Jimenez said before Nick had a chance to hang up, "You let me know if you talk to him and he tells you anything else. He's still my witness."

"Done." Nick hung up before Jimenez could get another word in. He opened the attachment in the email.

"How is this pressing, Archer?" Willie asked.

"If Ray's around, he'll be able to get into places we won't. He'll also be able to find out if there's anyone we should talk to in the area who has an eye for cars. Lots of chop houses do jobs as they come, but they also have a running list of specific items; luxury cars, rare cars, stuff that's in high demand. Homeless eyes are cheap labor," he said.

Willie nodded. Nick hated when he involuntarily dipped into "teaching moments," but Willie had spent more time on her criminal justice degree than she had on the pavement. She could've taken every opportunity to tell him to blow it out his ass, but always took in the information if she was unaware, or gave him a simple, "I know," if he was spouting common sense. Her ability to not let pride get in the way of progress made their partnership much easier. Nick wished he had the same resolve, but his mouth often got in the way when faced with a situation where he might look stupid or clueless.

"But why the nonsense with the picture. Either he's here or he's not," Willie said, "We can see that ourselves."

"Just a hunch. It might be nothing."

He showed his phone to the volunteer.

"This the guy they brought in cuffed this morning?"

The volunteer took the phone from Nick and squinted at it.

"Yep. His hair was in his face when he got here, but the beard's the same. That's the guy."

"Okay, thanks," Nick said, "We're going to ask around a bit, maybe see if he's here."

"Be my guest," the volunteer said, "But use a light hand in there. These people are here to not be bothered and I don't need to tell you they don't like police. Even if they know where Cobb is, they probably won't tell you. You're better off asking other volunteers."

Nick flashed the picture to everybody he passed, watching for a look of recognition to cross their eyes. Most of the volunteers from the breakfast line were long gone.

They went out into the yard. A handful of folks were shuffling around, but most people had already gone outside. Ray noticed a short volunteer at the exit, shooing people out. He had a pleasant demeanor and the people who interacted with him smiled when they talked to him. Nick remembered working with this sort of guy when he'd volunteered. For them, it was just another day dealing with people. Not homeless people. People. They were trying to get through their day like everybody else; get something to eat, get comfortable, and get somewhere to sleep.

"Better hurry up before the lunch line is too full, Jerry," the volunteer said to a tall guy in a knit cap, "They don't give out food based on height."

The tall man laughed at the joke and shook the volunteer's hand.

"Mama, you hungry?" he said, looking over to where a grandmotherly woman adjusted her glasses. She waved to him like she was meeting him for the first time. The volunteer called to someone in line, "Nyima! Bring out some rolls or something for Mama. She'll need it later."

Nick walked up to the wrangler and introduced himself. The man gave his name as Guillermo Torres.

"You won't get much outta these folks most of the time, especially now that they're hungry," Guillermo said.

"Have you seen this guy around today?" Nick held up his phone.

"Oh yeah. Remember him from this morning. Quiet. Left after breakfast. Walked right out these doors here," Guillermo said.

"And you haven't seen him back?" Nick asked.

"Nope. But they usually don't turn back up unless they need food or a bed. Something about the fences around these walls makes people uncomfortable. Heck, they make me wary sometimes, and I've got a home and a wife to get back to. Sometimes I think the only difference between me and the people who wander in through these doors is hope. You give 'em a little hope and it goes much further than a soft bed or a hot meal."

"You didn't happen to notice a white Audi coupe parked around here last night? Newer model?" Willie chimed in.

"Think I would've noticed something like that around. Car like that wouldn't last ten minutes parked around here without at least a busted window. Someone would try to snatch the stereo or just break in out of spite," Guillermo said, then turned back to the yard, "Last chance, Mama. Dunno if Nyima can sneak anything out for you."

"Thanks for your help," Nick said, "Keep up the good work here."

"Just trying to make every day a little better than the last," Guillermo said with a smile, "Hey, it probably won't be much help, but I saw your friend sit with Mama over there. Looked like she was doing most of the talking, and she isn't all there in the head most days, but it wouldn't hurt to show that picture to her, see if she knows anything. Just don't tell her you're police."

Nick nodded to Guillermo and the detectives went over to where Mama Nomad was sitting. She smiled as Nick sat down next to her. Willie stayed standing.

"Well, hello to you, handsome man and pretty lady. You two here on your honeymoon?" Mama Nomad asked.

Nick smiled at Willie, who was covering her mouth, either to stifle a laugh, or keep down vomit.

"Looking for a friend of mine, wondering if you've seen him," Nick said, showing her the picture.

"Oh, yes! That's the boy who looks like my Amos. Oh, he's a nice one. Left here just after breakfast, Amos did, but told me he'd be back to say hello," Mama said.

"If you see him again, would you tell the front desk? I'd love to get ahold of him," Nick said.

"Why for most certainly. You seem so nice and he's so nice, I think you two should be friends," Mama said, "I remember I had some friends, The Flying Ramirez Brothers, trapeze artists when I was a ring girl with the circus out in Topeka. They were nice boys, too. A bit darker of skin than you and your friend, but pleasantness don't know no race and I say that true a'fore God and everybody."

Nick thanked her and they walked back to the car.

"So, was your hunch right?"

"Nope. Ray was here, just as he was supposed to be. We'll see if he comes back tonight," Nick said.

"Maybe let's try to get a lead on our case before we go sticking our noses into a random murder at Central," Willie said, "If we can't talk to Rory Knapp or the twins tonight, I'm going to get started on the paperwork. I don't see this one being solved by the end of the day."

"Good idea," Nick said.

He didn't tell Willie, but he had a feeling that morning was the last time he would see Ray Cobb again for a long time.

15

Ray followed the twist of the L.A. River. It was early in the evening, the roads choked with cars, the streets filled with people. Rain darkened the landscape as night fell and Ray was soaked through. He was going to have to abandon No-Tongue's outfit soon. The mute hadn't transitioned from his summer wardrobe and the thin fabric wasn't doing its job. Ray figured if No-Tongue traveled light in January, he had probably already shed some of the layers Ray had given him that morning. He wouldn't feel too bad about upgrading his coat as soon as he passed a thrift store's donation bin.

The rain gave him another problem; Raccoon Man would stay underground for the night.

Few people knew about the abandoned tunnels under downtown Los Angeles. The Belmont Tunnel, the most well-known old subway entrance in L.A., had been blocked off and built over. Once a magnificent tapestry of graffiti art and a testament to the city's past, the terminus was now sealed up. The mechanical building had been repainted and locked, a park replacing the empty lot once filled with burnt barrels and passed out homeless. Red brick condominiums blocked the gateway and access to the new plot of green was as coveted as a key to Gramercy Park. But just because one tunnel had been sealed, didn't mean there weren't other ways down.

The subway ran from the late 19th century all the way through the 1960s, killed by the sprawl of highways that soon became synonymous with L.A.'s identity. Some of the tunnels were still accessible through the basements of apartment buildings and tours were given to the historically curious. Hip, urban archaeologists took cell phone pictures of the old track signs, posting them to social media, fascinated by the dirt and kitsch.

Service tunnels that weren't open to the public were harder to access. They were routinely cleared, preventing underground communities from taking hold. But in the woods off the 5 freeway, between Dodger Stadium and the police academy, an access panel grown over with brush provided an entrance to Raccoon Man's lair.

Believing himself to be some sort of figure out of fantasy, Raccoon Man kept to the shadows. Staying underground, surrounded by his cadre of masked minions, he fancied himself a beastmaster. Wizard Commander of the *Procyon Lotor.* Ray knew he was just an autistic eccentric who smelled like raccoon shit.

It didn't make visits with Raccoon Man any less dangerous. The raccoons appeared to be well-trained, but they were just acting on instinct, going where the food was. Any of them could've been carrying a dormant strain of rabies and were prone to attack to defend their territory. An advanced infection was likely the cause of Raccoon Man's delusions of grandeur.

Tagging along with his pets when the sun went down, he would "command" them to do his bidding. Find uncovered trash bins, tear open the bags, and look for any shredded paper—the long strips processed through a simple office shredder. The raccoons were just looking for food. Any time they happened upon shredded paper, it was either by accident, or they associated the tangle of straw with material used to build their insulated nests.

People shred their mortgage paperwork and old credit card statements and throw it all away. If someone picked through their garbage, they figured the scroungers were looking for discarded recyclables to exchange for a few dollars. The shredded documents they'd thrown in the bin had become an afterthought.

The bags Raccoon Man brought back were torn open and sorted through with calculating patience. Anything that looked like a credit card or bank statement became a treasured enigma. Raccoon Man entertained himself by putting together what he saw as nothing but a giant jigsaw puzzle. When a credit card or account number came together, the puzzle became an even more exciting challenge as he tried to pair it with another statement or social security number. Once he'd completed a puzzle, he'd tape it together and get in contact with the kinds of people who had the means to exploit that information. The identity theft would show up in Southeast Asia or Eastern Europe, some mysterious unknown person opening an account under the victim's name and ruining their credit.

Police cybercrime units assumed an email had been hacked, that a porn site or online poker service had a worm. The Luddite animal lover living in the sewers below their feet wasn't on any of their suspect lists. Because the identities were never used within the United States, no one ever suspected it was a domestic enemy. Raccoon Man didn't ask what happened to the people he stole from. For him, it was less about the money than it was the brain-taxing entertainment of going through the hundreds of thousands of strips of paper to find the elusive matches. Payments he received for services rendered might as well have been gold stars or bottle caps. To Raccoon Man, the world of humans made no difference. He did, however, care about his pets.

Ray had eliminated Benny 7-11, a man who used to torture Raccoon Man's furry family for fun. An evil mustachioed fiend, in Raccoon Man's words, protected by a lunatic who lived in the woods. Ray didn't even know he'd done Raccoon Man a favor.

Years earlier, haunted by the nightmares of the men he'd killed, Ray was passed out drunk and woke up surrounded by a dozen raccoons hissing at him. He thought it was an alcohol-induced nightmare until Raccoon Man stepped out of the shadows. He thanked Ray for his service to the community and offered him a place of refuge should he ever need it. He told Ray the location of the access grate, then disappeared into the night, his loyal followers in tow.

Ray hoped the offer had been in earnest. He'd never had the occasion to disappear from the world, even when he was posing as No-Tongue. People's alliances on the streets shifted without notice. He didn't know what to expect. Years ago, he was offered asylum, but in the time since, he could've done something that removed him from Raccoon Man's good graces.

The scars in Ray's belly tugged as he strained against the rusted grate. Lifting it was difficult, the rain making the metal slick, flakes of black and orange peppering Ray's palms. He wiped them off on his clothes and peered down into the darkness. There was a ladder there, but he couldn't see down more than a few rungs. He flicked on a cheap disposable lighter to try and illuminate his way, but what light he managed to shine into the hole was extinguished by the pissing rain. Water flowed at the bottom of the tunnel. It didn't sound like it was any more than ten or fifteen feet deep. If he slipped, it wouldn't be an easy fall, but he probably wouldn't die.

He clutched the edges of the panel as he went down a couple of steps and only put his whole weight on the ladder once his entire body was down the hole. After a couple steps down, the rungs stopped and Ray's foot swung out to catch nothing but air. He had misjudged the distance from the surface, down at least twenty feet, maybe more. The rush of running water was close and Ray figured the drop couldn't be significant. Hands slick with water and sweat, Ray lowered himself to the final rung of the ladder. His toes reached out for the water below and he felt nothing.

He was strong and scrappy, but his body was used to dealing with the endurance of daily life, not lifting his body weight. He heaved up as hard as he could, strain pushing on his forearms and biceps. Nothing. He tried to kick his feet up and hang there like he was a child on monkey bars, but couldn't get them above his waist.

"Great," he said, "Gonna break my leg and die in a sewer because I couldn't do a fucking pull-up."

"Let go," a voice echoed from behind him. It cut through the water, bouncing off the concrete, surrounding him.

Ray did as he was told and it made him feel like an idiot. If he were six inches taller, he would've been standing on the ground from the last rung on the ladder. The water rushed over his tattered shoes and soaked through his socks and pant legs. It would make for an unpleasant rest of his day.

They stood there in the darkness for a moment, facing each other, not saying anything. When Ray realized Raccoon Man wasn't going to provide a light source, he flicked his lighter. The first thing he saw were the dark reflective eyes of the raccoon perched on his shoulder and Ray jumped back thinking it was Raccoon Man's head. After the initial shock, he saw the outline of the man's face before his features came into focus in the low light. Dark freckles were peppered across the wide brim of his nose and natural black sandbags under his eyes made him look like the beasts he'd befriended. His large eyebrows grew together into a single tuft of fuzz at the center of his furrowed forehead. A tangle of hair hung in a ponytail over his shoulder and the raccoon perched there was playing with it like it was a dog toy.

"Come to get dry," he said, turning and walking down the pipe. Ray had to keep pace behind him to ensure he didn't lose him in the maze of sewers.

After one turn, the lighter in his hand was extinguished by a droplet from the ceiling. Ray stopped in the darkness, flicking the flint several times to get back into the light. When the flame reappeared, Raccoon Man was gone.

"Hey!" Ray called out. His voice echoed off the walls, but was swallowed up by the sound of rushing water all around him. Ray listened for the footfalls of boots against concrete, but heard nothing. Walking forward, he came to a split in the tunnel.

What was he doing down there? Every part of Ray's logical mind told him we would be free of the charges if he just let the police do their jobs. Then he could go back to life as usual. But the unanswered question would poke at him. A sharp pebble in his shoe. Who set him up? And if justice was served and Ray was cleared, what would keep them from trying again?

"You coming?" Raccoon Man asked in the darkness. His massive head stuck out of a large hole in the concrete, something Ray had missed in his wandering toward the split in the pipe. Raccoon Man pushed aside a piece of heavy canvas to expose the orange flicker of a fire.

The room was massive. It was the platform for track five pointing toward Hill Street. The abandoned subway line ran under the spot where Ray Cobb found the dead man who would change the course of his week. The pillars on the platform were crumbling, decay ravaging the old plaster, but the concrete and rebar underneath would hold up the tunnel until the big earthquake hit. There were no art deco tile designs on the walls or chandeliers long forgotten and covered in bats. No grand pianos covered in dust. It was just a concrete room. But instead of commuters, packs of raccoons ran back and forth.

Raccoon Man ignored Ray's presence, hard at work on one of his puzzles, a circle of paper on the ground spread out from the fire in the center. He carried a torn plastic garbage bag with him, pulling out a strip at a time, eventually finding a match, or starting another puzzle as an extension of the expanding spiral. In the tunnel behind him, Ray could see piles of shredded paper in plastic bags. Ray wondered how much of it had been collected and abandoned, enough time having passed that the information contained within would be worthless to Raccoon Man's buyers.

"Do you need any help?" Ray asked. He wanted to go into the center of the circle to warm himself by the fire, but was unsure how to enter the circle without disturbing any of Raccoon Man's hard work.

"Touch nothing," Raccoon Man said. On his way to a destination only he could see, he nudged Ray and said, "Come."

Ray followed him around the circle. When he took his gaze off Raccoon Man he could see the glowing eyes all around them, watching, waiting. When the large figure stopped abruptly, Ray almost ran into him.

"Here." Raccoon Man pointed at a small break in the swirl of the paperwork, avoiding eye contact. Ray never would've seen the trail through the mix of shredded paper, but there it was. He walked from the outline through the mess until he reached the warm center. He wished he were comfortable enough in the place to take off his shoes and socks to dry them in the heat, but he wanted to retain the ability to run for it just in case the raccoons grew weary of his company. He settled for warming his hands and trying to get close enough to dry his clothes without setting himself on fire.

"Why have you come to me? This is a debt not redeemed lightly. You will not have access to this place again."

The fire wasn't helping. Ray was now warm and damp, like he was wearing clothes taken out of the dryer too early.

"I need to find someone, thought you could help."

"These are my friends," Raccoon Man gestured to the animals scurrying at his feet, "I have no business in the world of men."

"Actually you do," Ray said. It came out in Ray's signature sarcastic clip before he could catch himself. Raccoon Man stared through him. The surrounding animals perked up, sensing his aggression.

"I mean," Ray said, trying to phrase his requests correctly, "The men you give your completed puzzles to, they're Russian, right?"

"Do I look Russian to you?" Raccoon Man asked. He looked like he was a sable hat and pogrom away from being a Cossack. Ray wasn't sure how to respond. The Politburo poster child's eyes focused on Ray in a way that made him wish the pony-tailed eccentric would go back to staring at the floor.

"I am Armenian," Raccoon Man said, "My clients are from Ukraine. As though I could say, you are from North America, you are Mexican."

"My mistake."

"Say what you want and leave."

Ray pulled out the cigarette butts. He walked from the center of the circle, trying to follow the path laid out for him, but it was harder to see from the other side. His foot slipped at one point, skimming the edge of an almost completed bank statement and he stopped, Raccoon Man never taking his eyes off of him. He lifted his foot carefully to make sure it hadn't disturbed the paper.

Raccoon Man took the butts and rubbed the filters in his dirty fingers. He licked the end, not caring it had been in the dirt, someone else's mouth, and a homeless man's pocket. He leaned down and gave one of the butts to the large raccoon at his feet. Turning it over in its monkey-like hands, the raccoon smelled it, made a loud screech, tore it apart, then disappeared into the shadows. Ray tried not to give away his frustration at the destroyed evidence.

"These are Belomorkanal. Very strong. Popular where I am from. Would be like having to identify a man who smoked Camels in this country," Raccoon Man mused.

"But?"

"These are not imported by many stores because of the use by children to make cigarettes from marijuana. The stiff board paper makes for sturdy use," Raccoon Man said, "I know many men who smoke these."

"Am I looking at a dead end?" Ray asked.

"If this were the cigarette of any other man, you would be. I had my suspicions as you handed them to me. Olga's reaction confirmed it," he said, referring to the raccoon that had shredded the butt and disappeared.

"Should I be worried?" Ray asked.

Raccoon Man let out a laugh, haunting and hollow.

"You should disappear. End this hunt now. It will not end well for you," Raccoon Man said.

"Just tell me who I'm dealing with. I'll do with it what I will."

"This man who smokes Belomorkanal, has a strong love of pickled fish. He is not a lover of animals. If it were not for the reputation he holds, he would be skinned alive for kicking Olga upon one meeting. She will never forget his scent. He is a mercenary. Though he now only works for one man."

"Do you know his name?"

"Viktor Mochulyak. Also known as Gravedigger."

Ray would've preferred to be going after someone nicknamed "Soft Hands" or "Snugglebear." Raccoon Man smiled at his guest's apprehension.

"It is not just a clever moniker. The word for "gravedigger" is *mohyl'nyk* in Ukrainian. You see how his profession and surname are similar, yes? One serves the other I suppose."

Ray searched his memory for the name, but came up with nothing.

"He is a man you should not wish to be involved with. Not one grave he has dug has ever been found," Raccoon Man said.

"What about his boss? Say I want to get involved with him? How do I find him?"

"This is not a man I deal with. I do not wish to know his place in this world. We... differ."

Ray was sure Raccoon Man "differed" from everyone on the planet. The Armenian refocused on his work, pulled a single strip of paper from the bag he was holding, and moved around the circle. From his demeanor, Ray assumed the conversation was over.

Raccoon Man found the puzzle he was looking for, knelt in the dirt, and aligned the strip to its match.

"You have not left," Raccoon Man said to Ray as if seeing him for the first time.

Ray nodded and walked back toward the hole in the wall covered by canvas. The horde of raccoons blocked his path, but scurried away when the Raccoon Man spoke again.

"The Truthseer will guide you on your dangerous path," Raccoon Man said, more to the ground than Ray.

Ray stopped, his hand on the busted concrete.

"What? No... wait... you don't mean—"

"Go, Raymond Cobb, and forget this place," Raccoon Man said.

Ray flicked his lighter and headed back out into the darkness. He hoped to find his way back to the surface before a raccoon sunk its teeth into his leg. The last thing he needed was to add punctures from rabies shots to the scars at his guts.

16

Rory Knapp was out of surgery, but the doctors had him in an induced coma. According to his blood tests, he had a complex cocktail of toxins flowing through his system. When he'd taken the leap off the ledge, he was either Shadow Dancing or had been recently. The blow on his head caused his brain to swell and the doctors were worried the trauma would be too much for his body to handle. For as far as he fell, and the angle he hit the exposed rock, the impact should have killed him. When Knapp woke up he would have some mild brain damage. No matter how Rory Knapp was involved, there would be no information from his camp for a while.

Once the detectives reported in for the evening, Lieutenant Jenkins made a courtesy call to the local DEA office. They didn't have any information on Shadow Dance either. The contact at the office wasn't surprised to hear about a new designer drug hitting the street. After the crackdown on pseudoephedrine purchases, junkies were coming up with different ways to get high every day; flesh-eating cocaine, bath salts, even cracking open smartphones and cooking up touch-screen plasma. The feds wanted to be looped in on any new information and would help to analyze the sample, but until the LAPD had proof Shadow Dance was spreading out beyond a small group of celebrities, they weren't going to get the Attorney General on the horn to classify it as a new harmful substance. Nick and Willie were to operate under the assumption that it was a Schedule I Narcotic until they got the full tox-screen back from the lab.

The rest of the day passed without much to break the case. There was a whole lot of hullabaloo around the office and Jenkins had to assure the press all of their resources were dedicated to finding out what happened. A few officers were allowed overtime to help canvas the homeless in Skid Row, but Nick knew they wouldn't have much more luck than he and Willie had that afternoon. It was more of a placating act than anything. A dog and pony show for the people who cared more about a celebrity murder than the millions around the world dying in genocides.

Nick was doing paperwork. Where evidence was discovered, how the scene looked, positioning of the body—all that information had to be put to paper while it was still fresh in the mind. Most detectives hated it, but not Nick.

Doing paperwork had led him to where he was now. It had made his career. If Nick hadn't been so good at paperwork, he never would've tied together the details of the Keller & Hoff case. Turning the words in his head to find a new perspective and a new angle was part of the game. He could've done the easy job, minimum effort to get the forms filed, but there was nothing waiting for him at home but a beer and an empty condo. If he went to go visit his mother, he'd get stuck in traffic and arrive right in time to watch her get her catheter changed. But milking the clock meant he had to get verbose. He would take extra care in describing the position of the victim's head on the street or the smell in the room. Jenkins knew Nick had nowhere to be when he got a report that read like a James Joyce novel.

Willie was going over the list of studio visitors, looking for any anomalies. Davidson and his assistant came to set on occasion to make sure their clients were being taken care of, along with the agents of other stars. A few studio execs, family members, and other random names on the list—each had a specific reason for being on set the days of their visits. If what Davidson said was true, and the pair of stars got their goods delivered on set, it was going to be a long list of suspects. Interviewing every person would take days. The guilty party would have the opportunity to disappear or get their story straight.

Nick had finally finished adding unnecessary adjectives to his report. Instead of analyzing the data Willie had put on his desk, he turned into a smart-ass in detention. He tossed pens in the air, sticking them into the cheap ceiling panels.

"Did you send that powder to the lab?" Willie asked.

A ballpoint fell and bounced off the top of his head.

"Yep. And Jenkins had some sent to the DEA lab, too. They'll need a few days to figure out what exactly is in it," Nick said. He tossed up another pen and pumped his fist in celebration when it stuck in the forest forming above his desk.

"Could they tell us anything just from sight?"

Willie removed the cup with the few remaining pens and pencils away from Nick's desk so he would focus on her.

"That's not gonna stop me," Nick said. He opened his lower desk drawer and pulled out a tennis ball. He whipped it at the ceiling and pens rained down around his desk. He made eye contact with her and flung another pen into the air. They didn't break their stare as it thunked into the foam.

"My partner is a child," Willie said, "You going to answer my question? Unlike you, I'd like to get home at a reasonable hour tonight."

"Hot date?"

"Archer."

"Fine," Nick said, "At first they thought it was some weirdo version of meth, you know like that pink Strawberry Quik stuff that made the rounds a few years ago."

"I thought that was an urban myth," Willie said.

"Nope, real thing. Didn't make it out here much, mostly it was around Vegas. There was a small period of multi-colored meth at the height of the *Breaking Bad* craze, everybody hoping for their own brand of Crystal Blue Persuasion, but it was just food coloring in the good old-fashioned poison."

"So it wasn't meth?"

"The tech I talked to said there was something in the consistency of the powder that didn't quite fit. Asked a couple of the guys over in Narco if they'd seen anything like it before and they had no idea. That, plus the apathy we're getting from the DEA, this is all us."

"Great. Hooray for teamwork," she said, "Did you finish the report?"

He slid the typed-up report over to her as he tossed another pen into the ceiling.

She read the first couple of sentences to herself, let out a breath of exasperation, and looked over at her childish partner.

"Seriously?" she said.

"I know. I'm brilliant. Call the Pulitzer people."

She read the report aloud, no inflection given to Nick's choice of words, "Secreted away in the neglected watch pocket of the faded designer denim, a small packet revealed itself. A taste of escape for our victim, a moment's respite from the crippling pressure of fleeting fame. A fine powder, purple, the color of clouds lined by the sunset of a late autumn—you're an idiot."

"Or am I so smart, I've fooled you into thinking that?" Nick said, "You find out who Seward was dating last?"

"Not yet. No luck on Seward's phone either. Called his publicist around six. Bunch of texts to Knapp and a ton of random girls to meet him at 3K. I assume that's the nightclub where witnesses saw him earlier."

"Our sexy Filipino twins in there?"

"Wouldn't know. All the women are listed with clever names like Tits1, Hairy Snatch, Tits2, and my personal favorite... CameInHer," Willie said.

"Gotta keep track of that kind of thing."

"Some real conversationalists. Don't know if there are any actual English words in these exchanges. None of them seemed more intimate with Seward than the others."

"Fine by me. I'd rather not have to call them all and find out if CameInHer saw anything suspicious," Nick said.

"Go home. We'll pick this up tomorrow." Willie shut off her computer and gathered her purse.

The elevator doors opened and she stepped in, running into Detective Jimenez.

"You know you could've just asked me to dinner, Grant. You didn't have to force yourself on me," Jimenez said with a leering smile.

She didn't answer him. Instead, she brought her middle finger up and waved it to include Nick in the collective fucking off before the elevator doors closed. Jimenez went over to Nick's desk and watched him toss a couple more pens into the air.

"You have nothing better to do tonight either, huh?" Jimenez finally asked.

"I'm about ready to go home. Just don't want to deal with the vultures," Nick said, a thumb flicked toward the plate glass.

Jimenez took a step toward the window and looked down at the parking lot. Willie was accosted by a group of reporters, lights and cameras in her face. Lowell Seward's murder had been confirmed by his lawyers earlier that afternoon.

"Bet she wishes she'd touched up that makeup job before heading out," Jimenez said, "I'll have to be sure to DVR TMZ tonight."

"You got an I.D. on your vic yet?" Nick asked, changing the subject.

Jimenez threw his file down on the desk and untucked his shirt.

"John Doe is staying John Doe, at least for now," Jimenez said. With all of the technology available for identification—fingerprints, DNA, and the like—it was shocking when someone didn't appear in their database. Unfortunately, if there were no previous arrests, sometimes it was hard to get a bead on a suspect.

"That's just the way they fall sometimes," Nick said. He wondered whether or not braving the reporters was a better situation than trying to make small talk with Jimenez.

"We're checking the international databases. He had a tattoo on his forearm. Cyrillic translators said it says, 'Property of The Bear'," Jimenez said, "So my guess is we're looking for a big hairy Russian fag."

When Jimenez laughed at his own off-color joke, Nick knew it was his cue to get going. He tossed the tennis ball into the air again and gathered up the rain of pens around his desk.

"So is this a social call, or did you need something?" Nick asked, knowing Jimenez didn't make the jaunt from Central Division just for shits and giggles.

"Wanted to apologize for being a dick this morning. I gotta get the fuck out of Central, it's making mc an insufferable prick."

"You said it, not me."

"Fuck you," Jimenez said without malice, "Also want to make sure you can control your CI. If nothing comes up on this guy, he's my only witness and suspect."

"If he were a suspect, you wouldn't have let him go so easy," Nick said, "Don't you have someone on him?"

"Those homeless, man, they live boring ass lives. Reese has been on him all day and he hasn't done shit. Picked through some garbage, took a nap. I'm heading over to relieve Reese now. Want to join me?"

Nick looked at his phone. Ray should've been checking in for his bed at Dawkins soon. It was strange for Ray to have been released from custody and go about his business for the rest of the day. He was probably playing on his tail's need for a little excitement in his life. If he convinced Jimenez to come to the conclusion he wasn't worth following, Ray could be a good little boy for a few days, then be left alone to pursue what he needed to.

"My hands are full with the Seward thing," Nick said. Even if he weren't exhausted, spending more time with Jimenez wasn't on the top of his list of fun things to do. He left Jimenez sitting at his desk as he made his own trip to the elevator.

"After they lock the doors, he's not going anywhere," Nick said, "Put another tail on him in a different car. Someone who doesn't look like a cop. If he didn't do anything interesting today, he knows he's being followed."

"You give this guy a lot of credit."

"I have to," Nick said, "He's smarter than me."

17

Night was the toughest time for the homeless. Psychopathic garbage found dark holes during the daylight hours, but slithered out once the sun went down. An uneventful night was dealing with lowlifes who thought taking someone else's dinner was a better choice than going out to find it themselves. A full night involved a murderer, or worse, a rapist. Those who preyed on street dwellers didn't discriminate in their choice of victim—women, men, elderly, young—it was all the same; a pussy or asshole for the taking.

Darkness also brought out a different kind of citizen. People who had homes and jobs, but released their primal urges on a community no one cared about. Bands of bored youths would beat a homeless person near to death for no reason other than to do it. It was less of a problem than it used to be, but sadistic people saw the homeless as no more than mangy dogs and would torture or murder them because they wouldn't be missed. It was the way it was out in the concrete.

Ray thought about these things as he sipped his coffee; the horrible crimes ignored by the police while they followed a dead-end lead. The unmarked Crown Vic was still sitting in the alley across from The Dawkins House, focused on tracking the decoy of an innocent man, instead of paying attention to the myriad of despicable acts happening mere feet from the car.

Crown Vic had been joined by his partner, the dickhead who wanted to book Ray and charge him with murder before Nick had stepped in. Even dressed in a hoodie and jeans, the dumb detective couldn't conceal the obvious. Ray wondered if the uniforms who dropped him off that morning had even noticed the detective tailing them. There was no reason for them to suspect anything, unless they knew the tail was behind them all along. But Ray's experience on the streets made him paranoid. He didn't like being in places where people could get the drop on him, always kept his peripheral vision acute. He'd had one too many concussions to do anything less. The number of times he'd been knocked unconscious, he doubted he would die of old age.

"Anybody know what time it is?" Ray said to no one in particular.

Wind ripped through the distressed nylon of the tents behind him.

"Round about 8:45," a voice said from one of the tents, "You wanna come in from the cold for a minute?"

Ray took his eyes off the Crown Vic for a second and turned around. Shake n'Bake's red-rimmed eyes stared up at him through the tent flap.

"I'll take you up on that in a minute, Shakes," Ray said, "Just need to toss my coffee cup."

Ray stepped off the curb and made his way to the overflowing garbage can on the corner, across the street from Dawkins. Once he was confident No-Tongue had passed for him, he ducked into Shake n'Bake's tent. He wished he'd waited longer.

Shake n'Bake had already started the evening's cook and they wouldn't be able to ventilate the tent without bringing the bike cops by. The smell would be diffused by some of the odors coming off the rest of the tent village—food cooked on hot plates, shit, piss, garbage—but people would know a cook was happening and they'd come running.

"Take your shoes off, would ya?" Shake n'Bake asked, a bandana over his mouth and nose.

The smell in the tent couldn't get any worse. He did as he was told, setting his dirty shoes next to Shake n'Bake's boots.

"You wanna get on some this when it done?"

Ray couldn't tell whether or not Shake n'Bake recognized him with his new haircut or if he was being generally hospitable. The fumes were overwhelming and Ray pulled his t-shirt over his face, breathing in the mixture of No-Tongue's body odor and his own.

"I'm good," Ray said, "But don't let me keep you from business."

He'd seen this sort of makeshift cook several times before and was intrigued by how resourceful junkies could be. The way Shake n'Bake made his meth was how he got his name.

Shakes took an old Gatorade bottle, filled it with drain cleaner, lighter fluid, and a couple of other things Ray couldn't identify. A couple of crunched up Sudafeds went into the bottle, then the inner strips of some lithium batteries, cut into little chunks with a tin snip. Usually, that was the last thing he tossed in before covering and shaking the bottle to start the chemical reaction, but he stopped for a second and his eyebrows went up.

"You get a bad rap, Ray, but I know I can trust you," Shake n'Bake said through the bandana.

The recognition verified that Ray's new look wasn't as severe as he'd thought.

"You know I won't rat on your cook, just like I know you won't rat I was with you," Ray said, thinking it might be a good time to leave.

"Got a brand-new secret recipe. Gonna put me back on top, son. Gonna be the Pablo Escobar of Skid Row," Shake n'Bake said, pulling a baggy of brown powder out of his pocket. It was a tan mixture, the consistency of beach sand, peppered with larger and sharper chunks of dark brown. Ray had never seen it before.

"I know you aren't gonna tell me what that is and I don't want to know. Thing I do want to know is... should I tell people to stay away?" Ray asked.

Shake n'Bake laughed, dumped in the last ingredient, covered the bottle, and started to do his thing.

The battery strips fizzed, slowly turning from silver to a dull rust. The smell of the chemical reaction was pungent, seeping through the tightened cap.

"No man. You should send 'em to me. Stuff gonna make this dirty sick reality of ours disappear," Shake n'Bake said. His arm moved in a constant motion to continue the cook, pausing slightly every few seconds to see if the powder was starting to form sediment at the bottom of the bottle.

"And how many people have field tested it?" Ray asked, opening the zipper on the tent flap a little bit, already starting to get a bit of a contact high from the fumes.

"I ain't Phillip Morris or Pfizer or nothing, so I is about to be the first customer."

The fumes were getting worse and Ray knew he had to bail. He didn't know if it was the addition of Shake n'Bake's secret ingredient or the emptiness of his stomach, but it was time to go.

"Hey, you wouldn't happen to know where I could find Crowley, would you?" Ray asked.

"Want to know your future?" Shake n'Bake asked, his eyes squinting in the grin hidden by his bandana.

"Something like that."

"Last I saw of him he got kicked out of the Family Arcade on Vermont, across from that City College there. Was accusing the pinball machines of being in a deal with the devil or some such craziness. But that was a few days ago."

Before he unzipped the tent, Ray nodded to Shake n'Bake's bottle, "What do you call this miracle? You know, just in case anybody asks."

Shakes put the bottle down and contemplated, eyes flickering around the tent for inspiration. Then he smiled, dug through his bedding, and found a little white packet. It was ripped at the top and crumpled. He hid it as best he could, adjusting his eyes to read something, then stuck it back under his pillow.

"You know how them rich folks got cocaine, real nice soundin' and all, then by the time it got on down to us, it was all cooked and fucked up and wasn't nothing but a ball of crack, like it came outta someone's stinky old ass? This ain't gonna be that way. It gonna be called Flying High. I'm gonna call it Flying High. Tell your friends," Shake n'Bake said, picking the bottle back up and finishing his cook.

"Isn't much subterfuge if 'High' is right there in the name, is it?"

"Subter-what now?"

"Nevermind. Good luck with your new business venture," Ray said.

"You be comin' on back when you hear how good this shit is. You mark my words," Shake n'Bake said.

Ray slipped his shoes back on and left the tent, zipping it shut behind him. The Crown Vic hadn't moved.

He made his way up 6th street, trying to get the smell of Flying High out of his nose.

18

Nick had managed to wade through the sea of reporters and get to his car. He'd recognized a few of them from the crime scene, including Carly Wentworth, the pretty one who'd asked him for an interview when he was out on the fire escape. He was a couple of blocks away when he dialed The Dawkins House.

"I was there earlier this afternoon looking for someone with a reserved bed," he said into the phone, "Ray Cobb."

He waited on the line as the person running the desk went to go check his cards. The receiver made a noise like someone was picking it up from the counter.

"Okay, yeah, we've got him," the volunteer said, "Checked in for a bed, traded in his clothes for a wash. He's in the dormitory now."

"Excellent."

Nick knew he could trust Ray to stay put. If he were guilty, he would've run. Instead, he was taking advantage of some time out of the cold and rain. As stubborn as Ray was, at least he had a little common sense.

"I know you lock the dorms once they're full, but would you make an exception for law enforcement?" Nick asked

"Those men aren't going anywhere. We monitor them all night and only let people out if someone gets unruly," the volunteer said, "Come by at 5:30 a.m., you can be the first one to talk to him when he gets out."

"Okay, thanks," Nick said and ended the call. With all of the strange details of the Seward case banging around in his head, at least he didn't have to worry about Ray for the next eight hours.

Daydreams of pizza, beer, and a comfy couch were whisked away as his phone lit up. He didn't recognize the number.

"Archer."

"Detective, this is Denise Parley, I'm the nurse on-call over at Good Samaritan Hospital. I was told to call you when Anita Mercado and Mercedes Pao were starting to come out of sedation. Both women are now awake and coherent."

"They're in separate rooms, correct? Not in an adjoining room separated by just a sheet? Is the officer still posted outside their rooms?"

Autopilot took over and the questions left Nick's mouth before he realized how blunt they were. When there was a break in oncoming traffic, he swung his car around.

"Yes on all accounts, sir. Should he not be?"

From the tone of her voice, Nick could tell the rapid-fire questions put her on the defensive, but he'd only have a small window to interview the girls. It was no time for idle chit-chat.

"Can he come to your station and still be in sight of the rooms?" Nick asked.

"No, it's around the corner, but there's an access phone at the room across the hall from him, I can transfer you," she said.

"That'd be great," he said, waiting for the call to turn over. He caught a stoplight and texted Willie. *Hope you aren't in your jammies yet. The twins just woke up. Headed to Good Sam now.*

"Villanueva," the officer on the other line said.

"Hey. This is Archer, RHD. I'm headed over now, I'll be there in ten minutes. Don't let anybody in those rooms other than medical staff, not even family. I want to be the first person to talk to them about what happened. I don't need some nervous mother chatting in their ears about respect and honor or some other bullshit before I can find out what the hell happened in that apartment. And don't let them talk to each other. I don't want to give them time to corroborate a story," Nick said.

"You got it," Villanueva said, "I just relieved the last guy. Shouldn't even have to leave to take a piss."

"Don't have any large coffees in the meantime." Nick hung up.

The phone buzzed with an incoming text.

Just got home. It'll take me 45 to get there. You need me?

The light turned green and he hit the gas, wondering if he could hold off any family in the waiting room for that long. The girls would be scared and out of it, having a female presence in the room would be a good idea, but Nick didn't want to risk losing time waiting for Willie.

I'll report to you when I'm done. Might call in a secondary just to be safe. Don't be jealous.

Nick was still a couple of blocks away from Good Samaritan. He put a call into the Rampart Division, right around the corner from the hospital.

"This is Detective Archer, RHD," he said, giving his I.D. number to the dispatcher, "I need a secondary for a witness interview. Any officers rolling close you can send over to Good Samaritan in the next five minutes, preferably female for the sensitive nature of the case?"

"Officer Sandoval just checked in. She will meet you there shortly," the dispatcher said.

"Rooms 237 and 239. I'll meet her in the hallway. If she gets there early, she is not to go inside."

He pulled his car into the "Reserved for Police" space in the parking lot, stuck his placard on the dashboard, and jogged to the entrance of the ER. Whatever story these girls would have for him was going to be more information than he'd gotten from anybody all day.

The doors of the elevator opened on the second floor and he trotted to the nurse's station. An old Filipino woman was arguing in broken English with the nurse Nick assumed was Denise Parley.

"You cannot keep me here! She's awake!"

Parley was trying her best to calm the frantic woman down, but was losing the battle. Nick took out his badge and lightly touched the woman's arm. She spun on him so quickly he had to take a step back.

"Don't touch me!"

Officer Villanueva peered around the corner to see if help was needed. Nick waved him off.

"Door, Villanueva. I got this," Nick said. It was clipped shorter than he'd intended, but he needed a guard on those women, not a looky-loo. Villanueva popped back into the hallway, the look in his eyes telling the detective to fuck right off.

"Ma'am," Nick said to the shaking woman, "Ma'am, I need you to calm down. I'm a police officer."

"Arrest her! Want to see my daughter!"

"This nurse is doing her job and acting under my orders. You'll get to see your daughter, but I have to talk to her first. She has some important information," Nick said.

"No! You cannot go in there with her. I know my rights," the old woman said.

The elevator doors opened and a young Latina officer stepped out.

"This is Officer Sandoval. She'll be in the room with me. We're trying to keep your daughter safe. The only way we can do that is if you cooperate," Nick said, trying to remain calm, but he wanted to talk to his witnesses as soon as possible.

The old woman broke down crying and Nurse Parley went to comfort her.

"Which one is your daughter?" Nick asked, his voice softening.

"Mercedes," the woman said through her tears.

"I'll interview her first so you can get in to see her, okay?"

The woman nodded, sobbing.

"She's just scared and wants to see her baby," Parley said, "I'll stay here with her. Make it quick."

"Is the family of the other girl here? Mercado?"

"They're on their way," Parley said.

Nick nodded and waved Sandoval down the hall with him.

"Archer," he said, holding out his hand. She shook it.

"Look, I don't need you to do anything in there but listen and watch. Don't interject. Don't ask any questions. These women were on some unidentified psychedelics less than twenty-four hours ago and we don't know what sort of after-effects the drug might have. They could be lucid now, but I don't know if they'll fall into another trip, or have a bad flashback or what. Oh, and everything you hear in here is confidential. Any of this I hear leaked anywhere I'll know exactly who it came from."

A silent nod and wide eyes answered back. Nick could tell she was a boot — a rookie with limited street time. Her training officer was probably glad to be rid of her for half an hour so he could take a shit in peace.

"No stories at the bar, no nothing, don't even tell your T.O. He asks, it was a rape interview and my partner was unavailable. Nobody knows what happens in there but me and you. And you'll only be asked what goes on in there to back me up or contradict me if I misspeak. You're just here to cover my ass and the department's. Got it?"

"Yeah," Sandoval said.

It wasn't Nick's style to be all business, so he broke the tension before opening the door, "And thanks for coming down on short notice. I appreciate it and I know it'll make these girls more comfortable having another woman in there."

The light was low in the room when Nick and Sandoval stepped in. Mercedes Pao was propped up in bed. She'd pulled the rolling tray over to her lap and was pouring herself a glass of water from a pink plastic pitcher, trying not to get her I.V. tangled in the bars on the side of the bed.

She looked different from the last time Nick had seen her. For one thing, she was wearing clothes. The hanging drapery of the hospital gown hid the lithe figure half the LAPD had been gossiping about that morning. Her hair was tangled into the pillow from a fitful sleep and the heavy makeup had been removed, exposing a naturally pretty face. Nick thought she looked better without all that gunk on and wondered if anyone ever bothered to tell her that.

"Ms. Pao," Nick said, approaching the bed, "I'm Detective Archer and this is Officer Sandoval. I was wondering if you would mind answering a few questions for us while your memory is still fresh?"

"I don't remember," Mercedes said, looking up at him with honest eyes, "Didn't even know where I was until the nurse told me. They had me strapped down when I woke up." Tears started to stream down her face. "What did I do?"

Sandoval went and grabbed the tissues without being asked and held the box up to Mercedes.

The girl dried her eyes, thanking Sandoval for the tissues.

"You didn't do anything," Nick said, "It's more important what you saw."

"I told you, nothing. I met this guy at a club and he asked me if I wanted to meet a movie star. I said sure. He led me out to a limo behind the club, opened the door, and that's the last thing I remember. I woke up here."

"Which club was it?" Nick asked.

"Um, Three Kingdoms Lounge, I think?"

"Can you describe the guy at the club?"

Eyes closed, lips pushed together in a thin line, Mercedes took a deep breath in through her nose. Nick was trying to remain patient in the silence. He knew he'd thrown a lot at the girl in a short period of time. Her mind was probably still fuzzy from the after-effects of the Grandpa in her system.

"He's a promoter. I've seen him there a bunch of times, taking girls up to the VIP tables. I go there with my girlfriends sometimes. Dress in a short skirt and get guys to buy us drinks," she said, heavy tears pooling at the corners of her eyes, "It's just an act. I'm a grad student. Sometimes I want to go out, but can't afford it. Have to look the part, you know?"

"My girls and I do the same thing," Sandoval said. It made Nick's mind flash to what Sandoval might have looked like in club clothes. It was a pleasant image, but he knew this was neither the time nor place for such fantasies.

"You aren't to blame for anything. You're the victim here," Sandoval added, taking the girl's hand. The boot hadn't listened to his advice about not talking, but he couldn't scold her in front of the witness. He shot a look at Sandoval as a warning, but she was focused on comforting the girl and missed it.

"What does this guy look like? The promoter?" Nick asked.

"He's short. Like shorter than me with my heels on. European, Italian or French, I think? And older, but hides it badly with bleached blonde hair. He wears eyeliner," she said, "Always thought he was a creep, but the place was always full so he must be doing something right. His name is Franco or Carlo. Something like that."

"That helps a lot, thank you," Nick said, smiling at her. Mercedes Pao tried to smile back, but it was a struggle. Nick knew it was time to get to the heart of the matter now that the girl was starting to trust them, but he would have to be careful. The interview could turn sour at any moment.

"We're gonna get these guys for what they did to you, but I have to know something," Nick said, "You remember getting into the limo. Do remember being offered any drugs when you got inside?"

She peered up at him with her big dark eyes and the look told Nick everything he needed to know. Problem was he couldn't do anything with a look. He needed her to say the words. And he needed her to say them before the word "lawyer" passed her lips.

Mercedes broke her gaze from Nick and looked to Sandoval, then at Sandoval's badge. Nick could see he was losing her. He opened his mouth to speak, but Sandoval spoke out of turn again. This time he was grateful for it.

"You can tell us the truth. You won't be charged with anything. You aren't in trouble. You were drugged and assaulted. If you can give us any leads to identify who drugged you, we can put them away quick," Sandoval said. She'd built an immediate trust with the girl. He'd have to give her training officer a call to let him know she'd done a good job, even if she was shit at following instructions.

"It's fuzzy," Mercedes said, "but I did snort something. I didn't think anything of it. Everybody was doing it. It looked like colored sugar. I thought they were messing around with candy. Like they'd gotten drunk and were doing the sugar from drink rims or something. Or maybe that's just what I told myself, I don't know."

"Was it purple?" Nick asked.

She nodded "yes" and started crying again.

"I wanted to impress him," she said through the tears, "I didn't want to be the only one who refused it. God, it sounds so stupid when I say it out loud. I deserved this."

"No. You didn't," Sandoval said. In three short words, Nick knew why this rookie had become a cop.

"Did Lowell Seward give you the drugs?" Nick asked.

Her eyes went wide. There was much more going on than she had been led to believe. Something had happened. She knew she hadn't just been raped and that these officers were investigating who did it. They knew who did it.

"I think I should wait to say anything else before I talk with a lawyer," Mercedes said.

The edge of Nick's mouth went up in a smile and he nodded slightly that he understood, but underneath he was seething. The girl was smart. She knew if she started throwing a celebrity's name around in a sexual assault investigation, she had better be 100% certain. Millionaire playboys had entire teams of people keeping their dirty secrets secret and without proper representation, a sneaky lawyer could turn the story completely around on her. Nick knew it was her story against a dead man's. He needed the other girl to corroborate the night's events.

"You did good, Ms. Pao. Thank you. We'll let you rest and—"

The end of Nick's sentence was cut off by an alarm outside the room.

"Stay with her," he said to Sandoval, as he ran to the door, throwing it open.

The crash cart doctors were running down the hall past him as a light above his head flashed a Code Blue. They were wheeling into Anita Mercado's room.

"What happened?" Nick yelled to Villanueva, who was still guarding the door, but keeping out of the way of the rushing hospital staff.

"She started having a seizure, foaming blood at the mouth, outta nowhere," Villanueva yelled over the panic of the crash team.

Nick couldn't see what was happening in Anita Mercado's room, but he could hear the flatline as the doctor called time of death. In the confusion, Mercedes Pao's mother made a break for her daughter's room and Villanueva caught her on the fly. She struggled against him, her fat elbows digging into his ribs as she struggled.

"Let her," Nick said, leaning his head up against the wall.

Villanueva let the woman go and she ran past the confusion into Mercedes' room. Sandoval stepped out of the way just in time to keep from being crippled by the charging hug and barrage of kisses.

Nick stepped into the doorway of the room and beckoned Sandoval out with the nod of the head.

"Is she okay?" Mercedes said, crying. Nick started to shake his head when she said, "Oh God! Is that the blonde girl? Is she okay?"

He lifted his eyes from the floor.

"What blonde girl?"

19

The blonde girl opened her eyes. They fluttered, bloodshot orbs lulling in dark pits, then closed once more. Her mind swam in the black, eyelids keeping out the nightmare, hoping this was just part of the Dance.

But she knew it wasn't.

She let the dim light in once more. Panic raised her heart rate until she realized a cot and recessed lighting weren't typical features of a grave.

All she remembered of her Dance was a phasing figure, shifting from angel to demon, wings of downy feathers morphing into stretched leather claws. He sprayed her with dragon urine, filling the bucket of her prison with his waste.

Or was it only water?

She screamed into the ceiling until her throat was raw, the dirt absorbing the sound. The girl crumpled into a ball in the muck, mud soaking through her jeans. The sheer lace crop top did nothing to protect her from the cold.

Knees hugged to her chest, shivering, the girl tried to steady her thoughts.

Where was her blazer?

The one she wore to...?

Her mind flooded with questions, an onslaught of mysteries. If she let them all in at once, she knew she would go insane.

What did she know?

"Katie Devon," she said. The raw sound coming from her throat had a different quality from her screams. Hearing her name, spoken by the voice she was used to hearing through her skull, helped her focus. If everything else was a nightmare, she knew one thing to be true. She knew who she was.

"And I'm..."

Where? And who was...?

The angel flashed in her brain. Then the demon. Then the man. The man in the garden.

The hatch above opened. It was dark outside and the insulation of the pit kept the wind whipping above her at bay.

"Still alive?" the man asked, the backyard light reflecting off the small pistol he held fixed on her.

Katie nodded. She wasn't sure if she was allowed to speak.

"I apologize for the inconvenience. The rain has interrupted my usual schedule," the man said.

His tone was light and articulate. If it weren't for the gun in his hand, Katie wouldn't have been surprised if he'd asked her if she wanted a cup of tea to warm herself. He stepped away from the edge, briefly disappearing, then slipped a wooden ladder down into the pit.

"Come on up," he said. Katie didn't move or speak.

Noticing her trepidation, he put the gun into the back of his waistband and offered her his hand.

"I don't intend to hurt you. But I want you to know I have it, just in case you get any ideas. Let's get some food in you, shall we?" he said, his hand still extended.

Katie didn't take his hand, but started up the ladder anyway. The man in the garden backed off, giving her room to roll up onto the grass.

"Pull the ladder up after you," he said, "And keep quiet. My neighbors have to work in the morning."

The backyard was surrounded by a wall of cinderblock, painted smooth in light blue. For any visitors, it must've given the yard a look of perpetual springtime, but the smooth surface would also prevent someone from climbing the wall and leaping over. Because of the barrier around the yard, Katie couldn't tell where she was, but the silence let her know she was no longer in Los Angeles. Even the quietest neighborhoods had both the low hum of traffic and the dark of the sky tainted by light pollution. There was a greenhouse in the yard that occupied almost half of the space. The small patch of grass was surrounded on all sides by a well-manicured garden.

Her captor was doing nothing to obscure his identity, which made her nervous. He had nothing to hide, which meant he was confident Katie wouldn't be describing his appearance to anyone any time soon. The man was thick, but not fat. Muscular in the way that middle-aged men who exercised were, not cut out of marble, but solid. His wire-rimmed glasses were perched on the brim of his nose and he was wearing designer jeans and a button down. He looked like he was about to host a dinner party rather than a kidnapping.

He opened the sliding glass door and gestured for Katie to go inside. She pondered making a break for it through the house, but was sure she would be shot before she took two steps. The gunfire would rouse the neighbors, but her entire plan hinged on her body being found in the man's living room. She decided to be patient and formulate a plan for escape that didn't end with her bleeding out on a suburban floor.

The house was well-decorated, someone had an eye for interior design. Original art pieces lined the walls, frames distressed by a hand familiar with arts and crafts. A blend of modern and antique furniture filled the living room. The benevolence of her environment, juxtaposed with the gun at her captor's back, made her wonder if she had merely transitioned into a different part of her waking dream.

"Sit down. Eat," he said, walking around the island in the kitchen.

Katie tentatively sat at one of the barstools and watched her kidnapper turn on the water in the sink and start washing the dishes. A sandwich had been pressed in a panini maker and placed on a paper plate. A lunchbox-sized bag of Taro chips, unopened, and a napkin, sat beside it. The sharp butcher knife he'd used to cut the sandwich glinted in his hand as he wiped the green oil of basil pesto from the blade.

"What's your name?" he asked. Katie didn't touch the sandwich, but she was starving.

"Is it important?" she asked, picking up the Taro chips, keeping an eye on the knife in his hand.

"I need to know what to call you. Give me a fake name if you wish. I just don't want to continue calling you 'girl'. It sounds strange," he said, placing the knife in the drying rack, but still within reach.

"Katie," she said, opening the small bag. She smelled one of the red chips, breathing in the salty flavor, detecting nothing strange, then eating it. Her kidnapper could've put anything in the sandwich, but the chips were right out of the bag, they had to be safe. The salt sent wild signals to her brain, revving up her hunger.

"My name's Edgar," he said, as though he was introducing himself at a cocktail party. He gestured to the sandwich.

"And that is a chicken pesto panini. Made it myself. Basil fresh from a neighbor's herb garden."

"What do you want?" Katie asked, never taking her eyes off of Edgar. She was ready to defend herself if he made any sudden movements.

"To give you a new life," he said.

"Just let me go, I won't tell on you, honest, I'll just say you saw me wandering the street and thought I could use some help," Katie said, becoming increasingly frightened by how calm Edgar was.

He ignored her plea.

"Here." Edgar picked up the sandwich and took a bite. "Does that show you it is okay to eat? I can even cut out where I took a bite so you don't get cooties."

Katie made no move for the sandwich.

"All right, but you'll be hungry later."

He cleared her plate, taking another bite of the sandwich before he placed the rest in a small piece of Tupperware and put it in the fridge.

"Time to get a look at your new accommodations." Edgar pulled the gun out of the back of his khakis and replaced it in the front band, so as Katie followed she wouldn't be tempted to make a grab for it.

"Please, what do you want? You want me to suck your dick, huh? Is that what this is? You don't need the gun. I'll suck it. Then let me go," Katie said, fear raising her voice. She didn't know why she'd said it. Another part of her had said it; a dark, panicking stranger. As soon as the words slipped her mouth, she wanted to pull them back. The thought of sucking off this button-down psycho made her gag, but the fleeting moment of disgust would be better than whatever alternative he was planning for her.

Edgar turned on her. He was too close.

"Here is the deal," Edgar said, his face red. Katie couldn't tell if it was from embarrassment or anger. "I will not be assaulting you sexually and neither will anyone else. If you do what I tell you, quietly and without incident, you will be treated well. Good food, good sleeping quarters, and even good drugs at the end of a long day, if that is your preference. I don't touch them myself, but some find it helps."

"And if I don't agree to the deal?" Katie asked, finding some courage now that she'd seen her kidnapper express a modicum of emotion.

The pistol was out quick, cocked, and to Katie's temple.

"This house is soundproofed and I know a discreet carpet cleaner," Edgar said, his eyes flashing with rage.

Katie dropped to her knees, shaking.

Edgar replaced the .38 in his waistband and pulled Katie to her feet.

"Down the hallway," Edgar said, gesturing for Katie to move, "Door at the end."

Katie nodded and did as she was told. She passed by several open doors. Bedrooms, an office. Typical house. When she reached the oak door at the end of the hall she stopped, not turning around.

"Go ahead," Edgar said from behind.

Her hand went out for the tarnished brass door handle and she held it a moment before turning it. Anything could be beyond the door. A killing floor. A porn den. An iron maiden. She pushed the door open and Edgar reached past her to flip on the light.

It was a bathroom. Small, but clean.

There was a standing shower, a sink, and a toilet. No mirror. No window. Sitting on the edge of the sink was an individually wrapped bar of soap, a travel shampoo, toothbrush, and a small tube of toothpaste. The only other thing in the room was a small travel alarm clock sitting on the back of the toilet, neon green numbers bright against black. Edgar had taken every precaution to make sure there was enough in the room for his captive to get clean, but not enough for her to get any ideas about MacGuyvering together an elaborate escape.

Katie stepped into the room, confused, examining the tile for pinhole cameras. Maybe that was the whole point. This guy sold videos of young women showering and sold them online. Katie figured that had to be his angle because thus far this weird suburbanite had kidnapped her, tried to feed her a good dinner, and now was going to let her get clean. The only thing keeping Katie from accepting her new situation were the hours she'd spent underneath a compost heap in the garden.

Edgar picked up the travel alarm clock, hit a couple of buttons, and showed it to Katie.

"You have seven minutes. I will leave. You lock the door behind you. I won't violate your privacy, but rest assured I will be able to gain access to this room if you do not emerge when those seven minutes are up. Use the facilities, get clean," Edgar said, placing the clock back on the toilet, the numbers already starting to count down.

Edgar left the bathroom, hearing the click of the lock behind him. He stood outside the door for a moment, listening to the girl sob. She wasn't going to undress. Most of them didn't the first time. He walked back to the kitchen and washed the dish he'd served the sandwich on.

He paused to listen if the shower was running as he drained the sink and dried his hands.

It wasn't.

Four minutes remaining. Just enough time had passed for her to realize she wouldn't be able to use the flimsy toothbrush as a weapon when he returned.

Wiping down the counter, he grabbed the dropper of liquid sedative from behind the flour container and put it in a junk drawer—right next to the butane lighter he'd used to reseal the bag of chips.

20

"I believe in witchcraft! I believe in the salutogenic properties of alchemy!"

Mr. Crowley was shrieking at a young couple emerging from the Vermont/Beverly station just as Ray was getting to the surface. He could see the girl, dressed for a night out, was yanking at her boyfriend's coat to pull them away. The kid was obviously a hothead and would get into it with anyone, even a crazy homeless man. Ray managed to grab Mr. Crowley by the lapels and pull him in the other direction before the kid overpowered his girlfriend.

"You think you can silence me?" Mr. Crowley yelled, spraying spittle into Ray's face, "You have shaved away your Sampson strength!"

In the past day, Ray had realized how observant the homeless community really was. A shaggy look-alike version of him had fooled the police, but a shave and a haircut hadn't kept anyone from identifying him on the street. Lucky for Ray, those weren't the people he was hiding from at the moment.

"Zip your yap for a minute, would ya, Crowley?" Ray demanded, as he pulled Mr. Crowley over to a set of benches.

"I smelled it on him, Cobb. Wolfsbane and witch hazel. The surly one there is obviously a warlock of the highest degree."

"It was Axe body spray," Ray said, putting a hand to Mr. Crowley's chest as he stood up again.

"It was either witch hazel or elderly vagina. I'd have to get closer to his crotch."

Ray had no idea what Mr. Crowley's real name was. He'd taken up the moniker of Aleister Crowley, the famous magician and occultist, but everyone thought his name was Mr. Crowley because of the Ozzie Osbourne song and his passing resemblance to guitarist Randy Rhodes. A European road map of veins ran up his arms. Curly blonde hair tangled down over his shoulders and his deep blue eyes were circled in red like spelling errors on a manuscript.

Mr. Crowley claimed to be tapped into a different world. A darkness below the surface of reality. He was adamant he could see demons, dragons, and people's true selves. A street mystic.

But it was all bullshit. Mr. Crowley and Raccoon Man lived in the same world of magical delusion.

Plenty of homeless bought into his abilities. Like a neon sign psychic reading palms and tarot cards, Mr. Crowley was excellent at reading people. He was a con-man like the rest of them, he merely lacked a storefront. But part of Mr. Crowley's mind had splintered enough for him to forget he was performing an elaborate con. For him, his observations and predictions were very real. They came from the great beyond. But Ray knew Mr. Crowley's powers to see into the mysterious ether were because he had a photographic memory. Whatever he saw or heard on the street, a small part of his fractured psyche stored for later, a gigantic database of organized madness. If Mr. Crowley read something, overheard something, or watched something, it all got put into the vault of information. The problem was finding the trigger that would release it from the vast storehouse, pulling the information out between the cracks in his broken rants.

When someone on the street came to him, seeking advice or predictions of the future, Mr. Crowley's unconscious mind would filter through his brain's database, find any pertinent information, and regurgitate it. He'd gotten so good, his reputation had branched out beyond the street. Common hustlers caught his act while they were scoring a dime bag and they told their friends. Those friends came to see for themselves. Then they told their bosses. Talk of Mr. Crowley's parlor tricks soon drifted into the cadre of criminals who profited from the streets.

Mr. Crowley wasn't a psychic, he couldn't pick the winning lottery numbers, but he'd overheard enough conversations to know which stocks would shoot up in price. Unfortunately, homeless people didn't have the sort of scratch to start investment portfolios. Everyone knew Mr. Crowley was the psychic advisor to any underworld players willing to listen and was paid well for his services. What he did with his cash when he got it was anybody's guess.

"If we're going to do this, you need to listen and obey, Cobb!" Mr. Crowley said, shaking free of Ray's grip.

"Do what, Crowley? I haven't asked you for anything yet," Ray said. This was what was frustrating about dealing with Mr. Crowley. He always seemed to have an idea of what you were going to do next, before even you knew what you were doing. It was because he was always paying attention when most people were drifting through their lives.

"Actions have consequences. *Fallor Ergo Sum*. Failure becomes us," Mr. Crowley said. The crumbling leaves from a small sapling in a city planter intrigued him and he pulled the leaves from it like he was picking precious fruit.

"Do I need to smack you upside the head to get you to stop talking in fucking riddles?" Ray asked, "I'm looking for—"

"Gravedigger will find you if you wait. All you must do is be still," Mr. Crowley said.

He threw the leaves he'd stolen from the small tree into the air and danced through them.

"I'd like to stay on the offensive if I could," Ray said.

The only comfort in the mystic's knowledge was that it let Ray assume the body in his car came from a logical progression of events and wasn't a random act. If it had come out of nowhere, there was no way the street mystic could perform his "predictions." The man was an actuary of the human condition.

"That is not likely to end well for you. The best offense is a good defense. And the best defense relies on drafting good tackles and ends."

"If I ask you why this guy is doing this, will I regret it?" Ray asked.

"He is doing it because if he wasn't doing it he would be doing something else."

"Like talking to the goddamn Cheshire Cat," Ray said to himself.

Mr. Crowley stopped for a moment and grabbed Ray's face, fingernails digging into the side of his head. He tried to struggle out of the hold, but it just made Mr. Crowley's grip dig deeper into his flesh. Ray kicked Crowley in the stomach and the dirty nails raked down the side of his newly shaven face, leaving trails of red and black.

"What the fuck!?" Ray yelled, clutching his face.

"You've opened something," Mr. Crowley said, gasping for air.

"You fucking opened something, Crowley! My fucking face, you sick fuck!"

"In search of your future, you say. But have dipped into your past. I told you, you shaved your power away."

"What part of my past?" Ray asked. He dabbed his fingertips onto his face and pulled them away, looking at the blood.

Mr. Crowley smiled and wagged a finger at him, waiting for more questions.

Ray had to tell himself to focus. It was what Crowley did. He put his subject off their game by saying cryptic things. He sees the lack of sleep, the bloodshot eyes, the lines deep from years of wear once buried by a beard. It was nothing but a Sherlock Holmes-type analysis.

"Get me in with Mochulyak. That's all I want," Ray said.

"Will you listen and obey as desired?" Mr. Crowley asked, his eyes focused on the stars rather than the knowledge he'd just dropped on Ray.

"Yeah. Fine."

"Yuri Karsenov."

"Who's Yuri Karsenov?"

"You are."

"I am?"

"Yuri is."

"Me."

"Right. No. Not you. Yuri."

"We're saying the same damn thing," Ray said, raising his voice.

"Just making sure, Yuri," Mr. Crowley smiled.

"Do I need an accent or an elaborate backstory?" Ray asked.

"No," Mr. Crowley said, "Wait. Yes. You don't have Hep C."

"I *don't* have Hep C," Ray said, confirming a true statement.

"You're better at this than I thought," Mr. Crowley said. Without asking Ray to follow him, he stormed down the sidewalk like he was leading Pickett's Charge.

Based the way Mr. Crowley doled out information, Ray began to worry if he actually had Hep C. Anything could've been under Mr. Crowley's fingernails.

It was also possible the scrawny mystic was fucking with him.

21

As he drove home from the hospital, Nick had trouble keeping his eyes open. The sheer number of things that had happened in one day left him confused and exhausted. He had two bodies, a brain-damaged movie star, a frightened girl with drug-induced amnesia, and a sketchy agent who could be obstructing his investigation. On top of it all, there was a mysterious blonde girl who might be able to put together all of the pieces of the puzzle. He knew he needed to get some sleep or all the details would start to become a horrible jumble inside his head.

The clock on his dash jumped past midnight. Underneath his eyes, the dark circles had grown so large he would have to start charging them rent. Stopped at a light, he rubbed the stubble on his cheeks and glanced at his droopy eyes in the rear-view mirror. He brought his gaze back to the road, the glowing red light taunting him with an empty intersection, then looked back to the mirror.

His suspicions had been correct. Someone was following him.

Nick took his foot off the brake. He crept through the green light to see if he could get a bead on the driver behind him, but headlights obscured his view. It was a late model economy car, the type that was doled out on the cheap at every rental agency in the country. He hadn't noticed the car earlier in the day, so there was a high probability the tail didn't already know where he lived. Turning off Wilshire, he headed up Vermont toward the hills to see if the car followed. It did.

The smart thing to do would be to try to get a read on the license plate and call it in, or give Willie a call and let her know what was going on. But Nick wasn't into doing the smart thing. If he called Willie and it had been nothing, he'd never hear the end of it.

At Franklin, Nick pulled into the 7-Eleven parking lot. He stopped at the door to give some loose change to a homeless man sitting on a milk crate and glanced up as the car passed. The driver was small. A woman. Blonde. Maybe his missing girl.

She drove through the intersection and pulled over into the red zone on the opposite block.

Nick went into the store and hovered by the window, pretending to be looking at the phone cards and magazines, glancing up to see if the driver got out of the car. She didn't move.

Moving further into the interior of the store, he poured himself a small coffee, wanting to be alert if his paranoia turned into a confrontation. About to grab one of the to-go lids, he thought better of it. A story he'd heard from Ray Cobb once about 7-Eleven coffee lids gave him pause. He reached down below the kiosk to where there were a couple of storage drawers, found an unopened package, and pulled one out. The man behind the counter didn't seem to notice one way or the other, which confirmed Ray's story about the other lids was probably true.

The small red car appeared in his rear-view shortly after he'd pulled from Franklin onto Hillhurst and headed up into the hills toward the Greek Theatre. Nick was dealing with an amateur. Shitty car, no effort made to disappear into the background. Nick could probably take her in a fight, but he kept his weapon unclipped just in case she had a black belt in the ancient art of *shoot-you-now*.

The Roosevelt Golf Course across the street from the glowing marquee of the Greek Theatre was dark. If he had any doubts about confronting whoever was following him, they were assuaged as soon as he got up into Griffith Park. The driver's lights turned off way too late into the tail, so Nick knew the car was there even when he couldn't see it. The moron didn't realize the dashboard lights illuminated her face perfectly for him in the rear-view.

He parked the car and wandered into the woods. The red car stopped a block behind him. The driver got out and followed.

"I hope you're a better reporter than stalker," Nick said, stepping out from behind a tree.

Carly Wentworth jumped and spun on him, her hand in her purse. Nick already had his gun on her. She looked scared out of her mind.

"You're lucky I don't like using this thing," he said, re-holstering his gun, "Please tell me you were going for mace and not a concealed weapon."

Embarrassed, she pulled out a small pink can. It looked like she had gotten it free at Urban Outfitters with the purchase of an ironic t-shirt. The only way it could have been less intimidating was if Hello Kitty was painted on it.

"You shouldn't sneak up on people. I could've blinded you," she chastised him.

"Sneak up on *you*? Seriously? You've been following *me*!"

"Is there even anything up here or were you just trying to get me alone?"

"I can't believe you're trying to use these cheap reporter's tactics to turn this around on me," Nick said. He was both amazed and impressed with the sheer volume of her balls.

"Which one of the girls died?" she said out of nowhere.

"Whoa. Timeout. First: What the fuck? Second: Fuck off."

"Can I quote you on that?"

"Listen, I know your biggest story to date is getting a scoop on what kind of puppy a reality star is going to buy and you think this is going to be your big break and make you the next Diane Sawyer, but right now we're looking into multiple suspects. That's all you need to report."

"Don't yank my chain. Just because I work for an entertainment news source doesn't mean I don't want to report the right story. And based on all of the running around you've been doing, you've got your head up your ass," she shot back at him.

"Wait," he said, realizing she had revealed too much, "You've been following us since this morning, haven't you? Who's your inside guy?"

"You play up being such a good cop, but this is the first time you've noticed me all day. I think that has something to do with your skill set."

"You risk interfering with my investigation, then you insult me? This is not how you get a news story, Ms. Wentworth. And while we're at it, don't avoid the question. Who's feeding you info?" Nick said, getting in her face.

"I can't reveal my source, you know that."

"You can if they're a member of the LAPD who's revealing confidential information to the press, compromising an investigation," he said.

She didn't say anything.

"You were at that crime scene early this morning. Nobody else had that information. You're putting your source's career at risk if they're found out. Think about that before you go using people for your own personal gain."

"If I had any real details on the case, do you think I would be out here getting yelled at by you?"

"If I see you in anything other than a professional capacity again, I'll have you arrested. Are we clear?" Nick said, trying to keep his voice steady.

"I won't get in the way. I just want the truth," she said, not backing off from him.

"I'm going home. I'm off-duty," he said, "If you want to follow me home to verify I'm telling the truth, be my guest, but when we get there, I'm not inviting you in for a drink."

"In your dreams."

She smiled and spun around, head high as she huffed back to her car. She sped off, leaving Nick sitting in the dark.

He didn't want to believe it, but it couldn't have been a coincidence.

On the back window of the tiny car, a decal was illuminated by Carly Wentworth's brake lights disappearing down the hill.

University of Maryland — College Park.

The school Willie Grant had attended for her criminal justice degree.

22

"Two of your best towels, please."

The man behind the counter didn't move. He was reading a worn paperback and his dark eyes lifted from the pages, staring through Mr. Crowley. The counter man's large head grew directly into his shoulders, swallowing his neck. Shoots of gray chest hair spindled up and tickled his clean-shaven third chin.

"We are closed. Members only," he said, his words buried deep in Slavic dialect.

"You should not be here," Mr. Crowley said, dropping his smile, "She should not be left alone."

"Huh?"

"You shall regret putting your duties before your love if you choose not to act," Mr. Crowley said, affecting his speech to the rhythms of a sideshow fortune teller.

A look of shock crossed the counter man's face. He realized who Mr. Crowley was.

"Are you... the seer?" the counter man asked. The tough exterior melted away, in awe of the man before him, eyes wide like those of a child meeting a birthday party magician for the first time.

Ray stood in silence behind Mr. Crowley, trying not to roll his eyes at the theatrics. Superstition did strange things to people.

"Depends on whether you believe me. And if I am right," Mr. Crowley said.

The hulk of a man stepped from behind the counter, moving quicker than his frame would indicate. He opened the door to the inner rooms, guiding Mr. Crowley and Ray in as though they were royalty.

The cavernous Russian bathhouse was empty. Puke green wall tiles were slick with condensation, sweating from steam rising from various pools of hot water. There was a constant drip coming from an unseen pipe. Ray couldn't get away from the damp, no matter where he went. Another large attendant guarded a door that led to the changing rooms. He raised his eyes from the game he was playing on his outdated phone, peering at the unexpected guests.

"The Truthseer," the counter man said, his voice echoing off the walls of the hollow room.

"You are not expected," the changing room guard said.

"Expectations are meant to be exceeded, otherwise we would always know what is expected of us," Mr. Crowley said. He sat down on the edge of the largest bath and dipped his shoe into the hot water. Ripples of dirt spread from the crusty soles as he moved his foot in circles like a kid at a neighborhood pool.

"He said I have to go. For Lucy," the counter man said.

The other one nodded ever so slightly and the counter man rushed out the door.

Mr. Crowley smiled up at the changing room guard, who had crossed the vast room and was now standing over the two of them.

"Who is this one?" the changing room guard asked.

"Don't worry about him. He is Yuri. He doesn't have Hep C," Mr. Crowley said. He was now splashing the hot water up onto his chest, seeming to have forgotten he was wearing clothes.

"Why would you say that?" the guard said, an eyebrow raised.

"To allay your worries," Mr. Crowley said.

"Seems odd to mention," the guard said, not moving.

"You run a clean joint, looks like," Ray added.

"Not when he's around," the guard pointed to the ring of brown floating on the water surrounding Mr. Crowley.

"Come in, Yuri. The water is here for you," Mr. Crowley said, yanking Ray down to his level.

"Are you here to test my patience?"

"I have nothing to offer you in exchange for your time. But Yuri here, Yuri Karsenov, with a 'K', he is someone who should be tended to."

The guard scanned "Yuri" from scalp to shins. Ray didn't shrink from the eye contact.

"Karsenov?"

"Yep," Ray said, "Our visit is time sensitive, so let's hurry this up, huh?"

The guard grunted, then disappeared behind the wall to the changing room.

"What did you see to get rid of the guy out front?" Ray asked in a hushed whisper.

"The truth," Mr. Crowley said.

Ray grabbed him by the lapels and shook him once.

"Don't forget, I don't believe in your gift."

The haze disappeared from Mr. Crowley's eyes for a moment and he focused on Ray, almost as though he was seeing his companion for the first time.

"An unusual amount of dander on his coat. His dog is dying. Probably thought I meant his wife. Perception is a funny thing."

Then the glaze over his pupils was back. When Ray let go of him, Mr. Crowley began to strip.

"What're you doing?" Ray asked.

"I should ask you the same," Mr. Crowley said, slipping off his pants and tossing them into the water, "I am leading by example."

"Not a chance."

"No place to hide a weapon. These are cautious fellows. Plus, free bath."

Mr. Crowley whipped off his stained underwear and stood before Ray. A crooked, uncircumcised member split his thicket of blonde pubic hair. He shook it out like it needed to be awakened from a long rest.

"Well?"

Ray made a face at the sinewy naked man before him. Mr. Crowley stood there smiling, his hands on his hips in a Superman pose, looking toward the changing room door.

"Jesus Christ," Ray said under his breath.

Shed down to his skivvies, stained yellow from sweat and piss, he couldn't remember the last time he'd gotten naked in front of another man several times in one day. In the corner of the room, the rest of his clothes drew in the moisture of the baths like estranged kin reunited.

"Everything," Mr. Crowley said.

"Is there anyone even here?"

"We are here."

Ray rolled his eyes, whipped off his last bit of clothing, and covered his crotch with his hands. Homelessness didn't usually breed modesty, but he didn't think he'd be able to have a comfortable conversation while his dick shrank from fear, giving away his resolve like Pinocchio's nose in reverse.

"Just to be clear, you don't have Hep C, right?" Mr. Crowley asked again.

"For fuck's sake, no!"

Then, Mr. Crowley was on him. His spindly legs wrapped around Ray's midsection, his genitals pressed hard against the small of Ray's back. Heels dug into Ray's testes, but he didn't register the pain as he clutched at the leathery skin of Mr. Crowley's forearm. It had enveloped his neck, the pressure of Crowley's elbow constricting Ray's breathing.

Ray slammed himself into the wet tile wall, but the slick surface didn't knock the wind out of Mr. Crowley as he'd hoped. The mystic gripped tighter at his neck, the only things going loose were the legs wrapped around his belly. Ray used the last of his waning strength to slam back into the wall once more, but Mr. Crowley anticipated the movement and braced his feet, pushing off the wall behind them and hurling their bodies into the hot pool at their feet.

Spinning in the steaming water, Mr. Crowley clung to Ray like an alligator drowning its prey. Black spots surrounded Ray's vision as water started to fill his lungs, his movement slowed by the tension surrounding his body. Fear and panic overtook him. As though Mr. Crowley had transferred his powers through strangulation, Ray had a brief flash of his own death.

His hand went to his neck in one final futile effort, then the body of Ray Cobb went still.

23

Exhaustion wasn't enough to send Nick home for the night. Between the coffee he'd bought, the adrenaline surge from the tail, and the anger swelling from Willie's apparent betrayal, all he wanted to do was eat. There was only one person in the world who would tolerate his company when he was this keyed up.

The night nurse smiled at Nick as he signed in at the front desk. Visitation hours were pretty strict, but with Nick's odd hours and his mother's precarious health, they let the rules slip when they could. It helped that he was a cop and brought the nurses late night snacks. He passed a plastic bag over the counter.

"Hey Maureen. Pad Kee Mao. Spicy."

"How do you always know what I'm in the mood for," she asked, opening the bag and smelling the food.

"Detective's intuition."

"Or you've been reading my diary."

"I fear that would be far too dirty for me," he smiled.

She humored him with a grin, but was avoiding his eyes. Something was off.

"How was she today?"

"Do you want the real answer, or do you want me to say 'fine' and be done with it?" she asked.

"Let me rephrase that. How was her health today?"

He knew his mother was a handful. If she had a tin cup, she would run it along the bars holding her in bed, screaming, "Attica!"

"Stable, but," she let out a breath, her tone changing, "I can tell you this, because it's you, but don't tell the resident doc I told you. She gets all high-and-mighty about bedside diagnosis, but I've been doing this long enough to know. Nick... she's fading."

Nick had heard this many times over the years. Doctors and nurses giving his mother months to live, telling him to prepare for the worst, asking him to start making arrangements. Every time they'd been wrong. But the look on the hospice nurse's face scared him more than any of those other warnings ever had. She was sure. Everything else clouding his thoughts disappeared into distant memory.

"She was fine this morning. How do you...?" he asked, not finishing the thought.

Maureen didn't answer right away. He could see her choosing her words before she spoke.

"Energy mostly. Like a battery losing power," she said, "You'll see when you go in and hold her hand. Her skin has the feel of thin wax. It's draining of vitality."

Nick had seen an abundance of bodies. He'd seen people killed. He'd witnessed suicides, shootings, and the effects of poison or overdose. But he'd never watched somebody die slowly over time. He thought he knew what death looked like, but he hadn't seen a body waste to nothing. A system shut down bit by bit. It frightened him.

"I don't like timelines. And I know you don't either," she said, having heard the whole story from both Nick and his mother, "but I'm saying from here on... relish these visits. You're only gonna have a few more."

"Which means no more Thai food for you," Nick said, trying to joke away his feelings.

"I'll be relishing the rest of your visits, too," she said.

Nick was glad this was the woman taking care of his mom. She knew how to offer comfort without sounding too sappy. He smiled at her and walked down the hall to his mother's room.

The television was on, as it always was, but the sound had been muted. Pictures flashed color across her weathered face every few seconds. Without sound, it projected a strange effect on the dozing figure, as though she had become an exhibit in a modern art museum. At any moment, a line of hipsters could be walking through her room, snapping Instagram pictures of the revolutionary piece, "Surly Woman on Deathbed."

The oxygen and monitors provided sound, accompanied by her occasional snore. The room had an antiseptic smell to it, a scent his mother may have always had, but was masked by decades of cigarette smoke. If he knew his mother, it wasn't the emphysema or cancer draining her of her final living moments, it was the absence of menthol lights permanently lodged between her fingers. His mother without a cigarette was like anyone else missing an appendage.

The doctors had no idea, but he'd been sneaking an e-cigarette in with him every time he visited. If he'd left it with her, she wouldn't have the willpower to hide it. He knew she needed the nicotine fix because it had been such a fixture in her life and he was worried about her quitting cold turkey. Along with all the other problems she'd suffered, it would've been a shock to her system. The doctors said it would improve her health not having it, that her body would adjust. Both of them took the opinions of doctors with a grain of salt. Nick knew smoking was horrible, but it might've been the only thing she was living for. A couple of puffs on the vaporizer would satisfy her high. It also gave them something secret to share.

He pulled the padded chair over and sat down next to her bed, his hunger and anger swept away by worry.

The fluorescent light above her head created an odd halo around her pillow. Her breathing was short, the exhales scraping against the back of her throat before passing her lips. The lack of makeup made her look older. The nurses would remove it before they put her down for the night, making sure she didn't smear the heavy applications on the starched white pillowcases.

Nick could see it—the fade. He didn't know if he would've seen it if Maureen hadn't mentioned it, but there was a hollow look about her now. She had been turned down, like the volume on her TV, a container harboring the last vestiges of life.

As he rubbed his thumb on her forearm to wake her, his rough callus dragged across waxy skin. It was more jaundiced yellow than the cigarette gray he was used to seeing; thin plastic wrap stretched loose to hold in her blood vessels.

"Ma," he whispered, his voice cracking. He wiped his eyes with his other hand. The last thing he needed was to have her wake up to him with tears in his eyes.

She awakened slowly, clutching his hand to verify she was still with him. The other hand raised up in a familiar gesture, the middle and forefingers pressed together, the tips slightly askew.

It was enough to chuckle his tears away. He reached into his coat pocket and pulled out the black stick with the glowing blue tip, checking to make sure there was enough liquid in the cartridge. He placed it between her outstretched fingers.

"Not even a 'Hello' first?" he asked.

She put the e-cigarette to her lips and inhaled. The water vapor puffed through her teeth, riding breath that smelled of sleep and rot.

"Could've used this a few hours ago," Janice Archer said. Finally opening her eyes, she took another drag.

"I'm running on fumes. Be glad I came at all."

"Saw you on the news," she said, gesturing ever so slightly to the television with the cigarette, "You need to grow your hair back out."

Only his mother could turn a celebrity getting his head blown off into an argument about the hairline he'd inherited from her side of the family.

"Anything interesting happen with you today?" Nick asked.

She handed the e-cigarette back to him. It was all the answer he needed. Usually he had to pry it out of her fingers when he left.

"That tastes funny." She made a face and stuck out her tongue like a toddler forced to eat broccoli. He noticed it was coated white.

"How you feeling?"

She let out a laugh that dissolved into a smoker's cough.

"Figure it out, Mr. Detective."

Nick had to clench his teeth to hold back the tension tugging in his throat. "Mr. Detective" was a dig on him she liked to save for when he was being a smart ass. But this time when she said it, there was something tender about it.

"I brought some Thai," he said, lifting the plastic bag from the floor.

She smiled and shook her head. That clinched it for Nick. Any other day she would've made a crack about coconut milk giving her the runs.

"You have anything else you want me to bring you?" he asked, holding back the implied words, *One last time.*

"Maybe a Philippe's dip? Don't know if I could take the hot mustard, but—," she stopped. She knew there was no point in ignoring the conversation they were supposed to be having instead.

"Nicky, I've spent so many years joking about this moment... I thought... hey, when it comes I'll be ready."

"Ma, they've been wrong before."

"Sure. Sure they have," she squeezed his hand, "But this time the diagnosis is coming from me. And, I'll tell ya, I'm scared out of my mind."

He wiped the tears from her face and kissed her forehead. It was hot, sucking all the heat from her cold fingers.

"What can I do?"

"You've done plenty," she smiled, "Do me one favor though, huh? Don't be one of those weirdos who hangs around here day and night waiting for me to die."

"I can't just go to work."

"Sure you can. Just like you will when I'm gone. You and I have had more goodbyes than necessary. Keep coming by when you can, let me get my nicotine fix, maybe a sandwich, until you don't have to anymore."

"I want to be here with you."

"I know. And that's enough," she said. The tenderness started to leave her voice, making her sound like her old self, "If you're underfoot for the rest of my life, we'll both want it to end sooner rather than later."

He laughed, knowing she was right. It was more likely for them to have a huge argument as their last words than a tender moment.

"You figure out what happened with this one?" she asked, pointing to the television where the story of the day had been Lowell Seward.

"I don't wanna talk about work."

"Since when?"

Nick swallowed, his throat dry.

"Well?" she asked.

Nick obliged. He could see she was grasping at the last straws of normal conversation. Anything to ignore the omnipresent specter of death.

"It was brutal. Whoever wanted him dead wanted him real dead."

"That agent of his keeps being interviewed about Lowell Seward's legacy. What legacy? His movies were terrible. James Dean, there was a legacy. Three movies. Three. Yet we still talk about him."

Nick looked up at the television where Shane Davidson was being interviewed. He'd managed to pluck the headset from his ear for the sit-down. Nick grabbed the remote from the end table of his mother's bed and turned the volume up.

"Do you have any idea who could have done this?" Nick recognized the voice of Carly Wentworth and a bit of anger flooded back, reddening his ears.

"Everybody loved Low," Davidson lied, "The world has lost a great artist."

Nick knew Davidson couldn't come right out and say Lowell Seward had been a consummate pain in the ass, holding up productions to go on drug binges, picking up girls at clubs then sexually assaulting them under the influence of psychedelic narcotics. But fluffing up Seward's legacy wasn't going to help anyone get closer to the truth.

"We have sources that say Lowell Seward was a whirling dervish on set, someone difficult to wrangle," Wentworth said. She was good, Nick had to give her that. Most entertainment reporters would just play into the sadness of the piece. But this girl knew how to get to the heart of drama, even if she got her information in sketchy ways.

"I'm not here to speculate, nor to speak ill of the dead," Davidson dodged, "My relationship with Low was one of mutual respect and friendship. I can't account for anyone else. I'd like to think his fans would remember him as I do."

The interview was edited there, likely because Davidson refused to answer any more of her leading questions. There had to be something more there than carefully woven PR.

"You can almost see him hiding his glee," his mother chimed in, "He'll probably make more money off him now that he's gone."

Davidson had already been leveraging Seward's legacy when they had arrived that morning. Could he really have had a part in killing Seward? Was it enough that Seward started costing him money and clientele?

Nick shut off the TV and set the remote back on the nightstand.

"You want me to stick around until you fall asleep?"

"Nah. I'll feel you watching me," she said, "One more drag though, huh?"

He handed her the e-cigarette and the blue tip glowed in the darkness of the room. She took a long pull of water vapor and handed it back to him.

"Remember. Philippe's. And maybe a red velvet from Doughboys."

"See you tomorrow, Ma."

"Yes. You will."

She smiled, closed her eyes, and turned over.

He stood in the doorway for a moment watching her, ready to disobey her request of leaving.

"Get outta here, would ya?" she said, not opening her eyes.

Nick smiled and closed the door behind him.

24

Katie's eyes fluttered, then adjusted to the dim light of the room in a series of staccato blinks. A figure hovered over her and a muffled voice struggled through the cotton of sleep to reach her ears.

"Take it easy, skinny. Gonna be all right."

There was a beautiful girl standing over her, no older than eighteen, long dreadlocks framing her face perfectly. She had large dark eyes, pools of deep brown encircled by crisp white. A dark scar ran the length of her forehead and bent to tickle the edge of her left eye. On any other face, the mark would've been ugly, but seemed to blend perfectly into her caramel skin. She wore no make-up, but didn't need it. Her smile and long eyelashes were enough.

"You won't have to go through this again, but we all have to do it once," she said, bringing a cup to Katie's lips.

Thirst took over as the cold water hit her tongue. It was cleaner than the hose water from the trough in the garden, but not cleansing enough to wash the sandpaper from her taste buds. The fog refused to drift from her mind and she did her best to focus on her surroundings.

She was in a small makeshift dormitory. Eight twin mattresses sat on top of military cots. The bed sheets were crisp and clean, smelling of detergent and fabric softener. For a moment, Katie figured it had all been a bad dream and she was in a shelter somewhere, back out into the world.

"Edgar is gonna take care of you. You hungry?"

The girl handed her a protein bar. Katie shook it off.

"Take it," the girl said, "You won't get no more tainted food. Like I said, it was just the once to get you into your quarters without a struggle."

"What do you want with me?" Katie said, her voice croaking from her throat.

"I don't want nothing from you, Sugar. Me and you is in the same situation. But in time, you gonna learn that down here you better off," she smiled.

"Where I come from, kidnapping and drugging people isn't the way to give them a better life."

She tried to stand, but her head was pounding. The girl offered the bar again. This time she took it. Katie was so hungry she didn't care if there were more drugs in it.

"Way Edgar explains it, we all were on the streets 'cause we running from something. Don't have our best interests in mind. Addicted to blowing in the wind, without realizing there ain't nothing beyond," she said.

"Edgar sounds like a Jim Jones cult leader," Katie said.

"Don't know who that is, but we sure ain't no cult. None of us worship Edgar or nothing. He's like a boss. Saving up our wages for once our work is done," she said.

"Sounds like a scam to me," Katie said.

"Nope. I seen it. He holds a little ceremony and everything. Like we graduating out of here to a better life. By the end of your time, you'll be grateful that man pulled you off the streets," the girl smiled, "He don't abuse us. No sexual favors or nothing. We get food, place to sleep. Ain't no different than being stuck in the corporate world."

Katie felt it would be okay to stand. Head clearing, she looked around the room for escape.

One door. No windows.

"All that and no sunshine? Sounds swell," Katie said.

"We get plenty of sunshine. But you gotta earn it. Once Edgar trusts you, he takes you to his flower shows. Even lets you walk around on your own, if you like. But like I said, you got to show you're worthy of that trust," she said.

"Listen," Katie said, pleading, "I'm no runaway. I'm not from the street. I have a job. I'm saving for a condo for Christ's sake. You've gotta get me outta here."

"It don't matter what you come from. You here now," the girl said, smile not leaving her face. Katie looked into the girl's dark eyes, searching for help, but could see she wouldn't find an ally in this girl.

"You want me to trust a maniac who brings me to his house in the suburbs and drugs me and throws me into an underground pit with one of his cult followers?"

"Emma."

"What?"

"I ain't no cult follower and my name's Emma," she said. The girl's pleasant tone was wearing thin. Katie didn't introduce herself.

"You wanna see where you'll be working, or you gonna sit here and be a pain? I guarantee that choice won't change your situation none."

Emma opened the wood door covered in chipped white paint. Katie took a step toward the larger room, her feet shaky beneath her. The way the floor bent, she could tell it was nothing more than plywood over uneven dirt.

Two long tables stood in the middle of the next room. A group of five workers, three girls and two boys, none of whom looked much older than Emma, busied themselves with their specific duties. All of them wore protective masks, which Emma had put on and was now handing to Katie. For as ramshackle as the door to the dormitory seemed, she was amazed at how much of the noise it kept out.

It was a typical assembly line. There was one girl emptying small packages into a large tub of water, then taking other tubs and filtering them through cheesecloth. The pebbles from the cloth were then taken by two of the other workers who placed them into coffee grinders, the loud whirr happening every couple of seconds, then dumping out the contents for another one to sort through. Once the piles had become large enough, the grinders joined the sorters in their tasks, pulling out the hard, dark brown shells and separating them from the light tan middles of what Katie deduced were seeds. The remaining worker was monitoring an elaborate group of chemical processes, checking pressure gauges and measuring out liquids and powders from unmarked jugs. The whole thing looked like a meth lab, but it didn't smell the way she assumed it would, the foul way it was portrayed on TV. It wasn't a pleasant smell, but there was something organic about it. Earthy. Katie figured the smell could have been filtered out or numbed by the large trays of blue, white, and purple flowers lining the walls.

"What is this?" Katie asked.

"The newest thing in nutritional supplements. Natural ingredients to focus the mind and spirit," Emma said, as though she was quoting a sales pitch verbatim. From Edgar's mind to her mouth.

"Pretty sure nutritional supplements aren't made in an underground meth lab," Katie said.

Emma ignored her and pulled out a chair at the long empty table. Katie wasn't seated with the others. A short girl working one of the grinders stood up and dumped her latest batch onto a tray on the table in front of Katie.

"The smell can bother some people, but you'll get used to it. We soak the powder in a petroleum-ether mixture to suck out the toxins before processing. Hopefully, the smell of the morning glories will overpower it," she said, "Separate the shells from the meat. Get rid of the dark brown stuff. Don't have to be perfect, but it keeps out the bitterness the less there is. Quality control."

"And if I don't work?" Katie asked, her arms crossed.

Everyone in the room stopped what they were doing and looked at her.

"Then none of us eat," Emma said, dead serious. No one else chimed in.

"Seems to go against your idea of Edgar taking care of you, doesn't it?"

"We take care of him, he takes care of us," she said as the other workers returned to their tasks.

Katie looked down at the pile in front of her, then back up at her fellow captives. Each of them kept glancing her way, waiting patiently for the new fish to take up her work. Katie could tell the threat was serious. Every second that ticked by without her touching the pile in front of her made them more nervous. The room breathed out a collective sigh when she started picking through the mixture, setting each type of grain into their own piles. No one else spoke to her. No one gave her a hello or a welcome.

As she kept to her work, she tried to take in as much of her new environment as she could. There were no windows in the lab. A wooden ladder led up to a heavy metal door in the ceiling. They were definitely underground somewhere. All the other kids in the room had the ragged look of runaways. She had to be the eldest among them at twenty-five. She didn't belong in this group.

She also noticed the smoke alarm and wondered who it would bring running in case of fire.

25

Nick rarely used his issued light and siren, but he didn't hesitate revving it up that morning. Though it was early, there was already traffic packed tight on the 10 and even with the siren, he found himself ducking onto the shoulder more than he should have.

He couldn't stop thinking about how Ray had trusted him. Ray told him he was being set up for something and he had just ignored him. Nick knew he should've called someone right away to cordon off the area, but he didn't want to admit to Jimenez he'd been wrong, that he'd let a witness die on his watch. It was the second day in a row where a phone call woke him up about a body.

When he got to The Dawkins House, he held his badge out in front of his chest, hoping no one would stop his forward momentum toward the dormitory. There was a different volunteer on duty for the morning shift. She was about as young as the previous day's counterpart, but must have been either more sensitive or a new addition to the team, because she was in between several long stints of crying. She had on a hoodie and her hands were tucked into the sleeves, the cuffs used as makeshift tissues when they weren't wrapped around her small body. Nick stopped his frantic run when he saw her.

"Are you the one who found him?" he asked, approaching her like he would a frightened kitten.

She nodded as she spoke, clear snot running to her lips before she swiped it away with her stained sleeve.

"Everybody piled out. Some were groggy like usual. It wasn't just me in here. They send us in teams just in case somebody is a problem," she said, holding back more tears, "Cam helped me try to shake him awake when we noticed how cold he was."

"Where's Cam now?" Nick asked, pushing past her into the empty dorm.

Bunks were crammed into the room tight and though everyone had bathed before bedding down, there was still a faint smell of body odor and feces. Though the latter was probably coming from Ray's corpse. She followed behind him.

"Cam stayed with the rest of the residents, shuffling them downstairs. Making sure they didn't make a big deal of the body. I said I'd stay with him... it... him," she said.

"What's your name?" Nick crouched down to where Ray's body had been covered with a wool blanket.

"Alison. Alison Ruck."

"Did you know Ray, Alison? Did you talk to him?"

"No. Not at all. I just got on shift an hour ago," she said, keeping her distance from the body, "I know it's ridiculous being so upset over someone you don't know, but..."

"It's hard to see. You want to help these people, but you don't know how," Nick finished her thought. The futility of it all was exhausting.

"Glad you were the first one here," she forced a smile, "Usually the police just come in, bag them up and go. Like they're taking out the trash."

"Yeah, well, he was my responsibility. And I let him down."

"He died in his sleep. There was nothing you could've done."

"I got this from here, Alison. I already called an ambulance. Do your best to let everybody know it's on the way."

She nodded and left the dormitory, sniffling as she went.

When he was sure she was gone, he pulled the blanket back. The greasy long hair came up with the wool and Nick went to smooth it back down before thinking better of it and grabbing a set of rubber gloves out of his pocket. There was something different about the vessel in life and death. Religious people would call it departure of the soul. A life force leaving the body. But Nick knew it was just science. The energy and heat were transferred out. The life gone, leaving a husk. A waxy shell. A different form.

He brushed the corpse's hair back.

It wasn't just a different form. It was a different person.

The hair was almost identical. The beard had the exact same mixture of gray and dark auburn tones. Even the nose was the same. But the eyes were different.

Nick remembered the day before, when the volunteer mentioned Ray keeping his eyes to the ground, not speaking, his hair flopped in his face. The son of a bitch had pulled a switch on him.

Whoever Ray Cobb's dead replica was, he could've easily fooled someone from a distance. The ringer was good.

"Motherfucker," Nick whispered to himself. The R.A. Unit would be there shortly, which meant that news would get back to Jimenez soon enough. He had probably just gotten out of bed and into the shower. Nick was going to need the hour to figure out what to do with this new information.

Ray wouldn't fake his own death. Or if he did, he would never kill someone else in the process.

Would he?

Nick stared down at the body, thinking. Ray had to have known that the ruse would be over as soon as the body was discovered. Which meant Ray never meant for his doppelgänger to die. Hell of an inconvenient time for a man's heart to give out.

Sirens grew in intensity as the ambulance approached. Nick took a couple of pictures with his cell phone, making sure to get a record of the scene before he disturbed it. Carefully folding the sheets down to the dead man's chest, Nick caught a glimpse of something. He stuck his fingers into the collar of the corpse's sleeping clothes. There was a red line cut into the man's neck. The volunteers must have been so distraught by finding the body, they'd just assumed he'd died in his sleep, like most of the other bodies they'd found.

It took a moment for his cop brain to catch up with his curiosity. His eyes went wide and he bolted down the stairs, looking for anyone of authority.

"You need to put this place on lockdown," he said to the tall guy at the front desk. This must have been Cam.

"We have to open the doors for breakfast," Cam said.

"Nobody gets in or out. The guy upstairs was murdered. You lock this place up for the night, it can stay locked for a few more hours."

"But—"

"Call whoever the fuck you have to call, just get it done!"

The kid complied, still confused as to what was happening.

Nick got on his phone and called Central Division, just as he met the EMTs at the doors.

"This is Archer, RHD," Nick said into the phone, "Body at Dawkins is a crime scene. Send a team. And call Detective Jimenez. He'll want to know about this."

A mess of disorganized volunteers struggled to keep the gathering masses of homeless outside the gates from rioting for their breakfast. Nick felt like he was standing at the base of a dam, cracks forming quickly as small sprays of water burst through. He'd have to plug the big holes first and hope he didn't miss the trickle that would let loose a deluge.

The analogy in his mind told him his next step.

The showers.

Nick barked orders at the approaching supervisor before he had a chance to speak.

"No one leaves. You had a murder upstairs. Come with me," Nick said.

The men from the dormitory were already clean and dressing.

"Everyone. I'm going to need you to stay put for a few more minutes," the supervisor said, standing up on a bench. The gathered homeless men were in various states of undress and a collection of confused groans filled the room.

"I'm sure you heard we lost one last night and unfortunately it was not natural," the supervisor said, looking down at Nick. His gaze wasn't met. Nick was scanning the faces, searching for the set of guilty eyes looking to the floor or focusing too intently on what was being said.

"How do you wanna do this?" he asked Nick, his voice lowered.

"We're going to have to interview everyone individually. Once I get a couple of officers here it will go much quicker than me doing it myself," Nick said.

He got up on the bench.

"Listen, I know you're hungry and you want to get out of here, but we need to find out if anybody heard anything last night, so we're going to have to hold you all here for a bit," Nick said to the crowd.

"I didn't hear or see nothin'," a short man wearing a stained t-shirt and not much else cried out, "You can't keep us here. This ain't no prison!"

There was a general consensus of agreement amongst the men and Nick could feel the tension in the room rising at a fever pitch.

"I'll tell you what," the supervisor jumped in, "We'll do the interviews in the cafeteria. So you all get to hop the breakfast line. That incentive enough for you?"

There was some more grumbling, but the forensics team and uniformed backup had arrived to control the crowd. The presence of additional badges silenced all but a handful of vocal conspiracy theorists. Nick made note of which of them to interview first.

The phone rang in his pocket. He answered.

"What the fuck is going on?" Jimenez said. The sounds in the background indicated he was racing through traffic just as Nick had half an hour before.

"We got another strangled DB and lots of potential witnesses and suspects."

"Cobb's dead?"

"No," Nick said, "Cobb's gone."

26

Air rushed into Ray's lungs after the water vomited out of his stomach. A combination of dirty water, snot, and spittle came up in raspy coughs. Oxygen was in short supply as his body prepared for the next dunk into the rusted tub. Whoever was gripping the back of his head couldn't get a hold on his newly shortened hair. Ray could feel the crescents of sharp fingernails digging into his skull, drawing blood from the loose skin of his scalp. To get as much air into his lungs as he could before he was shoved underwater again, he nearly hyperventilated with quick gasps. His breathing eventually slowed as he realized he wasn't going for another swim.

He took in the room between coughing fits. There was a dampness reminiscent of the bathhouse, but he had been moved. It was too run down, abandoned. Wallpaper was peeling from the water-stained walls. Every metallic fixture had a thick layer of rust around it and bled into the porcelain, crying tears of iron oxide onto the cracked and chipped surfaces, the sheen of new tile forgotten decades before. Flecks of old paint floated on the surface of the rust-colored water. He wondered if he was going to die by drowning or by ingesting a lethal amount of lead.

The hand on the back of his head spun Ray around. The tub was on a raised platform in a room larger than his original assessment suggested. Someone had pulled him back into No-Tongue's stained pants, but he was naked to the waist. Cracks in the old claw foot tub leaked water out onto the dirty floor, soaking through his pants, dampening his raw knees. Mr. Crowley was gone.

Standing over him was a gaunt man who looked like he could've been knocked over with a light shove. He wore dark suit pants and a white shirt that hung off him, rolled to the sleeves. His cheekbones jutted from his face, sharp promontories pocked with acne scars. Deep lines were drawn down to his mouth. His sour breath wafted through his discolored front teeth, fixed in the scowl of a hockey player ready to drop the gloves after a bad crosscheck. If Ray had been told this man was powerful enough to hold him underwater, he would've thought he was the victim of a cruel and terrible prank. But there the scrawny man stood, a sturdy skeleton wiping water from his oversized hands with a towel. The stringy sinew of his forearms twitched, making the Cyrillic letters in an old tattoo dance.

Ray had seen the tattoo before and the skeleton caught him staring. His eyes went back to the floor, lest he get dunked again for his insolence.

The skeleton rolled down his sleeves and put on a suit coat hanging from a steaming radiator. He tossed the towel at Ray's face and it landed in his lap. But it was useless. Ray's hands were tied behind his back.

"You are disturbingly resilient, you know this?"

Ray squinted to get a focus on the voice across the room. The accent was distant; the edges of Ukrainian shaved off by decades of residency, vocal chords run through a polish of good bourbon and better vodka. Sitting on a small stool was a bulbous man in his fifties, his gray hair crew cut to his skull. There was a dark ring of sweat around the neck of his Indiana

University sweatshirt and his hands, folded together like he was about to pray, were covered in thin knit gloves.

"And you don't look like any Russian mobster I've ever met," Ray said. He knew this was the end of the line. He wasn't going to beg for his life.

The skeleton man swatted him on the back of the head. Ray could feel the hard bones of his hand scrape against the divots his fingernails had left.

"When you hear the voice of The Bear, you listen," the skeleton said.

The Bear put his hand up to halt the assailant from any further attacks.

"Has he not suffered enough, Viktor?"

Ray kept his eyes on The Bear, trying to remain calm, but his pupils dilated and his breath quickened.

Viktor.

Viktor Mochulyak.

Gravedigger.

The skeleton who'd been drowning him was the man he was looking for, the man who'd left a dead body in his car. The man notorious for burying bodies where they were never found, but who chose to leave one in plain sight.

Ray had too many questions, but was afraid of catching this man's wrath again. He would be silent until he was told otherwise.

"Please excuse the attire," The Bear said, unconsciously rubbing his hands on the thighs of his yoga pants, "My wife thinks I have gone for an early morning jog."

Ray licked his lips, his eyes flicking between The Bear and Gravedigger, the strangest tag team on the planet.

"You must know, Mr. Cobb, that I owe you thanks," The Bear leaned in, "You are responsible for a wonderful wave of good fortune in my life. Mr. Crowley has told me so. This is the only reason you are not dead yet."

Ray had no idea what he was talking about. His mind lingered on the addition of the word, "yet."

"Some time ago you played a game of poker, yes? With a man who had no face?" The Bear smiled.

A smuggler and gambler named Pretty Boy D'Arby had once gotten in Ray's way and didn't live to see the next morning. Ray wasn't the one who'd killed him, but he'd made it easy for his murder to happen.

"In the vacuum left by Pretty Boy's enterprise, I was able to capitalize on some of the more... innovative aspects of his business. And I have you to thank. But you see Mr. Cobb, as business grew, so did complications. Not an uncommon thing in any business, there are growing pains to be sure. Someone in my employ made too many mistakes. This was the man we left in your car. No one of consequence."

The Bear stopped speaking and silence crept into the space, broken only by the drip of water. Ray looked up at Viktor, but Gravedigger's eyes were fixed on his boss.

"So..." Ray started, bracing for another clap across the back of his head. It didn't come. He continued. "If you owed me so much, why conspire to get me thrown in prison for murder?"

"A courtesy."

Ray's eyebrows went up in surprise. His tongue held back the sarcasm brewing in the back of his throat.

"You see, there were many who knew of what you had done to Pretty Boy. For a long time, I was the only one between you and assassination. Your relationship with the police force held back the men who would have their revenge on you. For a long time, your potential murder would not be washed over as any other homeless murder might. Law enforcement was still paying attention to you. However, tension was mounting and the years were shortening police memory. Having you on the street was a liability. And as we have seen from your escapades today, once you get curious about something, you have a hard time letting it go."

"So, what? You're my guardian angel? Funny way of showing it."

"I was saving your life by sending you to prison. I could've just had you killed and been done with it, but in prison, I could protect you. There is a much smaller area to cover there, fewer bodies to keep track of, you understand? To kill the man who had given me so much, I would risk losing both honor in my heart and the favor of fortune. I do not wish to tempt fate."

Ray noticed the fat man put a lot of credence in fate and destiny. It was no wonder he'd adopted Mr. Crowley as one of his pets.

"Then why am I here now? How're you not tempting fate?"

"There is a difference between relying on the universe to provide you with answers and giving in to superstitious stupidity," The Bear shrugged.

"And what did I do to warrant your protection for so long, only to have you turn on me?"

"Turn on you? I would say I came to your aid," The Bear said, leaning back on his stool, "It is the common opinion that those of us who operate outside the law kill people without care. This sort of moral assumption upsets me. Just because I would trade a human soul for labor or sex, or sell drugs, why does this automatically make me a murderer?"

"So the guy you left in my car died of loneliness?" Ray said.

Viktor punched him and blood flowed down his nose. He licked his lips, the iron taste mixing with the rust on his tongue.

"I would argue the lives I had part in taking were the cost of doing business. The man found in your car, he outlived his usefulness. Your friend at Dawkins, however, that was a mistake."

Ray closed his eyes and took in the information that No-Tongue was dead. And that it was his fault.

"Viktor got a bit overzealous," The Bear said, "He did not understand I have no reason to kill you. But, alas, Viktor has now provided a sound argument for your execution. He must atone for his mistakes. It can't be helped."

Viktor walked behind Ray and wrapped a length of wire around his neck. He could feel it cutting into his throat, the breath constricting as he started to suffocate. Black bursts appeared in front of his eyes as he watched The Bear stand from his sitting position and go to Viktor.

Using a straight razor, The Bear opened Viktor's neck.

Blood sprayed down his shirt as the wire loosened. Ray gasped for breath like a fish flopping on a dock, watching the life gurgle out of his would-be executioner.

Soon Viktor Mochulyak was still, blood pooling underneath him. The Bear had to step back to keep the puddle from getting onto his clean white running shoes.

He wiped the razor on Mochulyak's shirt, then pressed it into Ray's bound hands.

"Use that to free yourself."

"Why?" Ray coughed out. He could feel the small trickle of blood starting to flow down his own neck where the wire had sliced into his skin.

"If he had done his job correctly the first time, we would not have had this conversation. If he had not sought to remedy his mistake without consulting me, he would still be alive. It is unfortunate. He was good at what he did," The Bear said, "This is the second time I have chosen your life over the life of my men. There will not be a third. And since you have caused so much chaos in such a short time, I will not let you out of my hands to run rampant. You have forfeited your life to us. Someone will be here to collect you shortly."

The Bear walked out of the bathroom and disappeared. Ray stared down at the body in front of him and clutched the razor. In trying to get clear of one murder, he'd placed himself as the sole suspect in another. And he didn't have an alibi for this one.

Ray bent his wrist at an unnatural angle to get at the ropes. Trying to position the razor correctly, he accidentally sliced through his wrists a few times. They were superficial cuts, but if he wasn't careful, he'd make an epic slip and it wouldn't matter whether he got out or not.

As the ropes started to come free and more cuts started gathering on his skin, he realized The Bear had been beyond careful. He was wearing gloves, so his prints would be on nothing. Ray had been asking around town for Viktor Mochulyak and now he would be found dead in a room covered in Ray's DNA.

He knew he had to get to Nick. Start spilling a story and hope The Bear didn't have someone around to silence him in the holding cell. He'd spent the last two days avoiding being arrested and now that was what he wanted more than anything in the world.

Hands free, he sprung up, trying not to put his bare feet into the spreading puddle of blood.

Pushing out of the bathroom into the main room of the abandoned house, two pinpricks shot into his chest, a high voltage taser surging electricity through his body. The forms of two men were the last things he saw before once again losing consciousness.

27

The thick coffee from the Dawkins canteen wasn't doing the trick. Just as Nick had suspected, the interviews of every man in the dormitory came up with nothing. Nobody saw anything, nobody heard anything. Even if they had, they weren't going to tell the police. Nick knew as soon as he'd initiated the interviews it would be a pointless exercise, but it would give the team a chance to sit down and get a look at each of the men's hands. If the murderer had used a wire garrote, there would at least have been some marks on the suspect's hands. But there was nothing.

Whoever had killed Ray Cobb's doppelgänger was long gone. Even though the dorms were closed at night, it would've been easy for someone to blend in with the group shuffling to the showers and disappear. They did a head count and weren't missing anybody, so the killer didn't check in then leave an empty bed. Whoever framed Ray Cobb had upped their game to make him the new target. They were going to take him out one way or another. Which meant wherever he was hiding, Jimenez was going to have to find Cobb before the assassin did.

Nick stepped out onto the street as the shelter opened the doors for people who still wanted breakfast. He could hear them swearing at him, cursing the LAPD for fucking up their morning. Some of the more conspiracy-focused detractors hissed comments about a police state holding people against their will.

As soon as the team from Central Division showed up, he'd checked in with Jenkins to let him know where he was spending his morning. He had yet to connect with Willie. The chaos was a welcome distraction from confronting her about being a press informant, but he knew he would have to have the awkward conversation soon after arriving at the station. He wouldn't be able to hide his disgust and she would see it on his face.

He got into his car and turned the ignition, trying to remember if he had a clean change of clothes in his locker. As he was about to pull out of the spot, his radio buzzed.

"DB found in a tent on 6th and Wall. Possible O.D. Officers on scene."

It was the usual noise and Nick tried to ignore it. There was another squelch.

"Contact RHD primary. Possible evidence in Love Nest investigation."

"Love Nest" was the code assigned to the Seward case. There were too many people tuned in to police radio scanners to say the name out loud. Not that the code names deterred anyone who was paying attention, but it warded off tourists.

As Nick was about to radio dispatch, his cell phone rang.

"Heard it on the radio. I'm around the corner, show me responding," Nick said.

The bicycle cops had already cordoned off the tent and cleared the other settlements around it as best as they could. It was their usual task to pedal down the streets of Skid Row and clear the tents. They knew there wasn't much they could do at night, but at least they could get some of the homeless off the streets before the local businesses opened for the day.

"Archer, RHD. What do you got?"

"Williams and Tufts," Officer Williams said, introducing himself and his partner, "Doing our usual morning clear and this one didn't move. Obvious O.D., but we caught something in the corner that made us think twice. We checked to make sure he wasn't breathing, but didn't touch anything else once we saw it."

Nick took a step inside the tape and the smell coming from the tent washed over him. It was days like these he wished his mother was still in his house, burning his sense of smell out with secondhand cigarette smoke.

"You got a mask and gloves I can use?"

Williams dug into his bicycle's fanny pack and handed them over. Nick unzipped the flap of the tent.

On first glance, the bike cop's call of an overdose was accurate. The body was splayed across a makeshift mattress of blankets, his ball cap askew from thrashing. The dried foam of saliva mixed with a black line of blood from the victim's nose, forming a sticky mask over his dirt-stache. An old Gatorade bottle sat in the corner, a brownish residue collected in the basin. A mason jar with a coffee filter over it was filled with runoff liquid that gave off a strong, distinct smell. The discarded battery casings and small bottle of lighter fluid pointed to a shake cook. But if it had been purely meth, the gunk in the Gatorade bottle would've been a different color.

The victim had emptied his powder out onto a flattened box of generic Rice Krispies and had put the powder up his nose with an old drinking straw. It wasn't purple, so Nick could rule out that this wasn't his mysterious movie star killer. That was until he saw why the bike cops had called it in.

Flopped open in the corner of the tent was Lowell Seward's wallet. The officers wouldn't have had to do much investigating to see whose it was. The driver's license was displayed open in a clear plastic pocket, Seward's bleached white teeth flashing at the camera. The credit cards were all there. The department hadn't gotten a ping on their use the day before, so the dead homeless man was smart enough not to use them. The back flap was empty, whatever cash was in there was probably used to buy the cook materials, or was stashed somewhere else. There wasn't much else inside it. Gym membership. AAA card. No bright and shining business cards from a dealer that said, "Call Me For Drugs!"

It was another damn dead end. The wallet probably fell out of Seward's pants when they were flung off the balcony and was picked up by the first soul who happened by.

Nick looked over at the dead man. His eyes were wide open, staring up at the dome of dirty nylon. Whatever shock had come from his thrashing overdose had subsided once the life had left his body, his face going slack. Rigor Mortis had yet to set in, so his muscles were still loose, the body flopped into its final position. A couple pairs of ragged socks hung off the dead body's feet, his shoes kicked off in the seizure.

No. Not kicked off in the seizure. Nick could see them set just inside the flaps of the tent.

Homeless people had some weird habits. Hell, everybody did. Strange leftovers from another time in their lives. The dead man had probably been trained at some point in his life to take his shoes off when he went into somebody's house. An OCD mother who didn't want her carpet stained, maybe a wife who'd hen-pecked him to drug use. Or it could've been simpler. He might've stepped in shit and didn't want to rub it on his bed. The victim hadn't taken anything else off. He was still in layers of coats, pants, and a ball cap. He even had on fingerless gloves for his cook. Why would he take his shoes off?

Nick picked up one of the ratted, stinking boots and shook it. The loose rubber sole flapped against the leather with a slap. Nick did the same with the other. Nothing.

He looked inside each shoe before sticking his hand in. Last thing he needed was a dirty needle in his finger first thing in the morning. Seeing nothing, he felt around the insoles. The left shoe felt funny. He pulled up the cloth insert and shook the shoe again. A folded piece of paper flopped out onto the base of the tent.

The curved edge indicated it had been inside of a wallet, the natural formation of a butt cheek bending the sides ever so slightly. Unfolding it, Nick recognized the handwriting. He'd seen it on a stack of signed photographs on Lowell Seward's desk.

The dead man had to improvise with the resources available to him, get creative.

The contents of the small piece of paper had killed him.

The last words of Lowell Seward.

A recipe for Shadow Dance.

28

Ray was roused from his sleep by the sound of rainfall spattering against leaves. The jolt of electricity made him piss himself and his teeth were chattering from the cold. Wherever he was, it was dirty and damp. He smelled rotting food. A single light was buried in the earth below him, recessed in the soil and covered in a piece of weather-resistant plastic.

He was on a small stained cot and shared the room with nothing but two buckets. One appeared to have clean water in it, the other smelled like the depository for the water once his body processed it. He took a small comfort in the first bucket being full and the second empty, rather than the other way around. But access to rudimentary restroom facilities gave him cause for panic. Whoever had buried him in the hole wasn't expecting to return to him any time soon.

There was a bandage covering the underside of his forearm. He didn't remember injuring it as he fell, but it stung like a second-degree sunburn. He itched around it a little, but stopped when the pain became too much.

What was The Bear doing with him? Ray had offended him, but hadn't done enough to warrant a death sentence. The Bear believed so much in his strange moral code, he was willing to take out one of his soldiers for disobeying him. Either that or Viktor Mochulyak had outlived his usefulness. For as averse to murder as he'd said he was, The Bear didn't appear to have any trouble disposing of those in his employ at the slightest affront. It was as though they were property rather than people.

Property.

Ray yanked the tape from the bandage on his forearm and peeled it back like the top of a sardine can. Etched in his skin were familiar Cyrillic letters, ringed red with the new sting of needles and ink. He didn't know what it said, but he knew the other people he'd seen with the same tattoo were now dead. He had been marked. The Bear didn't kill him because Ray Cobb was now his property.

Of all the indignities Ray had suffered on the street, this one was the most heinous. Beatings, framing, kidnapping—none of them fundamentally altered his appearance, aside from a few scars. The tattoo was deeper than a mark on skin. It was a permanent alteration of his existence. Whether he was indentured to The Bear until he died, or if he managed to find a way out from under the gangster's thumb, some remnant of the mark would always be there. A constant reminder. It would be a memory he'd never be able to shove down into his subconscious and ignore.

Ray felt a familiar twinge below his waist. He hadn't let go of as much piss as he'd thought when the tips of the taser hit his bare chest. He untucked himself and voided his bladder into the empty bucket, the acrid orange flowing from him like it would never stop. Just as he had filled a quarter of the bucket, he heard a strange creak above his head. A shred of light came in from a crack in the surface. He turned, his dick still in his hand, to see the outline of a man hunkered down above him. The only thing Ray could make out from the backlit form was the outline of a small caliber pistol in his hand. The silhouette chucked down a couple of protein bars.

"Good to see you're awake," the man above him said. The Ukrainian accent he'd associated with his previous opponents was absent from this man's speech.

"You won't be down there forever. Hold tight and I'll retrieve you after dark."

The top of the pit closed once more and the lines of sunlight hovered in negative colors across Ray's vision. He tucked himself back in and wiped his hands on his pants before dipping them in the other bucket and bringing a gulp of water to his face. When the latch of his prison was open, he could've sworn he'd heard the faint sound of children playing. Was that possible?

He unwrapped one of the protein bars, sat back down on the cot, and tried to process how he'd gotten there.

When he let Pretty Boy D'Arby die, he'd made some enemies, but also made an ally. The Bear. A man who had been secretly protecting him from Pretty Boy's former colleagues out of a sense of misplaced honor. But when The Bear couldn't protect him in the wide world, he made the choice to frame Ray for murder, setting him up in prison where he could keep a closer eye on him. As luck would have it, one of The Bear's lackeys had screwed up somehow and was killed by Viktor Mochulyak, then placed in his car. But Ray had started snooping around, making Viktor nervous. Viktor panicked and set out to have him killed. But it wasn't him. It was No-Tongue Duggan. Watching his network of lies thwarted by an annoying homeless man, The Bear should've just killed him. But his karmic superstition kept Ray alive. Now, The Bear had no choice. He had to take possession of Ray and create a prison of his own making.

He couldn't believe his current situation was the result of a fleeting decision made years ago.

What did Mr. Crowley say?

Actions have consequences.

Failure becomes us.

He itched his forearm again, the stinging burn keeping his mind focused. The Bear was soon going to realize he should've killed Ray when he had the chance. Toying with his life was going to bring a retribution the likes of which he'd never seen. Actions have consequences.

The Bear wanted to bring Ray into the fold? Take possession of him? Fine.

The Bear was going to learn that some animals don't take well to captivity.

29

"You done over at Dawkins?" Willie's voice cracked on Nick's voicemail, "I'm gonna go interview one of Seward's exes. Meet me at the Vidala Spa in Beverly Hills if you're out soon."

He knew where she'd gotten the name of Seward's former paramour. Late night talks with Carly Wentworth over a bottle of cheap red wine. Which celebrity was dating which? Who wore it better on the red carpet?

How to be first to a crime scene?

Who better to consult about a list of Low Seward's jilted lovers?

Nick sat in his car in the parking lot across from the Three Kingdoms Lounge. He'd managed to avoid Willie for most of the day, but he knew they would have to compare notes as the afternoon wore on. He was replaying every conversation they'd had over the past few days in his head.

There were plenty of people on the force who gave up information here and there for a lead. Sometimes they did it to line their pockets, but most of the time it was a Quid Pro Quo barter, an exchange of information. Maybe that was all it was. Maybe Willie gave Carly a head start, knowing she'd be able to provide an inside look at celebrity culture later in the investigation, but didn't reveal any details.

But why would an entertainment news organization hold back info about the nature of Seward's death if they had the inside scoop? It was their job to be the first out with gossip and beat their competitors to the punch.

All of the ruminating was pointless. Nick knew why he was pissed. He was beating himself up about not seeing it, duped by his attractive partner. She had a mouth like a sailor, they got along, and always seemed to be on the same page. Willie was right. A pretty face could still distract him.

How could he be so stupid to think she wouldn't have her own contacts? He had his—or he thought he did. But the thing that stuck in his craw the most was, if Willie was so good at hiding her association with Carly Wentworth, what else was she hiding from him?

A black Range Rover pulled into the Three Kingdoms parking lot, yanking Nick from his thoughts. A doughy Korean man got out of the driver's side. He was wearing pressed slacks and a loud shirt, unbuttoned to mid-chest. Out of the passenger side, looking like he had just emerged from a photo shoot for *Douchebag Monthly*, was Franco Esplanade.

Nick recognized him from his mugshot. Franco was aggressively dying his hair and wearing more eye makeup than Keith Richards, but it was him under the scarf and porkpie hat. His probation for recruiting underage girls to frequent the clubs he'd promoted had passed, but with guys like him, there was always something brewing under the surface to put more dollars in their pockets.

Nick got out of his car and jogged across the street, knowing he'd have to catch them before they went inside the club or he wouldn't have access until business hours. By that time Franco would've had enough of a lead on him to get rid of any incriminating evidence.

"Yo, Franco," Nick said.

Both men turned around. The doughy man's eyes shifted between Franco and Nick, his look betraying that he wanted nothing to do with what was about to happen. Franco didn't break eye contact.

"I know you?"

"Nope. But you know Low Seward, right?"

The .45 was out before Nick had a chance to pull his own weapon. He dove behind the Range Rover as bullets passed over his head.

His back against the bumper, sweating, he pulled his own piece. Breathing heavy, he readied himself to poke his head out.

The doughy man yelled at his compatriot in Korean as Nick heard Franco's footfalls running away.

He looked out, seeing Franco running down the alley, and got to his feet.

The doughy man cowered in the parking lot, his hands over his head, yelling to Nick, "I have nothing to do with this!"

"Stay put!" Nick said, pumping his legs to catch up with the fleeing suspect.

Franco ran across Pico, dodging cars as he went. Nick was nearly clipped several times as he followed, a cacophony of honks and curses left in his wake.

The gun was still in Franco's hand, scaring away pedestrians as he passed, but he didn't fire back in Nick's direction. Lungs burning as he ran, Nick took it as a sign he wasn't dealing with a complete psychopath.

Flinging open the glass door of a Korean BBQ, Franco ran inside. Nick could hear the screams from the diners as he followed.

His gun up as he opened the door, he found Franco standing in the center of the restaurant, weapon fixed on Nick's head. With the rest of what Nick was dealing with, he didn't need to be stuck in a hostage situation.

A bustling lunch crowd filled every booth, people hunkered down in their plush seats as meat sizzled on the grills set in their tables. Everyone's eyes were shifting between the man in the middle of the restaurant and the other who had just followed him, both of them brandishing weapons.

"You going to shoot me? With all these witnesses?"

"Put the gun down," Nick said, trying to catch his breath from the unexpected sprint.

"Memorize his face! Call the police!" Franco said, then repeated the same in broken Korean.

It was in that moment that Nick realized he'd never identified himself.

"I'm Detective Nick Archer. Whoever you think I am, you're wrong."

"Bullshit."

Meat was beginning to burn at several tables.

"Can I grab my badge?"

"No."

A squad pulled up in front of the restaurant and two uniforms piled out, service pistols drawn. They stood behind their open car doors, using them as shields in case the gunmen turned their attention to the street.

"Put down your weapons!"

"Him first!" Franco yelled back.

"I'm a cop," Nick said, "I'm tossing my weapon. Don't shoot."

Nick kept his eyes on the barrel of Franco's pistol as he bent down slowly. Whoever was in the car behind him, he hoped they didn't have itchy trigger fingers. He dropped his gun to the ground.

Franco held his gun on Nick for another moment, his eyes shifting to the officers behind the plate glass. Nick could see Franco weighing his options and felt a line of cold sweat run down his cheek and soak into his collar.

Slowly, Franco knelt down, placed his gun on the ground, and put his hands in the air.

The officers charged in, each of them taking one of the suspects. Nick was slammed into one of the tables, his head inches from a sizzling grill. He was frisked and the arresting officer came up with his wallet. When he saw the shield, he picked Nick up from the table and uncuffed him.

"Sorry, Detective, but, we—"

"No worries," Nick said, rubbing his wrists, "I would've done the same. But next time watch where you slam down a perp. Any closer to that grill and I'd be drawing on my eyebrows tomorrow morning."

The officers pushed Franco out to the pavement. Nick followed after mumbling a half-assed apology to the owner of the Korean BBQ.

Franco strained against the officer's hand pushing his head down into the car.

"I didn't know! I didn't know he was a cop!" Franco yelled over his shoulder.

"Can you give me a few minutes with him?" Nick asked.

The officer's wary look told Nick he didn't want to give him the alone time, but Nick knew if they balked, he'd only have to hint at how the uniforms had handled the situation. How it would look in the official report. They would be in a world of hurt if they gave him more trouble, so they relented.

"On the sidewalk where we can keep an eye on you."

"Fair. Miranda him first."

The officers conferred and sat Franco down on the concrete. They took a couple of steps back, but stayed close enough to act if Nick wasn't who he said he was.

"I swear, if I'd have known you were a cop, I wouldn't have taken a shot at you."

"Who did you think I was?"

"I dunno. Seward dies. Knapp is crippled. One of the girls is dead, the other in the hospital. You see how I might be worried?"

Franco had been watching the news. Anita Mercado's death was the breaking story that morning.

"Lay the night out for me."

Franco said nothing.

Nick was tired and in no mood to get stonewalled. Good cop was no longer in his repertoire.

"Here's where we stand. With your record, I'm going to assume you don't have a license for that weapon. I've got a witness who said you coerced her into Knapp's limo, which could make you an accessory to the murder of the dead girl. On top of that, you resisted arrest and attempted to kill a police officer. See how all of that sounds? Or... you were acting in self-defense and all you're facing is a possession charge. You're gonna get punished, Franco. Whether you cooperate will determine how much. Just be glad you're a lousy shot."

Franco glanced at the two uniforms and back at Nick.

"What do you want to know?"

"Who was in the limo?"

Franco gnawed on his lower lip, nervous.

"Knapp, Low, and some blonde. The way she was crawling over Seward in there, thought she would've been pissed when I brought in the other two, but she was in her own little world."

"You'd never seen her before?"

"I see a lot of blondes in my business." Nick's stare told Franco he wasn't in a joking mood. Franco elaborated. "I'd seen her with Low in the club once or twice, but she always had this look like she didn't want to be seen with him. Weird, considering every other cooze in the place wanted nothing more than a phone snap with him."

"Any chance there's a paparazzi photographer with her picture somewhere?"

"Sure, there's a chance, but they never came in together. Only left together, always out the back, right into the car."

"Did you give them the drugs?"

"No way. I'm not incriminating myself."

"I don't fucking care about weed or coke or ex, Franco. Shadow Dance. The purple powder."

"Never heard of it," Franco said, dodging eye contact.

Nick grabbed Franco's chin, gripping his jawbone and forcing eye contact. He could feel the officers behind him ready to stop the street interrogation.

"Purple. Powder," Nick said through clenched teeth.

Nick held Franco's gaze and made no attempt to hide his fury.

"I... I don't know..."

Nick let go of his face and stood up.

"Get him outta here," he said. The collective sigh from behind him told Nick the uniforms were more than happy to get Franco into their cruiser.

"Hold up," Franco said, the officer's hand already on his head to duck him into the car.

"What?"

"I... I brought a couple more girls out... you know, later, after those other two. Knapp was talking some crazy shit. Lunatic shit. Scared the new girls off. While Knapp is berating me, Low and the three girls climb out of the sunroof of the limo, pile into his car and bail. Does that help?"

"The white Audi?"

"Yeah."

Nick nodded to the officers to put Franco into the cruiser.

"Fuuuck!" Nick yelled into the sky. His hands were shaking, his body finally processing that he could've just died. Before his legs went out from underneath him, he sat down on the curb.

There wasn't much more to go on from his confrontation with Franco. Not a comforting feeling, considering he was almost shot, his face nearly burned off for his trouble. At least he had a secondary confirmation of the blonde girl. If what Franco had said about the photo-happy club kids was true, there had to be a picture of her somewhere. With a few deep and steady breaths, he got back to his feet.

On his way back to his car, he opened Instagram on his phone and searched hashtags, flipping through any pictures that could've been taken by fan girls at the club two nights before.

#Celebritysighting #GetLow #LowellSeward #RIPLow.

There wasn't much to work with. Lots of girls making duck faces or kissing Low on the cheek. Low Seward flashed his winning smile in each of the photos, happy to cater to his fans, but there was a far-away look on his face. The same one Nick had noticed in Rory Knapp's eyes right before he took a flying leap from his balcony.

Swiping down in the feed, he wasn't finding much. Then his eye caught something.

He swiped the feed back up. In the background of a photo, obscured by waving hands and flashing lights, a hint of blonde hair filled the side of the frame. One blue eye focused hatred on the photographer, the edge of a mouth turned down in a scowl. Nick put two fingers to his touchscreen and expanded the photo out. It was only part of her face and zooming in did no good. But his mysterious blonde was real.

His search was interrupted by an incoming call.

"You okay?" Jenkins asked. Word of officer-involved shootings traveled fast. There wasn't concern in Jenkins' voice. He just wanted to know whether he'd have to put Nick on psych suspension.

"Still have the same number of holes in me, if that's what you're asking," Nick replied.

"You fire your weapon?"

"Nope."

"Good. I'd hate to have to take it away from you for a few days. We got some info on that recipe you found this morning. Get here pronto."

30

"You wanna tell me what the hell we're dealing with here?" Detective Ken Marconi asked.

After the death of the girl in the hospital, Nick's discovery of the recipe in Lowell Seward's wallet, and the shootout in Koreatown, Lt. Jenkins thought it would be a good idea to bring in someone from Narcotics to consult on the case. The department was getting more questions from the media than they could handle. Marconi, a brash cop who was used to undercover work, had seen just about every substance on the streets. He took down a perp on bath salts long before the guy in Florida started chewing people's faces off. He'd never seen the purple stuff before, but at least now they knew they were dealing with a Schedule I Narcotic.

Nick relayed Shane Davidson's account of how Seward and Knapp acquired the substance to the small group sitting around the briefing room. Based on what Franco and Mercedes Pao had told him, the two stars had taken the drug with the three girls in the limo at the club, then Seward and Knapp went their separate ways.

"This blonde girl your main suspect?" Marconi asked.

"Could be another of Seward's sexual conquests, but doesn't mean she didn't have something to do with it," Nick said.

"And the Audi hasn't turned up yet?" Marconi asked.

"Nope," Willie said.

"Sounds to me like we should be watching this Davidson guy," Marconi said, "You don't get that detailed a look at a drop if you don't have some hand in it."

"We've got a car on him, but he appears to be forthcoming with his information," Nick said, "Right now there's nothing we've gathered to justify official surveillance or get a search warrant issued. We did get a subpoena of his phone records, since Seward called him not long before he died, but he was honest with us. The only calls that night were the one he confirmed from Seward, then the text he sent to his assistant to set the meeting he was expecting us for in the morning. His phone started ringing soon after the media frenzy we saw at the apartment yesterday. The timeline checks out."

"I'll see what we can get on his financials," Jenkins said.

"Don't know how much good they'll do. My guess is his cash flow is tied pretty tight into his business. If the IRS doesn't see anything strange and unusual happening, I don't know if we will," Willie said.

Nick hadn't had a chance to talk to her yet. They had been shuffled into the briefing room as soon as Nick got back to the station.

"Can't exactly say I trust the IRS to have their heads out of their asses," Jenkins said.

"If Lowell Seward was murdered because he was trying to undercut the supply of a new drug from a larger organization, the entire department is going to have to tread lightly. At this point, we don't know if we're dealing with a small group of local suppliers, or a branch of a Mexican drug cartel. The severed penis would definitely imply the latter," Marconi said.

"Don't they usually cut people's heads off?" Nick asked.

"When it comes to removing appendages, they aren't picky," Marconi said.

"Can we take a look at this?" Dr. Greta Peete chimed in.

The detectives stopped their chatter and turned to the chemist. Usually, tox-screens on bodies took a while, but between the blood work done on the Filipino girls and the recipe laying out the components of the substance, Dr. Peete was able to do a bit of research on her own. Given the size of the packet in front of Nick, she had done plenty with the half-day she had.

She pulled up a barebones PowerPoint on the projection screen. Nothing fancy, just enough to accompany the reports she'd handed out to everyone.

"Morning glory seeds can be used as a mild hallucinogen. They contain a much weaker version of LSD called ergine. It was commonly used by Aztec priests in religious rituals to enhance their understanding of the beyond, or put into a paste and rubbed on the skin of warriors," she said, showing some basic pictures of the common varieties of morning glory flowers that contained higher concentrations of ergine. Nick wasn't surprised to see the names of the flower's varietals; Flying Saucer, Heavenly Blue, Shadow Dance, and his personal favorite, Grandpa Ott.

"Anyone can go down to the Home Depot and pick up as many packets of morning glory seeds as they want," Willie said, "I think I've got some in a window box at my apartment. How's this possible?"

"In the same way that someone who's determined enough can go out into the woods and find magic mushrooms or scour the desert for peyote buttons. Even though those things have been classified as illegal substances, they're still out there in the natural world."

"But morning glory seeds don't have an official classification as dangerous? Shouldn't we have driver's license scans when people go and buy seed packets the same way we do with cold medicine?" Marconi asked.

"Do a quick Google search and you'll find plenty of recipes for extracting the psychedelics in morning glory seeds. It's as simple as having some patience and grain alcohol," Dr. Peete said, "But that's just for mild highs, kids already doing harder psychedelics looking for something to supplement the experience."

"So are there restrictions in place?" Nick asked.

"Not officially. Morning glory seeds are typically doused in highly poisonous pesticides and go into the packets that way. There are organic ethnobotanical options sold online, but if you get them in the store, they've been treated," Dr. Peete said, referencing back to her presentation, "Also, the outer shell of the seed is bitter and indigestible, they have to be ground up, the meat separated. Get through all of that, and someone would still need several hundred seeds to even make the experience worthwhile. Most stoners aren't that patient."

Flipping through the packet in front of him, Nick couldn't make heads or tails of the jargon Greta Peete put into her preliminary analysis. A lot more work was going to have to be done on the substance before they knew what they were dealing with.

"We picked up Shake n'Bake a few times on meth cooks. He made his own stuff and distributed to friends. Never more than he could handle," Marconi said, "But he never gave a bad cook. Nobody O.D'd on his shit."

"Just like a meth shake cook uses household items versus a lab cook, we saw the same thing here," Dr. Peete said, pulling up a close-up of the recipe, "Several of these items he was able to get the street equivalent of, but there are a couple of things on this list he wouldn't have access to. It's early to say, but if I had to guess, I'd say the overdose was due to the absence of these key ingredients, exacerbated by his failure to rinse the pesticides off and separate the seed shells from the meat."

"So, we start tracking some of the harder to find stuff and we're good to go, right?" Nick said.

"Not exactly," Dr. Peete said, "Most of these ingredients are difficult to come by, but not rare. Sure, someone could've been stupid enough to make orders of some of these chemicals from China, but none of the separate parts are illegal or severely regulated. You're better off looking for a chemist smart enough to put this combination together. It took quite a lot of planning to get this particular cocktail."

"What about people ordering bulk seeds online?" Willie asked.

"Farmers. Gardeners. Hobbyists. Florists. Or they could've been ordered out of country and brought in. It's a possible trail, but there'll be a lot of dead ends," Dr. Peete said, "What we need to focus on is the problem of the purple."

"I thought morning glories were purple?" Nick asked, aware it was a stupid question.

"But the processing of the seeds wouldn't yield that pigment and, again, I need to do a lot more tests, but at first glance, I'm fairly certain this combination wouldn't result in that color naturally."

"So this might not be the final recipe," Willie said.

"Precisely," Dr. Peete said.

"Thanks, Doc," Jenkins said, taking the floor. His short waddle to the front of the briefing room caused him to break out in a light sweat.

"We'll get somebody researching the seed buyers, might take too fucking long, but we don't have much else to go on right now," Jenkins said, "Let's see what we can do about the chemistry."

"I'll ask around, see if my guys know of any cooks branching out," Marconi said.

"Keep the talk general on this one. Last goddamn thing we need is a rush on this thing if word gets out there's a new possible revenue stream on the street. If Marconi hasn't seen the substance out there, likely there wasn't wide distribution yet, backing up what Davidson told us."

"How do we know he didn't give us a load of shit?" Nick asked.

"Go back and find out," Jenkins said before leaving the room.

Marconi and Peete packed up and followed him out, leaving Nick and Willie alone.

"I didn't get anything out of Seward's ex. Seems like he got around enough that we'd have to scour through half of Hollywood before we found a lead," Willie said.

"Mmm-hmm," Nick said, flipping through the pages of his packet.

"But while you were out gallivanting with Jimenez and getting yourself shot at, I did some digging into Shane Davidson's drug history. An unreported dealing snafu when he was in college. No charges were ever filed, but it could come in handy to brace him, even if it's from a couple of decades ago."

"Sure. Okay," he said. He knew his indifference act wouldn't work long.

"Spill."

"No, that's good work."

"I do something to piss you off? You've been avoiding me all day. Talk."

Delicate ease into the conversation would've been the correct tactical move, but Nick stewing in frustration all day sucked every bit of delicacy from his reaction.

"I'd rather not have what I tell you end up on Carly Wentworth's desk."

"What the hell is that supposed to mean?"

"Don't give me that shit. I know you tipped her to the crime scene."

"Excuse me?"

"You get there early. Put the call in to me. Put the call in to her. She gets there moments after I do. Is the paycheck really worth it?"

"Fuck you."

"Fuck you! How the hell am I supposed to trust you if I don't know whose pocket you're in?"

Willie punched him hard in the nose. His chair flipped over backward and blood spurted out of his nostrils.

"You fucking asshole! I can't believe you would question my integrity like this. I would never—you know what, fuck it. I don't have to explain myself to you."

She slammed out of the briefing room. Nick ripped the back page off of his Shadow Dance packet and dabbed the blood flowing from his face. Other officers were glaring in at him through the blinds of the windows, some in shock, some giggling.

His phone rang.

"Yeah," he answered, slightly stuffed from his swelled face.

He listened to the voice on the phone, said thank you and hung up.

Outside the briefing room, he grabbed a couple of Kleenexes from a co-worker's desk and applied them to his bloody nose. Willie was at her desk pretending to be focused on her computer, but she was still fuming over his accusations.

"Knapp's awake," Nick said, his voice low.

Willie got up, grabbed her coat, and went to the elevator without answering him. Jenkins came out of the staff kitchen, eating a burrito he'd just heated up in the microwave.

"What'd you do?" Jenkins asked.

"Why do you always assume it's my fault?" Nick asked.

"Because it usually is."

Nick grabbed his own coat and a file from his desk. Willie wouldn't be waiting for him. He'd have to take his own car to the hospital.

31

When Nick got to Hollywood Presbyterian, Willie was waiting for him outside Knapp's room. The bleeding had stopped, but his nose was red and swollen, making him look like W.C. Fields.

"Is it broken?" she asked.

"Stings like a bitch, but I don't think so," Nick said.

"There's a lawyer in there hovering over him. Davidson called him."

"Of course he did."

"I want us to be on the same page. In that room, we're on the same team, okay?" she said.

"But our other conversation isn't over," Nick said.

"Not by a long shot," she said, opening the door to the hospital room.

Rory Knapp was awake, but he wasn't speaking. His movement was stilted, labored, like someone who had just suffered a major stroke. When his eyes were open, they stared off into the distance. He had so much of the hallucinogen in his system the doctors couldn't tell if he was in a semi-catatonic state from the accident, or if he was locked into a trip, a waking dream where he was unaware whether he was in the hospital or even injured.

Knapp's lawyer, Paul Abof, was an overweight man in his early fifties. His labored nose-breathing filled the silence of the room. Poured into his suit, his dark tie bending over his belly, he sat in the corner, squeezed tightly into one of the guest chairs. He was obviously working on another case and had all the files spread around him.

"We're just going to show him a couple of pictures and see what sort of reaction we get," Nick said to Abof, who was reading a brief and not really paying attention. Abof flapped his hand in Nick's direction, beckoning him over without looking up. Nick placed the file of pictures into Abof's sausage fingers.

"As long as you know grunts aren't admissible testimony as they could be interpreted any number of ways," Abof said, flipping through the pictures. He couldn't sound any more bored.

Nick opened his mouth to get into it with Abof, but Willie put her hand firmly on his arm. He seethed for a moment, but knew she was right. There would be nothing he would gain by getting into a verbal spar with the lawyer. Besides, the fat prick was right.

"We're just gauging to see if we're on the right track," Willie said.

"Do what you will," Abof said, handing the file back, "Careful with the more graphic pictures. We don't know where his mind is right now and one of those could put him over the edge."

"Those are key to the investigation," Nick said.

"That may be, but my client is in no state to give consent to an interview. This is being done as a courtesy to your department only because it's uncertain if he will get better or worse," Abof said, getting agitated enough to take his eyes off the paperwork.

Nick pulled his phone out of his pocket and zoomed in on the picture of the blonde girl at the edge of the frame.

"Can I show him this?"

"What am I looking at?"

"This blonde here," he said, pointing at the Instagram photo.

"Just looks like a blur of hair to me, but if you want to show him, go ahead."

Knapp hadn't acknowledged all the people sitting around his bed. He stared at the ceiling with an occasional twitch. One hand clutched a pen and was absentmindedly doodling on the cast that went up to his crotch. Knapp couldn't reach very far down his leg and the single spot was black with mark over mark in continuous motion. The ink of the cheap disposable pen stained his fingers as he rubbed his hand against the plaster.

"Mr. Knapp, we're going to show you some pictures and if any of them look familiar, or register a reaction from you, just give us a sign as best you can," Nick said, a little too loud.

"You'll need to be more specific. Any movement could be misconstrued as a reaction in your vague interpretation," Abof chimed in once again. Nick was beginning to wonder if Abof had a desire to get him to leap at his throat in an excuse to sue the department for assault.

"Mr. Knapp. Snap your fingers if anything seems familiar." Nick punctuated his words in Abof's direction.

"There is no way of gauging—"

"Will you shut your—"

"Just let us show him a couple of pictures," Willie interrupted. Nick was on the verge of ruining the questioning before it began. As much as it pained him to admit to himself, he was glad she was there to keep him in check.

"Fine," Abof said, now huffy and fully focused on what the detectives were doing.

Willie took the pictures and phone out of Nick's hand. He walked to the other side of the room, trying to put as much distance between himself and the fat lawyer.

Sitting down in Nick's place, Willie sorted through the pictures. She pulled out shots of both the Filipino girls from the hospital, Shake n'Bake's mug shot, a shot of the purple powder, and finally a blown-up picture of the recipe from Seward's wallet. The rest of the pictures of the crime scene she put back in the folder and handed to Nick.

Knapp's head lolled from the ceiling back down to where his hand was tracing heavily on his cast—the same spot, same pattern repeated.

Nick tried to refocus, channeling the anger he felt toward the lawyer into doing something productive. If Knapp didn't make a definitive movement, there were other tells someone could give, even if part of their mind had disappeared and floated away.

"Mr. Knapp, do you recognize this girl?" Willie asked, holding the phone in front of his face, "The blonde girl?"

Nothing.

Willie manipulated the picture on the phone, zooming back out so that the main photo was of Low Seward and the girl making the duck face.

"How about Lowell Seward? Do you recognize him?"

The continued lack of reaction didn't bode well. She handed the phone back to Nick.

Each of the pictures didn't seem to register anything. Willie could've been showing him a blank piece of paper. Knapp's eyes didn't dilate on recognition of Shake n'Bake. The corner of his mouth didn't register a smile when he saw the two girls. The same with the drugs and recipe. They might as well have been interviewing a brick wall.

"Are you quite finished with this exercise in futility?" Abof said, "Because I'd like to get some dinner and rather not have you alone with my client."

Willie stood up, trying to maintain the composure her partner refused to exhibit.

"Thank you for giving us the time. Let's go, Archer."

She moved past where he was standing and opened the door to the hospital room, expecting him to follow. Nick chewed the inside of his bottom lip, not moving to leave. Willie and Abof hadn't seen it, and maybe Nick was imagining things, but he had to double check. Dead ends were becoming too commonplace.

"Would you mind if we showed him one of those pictures again?" he asked Abof.

"What do you expect to glean upon a second glimpse? Clearly my client is in shock, if not beyond repair. Whatever possible recovery he'll be able to endure won't be helped by constant police harassment."

"Humor me. Then we'll go," Nick said. He took the pictures from Willie. The look on her face told him she had no idea what he was doing, but she knew he had some reason for doing it.

Nick went through the photos, changing their order.

"Actually wonder if you could show these to your client for me?" Nick said, handing the reordered photos to Abof.

"Why?" Abof said with suspicion.

"I need my hands free. Plus, I want you to see what's happening and that it's happening without the coercion or prompting of me or my partner."

Abof took the photos. Nick pulled his notebook out of his coat pocket and flipped it to a blank page. He gently lifted Rory Knapp's hand up from where it had been drawing on the cast and slipped the notebook under the pen. Knapp's hand didn't stop moving the whole time, like a needle lifted from a record, ready to be replaced and serve its purpose.

Once the pen reached paper it continued the scribble it was doing in the air. There was nothing significant about it. It was just a zigzag line. A reflex.

"Show the first picture," Nick said.

Abof did as he was told and Nick moved the notebook slightly so that Knapp was drawing on a different axis.

"Next."

Abof turned the picture and Nick once again shifted the paper.

"Another."

Abof did as instructed. Once again Nick moved the paper. He nodded for Abof to continue and they did the ritual two more times. When Abof was out of pictures, he shrugged and handed them back to Willie.

"You want to tell me what the point of that was?" Abof asked.

Nick lifted Knapp's hand one more time and showed the notebook to Abof.

There were three distinct zigzag lines where the pen began and the first two pictures were shown. But in the moment when Abof held up the picture of the purple powder, something changed. Instead of the distinct zigzag, the same pattern that reappeared once the picture of the powder had been removed, there was another pattern. A figure eight. But it wasn't any figure eight. There were straight lines, creating a pair of diamonds stacked on top of one another. It wasn't a shift in the doodle. It was a deliberate change.

"What does that mean?" Abof asked, baffled.

"Your guess is as good as mine, but it probably doesn't mean your client likes the color purple," Nick said. He took the picture of the drugs and placed it once again in front of Rory Knapp. Moving Rory's hand ever so slightly, the double diamonds began to take shape on the ridges of hard plaster.

"Thank you for your time, Mr. Abof."

Without saying another word, Nick left the hospital room with Willie in tow. He waited for her to ask the obvious question, but his phone rang before she could get the words out. He answered it, turning his back to her.

"Archer."

"Got a lead for you."

"I need some good news, Marconi. Lay it on me."

"No sign of your Shadow Dance on the street, so we're dealing with a small, or at least burgeoning, operation. But get this. Got a CI in Boyle Heights tells me he's at this cat's house six, seven months ago, mid-level dealer, and this dealer's cousin comes knocking at the door. The dealer makes a huge deal of him coming home because the kid got out of the shitty life and never wanted to come back, you know. They're sitting in the living room, getting high, cutting the product for the week's distribution and this kid pops up out of nowhere, dressed like he's coming over for a fucking quinceañera. Well, this cousin starts talking about distribution costs, putting together a network, all the shit people who stayed in the neighborhood learned by being there. This cousin says he's doing some research for his boss, they're financing a movie and they want to make sure everything is realistic. Want to get all the details of how dealing is really done. Gives some bullshit story about bringing them on as consultants. Dealer lays out the info, the cousin leaves."

"And how is this connected to Seward?"

"Seward gets mentioned in the deal as the guy who's gonna to star in the movie."

"That doesn't help much. He get a name on this cousin?"

"Course not. Primo this, Primo that. Wetback Spanglish. He said he didn't get it and wouldn't give me a name on his dealer either. He's an informant, he's not stupid."

"You want to quit dancing around this and tell me why this is important?"

"You know how I said the kid managed to pull himself up by his bootstraps and get off the streets? Living the high life? Guess who he works for?"

"You'll make me a happy man if you say Shane Davidson," Nick said.

"The gentleman wins a prize."

Nick gritted his teeth at the sheer arrogance of Davidson when they were in his office, the peacocking that he wouldn't be found out.

There was something bigger at work. Davidson and Seward were both millionaires. Sure, a million dollars today can't buy what it used to, but it wasn't chump change. Street hustlers usually made their money in black market enterprises and when they got a taste of the good life, they did everything in their power to become legit. It didn't make sense that two players who were already making good paper would start warring cartels on the boulevards of Beverly Hills. Maybe they had both gotten so buried in drug debt, they were beholden to their suppliers to try and dig themselves out.

"We may have something else," Nick said, "You ever seen a tag out on the streets, like a figure eight of two diamonds stacked on one another?"

There was a pause on the other line as Marconi thought.

"There's a law enforcement gun supplier called Double Di-amond, but their logo is side by side, like a ski hill. Could also be a brand, like the ones pressed into an ecstasy pill, but there are about a zillion of those. I'll ask around."

"Pretty sure we're reaching the end of this murder investigation, but that symbol may be the key to closing the drug case before it opens. I'll text you a pic."

Nick took a picture of his notebook and sent it to Marconi. He put the phone back in his pocket.

"You want to maybe let me in on the investigation you're running in your head?" Willie finally got to ask.

"Shane Davidson just became our lead suspect."

"Then we should get to him while his lawyer is getting dinner," Willie said.

"Race you there."

32

"Because he's fucking brain dead, that's why," Shane Davidson said into his headset, "Abof says he's doodling and that's about it, otherwise he's full-on *Awakenings*... fuck you, no... on the outside he's a drooling retard. Stephen Fucking Hawking couldn't drive a car through an explosion and now neither can Rory Knapp."

Nick and Willie pushed into his office with a sniveling temp close behind.

"He's very busy right now, you can't—," the overwhelmed temp said.

Davidson gave her an upset look, but nodded to the detectives to sit while he finished his phone call. They remained standing.

"The goddamn new girl just let some people into my office. I'll call you back. I got another guy we can slide in his place. Up and comer, done some good guest stars. Don't call another agency until you hear from me."

He hung up the phone.

"Sorry about that. These last few days have been shit. Two stars gone. My entire fucking roster is clambering to take their place. And my goddamn assistant has the fucking flu, leaving me with a cunt moron from the mailroom who apparently has never used a telephone!"

He yelled the last part of the sentence so the whole office could hear. Through the glass, the detectives could see her back heaving in spasms of tears.

Nick and Willie shared a look. This Shane Davidson wasn't the calm, helpful man they'd met the day before. This shark was capable of murdering his friends to get ahead.

"Has Abof reported back anything we should know about?" Nick asked.

"Just so you know, I didn't send him there to get in your way. I'm the only person looking out for Knapp right now, even if his brain's mush."

"You seem to take a rather complete role in your clients' personal lives. Rare, isn't it?" Willie asked.

"Like I told you before, these two were involved in some heavy shit and I was unlucky enough to know about it. Yeah, I took a special interest, but when you're making a couple million a year off of two guys, you give them special attention."

"And your relationship trumps friends, family, business managers?" Nick asked.

"I don't like your tone."

"And what tone is that?" Nick asked.

"The accusation that I've got my fingers all over this to cover something up."

"And what if I told you we had enough evidence to bring you in on suspicion of murder?" Willie asked.

"I'd say you better check your evidence."

"So, do you want to come with us, or do we need to break out the cuffs?" Nick asked.

"Look," Davidson said, his tone changing, "I didn't kill Low Seward and had nothing to do with it. You take me into an interrogation room with my lawyer present and I'm going to tell you the same story. But reputation is everything in this town. Even the suspicion that I had something to do with this could ruin me. You waded through the vermin reporters to get up here. You know they want a story more than they want the truth."

"Can't say I'm worried about your reputation," Nick said.

Davidson picked up the phone. The teary temp answered on the other side of the glass.

"Get Abof on the phone. Tell him to meet me downtown. I have to provide more information to the police."

He slammed the phone back down onto the cradle and buttoned his coat.

"Would you let me get a statement out on camera, control the narrative?"

"We're not in the business of public relations," Nick said.

"I'm coming willingly and I'm innocent. Let me salvage some of my dignity for when this is over, or the LAPD will find itself with a defamation lawsuit on its hands."

Both of them knew what they had on Davidson was speculative and circumstantial. They'd have to hedge their bets.

"You get a smile and wave," Nick said, "I'll make the statement that you're cooperating and providing information. But if this is a ploy to slip away, remember you're pretty recognizable out in the world and I won't hesitate to shoot you if you run."

Willie opened the office door and Nick guided Shane Davidson out.

He was worried. Either Davidson was a liar of the highest degree, or they had the wrong man.

33

"This is it. This is where I saw him," Mr. Crowley sing-songed from the backseat of the Crown Vic.

Jimenez and Reese were getting sick of his babbling and smell, but he was the only person claiming to have seen Ray Cobb in the last twelve hours. They pulled the car up in front of the abandoned house on Crenshaw.

"You followed them here?" Jimenez asked, still not believing the rail-thin homeless man. He didn't seem like the type who would be acting as a good citizen with no reason.

"The suspicious one is keen, but assumes too much," Mr. Crowley said, slipping back into his fortune teller voice, "It's a place out of the rain, but when I came to claim it, I found it occupied."

"You're sure it was Cobb?" Reese asked.

"Hair cut and beard gone, but his filthy life still shines on," Mr. Crowley said, then giggled at his own rhyme.

Jimenez and Reese got out of the car, leaving Mr. Crowley in the back seat. He didn't seem to mind, content to have a conversation with himself.

"What do you think?" Reese asked.

"I think that guy's out of touch with reality. We'll be lucky if we find more than rat turds in there," Jimenez said.

They knocked on the door of the old house. At one time, it was probably one of the more lavish homes in the neighborhood, but it had been abandoned around the time disco died. There was no answer.

Reese tried the doorknob as Jimenez pulled his weapon. They shared a nod as they opened the door and pushed into the dark house.

The gray wood creaked beneath their feet. Dust motes hit the light that escaped the clouds as the sun rushed toward the horizon. There was some rotting furniture strewn about the main room, arranged by squatters into a semi-livable space. The appliances had long been ripped out of the kitchen and the spindly fingers of the crinkled yellow gas line poked out of the stained paint. The rusted faucet was dripping water into the sink and Jimenez hoped the city hadn't been as neglectful turning off the gas.

"Jimenez," Reese said. He followed his partner's voice through the master bedroom and into the bathroom.

"Jesus," Jimenez said.

A gangly man was sprawled out on the tile in a shallow brownish pool. A puddle of blood had drained out of the corpse's neck and mixed with rusty water dripping from the raised tub. The body fit the exact description the crazy homeless guy had provided. The man he saw Ray Cobb drag into the abandoned house.

When Jimenez went back out to the car to get equipment to secure the crime scene, Mr. Crowley was grinning at him from behind the closed car window. As he called it in, Mr. Crowley didn't make a peep, as though he wanted to be certain the call went in clear.

"May I go now?" Mr. Crowley asked.

Jimenez let one homeless asshole out of his sight too early, he wasn't going to make that mistake again.

"Sit tight."

"You will let me go," Mr. Crowley said, the smile never leaving his face. Jimenez was so creeped out he couldn't wait to return to the corpse.

Back in the house, he handed his partner gloves and booties. The first thing they looked at was the wire wrapped around the corpse's hands. There was some blood on it, but not enough to match the severity of the wound.

"Think that's what Cobb used?"

"Nope." Reese picked up the open straight razor he found under the tub. There were smeared fingerprints all over it, but in the dried blood there was one that was almost complete.

Jimenez bent down to examine the body. The gaunt man's eyes were open in a look of surprise, his discolored teeth loosely clamped down on his tongue. Jimenez rolled up the corpse's sleeve and wasn't shocked to find a tattoo there.

"Son of a bitch," Jimenez whispered.

"Another one of those Bear tattoos?" Reese asked. He ceased scanning the room for any other evidence.

"Whoever this Bear is, he's out another piece of property," Jimenez said, rolling the sleeve back down.

He looked down to the soaked pants of the corpse, seeing he had something flat and square in his pockets.

Two Ukrainian passports, stained from the blood and rust water.

"Say hello to Viktor Mochulyak," Jimenez said.

He opened the second passport, "And Yuri Karsenov."

"Who the fuck is Yuri Karsenov?"

Jimenez flipped the passport around and showed it to his partner. It was a picture of the man found in Ray Cobb's car.

"Convenient he would have those on him, huh?" Reese said.

"Murderers and their mementos. Bunch of fucked up ass-holes. He's probably been jerking off to it for the past twen-ty-four."

Making his way to the other side of the body, Jimenez patted Mochulyak's other pocket and found something else.

A small packet of purple powder.

"Fuck me."

"RHD sends out a memo on this stuff and it shows up in the first body we catch?" Reese asked.

"Far as I'm concerned, RHD can have this one. I'm done with it," Jimenez said.

"So what's our narrative here?" Reese asked.

Jimenez picked up the corpse's hands. There were distinct cuts in the skin of his palms. Those of someone pulling hard on a garrote wire. Also, deep scars of the same ilk. Mochulyak had used wires like this several times before.

"I think this guy, Mochulyak, killed Karsenov and tried to pin it on Cobb. Then he tried to kill Cobb, but killed Duggan instead. Pissed off that his double got dead, Cobb went after him and took matters into his own hands."

"Won't take long to get a print match on the razor, if it's Cobb," Reese said.

"It's Cobb."

Jimenez stepped out of the bathroom into the empty master bedroom, slipped off his glove, and made a call to RHD.

"Lieutenant Jenkins, please," Jimenez said, trying hard to hide the rage in his voice.

"Jenkins," the Lieutenant answered, his mouth full of something.

"It's Jimenez from Central. Could you tell Archer I'm sick of him fucking up my life and that he can go fuck himself?"

Jimenez heard Jenkins wipe his face with a napkin.

"That's a message I'd be happy to deliver. You wanna tell me why?"

34

"You keep talking about being cooperative, but you're making us wait here with our thumbs up our asses," Nick said, "Can you see why this doesn't make me like you?"

Davidson was waiting patiently for his lawyer to make the drive across town. He leaned forward in his chair, a smug smile on his face.

"I need you to understand something about me. When I'm not working, I'm thinking about working. I don't take vacations. I don't take lunch. Business hours may be over, but if I don't have some deals in place by the time the phones are open in the morning, I'm out millions in commissions. And right now, there's a jackass idiot from the mailroom taking calls at my desk because you took my phone. Every second I'm here, I'm losing money. So don't talk to me about inconveniencing you. You can be damn sure every minute Abof makes us wait here is a minute I will refute on his bill."

"Then why bother waiting? Why not just tell us your side of the story?" Willie asked.

"Because I didn't do what you think I did, but I can't say you won't twist my words to extract an explanation that could be misconstrued as guilt," Davidson said, "What I can tell you is you're wasting your time."

At that moment, Abof stepped through the door of the interrogation room. He mopped his forehead with a handkerchief, but the beads of sweat reappeared in an instant.

"Fucking 110," Abof said, "You haven't been interviewing my client, have you?"

"Nope. Not that we haven't tried," Nick said.

"Can we have a moment alone?" Abof asked.

"That won't be necessary," Davidson said, "You can stop the line of questioning if you're uncomfortable with it, but I need to get this over with."

"I wouldn't recommend that."

"I don't fucking care what you recommend," Davidson snapped, "If you'd been here half an hour ago we would've had time for your little sidebar."

"Don't rush on our account," Nick said, "We could be here a while. You may want to advise your counsel to make arrangements so you aren't worried about your business for the rest of the evening."

"This is going to take much longer if you refuse to listen," Davidson said, "So ask away."

Davidson's confidence made Nick nervous, but he did his best to bury the thought.

"You were kind enough to give us a lead on this purple powder we're now identifying as Shadow Dance. Your intimate knowledge of the distribution process raised a red flag. I'll ask you again. Have you ever used Shadow Dance?" Nick asked.

"You don't have to answer that," Abof chimed in, "It isn't relevant to this murder investigation."

"It would establish motive," Nick said.

"I don't have to answer any of the questions they ask if they incriminate me," Davidson said, "I read contracts for a living. I know the basics of the Constitution."

"You wanted me here," Abof said.

The agent and his lawyer were bickering as though it was a planned distraction to buy time. Nick was done with their horse shit. He snapped his fingers at them like they were a couple of first graders who needed time-outs.

"Hey! People are dead. Let's talk about finding out why."

Davidson took a deep breath.

"I have used it," he said, "Low gave it to me at the premiere for *I Am Become Death*, about a month ago. I was stressed out, more than usual, and was going back to NA meetings. They weren't working. I knew Low could get me the pills I needed, so I asked him. He said he had something better. Something that turned your brain in on itself, but wasn't addictive."

"And you just took it from him, no questions asked?" Willie said.

"Quite the opposite," Davidson said, "I asked every question under the sun. Where he got it, what it was, how it worked. If you haven't noticed, I'm a bit of a control freak. If I'm going to put a substance into my body, I want to know what it's going to do to me. That's why I had intimate knowledge of how it worked. We had one of those full disclosure relationships."

"Full disclosure relationships, eh? So, would you know who this is?"

Nick held out his phone. Davidson squinted at the smudge of blonde hair.

"Are you serious?"

"Maybe you'd know who he was dating recently?" Willie asked, "This blonde?"

"Jesus Christ. When it came to his dick, Low was the United Nations. He didn't discriminate. He may have been fucking a blonde recently, I wouldn't know."

"Thought you talked about stuff like that?" Nick asked.

"Let me rephrase. He wasn't dating anyone strategically on a regular basis."

"Strategically?"

Davidson let out an exasperated sigh.

"People like Low date public figures for the public and take care of their other kinky shit behind closed doors."

"Kinky shit like drugging a couple of girls and gluing them to the floor?"

"I have a client who only fucks pregnant married women in the parking lots of Babies R' Us. Nothing is too weird anymore. But I wouldn't know anyone on that secret list of lovers."

"And he never gave up his supplier?" Nick asked.

"He'd been sworn to secrecy, so he said. He said I could get more from him if I wanted it."

"And did you?" Willie asked.

"No. I only used it once and it scared the shit out of me. If your mind is ready to accept the release, apparently the dream flow is a pleasant experience, like a good LSD trip. If you're prone to stress dreams or nightmares, then that's what's reflected in your Shadow Dance. But it did the trick. After that, I didn't pick up pills or a bottle. I never wanted to feel like that again. Whatever state it put me in, my reality would never be that bad. Ever."

Davidson's romanticized response sounded rehearsed. If he was the primary Shadow Dance dealer, Knapp and Seward could've been at the top of his pyramid scheme. Word of mouth was the best advertising.

Nick wondered if there was a way he could manipulate the agent into making sense of the hodgepodge they'd unearthed in the past few days. Davidson was in the business of telling compelling stories. Finding interesting ways to help fill plot holes was in his job description.

"Seems convenient. You learn all this stuff about a mystery drug and then abandon it. See how that might come off as far-fetched?" Nick asked.

"This is why you're here," Davidson poked Abof, "Twisting speculation."

"Oh, so I can talk now?" Abof said.

Davidson gestured his hand forward, giving Abof the floor.

"Detectives, please restrict your line of questioning to the murder of Lowell Seward. My client's use of substances is not the issue. He's been cooperative, admitting to ingesting an illegal substance for the sake of your investigation."

"Did you Shadow Dance the night of Lowell Seward's murder?" Nick asked.

"I only did it once. December 7th. When my assistant is back at his desk, you can check my calendar. I called in sick that day. The first time in three years."

"Your alibi for the night of the murder checked out, just so you know," Willie said, trying to keep Davidson on their side. Nick was too good at pushing suspects and he could see Willie struggling to keep the conversation amicable.

"But you want to know if I hired someone to take Low out?" Davidson said.

"Are you acquainted with a man named Viktor Mochulyak?" Nick asked.

Davidson paused and Nick studied his face.

"Not that I can remember," he answered.

Nick met Willie's eyes and nudged his head to the side in an almost imperceptible movement. Davidson wasn't lying.

Willie pulled a picture out of a file folder and slid it across the table. They'd gotten it from Jimenez only a few minutes after arriving at the station.

"Him?" she asked.

Davidson concentrated on the gaunt, lifeless face, then looked up at the detectives in realization.

"It's him, isn't it? He killed Low," Davidson said.

"We've seen Shadow Dance twice. Once in Seward's pocket, once in his. You said it was an elite drug. He's no movie star," Willie said.

Davidson wouldn't take his eyes from Mochulyak's face. It was the first time Nick registered the fatherly affection Davidson felt for Lowell Seward. It took seeing the face of his possible murderer to get it to bubble to the surface. It was also the moment Nick realized they had the wrong guy. Problem was, all of the evidence pointed in Davidson's direction. There was something missing.

Nick picked up the photo and handed it back to Willie, clutching her lightly by the elbow.

"Excuse us for a second," Nick said, then looked at Abof, "You can use this time to confer with your client."

Outside the interview room, Willie spun on him.

"What're you doing? That picture affected him. You saw his face. We should be attacking," she said.

"It's not him."

"Don't give me your intuitive bullshit, Archer. Everything is pointing at Davidson. He spends his whole day around actors, you don't think he picked up a technique here and there?"

"I want it to be him, too, Will, but it's not. I've done what you're doing. I'm trying to make the evidence fit my conclusion rather than the other way around."

"You mean like with me and Carly Wentworth?"

"I didn't call you out here to argue with you," he said, "This is about the case, not our other shit."

Willie collected herself, but there was fury boiling beneath the surface.

"When we're done here, you and I need to have some serious fucking words, but we need to get back in that room. I'll follow your lead. But I'm done after this. I want a partner I can trust. Not someone who's gonna shut me out, disappear into their own brain, and go solo," she hissed. She opened the door to the room and slammed it behind her. Nick let out a frustrated breath into the floor and followed her in.

"From this point forward, anything establishing arbitrary details of my client's personal life will bring me to shut this line of questioning down. Understood?" Abof said.

"You know what? You're right," Nick said, "Enough dancing around the issue. You've been cooperative, so I'll lay it on the table for you."

Willie shifted uncomfortably in the corner, but figured Nick knew what he was doing, considering he was being such a dick about it.

"Based on everything we've collected outside your testimony here today, the D.A. could easily prosecute you for conspiracy to murder Lowell Seward."

"More holes in your case than you think there are," Abof said.

"I know," Nick said, "And the biggest one of all is I believe you. I know you didn't do it."

Davidson looked at Nick through squinted eyes, searching for the trick to get him to reveal something.

"So why are we here?" Abof asked before Davidson could.

"I'll lay out a scenario for you. But only if you promise to listen. You or your lawyer decide to interrupt, I'll keep the rest of my secrets to myself and let the prosecutor listen to the rest."

"Agreed," Davidson said.

"Wait," Abof said, "Why are you giving away the details of your investigation?"

"Because I've got a story and it's a good one. But all the pieces don't fit together," Nick said, "I want you to hear this from the premise you're innocent and tell me whether or not you'd believe it."

"Go ahead," Davidson said.

Nick paced the room. He had to weave the story together as he spoke. If he put in enough speculation and detail, no one in the room would realize he was full of shit.

"We've got a high-powered Hollywood agent whose star client has recently become a financial liability. Even if he kicks his new drug habit, he's scorching the earth everywhere he goes. This is a problem, not just for the movies he's working on, but also the relationships his agent has with other clients and studios. The agent learns the details of how this drug is delivered. His knowledge seems too ready, too specific. So much so that it could be the agent himself who's dealing the drugs. He's created a monster he can't control. On top of it all, the agent finds out that the star has the recipe for his brand new special concoction and has plans to cut out the middle man. So, this agent puts one of his enforcers to work, a Ukrainian hitman, to take out the star in what looks like a drug deal gone bad. Plus, the final film in a profitable trilogy is already in the can. A dead star can't do anything to undermine the success of the film, his memory can only get more butts in the seats, and the marketing will reflect that."

Nick pointed to Abof. "If you haven't noticed, your lawyer is starting to squirm. That's because he's agreed not to interrupt. But about halfway through my little tale, if we were in a courtroom, he'd scream out 'speculation' and he might be overruled, he might not, but he'd be right. This is all a bunch of 'what ifs' because we don't have any evidence Mr. Davidson has been involved in dealing drugs. That was, until my partner had your college transcripts pulled," Nick said.

He pulled a sheet out of a folder and slid it across the desk.

"Suspension for dealing illegal substances."

"Can I explain myself now?" Davidson asked.

"You don't have to," Nick said, pulling the transcript back, "Your suspension was short-lived. Only one semester. So, my guess is, you had the pills, somebody bought a dose from you, got caught with them, and panicked. You're no drug dealer. It was an isolated incident."

"Precisely," Abof said, not sweating the new evidence.

"But our D.A. is a sneaky dickhead. By the time he produces this evidence and it's been objected to, the jury will have it in their brains you have a history of dealing drugs."

"Sounds like most of your courtroom knowledge you got from watching *Law & Order*," Abof said.

"You're not wrong," Nick said, "But I've got one piece I'm missing. That's why I need you."

He looked up at Willie, who knew he was about to reveal their prize piece of evidence, but she didn't move to stop him.

"I've got a witness who said you sent your assistant into his old neighborhood to do 'research' on a new film you're developing for Lowell Seward. The drug distribution information follows damn close to what you've told us about the distribution of Shadow Dance."

"I never sent my assistant anywhere for anything like that."

"We have yet to confirm that with him. He's next on our list."

"Whoever your witness is, they're lying," Davidson said, "First off, I would have no idea how to get in contact with a Ukrainian hitman. The concept is absurd. Secondly, you don't think people can get information about who I am and who my assistants are off the Internet? It's everywhere for the whole public to see. Plug our names into the right story and you're done."

"This is a trusted source," Nick said, "You see my problem."

"The whole thing is a lie," Davidson said, "I don't know if you know how the entertainment business works, but I'm not allowed a piece of a movie. I'm in the business of selling a star or writer or director once something is in place. Development is someone else's department. It's illegal for me to produce something while acting as an agent. If I were a manager, it would be a different deal, their agreements are a bit more fluid, but I've got strict union rules I've got to adhere to. If I'm going to be doing something as illegal as starting up an underground drug smuggling ring, I'm not going to get busted for a union violation."

Nick frowned and sat back down in the chair across from the agent and his lawyer. He was lost.

"Now you see my problem," Nick said, "You or our witness must be lying, but there's nothing to indicate you aren't both telling the truth."

"They *are* both telling the truth," Willie said, breaking her silence.

She had been standing quietly in the corner for so long, the men had forgotten she was there.

"It's clear that you, Mr. Davidson, didn't send your assistant to collect intel on drug dealing, but there's no way for our source to have had the information provided him without actual contact with your office," Willie said.

She looked down at Nick, pure hatred for not letting her into the story going on in his brain.

"You see your missing piece now?" she asked.

"Bernard," Davidson whispered.

"Motherfucker," Nick said, standing, "The whole story works. Just replace disgruntled agent with disgruntled assistant. Bernard would've had all the same access to Knapp and Seward as you would have."

"And it explains why we didn't see any strange names on the set visitors lists. Every time Davidson visited the set, Bernard was with him," Willie said.

"Jesus Christ," Abof said, flipping over a page in his legal pad. He drew the triangle pattern Rory Knapp had been obsessed with and slid it over to Davidson, "Look familiar?"

"Looks like those goddamn argyle sweaters he wears every day."

"Not a drug brand," Willie said.

"Knapp was trying to tell us all along," Nick said.

"Thanks for your patience, both of you," Willie said, "But we have to go. Do you know where Bernard is now?"

"Out sick," Davidson said, "He could be anywhere."

35

Katie stared up at the ceiling as she listened to the other captives sleep. The tips of her fingers were chapped and raw. She wasn't used to doing manual labor. The most intense job she'd ever had was at American Eagle Outfitters in high school. She never could've imagined how good she had it when she was folding flannel shirts four hours at a time.

Emma was right. The food Edgar brought down to them wasn't gruel and when he spoke, it was in a soothing manner, like a foster parent talking to his children. Katie did her best to keep her head down and focused on her pasta. The one time she did raise her eyes from her plate to look at Edgar, she caught his piercing gaze.

From what she'd picked up in conversations throughout the day, all the other workers had been homeless runaways. They had the impression they'd been plucked from their dull existences and given better lives. She wasn't one of them and they could tell by the way Edgar looked at her. He wasn't accustomed to kidnapping regular citizens with regular lives. Katie was never going to be one of those girls he took to garden shows. She was never going to stop being a problem.

Edgar was making Shadow Dance. He'd managed to convince the rest of the workers they were making a nutritional supplement, though she doubted any of them really believed the obvious lie. He was taking the converted raw materials back out of the hole with him. Whatever he was doing to turn the morning glory paste into Shadow Dance, he was doing it on the surface. But the dangerous processes were happening below ground. He must have trusted Emma because the amount of flammable liquid available to them wasn't something Katie would trust a bunch of runaway kidnap victims with.

From her spot in the assembly line, she had watched as several of the ingredients were measured in beakers and flasks, poured with chemist's precision. Many corresponded to the recipe Low had shown her when they were at the Three Kingdoms. He was bragging about how his movie money was going to pale in comparison to what was coming next. His retirement plan.

Dating a movie star was exciting. Dating a burgeoning drug kingpin, not so much.

Low would be looking for her. Wouldn't he? Whatever happened between snorting the purple powder after a quickie in the Three Kingdoms bathroom and her waking up in a pit in the ground had to do with that recipe. Had Low traded her for it? Did they take her from him until he gave it back?

She swung her legs out from under her bedding. They'd given her a hoodie to sleep in, but without the blankets, the room was chilly, cold as an empty tomb. As she stood up, the cot creaked, canvas pulling against steel. None of the other captives stirred as she crept out of the dormitory. They'd earned their sleep and the chorus of light snores was the sound of their recharging batteries.

Emma was a true convert to Edgar's cause. The Bunsen burners and chemicals had been locked up in their proper cabinets, no keys, the combinations stored inside her head. The room looked like a high school chemistry classroom at the end of the day. Lights off, counters clean.

"They all wander in here the first night."

Katie whipped around in a defensive position to see Emma standing in the doorway of the dormitory, her arms crossed.

"I don't know how you can accept being trapped in here."

"Freedom didn't work for me," Emma said, "When I could do whatever I wanted, I did. Got in a lot of trouble."

"He kidnapped you. Drugged you. Forced you to work for him. How can you look at him like a savior?"

"Not any worse than the world I came from. You gotta know that. We all got a story like mine."

More rehearsed bullshit. A sales pitch to create camaraderie and quell fear. There was no way for Emma to know she was dealing with a different situation. Katie had to convince the warden she was a new kind of inmate.

"I'm not like you. Any of you. I had a life before this. I wasn't a runaway. I wasn't on the street. I had a job. I'm twenty-five for Christ's sake. What're you? Sixteen? Seventeen?"

Emma said nothing, but there was a slight twitch in her cheek, a curious pause. Katie could tell Emma was searching for the lie.

"I don't know how I got here. One minute the guy I'm with is handing me this purple powder, then I wake up in a dungeon."

"Edgar must've thought you needed saving," Emma began to justify, her faith wavering.

"Edgar doesn't get to make that choice for me. He doesn't get to make that choice for you, either. You want to stay here, stay brainwashed, fine by me, but I have people who are going to notice I'm missing. And you don't know it, but there's probably someone out there who noticed you'd disappeared too."

"Doubt that."

"Emma, I have a life I want to live and it isn't this one. I'm all for being saved, but that isn't what's happening here."

"Just got to give it time," Emma said.

The docile calm of Emma's previous behavior was wiped clean. Katie could tell she was used to coming into this room and comforting a scared rabbit, convincing them this was the best course, just as Edgar or another girl had convinced her of the same. But Katie wasn't a broken girl with no choice but the street. She had made the mistake of getting caught up with the wrong guy, but that didn't mean she deserved to be sold into slave labor.

"You can come with me."

"And do what? Go back to my old life? Starving and turning tricks?"

The cracks were starting to show. Katie peered into the deep, root beer brown eyes looking back at her. If Emma fancied herself a matron, then Katie would treat her like one.

"I can't get out of here on my own. I need your help."

"Edgar will be angry with me. He won't let me graduate," Emma said, tears forming. The strong woman act was gone.

"Listen to what you're saying," Katie said, putting a hand on Emma's shoulder, "You should be able to do whatever you want."

"You're right," Emma said, wiping away the tears.

"Good," Katie smiled and pointed up at the smoke alarm in the corner of the room, "I'm going to guess that thing doesn't make a whole lot of noise when the wrong kind of smoke hits it. It probably triggers a silent alarm in the main house and that'll bring him running. We can get the jump on him when he comes down to check it out."

Emma bent down and opened the combination lock on one of the cabinets. She pulled out a rag, a Bunsen burner and a jar of ether. She plugged the Bunsen burner into the gas valve and soaked the rag in ether.

"A rag fire should do the trick," Katie said, "Good thinking."

Grabbing Katie by the hair, Emma pressed the ether soaked rag to her mouth, muffling her screams. She kicked out at the cabinets, her flailing arms making dull thuds against the wood. The noise brought the other captives from the dormitory as Katie lost consciousness and slipped to the floor.

"She was going to ruin everything," Emma said, panting, "She doesn't belong here."

The rest of the crew stared at Emma, neither helping nor admonishing her.

Following Katie's original suggestion, Emma unlocked the gas valve and lit the Bunsen burner, lifting it to the sensor on the alarm. The green light soon began to blink red.

Edgar would know what to do.

36

"Call her."

"I can't fucking believe after all this shit, you still don't believe me. I didn't call Carly Wentworth!"

"Then how did she know about the crime scene so early?"

"All those damn gossip sites have police scanners going 24/7. The first officer on scene said Seward's name in his call. It was a fucking rookie mistake because he saw that goddamn tattoo. Why aren't you on his ass? You think maybe if he's the kind of person who recognized that shit, he'd be the kind of person who'd want to endear himself to a celebrity gossip show?"

Nick opened his mouth to say something, but no words came out.

"Let's find Bernard. When the paperwork is in on this one, I'm done with you," she said.

"You didn't know her when you were at College Park?"

"It was a big school, asshole."

"You know what? Forget it. Forget it all," Nick said, changing tactics, "Just let me tell you why I want to call her. Even if you don't have her in your phone."

Willie looked like she was going to punch him again.

"Go ahead," she said, annoyed.

"Bernard checks her blog. All of the gossip and news blogs, remember? We feed her a piece of info to write and see if he bites."

"Sounds like a roundabout way for me to admit guilt."

"It beats running all over the city looking for him."

"He's probably in a country with non-extradition by now," Willie said.

"If he thinks we've arrested Davidson, with all the evidence pointing his boss's way, Bernard will go back to life as usual. He's the inside man on Shadow Dance. You think whoever he's getting these drugs from is going to like it if he cuts and runs at the first sign of trouble? If he disappears, he'd lose everything he's been building behind Davidson's back and the suspicion would be back on him."

"It's a long shot."

"I'm calling," Nick said. He pulled up the number for the *For What It's Worth* tip hotline on his phone.

"Wait."

Nick stopped and looked at Willie who already had the phone to her ear.

"Carl, it's Will. I need a favor. Meet me at the munchkin statue."

Nick couldn't believe what he was hearing, after all her protests.

She ended the call.

"Don't you say a fucking word until she gets here," Willie said.

Carly Wentworth trotted out of the parking garage. Nick and Willie were leaning against the munchkin statue outside the Culver City Hotel. The lights of the movie theatre marquee cast the three of them in an orange glow. There just happened to be a special showing of *Blade of the False King* that night. Apparently, Shane Davidson wasn't the only one trying to cash in on Low Seward's sudden passing.

"Hey."

The women hugged. Nick stood to the side, finding it difficult to keep his mouth shut.

"I need you to do something for me," Willie said.

"All this time stonewalling me and now you want something?" Carly asked.

"Tell him how much info I gave you on Seward," Willie said, nodding in Nick's direction.

"Why do you think I followed you into Los Feliz? I figured she wouldn't give up any info, maybe her dumb, cute partner would," Carly said.

"Her words. Not mine," Willie added.

"You expect me to buy this?" Nick said.

"Fuck you, Archer. Even now?"

"You're right. He is stubborn," Carly said.

Nick shook his head in frustration.

"Listen. Will and I went to school together. We collaborated when I needed some research on a paper I was writing and we became friends. And no matter how much wine I ply her with, she hasn't given me jack squat about any of her active cases. Ever."

"Sure."

"Asshole!" Carly clapped at him, as if to wake him from a stupor, "I guarantee you. It isn't her."

"Who then?"

"Nobody," she said, averting her eyes.

"I didn't tell him," Willie said.

"What the shit is going on?" Nick said, too loud. The few stragglers piling out of the movie theater noticed the agitated man yelling at the women.

"It's fine. He's fine," Willie called out to them. Then, turning back to Carly, "You don't have to tell him."

"Will it get him off your back?"

"I don't care what he thinks."

"Now who's lying?"

Willie avoided Nick's eyes.

"I'm sleeping with your Lieutenant," Carly said, sighing.

Nick physically recoiled.

"What?! No. Gross. What? No. Why? I don't wanna know. What?"

"See?" Willie said, "Why would anyone freely admit that?"

"Hey!" Carly said, swatting her across the arm, "He's cute."

"Said no one ever," Nick said, trying to hold back the vomit. It was less from Carly saying Jenkins was cute, and more from her also saying he was cute. It made him sick to his stomach to share that category.

"We were out one night at The Rusty Kilt and Jenkins came in. They hit it off."

"How? Do you both have an extreme love for ham?"

"Wow. You are super judgy," Carly said.

"Okay, Will, I'm a dumbass. You're exonerated," Nick said.

"Great," she said, her response dripping with sarcasm.

"But Jenkins isn't the kind of cop to drop info to the press. Even if they let him... eww... thinking about it is... blech... sorry."

"He's a good cop. Like your partner," Carly said, "But when he gets a phone call about a murder scene at 4:30 in the morning, he isn't exactly filtering his conversation to the sleeping woman next to him."

"Well, I'm a fucking idiot," Nick said.

"Yep. You blew it," Carly said with a smile, "So is this why you made me drive all the way the hell down here?"

"We need you to run a story on your blog," Willie said.

"About?"

"You already ran a piece about Davidson being taken in for questioning, right?"

"Oh my god. Did he do it? I never trusted that guy," Carly said, excited.

"We need you to run a piece saying we have a suspect in custody. Put it right next to the piece about Davidson."

"Is it Davidson?" Carly asked. She was in full-on reporter mode.

"We can neither confirm nor deny that," Nick said, "And he's got a lawyer at the ready if you imply otherwise."

"So, what's the point? You're not giving me anything more than I had a few hours ago."

"A favor for a drinking buddy," Willie smiled.

"Also, here," Nick handed her a slip of paper, "That's the cell number of Davidson's assistant. Call him to get a statement about his boss being brought in for questioning."

"That's not much of an exchange. He probably won't answer."

"Leave him a message."

"I could tell you to go screw yourself," Carly said to Nick, then looked to Willie, "But I'll do it for her."

"Yeah, yeah," Nick said.

"I'll have it posted within the hour. You guys must be close to finding the guy, huh?"

"Only if your readership is as dedicated as you imply," Nick said.

"Four million unique visitors a day."

"We're looking for one returning customer," Willie said.

37

Ray sat on the moist cot trying to focus his energy. He'd been down in the hole most of the day and could feel the nip of the night air seeping through the small seams in the cover of his prison. He tried to keep moving, but the sweat droplets on his skin made him colder.

Scenarios of sweet revenge played out in his head. Skipping over the part where he accomplished a daring escape from his mud dungeon, he kept thinking of new and interesting ways to punish The Bear. One particularly gruesome fantasy, where he mined the fat Ukrainian's chest with a pickaxe, was interrupted when the latch above him opened.

Ray peered up into the night. Instead of one formidable captor, he saw two. Between them, they held a third body. The accomplice was a young African-American girl, wearing much shabbier clothes than her counterpart.

"Catch her," the man said, lowering the third party into the hole without waiting for Ray's response. He did as he was told, if only to prevent the limp body of the blonde girl from collapsing on him. She was already beginning to groan back to life as he eased her down onto the cot. Ray turned back to the two above them.

"My piss bucket's nearly full," he growled, his voice as dirty as his cell from lack of use.

"Don't drink as much," the man said and closed the lid.

The girl was coughing and Ray sat down next to her. As soon as she opened her eyes, adrenaline took over and she kicked out, landing one foot square in Ray's chest and knocking the wind out of him. She huddled in the corner of the cot in a tiny ball, trying to protect as much of her body from attack as possible.

Ray gasped for air on his hands and knees. When his diaphragm remembered how it worked, he sucked in a deep breath and let out a hardy, "What the fuck?!"

"No. No. No. I don't want to be back in here. No!" The girl clutched the sides of her head and started crying.

He moved to his feet, holding the scars at his belly, trying to take in shallow gulps of air. His hands went up in supplication, doing his best to show the girl he posed no threat.

"Are you one of Edgar's flunkies? You going to tell me the error of my ways?" she spit out at him.

"I assume Edgar is the pretty boy up top?" Ray said, "And if you'd take a closer look at me, you'd see I'm as happy to be here as you are."

Her guard lowered a bit, but she wasn't ready to trust her cellmate just yet.

"Did you try to escape too?" she said.

"You want to give me some idea of where I'm trying to escape from?"

"I don't really know," she said, "I've been moved three times. Here, a house, and a lab. The lab and house could be connected. It was underground like this."

"What's your name?" he asked.

"Katie."

"Ray." He held out his dirty hand for a shake. She didn't take it. He didn't blame her. "You said you got here, then were moved, right? Were you unconscious both times?"

"Not from here to the house. He let me out with a ladder, but drugged my food. I don't know where the lab is, but it has to be close. The other girl, Emma, was down there with me. Bitch turned me in for trying to bolt," she said.

"Okay," Ray said, thinking about it, "This is going to sound like a strange question, but can I see your arm?"

"What?" she asked, backing off again.

"I want to know if you have one of these," Ray said, showing her the raw skin.

She pulled up her sleeve to show him nothing but a couple of minor scrapes and bruises.

"What does it mean?"

"Couldn't tell you," he said, "But I'm pretty sure it's a brand of ownership. One of us is expendable. And sorry, sweetheart, I don't think it's me."

"If they were going to kill me, they would've done it by now. I've been nothing but a pain in the ass," Katie said.

"They've got some reason for keeping you alive. You one of these Ukrainians' girlfriends?"

"Ukrainians? What?"

The look of confusion and disgust on her face gave Ray his answer. Her teeth were chattering from the cold of the hole. A threadbare hoodie covered her dirty club clothes. The quality of her shirt and jeans, though muddied, were too nice for her to be an underpass wandering professional. There were no track marks when she pulled up her sleeve. Whoever this girl was, familiarity with the underworld wasn't part of her daily life. Any knowledge she had of the darker side of Los Angeles she'd probably gotten through articles in news magazines and her Netflix subscription. But between the two of them, she was the one who had been out of the hole.

"How many are we dealing with up there?"

Katie paused. The time she was taking to count bodies in her head made him nervous.

"Edgar is the leader. Four more runaways in the lab, but nobody ever leaves, I don't think we'll run into them. I was surprised to see Emma out. The rest of the kids aren't quite as all-in as she is. She's, like, his henchman or something, but she's been brainwashed into thinking he's helping her. We can't trust her, but she's just a kid. I owe her a smack for attacking me, but that's all she deserves."

The girl was observant, he'd give her that. Maybe he'd underestimated her.

"Were you a runaway too?"

"Why does everybody think I look like I'm in fucking high school? I work for a PR firm. I went out with this guy, my boyfriend—or whatever, we weren't calling it anything specific—next thing I know, here I am. In a horror movie."

"Hmm," Ray said, processing what she'd given him, "We're interrupting a pattern then, you and me. From what you said, this Edgar guy has a ritual he follows. What're they making in this lab? Meth?"

"A nutritional supplement," she said, dripping with sarcasm.

"Well, they don't need illegal labs for that."

"No shit," she said, "If I'd have known this was how it was made, I never would've done it."

So that was it. She was just a club kid who'd stumbled into the wrong room where the wrong group of people were doing the wrong kind of drug. She'd lucked out that The Bear had gotten rid of Gravedigger before he could make her permanently disappear.

"This drug, what're we talking about?"

"It's like ecstasy, LSD, and mushrooms all rolled into one."

"You on it now?"

"Fuck you."

Ray snorted out a laugh and turned his attention to the hatch.

"Here's the deal, Katie. You and me? We're leaving."

"You think I didn't try to get out of here before?"

"This room wasn't meant to hold two of us."

"What do you mean?"

"Sounds like Edgar's using an old POW tactic. Isolate the prisoner and show them a bad situation, then give them a shower, a nice dinner, entice them with comfort. When the lambs are nice and sated, the captors give them the illusion of choice. Give up information or return to the hovel."

"Whatever Stockholm Syndrome crap he's playing with the others, I won't bite. I don't remember being given a choice after the nice dinner."

"The isolation is key, so single room, single bed. Edgar is bringing in kids one at a time, establishing trust, otherwise he'd kidnap kids and drop them right in the lab. My guess is you pulled up that cot and tried to climb it out of here?"

Embarrassment flushed in her cheeks, "I didn't really—"

"Not much of a survivalist, huh?"

"I was scared," she said, lowering her head, the tears coming again.

She wouldn't be much good to him as a whimpering mess, but he didn't have time to play nursemaid. There was no telling when Edgar would be back for them.

"Listen, kid, it's fine. It wouldn't have done you much good. No matter how much I arranged and stacked, I was still a good five feet short of the top. But now there's two of us. And if he's got two people gumming up his works, Edgar's liable to make some stupid mistakes."

Ray flipped over the cot and lodged it against the wood floor and dirt walls. He tested the metal braces with his weight and it seemed like it wouldn't slip out from underneath him.

"What're we looking at once we get outta here?" he asked.

"Uh, a yard. Walled in. There's a greenhouse. The house is to the left."

"Windows?"

"A sliding patio door, but when I was in there he had the shades pulled. If he's still got Emma up out of the lab, he probably doesn't want the world to see she's there."

"If the world can't see in, then he can't see out."

"One thing," she said.

"Dog?"

"He's got a gun."

"Yeah, I saw it. But this," he pointed to his arm, "I think it makes me bulletproof. At least until his boss says otherwise. And if this guy's holding me, he'll know better than to go against his employer. They haven't killed you yet, but that doesn't mean they won't. As soon as we're out of this hole, you need to disappear from sight."

"But—"

"I know you're pissed, Katie, but you've done nothing to show me you've got a killer instinct, aside from kicking me in the chest."

"Sorry about that."

"If it comes to it, I'm prepared to do anything to get us out of here. If we get out of this, the experience is going to be scarring enough without you hurting someone."

She looked at him, a mixture of confusion and curiosity.

"Who *are* you?"

"Someone who got wrapped in some shit he shouldn't have. Just like you," he said, "Get on my shoulders."

Ray crouched down and let her climb on. When he stood back up, he had trouble keeping his feet, the weight pulling on the scars in his gut.

"You okay? I don't weigh that much," she said, trying to keep from falling headfirst off his shoulders.

"Old war wounds," he said, "I have to use my balance to climb the cot, think you can stay up there?"

"I'll do my best."

Sweat poured down his forehead. Once he was sure the cot could take his weight, he climbed the braces. Every foothold was a struggle as he pushed up the extra weight. The tips of Katie's fingers scraped the ceiling. Even if he stood on his toes, giving her a few more inches, there would be no space for her to lift.

"Let me down," she said.

While Ray fiddled with the cot to try to get them some more room, Katie looked at the two buckets, then up at the lid. She grabbed one.

"No! That's the—"

Before Ray could finish his thought, Katie had sloshed an entire bucket of Ray's urine over the floor, wetting his bare feet.

"Why the hell would you choose *that* bucket?" Ray yelled at her.

"That's where the water was when I was down here!"

"You can't tell the difference between water and piss?"

"The way it smells down here, I can't tell the difference between you and piss!"

"Goddamn it. Just—empty the other bucket too. If you turn that thing over up there I don't want to be drenched in my own stench on both ends."

She did as she was told and grabbed the water bucket, getting back on Ray's shoulders. His knees were shaking beneath him, but he got her back up. At the top of the cot, she raised the bucket above her head and pushed. It didn't seem to do much good.

Ray pushed his legs out to the far edges of the braces, trying to get his balance as best as he could. Above them, they heard the rain start again. There was even the faint sound of thunder, an extreme rarity during the rain storms in Los Angeles. There would be mudslides in the hills.

"I don't know how long I'll be able to hold you."

Ray stood up, taking his hands off the rungs of the cot. The military grade bed held underneath him, but he could feel it starting to shake free from its fixed position with every breath he took. He put his hands up underneath Katie's thighs and pushed. He couldn't remember the last time he tried to bench press anything, let alone the unbalanced body of a 115-pound girl. A small shriek escaped his lips. Strain tugged at his waist and burned his shoulders.

The rain poured into the hole from the opening. Katie had the wherewithal to lodge the bucket between the lip and the door, leaving a crack in the surface.

She let out a first laugh of success, but the second one didn't have a chance to come. The cot slipped from underneath Ray and Katie fell backward, hard. She had much further to fall and Ray could've mistaken the crack of her ulna for another crash of thunder from above. She let out a howl that was covered by the sound of rain.

Huddled in the growing puddle of water and piss, the tears streaked down her face as she clenched her teeth. Ray could see that the bone was jutting up through the skin of her forearm. It was a nasty compound fracture. Now they really needed to get out of there. A doctor was going to have to splint and reset the bone.

Without thinking, he whipped off his dirty pants and flopped them over her shoulder. He tied the pant legs together and pulled the knot tight. Katie whined in pain as her broken wing was bound to her chest.

Standing before her in his skivvies, shivering, Ray needed nothing more at that moment than for the girl to suck it up.

"I know it hurts, Katie. I know you don't want to do anything, but you need a doctor. I've seen breaks like that before. You're bleeding just as heavily under the skin."

Katie cringed in pain, but nodded that she understood.

"I think I've only got one more in me. Make it count," Ray said.

Back in their previous position, Ray moved his hands to the bottom of Katie's feet dangling at his chest.

"On three, stand up and I'll push."

"K," she said, her voice weak but determined.

Ray counted and heaved. Beneath him, the cot shook once more and shot out from under him. He landed hard on his tailbone in the water, soaking his stained underwear. But Katie didn't fall with him.

She had a grip on the grass outside the hole, but was wailing with pain at her crooked arm trapped beneath her body and the edge. Her feet were kicking out to gain some leverage, but were finding nothing.

Ray scrambled to his feet and grabbed the cot. He stood on the other overturned bucket and lifted it above his head, giving her something to push against.

Her struggling feet found the rusted metal of the cot and Ray shoved. He dropped the bed underneath him as he watched her wriggle through the small opening and out of sight.

There was nothing for what felt like an eternity. The streaks of rain fell down, illuminated by the spare light now submerged underneath the growing pool of water at his feet. He was having trouble keeping his teeth from chattering as he stood in the puddle of his own sewage.

Had she been caught? He figured the rain had been loud enough to hide her cries of anguish, but if Edgar had been paying attention, he would've seen the sliver of light illuminating the darkness of his yard or the small girl with the broken arm slithering out of her prison. Maybe she had made a break for it, not trusting Ray any more than her kidnapper. Or she'd passed out when her body hit the wet grass, lying prone inches from the opening.

The bottom rungs of a ladder slid down into the hole. Ray grabbed it when he could and ascended out of the water, struggling through the small opening and beyond, glad to be breathing in the open air again. All thoughts of humility had been abandoned a long time ago, otherwise he would've felt like an idiot scrambling around a suburban backyard in his underwear.

Brick wall, greenhouse, and a hell of a lot of flowers. He grabbed Katie's free hand and pulled her into the shadows of the wall as they made their way around the side of the house. A wooden gate blocked their way, padlocked, almost as tall as the cement surrounding them. It couldn't be easily scaled.

There was a possibility Ray could make it over without too much noise, but Katie would be trapped. He was surprised she'd had enough energy to grip herself out of the hole, there was no way she'd be able to scale the fence.

"Wait here, I'll go get the ladder," Ray said.

He took two steps back into the yard and a light went on in the house. He squeezed back against the wall and over to where she was waiting for him. The blood had drained from her face and she was taking in short breaths.

If Ray ventured back to the hole, he'd be seen. They were running out of options.

"Only way out is through the house," he said.

She didn't respond, but Ray could tell she didn't want to go in there.

Almost naked, a whimpering, broken girl as his only ally, he was going to have to attack an armed suburbanite drug dealer head on. Hard for him to believe, but he'd faced worse.

He looked around his feet for anything that could be used as a weapon.

Nothing.

Just his luck, Edgar kept his property tidy. Everything was likely racked and organized in the greenhouse. He waved her toward it.

"We need to go in there with something more than your broken arm and my dick sticking out the flap in my undies."

The dry warmth of the greenhouse was a welcome respite from their previous lodgings. He wanted to sit Katie down and leave her there, but it was only a matter of time before her adrenaline drained. As soon as that happened, she would go into shock. Then he'd have a whole new set of problems. He needed to keep her keyed up at a high pitch until he could get her to a hospital.

"Garden tools. Shovels, hoes, trowels. Whatever you can grab."

Ray found a small trowel and a clawed tilling tool. The three sharpened prongs would hurt like a motherfucker scraped across someone's face and the trowel could easily be used as a dull blade.

"Ray."

She was holding a shovel and staring at the floor. A circular trap door was cut into the ground. It looked like a smaller version of a bank vault. The turning crank could only be opened from the outside. Surrounding the door were several vents to let in fresh air and out toxic chemicals. The lab was below their feet.

Without saying anything, Ray crouched and started to turn the crank, but Katie stayed his hand.

"We'll get them later," she said, her voice cold. Streams of her wet blonde hair hung over her steel eyes.

"Strength in numbers," he said.

"Yeah, but we don't know whose side those numbers would be on," she said, her voice weakening, "He's been brainwashing these kids. I don't know how many of them tip on my side of suspicion or Emma's side of devotion. Last time I tried to trust one of them, I ended up in a hole with you."

He traded her the claw tool for the shovel, figuring it would be much easier for her to wield.

"Stay behind me. If you get dizzy, don't fight it. Just bail."

The strange pair crouched along the side of the house, both of them drenched. When they reached the sliding door of the patio, Ray looked in through the foggy glass.

The woman Katie had identified as Emma was sitting with her back to them at the island counter in the kitchen. Edgar stood on the other side, explaining to her something she was having trouble agreeing to. Ray couldn't see the gun, but that didn't mean it wasn't close.

He tested the door by giving it a slight pull. There would be no way for them to sneak up on the two in the kitchen. Once they slid open the door they'd be sitting ducks. Between the noise of the door moving open and the sound of the rain coming down, there was no way Ray and Katie could ambush them in silence.

Ray ran strategies in his head. Creative problem solving was a positive byproduct of life on the streets. The last thing Edgar wanted was for Ray and Katie to escape. The dungeon proved that. Ray had to convince Edgar that their getting out wasn't an escape attempt. He only needed a moment to gain the advantage.

"Change of plans."

He took the shovel from her and set it down on the bricks of the patio. Between her arm and the makeshift sling, he slid the trowel up her sleeve, handle facing up.

"Wrap your hands around that, but clutch it to your chest, like you're holding your arm. Whoever goes to you, don't try to stab or slash them. Smash it across their face with the broad side, if you can. It won't do much more than stun them, but we need an advantage."

She nodded like she understood, but was scared and shaking. He tucked the claw tool down the back of his undies, the handle clenched between his butt cheeks, hoping the crude elastic would hold.

"Follow behind me. Slow."

Ray opened the sliding glass door. Emma was on her feet at the sudden sound and Edgar had the .38 snub out of his waistband, pointed at Ray's chest.

"How in God's name did you get out?" Edgar asked, panicked, but genuinely curious.

"The girl's hurt," Ray said. He didn't raise his hands above his head, just kept them flat at his sides.

Shivering, Katie walked in as she was told.

"Oh God," Emma said, her motherly instincts taking over as she went for Katie.

"Don't—," Edgar could barely get out.

Katie channeled all the rage she had into the garden trowel and whipped it across Emma's face. There was a dull thud as metal hit skull and Emma went down. The blow wasn't enough to knock her out, but the blade of the tool caught her under the hairline and blood flowed into her eyes. She stayed on the ground, crying.

Edgar swung the gun around to Katie, but Ray stepped in front of it, pressing the muzzle into the hollow of his sternum.

"Think for a minute," Ray said, his hands still at his sides, eyes fixed hard on Edgar's.

"I will put a bullet in you."

"I don't think you will," Ray said, lifting his arm and showing off his new tattoo, "I'm not yours to dispose of. Also, I think the shot will alert the neighbors."

Edgar's breath quickened as he realized his bluff had been called.

"You sure as hell look like a crazy intruder to me."

"And what'll you tell The Bear?"

Edgar smiled. It was Ray's turn to realize his bluff was worthless.

"Cost of doing business."

Ray barely managed to swat Edgar's hand away as the gun fired. The sting of the bullet scraped against the skin of Ray's ribcage and lodged in the masonry of the fireplace. He didn't have time to register the pain; he was too busy pulling the garden tool from his drawers and embedding it in Edgar's face.

Edgar yelped as Ray ripped the garden tool out of his cheek and thrust it into tendons of Edgar's wrist. He dropped the gun and Ray leapt for it.

Punches bruised Ray's kidneys as they grappled. He kicked out, catching Edgar in the groin and getting hold of the gun. It was upside down and Ray was afraid of shooting himself, so he flipped it over and swung it across Edgar's face. The gun metal scraped cheekbone, blood and saliva spraying from the open holes. Edgar was knocked prone by the blow. Ray was on top of him at once.

"You like kidnapping girls?" Ray slammed the gun into Edgar's nose, "Trapping people in your fucking garden?"

Blood gushed up and nearly blinded him.

"You ever think about their families?" Ray kneed Edgar in the groin and cracked him in the forehead again.

"Have you ever lost a daughter?" Ray said, punctuating each word with the hard metal denting Edgar's skull. He would've beaten the man to death if it weren't for a hand on his shoulder. He turned, ready to strike.

Emma jumped back. She held the trowel in self-defense, but was shaking, not ready to use it.

"She… she fell over," Emma said, her voice unsteady.

Ray glanced over to where Katie was.

"I'm okay. Dizzy. Bailed," Katie said.

The break was worse than he'd thought.

"You need any more convincing he's the bad guy?" Ray asked.

Tears filled Emma's eyes. Edgar's face was swelling from all the shattered bones in his face. Purple, bloated, and asymmetrical. His exterior was transforming, the monster he'd hidden below the surface emerging from the depths.

Ray stood up and went back out into the yard, grabbing the shovel.

Emma hadn't moved to comfort Edgar and he figured she didn't pose much more of a threat, but needed to be sure.

"You do anything, I won't waste a bullet. I'll bash your skull in," Ray said, shaking the shovel at her, "Get that one to her feet. Keep her awake."

She cowered from his rage, nodding. Convinced she wouldn't be a problem, Ray headed for Edgar's bedroom.

He pulled on the first clothes he could find, jeans and a stained Texas A&M t-shirt, and slipped on some ill-fitting shoes. Before leaving the bedroom, he did a quick scan. He knew The Bear would send someone to collect him at some point. He needed another weapon.

Ray tossed open a couple of drawers, making a mess out of Edgar's tidy folding system. The dresser yielded nothing but an obsession with silly socks.

In the closet, there was a small leather trunk, locked.

Shunk!

He brought the shovel down on the lock, breaking it off. Flipping open the top, he didn't find any weapons. It was full of hundreds of packets of purple powder.

The rage he'd unleashed on Edgar was subsiding, realizing he'd focused his hatred on the wrong man. If this was the drug Katie had described, it might come in handy in his pursuit of The Bear. Open some doors. He grabbed a couple packets and shoved them into his jeans.

"Hurry, she's not doing good!" Emma yelled to him from the other room.

Ray went back into the living room.

"Stay awake, kiddo," Ray said to Katie as he passed.

He grabbed Edgar by the scruff of his shirt. The broken body slid easily on the hardwood floors.

"Where you going?" Katie said, barely audible.

"Making sure he doesn't leave," Ray said, pulling Edgar through the patio door.

The adrenaline was still driving everything Ray did and he was worried he might pass out from the spike. He patted Edgar down, grabbing his keys and wallet, then kicked him over the edge of the grass.

Edgar's body flopped into the hole. He landed face down in the muck, something cracking as he landed. The pain was enough to jar him out of his unconscious state and he gasped to get his bearings.

"Enjoy your stay," Ray said, pulling up the ladder.

He slammed the lid of the compost heap down, silencing Edgar's scream and shrouding him in darkness.

38

Edgar's SUV wove through the Pasadena traffic. Ray didn't care how fast he was going. He needed to get the girl to the hospital.

He was surprised at Emma's sudden change in allegiance. Once she'd seen Katie was hurt, even though the girl had gone after her head with a garden trowel, all Emma cared about was keeping her safe. Whatever brainwashing Edgar had put her through, at her core she thought he was helping the runaways. Her need to help Edgar had come from a place of giving those kids better lives. Anyone deep into that lie would've seen Ray's coup as a threat to her delicate balance of existence, but having Katie with him must have knocked something loose in Emma's illusions, seeing that if Edgar really cared about them, Katie's safety would've been his highest priority. Even as they loaded a nearly unconscious Katie into the back of the car, Emma wouldn't stop crying.

Ray hadn't driven a car in nearly a decade, let alone one so large. He wasn't used to all the gadgets and gizmos built into the dashboard and his idea of finding the closest hospital was to open the glove box and look for a local map. Emma pulled up the directions on the in-dash navigation system.

The brakes screeched as he pulled the SUV into the emergency turnaround. He'd watched Emma fiddle with the navigation system enough that he knew where the "Home" button was. He pointed to the screen.

"Memorize that address. Get the police to take you back there to release the others," he said.

"What about Edgar?" she asked.

Ray could see her worry, the wavering voice of a wife unsure whether to press charges against an abusive husband. He wanted to tell her to forget where he was, let him rot in that hole and starve to death. A fate he more than deserved. But even if he said those things, he knew she wouldn't listen. She would go whatever direction her conscience decided to swing in the moment she reentered Edgar's house with the police. It was a toss-up whether she felt enough of a kinship to her captor to defend rather than condemn him.

"Let the police know he's there, but not until the others are free. Understand?"

He helped her get Katie out onto the sidewalk and ran back around to the driver's seat of the car before anyone else saw him there.

"You're not coming? You're hurt too."

"Not bad. Besides, I've got other business."

He slammed the horn and sped off. In his rear-view, he saw a group of orderlies run out onto the curb and load Katie into a wheelchair. Now Emma was the only one who would know how to get back to the house. He hoped her love for the others was enough to override her devotion to Edgar.

Ray drove through the empty streets, not sure where he was. In all of his time in Los Angeles, he didn't have many occasions to get deep into the San Fernando Valley. He was shocked at how suburban it all was. Like Mayberry existed only a few miles from the shit of downtown.

Once he was far enough away from the hospital he pulled the SUV over. He lifted the shirt he'd stolen from Edgar and looked at the wound in his side. The blood had dried black and left a streak on the t-shirt, but it didn't appear to be life-threatening. Another couple of inches and the bullet would've punctured his lung. Then it would've been bye-bye, Mr. Cobb.

He stared at the sore tattoo as he played with the GPS system. Priority one was taking care of The Bear. As long as the gangster was around, he would own Ray. It didn't matter where he went or how far he ran, Ray was a branded man. Property of the Ukrainian prick as long as both of them lived. There was only one way to be free of it.

One of them had to die.

And it wasn't going to be Ray Cobb.

Staring at the glowing map in the dashboard, Ray knew he'd have to jump right back into the belly of the beast to get the job done. Which left him with one direction to go. He typed the address into the navigation system and let it calculate.

"Twenty-five minutes to your destination," the pleasant electronic female voice informed him. He pulled on his seatbelt, put on his turn signal, and turned onto the empty street. Now that he didn't have a dying girl in his car, he was going to obey all of the rules of the road. Nothing was going to stop him from ending this.

39

The SUV hit Mr. Crowley from the back, pinning him under the front tire. There weren't enough people out on the sidewalk to mistake Ray for anything other than an early morning drunk driver, and those who did see what happened weren't the types to get involved in somebody else's business.

Crowley howled in pain, trying to extract his crushed shin out from under the heavy tire. He wrenched the skin further from the muscle with every twitch and was frantically trying to figure out the best way to escape when Ray opened the driver's side door and caught him in the face, denting the metal.

"Didn't see that one coming, did you?"

"A life of crutches will be short. But yours will be shorter."

Ray opened the back of the SUV.

"My guess is you don't want me backing the car off you, so you've got a choice."

A jack in one hand, a tire iron in the other, he held them up in front of Mr. Crowley.

"The Bear will make you burn. You are their property to do with as they wish."

"They?"

"You have no clue."

Ray dropped the jack and kicked it away.

"I didn't want to have to crank that sucker up anyway," Ray said.

He swung the tire iron, catching Mr. Crowley across the face. The chrome shattered his cheekbone where a bruise from the door was already forming. It burst, sending blood running down Mr. Crowley's face as he blubbered.

"You want to read my mind? Guess what? I hate getting fucked over. And I've seen you naked, you ugly fuck, you don't have one of these shiny new tattoos. Which means you turned me over on your own. You weren't bound to The Bear like those others."

Ray raised the tire iron to swing again.

"Wait!" Mr. Crowley shrieked, "I have foreseen something new. The Bear's ultimate end."

Ray got back into the SUV and tossed the bloody tire iron into the back seat. He put the car into gear and backed off of Mr. Crowley's leg. The street prophet screamed in new pain as the threads of rubber spun chunks of skin and blood into the piles of garbage surrounding him.

Ray grabbed him by the back of the shirt as Crowley made a futile attempt to crawl away. The base of his leg hung at his knee, gore dripping down to the sidewalk. Ray pressed Crowley's face into the hood of the car, the muzzle of Edgar's .38 at his Adam's apple. It danced on the small bulge as Crowley gulped in air.

"The iron would be more effective," Mr. Crowley said. The side of his face that wasn't broken curled into a smile.

Ray cocked the gun and pressed it into the bleeding hole in Crowley's cheek. The prophet gritted his teeth in pain, but the fear was gone.

"Your predictions are getting worse and worse. Looks like it was nothing more than a parlor trick after all."

"You used a pistol once and death followed. Not before or since have you picked one up. Even as you disappeared into the hills."

Trying to remain threatening, he knew the scrawny bastard was right. Ray wasn't going to shoot Mr. Crowley. He never wanted to shoot anyone ever again. But that didn't mean he wasn't going to stop hurting him. Ray replaced the hammer and put the gun into Mr. Crowley's mouth, then kicked where the exposed bone stuck out of the mystic's shin. Crowley's teeth bit down on the gun metal, muffling his screams.

"Where is he?"

Mr. Crowley was pale and sweating. Ray could tell he was dealing with the second person that day about to go into shock from a broken bone. He pulled the gun out of Crowley's mouth.

"It will not end there," the prophet sputtered out.

He slammed Mr. Crowley's hand into the grill of the SUV and yanked it back the wrong way, snapping several fingers at the knuckle. Tears ran down Crowley's face, but he had dipped into a place beyond pain.

"The bathhouse," Crowley squeaked.

"Last time we went there, the guards didn't respond well to 'Yuri Karsenov.'"

"It was a code for him, they did not know it. Those who guard him are marked as you are and just as stupid."

Ray punched him in the kidney and threw him down into a pile of garbage bags. Bottles broke underneath him, shards cutting him through his clothes.

"Time to predict whether or not you can crawl to a hospital before you bleed out."

Getting back into the car, Ray threw it into reverse, then into gear, and sped off down the alley.

He didn't bother looking back in his rear-view mirror.

40

Ray rolled the car along 6ᵗʰ Street, looking for Shake n'Bake's tent, but couldn't find it anywhere. He'd made a pact with himself that he wouldn't come down to Skid Row ever again, but he needed something.

It was his fourth circle of the area and he still hadn't caught sight of the familiar red nylon. It wasn't like Shake n'Bake to not set up camp. Maybe the drug enterprise he'd gotten so excited about had taken off suddenly, letting him set up in a transient hotel somewhere.

Wherever he was, Ray couldn't hang around anymore. The SUV was conspicuous. If he couldn't get a bead on the junkie, he'd have to make other arrangements.

On his third crawl past Wall Street, he saw the familiar waddle of Mama Nomad, pushing her cart down the center of the road. She must've missed her chance at a bed for the night, but no one would know it from the bright smile she had on her face. He rolled down the window and called out to her.

"Mama!"

"You just gonna hafta keep on moving, Sugar. I know I got a rear end to stop traffic, but them working girls don't tramp this block. I sure am mighty flattered, though, I tell you what."

"No, Mama. You seen Shake n'Bake?"

"That the fella they pulled out his tent this morning?"

"What do you mean?"

"It's all sorts of a shame, child. First, that nice boy, the Ray Cobb fella who looked like my Amos, he got hisself dead inside the shelter. Then, they find that nice Hispanical boy with foam coming down from his mouth. I tell you, when I ran in the circuit in New York City, the jazz circuit that was, the boys certainly did love their horse, but you didn't never find one of them like that, that's the God's honest. I do my best to avoid the junk. And you should too."

It wasn't easy making friends out on the street and in one day Ray had lost two. Los Angeles was becoming hazardous to his health and he was running out of allies.

"Who're the junk peddlers you avoid, Mama? So I know who to stay away from."

"Well, shoot, I ain't never been one to spread no gossip, but if you is trying to be good, keep yourself with a program, you best avoid the tent at the end of the road. Yellow tent. Means caution everywhere. Best steer clear."

She waddled away, not looking back at the man in the SUV, one of the only people who didn't recognize him without the beard and long hair.

He found a parking space and pulled into it. When he got out of the car, a junkie chick in a sequined skirt ducked into the yellow tent and zipped the flap up behind her.

There was already a scoper examining the SUV. He tried not to register his surprise when he saw that Ray was the driver, either expecting a rich dude who was lost, or someone from the neighborhood collecting taxes from the local dealers. Ray walked right for him, pulling out Edgar's wallet.

"You scoping for Gomez?" Ray asked. The scoper averted his eyes. He could easily take Ray and ten other guys in a fight, but protecting his face from future identification was what concerned him.

"Don't know who that is," he said.

Ray pulled out two credit cards and held them out to the scoper.

"Those won't be reported gone for a few hours. Get what you can with them between now and then. But first, watch this car for five minutes. Don't call Gomez. He's gonna get it soon enough, but I need it for the rest of the night."

The scoper looked Ray up and down, then grabbed the credit cards.

"Lemme guess? You ain't Edgar Parrish?"

"Edgar is... indisposed."

"Yeah, right," the scoper grunted, "You got five minutes, then it's gone. Got a funny feeling you ain't gonna report it stolen." He stepped in front of the SUV and leaned on the grill, now completely unconcerned whether or not Ray saw his face.

Slurping noises from the yellow tent told him the junkie chick was paying for her shit with her mouth. He hoped the dealer was a quick comer or his five-minute grace period with the scoper would be over before Ray had a chance for a pow-wow.

Lucky for Ray, the sequined junkie was good at her craft. She unzipped the tent and stepped out, one hand stuffing her product in her cleavage, the other wiping the dealer's jizzum from the edge of her rotten mouth.

Based on his suspicious look when Ray stepped through the flap of the tent, the dealer didn't know him. He tucked whatever visible packets he had under his leg and stared hard at his tent's new occupant. The smoke from his cigarette filled the tent, not doing a proper job of masking the smell of sex and cooked heroin.

"What you want?" the dealer asked. He pulled the stained beanie cap he was wearing over his eyebrows and took a long drag. He should've been paranoid about Ray's presence in his tent, but he had the laid-back attitude of someone who'd recently spiked and gotten their dick sucked. Ray was also sure he had a deadly weapon within close reach.

"I need a kit," Ray said.

"Don't know what that is and I don't know you," the dealer's words slithered out of his throat, punctuated by an involuntary chuckle. Ray wanted in on the private joke.

"I'm pals with Shake n'Bake."

"No, you ain't. Bake's dead."

"So I heard. He tell you what he was working on?"

"Like an art project or something?"

There was that chuckle again. It made Ray want to break his nose.

"Flying High, I think he called it."

"Who you?"

"Ray Cobb."

"Cobb's dead too. Found him right across the way. Fuck off outta my tent."

Ray started to lift up his shirt.

"If you Five-Oh you gotta tell me."

"That's a myth."

The dealer pulled out a Glock and pointed it at Ray's head. Ray stopped moving.

"Cobb shot Benny 7-11. 7-11 tore up Cobb's guts," Ray said, "You think I can fake this?"

Ray lifted the sweatshirt, exposing the crisscross of scars. The dealer put the gun away.

"Resurrected from the dead, eh Cobb? You'll hafta teach me that trick."

"Give me a kit for twenty," he pulled the only bill out of Edgar's wallet, "And I'll also give you this."

Ray held up one of the purple packets he'd pulled out of the chest in Edgar's closet.

"Looks like candy."

"Does it smell like candy?"

Ray handed the packet over and the dealer opened it up. He smiled.

"Smells familiar."

"Maybe this is your ticket to a new market share. Move out of this tent and into Bel-Air."

"What I look like, the muthafuckin' Fresh Prince?"

"If you don't trust it, here," Ray tossed him the other two credit cards in Edgar's wallet, "Usable until morning."

The dealer scoffed, but picked them up.

"All I got is my personal kit and you don't want to use it. I got the bug."

"You tell that whore that before you came in her throat?"

"Buyer beware," he chuckled.

"I'll take it. It isn't for me."

The dealer pulled a cigar box out from under his bedroll. He checked the blackened spoon, the rubber tubing, and replaced the cap on the needle with dirty fingers. He closed the top and handed it over to Ray.

"Sure you don't want some product to go with it?"

"Nothing better than that purple stuff I just handed over. But go easy, don't want to see you end up like Bake," Ray said, shuffling to get out of the tent.

"We all gonna end up like Bake. Just a matter of when."

Ray clutched the kit under his arm and made his way back to the SUV.

"Just in time. Was about to make the call," the scoper said.

"Make the call anyway. Tell him it's Ray Cobb."

The scoper pulled out his phone and dialed.

"Escalade. Five years old," he said into the phone, "Delivery by Ray Cobb."

A voice at the other end of the line spoke.

"Cobb's dead," the scoper relayed.

There was a time Ray thought being dead could be used to his advantage. Now it was pissing him off.

"Can I talk to him?"

The scoper's look told him the answer. Ray let out a sigh.

"I distracted the stoner valet for him at The Dresden on Labor Day. Was paid by a guy named Skippa. Tell him."

The scoper relayed the information and ended the call.

"814 W. Adams. They gone at 8 a.m.," he said, then lumbered away to go use his new credit cards before they were deemed worthless.

Ray got back into the SUV and started it up, tossing the kit onto the seat next to him.

He had one more stop to make before turning the car over to Gomez.

41

Bernard had his face locked on his phone. He jumped when he saw the dark figure sitting in his living room chair.

"Considering the company you keep, you should up your security," Nick said, turning on the TV to illuminate himself in a blue glow.

The young man clutched his chest and lowered his bag to the ground slowly.

"I haven't just been sitting here in the dark. I was watching SportsCenter and heard you come up the stairs. Thought it would be more dramatic this way," Nick smiled.

"You aren't allowed to be in my apartment without my permission."

"You spend too much time reading scripts about cops. I've got probable cause. And a warrant," Nick said, tossing the folded paper down onto the coffee table.

"You got Davidson. I don't have anything to do with it," Bernard said, his eyes darting around the room, looking for an escape route.

"Wouldn't worry about your boss. Though I'm pretty sure you're fired."

Bernard twitched and swallowed hard. If he'd been a cat, the fur along his spine would've been standing on end.

"Sit," Nick said, gesturing to the ragged leather chair across from the couch.

Bernard slumped into it, his stare boring a hole through the floor.

"Shadow Dance, huh? Don't know why you didn't just go with 'Purple Stuff', though I suppose those commercials were before your time. How old are you anyway? Twenty-three? Twenty-four? What the fuck, kid?"

"I'll make her disappear," Bernard said, his eyes still fixed on the floor.

Nick squinted at his suspect.

"Katie? Our missing blonde? Showed up at a hospital in Pasadena about an hour ago. Apparently, your supplier was holding her captive. So, no leverage there, pal."

"The fucking cunt had to go and cheat on me and screw everything up," Bernard spit out.

The change in his tone made Nick instinctively go for his weapon. There was so much venom in what the kid said. Unfettered rage. Nick saw the man inside Bernard who was capable of the horrible things he'd done.

"You can keep your gun at your hip. If you pull it out, I'll make you use it," Bernard said. The rage was gone. Now it was all calculation.

Nick had just seen three different people and he could only reason with one of them. There was nothing in Bernard's history indicating he had split personalities and Nick hadn't noticed any medications when he was poking around Bernard's apartment looking for weapons. There was a chance his mind was splitting from the pressure. The single act of violence splintering his emotions to compartmentalize the life he was trying to conceal.

Nick could deal with someone who'd made an innocent mistake. Someone who couldn't take his shitty assistant job and decided to deal drugs to his celebrity clients. But he'd overestimated Bernard's inexperience. He hoped Willie would pick up on whatever bullshit telepathy he was sending out and she would come help him deal with the new situation.

"I was a fucking moron to think I could've been happy, even for a moment," Bernard said, leaning back in his chair, despondent once again.

He was running through a gamut of emotions quicker than Nick could keep up.

Nick's eyes darted from the door and back to Bernard, who seemed to be finding exquisite comfort in the cushions of his easy chair. When Bernard's eyes rolled back to focus on Nick, he saw the change.

Bernard didn't have multiple personality disorder.

He wasn't a psychotic killer hiding behind the mask of an obedient assistant.

He was Shadow Dancing.

The purple powder must've hit his system shortly after he'd entered the apartment. Thus far, Nick's experience with Shadow Dance had been with its after-effects. A brain-damaged movie star, two girls with memory loss, another dead from cardiac arrest. Odds weren't good Bernard's trip would be a pleasant one.

If the high was like what Davidson and the other victims had tried to describe, Bernard was consumed by a living dream. He was transitioning through fantasy, his reality shifting. People and events morphed into one another. Nick cursed himself for being overconfident in coming to pick Bernard up. It was time to remove him from the apartment, threats from the dangerous side of Bernard be damned.

As Nick stood to pull out his cuffs, Bernard was on him in a flash, tackling him in the midsection, fists flying.

"You think you can take her from me?" he shrieked, his hands clutching at Nick's throat.

Nick swatted at his attacker, but his blows didn't seem to do anything. Repeated knees to the crotch and smacks to the face drew plenty of blood, but Bernard was unphased by the blows. The fire raged in his eyes, saliva foaming onto Nick's face.

Nick went for his weapon, firing once into Bernard's leg.

The pain didn't register. The grip didn't loosen. Bernard was right. Nick was going to have to kill him. But he wouldn't get the chance.

Bernard pulled his hands from Nick's throat and went for the gun, dark blood pumping out of the hole in his thigh. Instead of trying to wrestle the gun from Nick's hands, he sunk his teeth into the meat of Nick's thumb.

Nick's wail of pain was covered by another shot, this one taking a chunk out of the top of Bernard's ear.

Dental work met bone before Bernard spit out Nick's hand and grabbed for the gun. If Bernard had been hungrier, Nick would've been down one digit.

Before Nick knew what was happening, the barrel of the police issue had broken his front teeth and was tickling the back of his throat. Nick stopped moving, trying not to gag on the gun metal and shards of broken incisor. He almost forgot the pain in his hand, sweat running into his wide eyes as he watched the wild man kneeling on his chest.

"I gave you everything, Low!" Bernard hissed, "I saw you in that fucking commercial and recommended you to Shane. I made you! I made your career! I brought you in on Shadow Dance. You could've had any woman in the world. Anyone! But you had to have mine."

Nick realized Bernard hadn't known Lowell Seward was going to steal the drug recipe, shortly after he realized his bladder had let go.

"I'm going to make sure you never use that dick of yours to fuck anyone over ever again."

Nick tried to speak into the gun, but it just came out as a series of muffled growls.

"Them? They'll never remember this," Bernard said, "Neither will you."

His tone changed ever so slightly. Nick could see he was talking to someone else in his fantasy.

Bernard pulled the gun out of Nick's mouth and pressed it into his chin. His face was inches from Nick's, lips brushing against Nick's cheek as he spoke. If he wasn't so afraid of dying, Nick would've been creeped out by the forced cuddling.

"Do it," Bernard whispered, "End his suffering. He'll bleed out. Pain until you put him down like a dog. Your choice, Katie."

Bernard started cackling, his free hand slipping around Nick's neck.

"It's not your fault this fucking prick seduced you... no... only one person in this room deserves to die... you're lucky I love you or you'd be dead already... I can make you disappear... give you a few years to think about what you've done to me. And somewhere in the back of your mind, whether you remember or not, you'll always know you murdered a man."

Nick tried to focus his thoughts. Katie had killed Lowell Seward. Her disgruntled ex had put the shotgun in her hands, held a gun to her chin, and made her do it. In the end, Bernard had decided selling his girlfriend into slavery was a better fate for her than death or prison.

Bernard was still giggling, his grin sadistic and sad. Nick wasn't sure he could appeal to the drugged-out kid before he played out the rest of the murder scene in his head. The one advantage he had was Bernard was losing blood and the life was draining from his face.

"She's going to make you famous one last time, you sick son of a—"

Bernard's forehead exploded onto the couch and his body slumped over onto Nick's chest. Gore and gray matter filled Nick's mouth.

He turned his head to the side, vomited, and shoved the dead man off of him. His hands wouldn't stop shaking from how close he had come to death.

When he looked up, he saw Willie standing in the open doorway. Blood was caked to her dark hair and her brow bone looked like it had been broken. Her left leg was turned at an unholy angle.

"Motherfucker hit me with his car," she said before slumping down to the ground.

"I peed my pants," he croaked out, his larynx scraped raw.

"Me too," she said.

They both let out an involuntary laugh, but simultaneously groaned as they felt pain ripple through their chests.

Nick's phone rang.

"If you take that before you call 911, I'll kill you myself," Willie wheezed out.

He pulled his phone out and looked at the caller I.D.

Garden Commons Assisted Living.

Nick accepted the call and put the phone to his ear.

Willie watched his face sink as the voice on the other end of the phone spoke.

"Thank you," he said, a slight lisp in his voice where his front teeth were destroyed. The call ended and he dialed 911.

"Officers down. 3615 Wateska Ave."

He looked at the screen of his phone for a moment, then threw it full force against the wall, shattering it.

"Jesus!" Willie jumped.

He slung his arm over his eyes.

"What—"

But she didn't finish the question. She just watched Nick's chest shuddering and heard the sobs muffled under his sleeve.

42

There was no way for Ray to tell which of The Bear's body-guards were there by choice and which were indentured. They were all clad in dark suits and wore stone faces.

He was so filthy from the night's encounters, there wasn't much distinguishing him from the other homeless wandering Pico in the early morning hours. Dirt streaked his face from crawling out of the hole in Edgar's yard. Red-brown droplets sprayed from Mr. Crowley's broken jaw speckled the chest of his stolen shirt. Sweat rung the armpits, wet stains from his efforts dragging Katie to the SUV. He hoped to keep his head down and walk into the bathhouse uninterrupted, but he wouldn't be so lucky.

"Keep moving," the guard at the door said. He was different from the man who'd been at the door when Mr. Crowley had lured him there. Ray assumed the staff shifted when The Bear decided Viktor was a liability. It was a smart play, keeping everyone in the dark, preventing them from forming alliances.

The guard noticed the line of blood under his arm soaking through the cotton.

"We've got a problem," Ray said, meeting the guard's eyes.

"You'll have a problem if you don't start moving."

Ray rolled up his sleeve and showed the guard his fresh tattoo.

"There was a problem with... one of the other enterprises. The longer you keep me here, the more will go wrong. I'm going to guess because you're on door duty that you're disposable. Open the door."

Ray held his gaze. The guard's tough exterior waned as he took a step back and opened the door. Ray stepped into the dark corridor and slid the lock behind him. One barrier down.

The towel attendant Ray had met the night before sat at the front desk. He seemed more upset than shocked to see Ray.

"You can tell your friend, the goddamn Truthseer, I am angry with him. He had me nervous there was something wrong with my wife. Instead, my dog died. I did not even like the thing."

"I'll let you in on a little secret. He's no mystic. He saw the dander on your sweatsuit and smelled the sour urine of a dying pet. I could've told you that."

"He's going to get it next time I see him."

"He's already paying for his mistakes."

"We weren't expecting you."

"I wouldn't think so," Ray rolled up his sleeve. He was surprised how much access the tattoo was giving him. If at any point it backfired, he still had Edgar's .38 in his waistband. Not that he wanted to use it. It would alert his prey to his presence and bring undue attention.

"Roll up your sleeve," Ray said.

The towel attendant did as he was told. The tattoo there was faded by years of sun. Because of his duties, it was obvious The Bear didn't trust the gullible guard, he just didn't hate him enough to imprison him under a garden in Pasadena.

"As you can see, mine's fresh, so I'm still learning the ins and outs here," Ray said, "What does it mean, anyway?"

The towel attendant looked at Ray's arm, running a calloused finger along the skin to make sure the ink was real. Ray's other hand went to his back, ready to pull the pistol.

"It means, 'Property of The Bear.' And even if you get it removed, that will never change."

He let go of Ray's arm.

"Figured," Ray said, "Got placed out in the 'burbs. Soon after, everything went to shit."

"I have not heard about this."

"You're hearing about it now, me telling you, that's you fucking hearing about it." Ray moved toward the door to the baths. "I'm going back there. You want to stop me, you go ahead and think about where the Gravedigger has been for the last twenty-four hours. I watched The Bear slice his throat myself."

The towel attendant didn't stop him.

Entering the steam room where he'd nearly drowned the night before, he found The Bear sitting on a bench, the back of his head resting against the green porcelain. He was wearing a damp terry cloth robe and had a towel over his eyes.

"What is it?" The Bear said, not moving from his spot. Ray stepped silently over to where the gangster sat, standing over him.

"There have been some operational issues," Ray said.

The Bear flung off the towel and lunged for Ray's midsection. Ray thought he was ready for the attack, but The Bear was quicker than he looked. Ray slid to his ass, landing hard on his bruised tailbone.

The syringe, filled with a clear purple liquid, was already out and ready to strike. When The Bear tackled him, Ray had to hold it out from his body to avoid cracking it or sticking himself as he lost his balance. The Bear yanked at his legs, pulling Ray into the foaming water of the whirlpool. His robe opened up and The Bear didn't seem to take any issue with being naked, his bulbous belly pressing against the rim of the tub.

"This is how you repay my kindness?" The Bear huffed, shoving Ray's head under the froth.

He grabbed Ray by the scruff of his soaked shirt and slammed his face into the edge of the tub, opening a gash under his eyebrow. The blood flowing from the wound turned the water pink as The Bear dunked him once more.

Inhaling the salty water, Ray jabbed blindly, hoping he didn't stick himself in the process. As soon as he was certain the syringe met flesh, he depressed the plunger, sending the entire contents flowing beneath The Bear's skin.

The Bear continued to pull at him, but the drug entering his system slowed his movements.

"What have you—?" The Bear slurred as he pawed at Ray's legs, his grip loosening.

Beneath the water of the gurgling pool, The Bear's legs went out from underneath him, his gut floating to the top of the water as his head dipped beneath the salty foam. Ray sputtered to the surface, coughing, and lifted himself out of the water.

As he stood over The Bear, he watched as the hot water scalded the obese man's still open eyes. The drug flowing through his veins wouldn't let his mind register the pain.

Ray watched him float there for a while, then spit on him.

"That was for the fucking tattoo."

"The Bear will not be pleased."

"What?"

Ray looked to where the terry cloth robe had loosened around The Bear's body. On his forearm, at the edge of the sleeve, was the bottom of a familiar tattoo.

Ray jumped back into the water and yanked the sleeve up.

There, in familiar Cyrillic: Property of The Bear.

"What the fuck? You're not The Bear?" Ray grabbed the fat man by the neck and pulled him close. "Who the fuck is The Bear?"

"You ask... the wrong question... *tovarysh*... the lake it is lovely... all of us fish think so... *moyi zyabra dosyt'*... Malkin... he will know... where the purple will go..."

"Who is Malkin? Is Malkin 'The Bear'?"

Ray smacked him across the face, hoping to get one more lucid answer out of him, but soon there was nothing but giggles and gurgles as the fat man rolled over onto his belly into a dead man's float.

The gun had slipped out of Ray's waistband, down his pants, and was soaking at the bottom of the tub. Ray dove for it and lifted himself out of the water once more.

The fat man's body started to seize, water thrashing out everywhere. But he never lifted his face up from below the surface of the water, even as the hot foam mixed with vomit.

Vengeance was replaced with disappointment and frustration. This was supposed to be the end of the line. The answer to his problems. Instead, it was just another stone turned over, the underside covered in more grubs and worms.

Ray palmed the .38 and poked his head back out into the hallway.

"Could you come in here?" he asked the towel attendant, who was still cowed a bit from Ray's earlier diatribe.

Ray stood at the green tiled wall behind him, pistol at the ready.

The towel attendant's eyes went wide as soon as he saw his boss, but it was obvious why the fat man hadn't trusted him with more responsibility. He was stalled trying to decide whether to help the man who was floating face down or attack his assailant.

"Don't know how you earned that tattoo and I don't care. You can walk away now," Ray said.

"They will come after us," the towel attendant said, panicked.

"Who will?"

The attendant didn't have an answer. He'd been under the shadow of The Bear for so long, he couldn't register that with this man's death he might finally be free. He just stared at the floating whale, the syringe sticking out of his thigh like Ray had planted a flag on an undiscovered island.

"Is he dead?"

"One way or another," Ray said. He was certain he'd pumped the fat man's veins full of enough purple stuff to fry his brain, but on the off chance someone brought him back to life, he'd have contracted the tent dealer's HIV. The fat man had given Ray a mark for life, Ray felt it necessary to return the favor, no matter how short that life might be.

"You have a choice. Save him and be indentured forever, or disappear and hope he was the only person you owed," Ray said, "I'm leaving. Tell the guy at the door he's got the same choice. But ask to see his arm first."

"It does not end with him, you know this?"

"Who does it end with? Malkin?"

"I..."

Ray put the pistol to the quivering man's head.

"Who is Malkin and where can I find him?"

"Never heard of..."

The gun clicked as Ray thumbed the hammer back.

"Who is The Bear?"

"The Bear is a place. Not a person," the towel attendant sputtered, "This... this... Malkin might be with them. There is no knowing how many of them there are."

"Where do I find them?"

"Big Bear Lake. But you do not need to search for them, they will find you."

Ray tried not to register any emotion on his face as he walked out of the room, leaving the attendant with his choice. He hoped the guy at the front didn't ask him why he was all wet.

"Issue resolved?" the guard asked, lighting a cigarette.

"One of 'em," Ray said, "Can I bum one of those?"

"They're Russian, a bit harsh," the guard said, offering the pack of Belomorkanals.

"I'll risk it."

Ray took the cigarette and cupped his hand for a light. He strolled down the street and got into the SUV, rolling down the window to keep the interior from smelling worse than it already did.

He looked at the tattoo again.

In a pattern around the writing was something faint he hadn't noticed before. Stars. A constellation.

Ursa Major.

The Great Bear.

"Motherfucker," Ray cursed to himself.

The sun would be up soon. He had just enough time to drive to Echo Park and toss Edgar's gun into the lake. Much like Ray's shaved visage, by the time the .38 was dredged up, it would be too rusted to recognize.

43

"How much of that blood is yours?"

"Does it matter?" Ray asked.

Gomez inspected Edgar's car, unfazed by the dirt and smell of watered down urine coming off the driver's seat.

"Not really, but I can't resell the seats. Going to take something off the price," Gomez said, popping a piece of gum into his mouth.

"Just need some get out of town money," Ray said. He didn't mean to sound impatient, but the blood around his eye was drying into a crust and he couldn't see out of it. Gomez never asked him what happened.

"From the look of you, you need disappearing money. Don't think I can provide that."

He tossed Ray a cleanup rag to stop the blood flow.

"Be sure to take that with you when you go. We've got enough shit to worry about without you getting your dirty DNA everywhere."

Ray didn't spend a lot of time in the chop shops that rotated around the south of downtown, but he had done some work for Gomez here and there. The shops didn't use the same place twice for obvious reasons. You had a car to give up, you got a location. The next day, it'd be gone. The constant movement helped Gomez know who he could trust. Ray was on that short list.

If some rich prick on the street was exceptionally nasty, Ray made a phone call to teach him a lesson, getting Gomez to extract the asshole's Benz. He never chose random cars off the street to turn in because he wanted to know who he was victimizing. It didn't weigh well on his conscience to screw someone over for no reason.

"How hot is this thing?" Gomez asked. He opened up the back and scratched at the soil ground into the carpet with his fingernail.

"Right now, it's not, so you've got some lead time," Ray said, "But by noon it's going to be as sought after as that."

Ray nodded to the Audi in the corner with the new black paint job. The canvas of Skid Row from the day before had the street abuzz. Gomez had redone the paint, but he was going to have to ship it overseas. The model was new and rare enough he wouldn't be able to switch out the frame or VIN with a wreck from a junkyard.

"Yeah, well, I bought it before I knew what it was. Probably shouldn't make the same mistake here, but I know I can bury this in the system. Plenty of turned over tanks like this one in the boneyard," Gomez raised an eyebrow at Ray, "Any bodies attached to this? You know what, don't answer that. Last thing I need is an accessory after the fact if things go south."

Ray glanced over at the Audi again. Hitching or walking to Big Bear wasn't going to be a treat. The snow at that altitude was already coming down thick and heavy.

"Want to trade straight up?"

"That car is worth a hell of a lot more than what you brought me," Gomez said, closing the back gate on the SUV.

"Actually, I think it's worth this Escalade plus $100."

"Or I could tell your crack smoking ass to get the fuck out of my shop," Gomez said. His tone made the crew stripping a pickup truck behind them stop their work and listen.

"The Audi is a liability. Mine isn't. Plus, I'm going to get it the fuck out of town for you. Can't do that with no money for gas, can I?"

"And the second you drive a little wonky and get pulled over, this puppy is back in the system. Pretty damn risky."

"When I get to where I'm going, I'll leave it with the keys in it. It'll end up in a shop just like this one, scrubbed down, somebody else's problem. I'll go five miles under the speed limit the whole way."

Gomez didn't answer. Instead, he rolled the piece of gum back and forth between his cheeks, weighing his options. Ray pushed again.

"The moment I leave here, it's my problem. Even if I get pulled over, you got nothing linking you to this car but the paint job. Any shop in town could do that. You know I'm doing you a favor."

Gomez snorted out a laugh. "You're too smart for your own good, you know that?" He reached into the pocket of his jeans, pulled out a money clip, and peeled off a bill. "Quit bleeding all over my garage."

He whistled to his boys to get the SUV into one of the service bays and got on his cell phone to look for the frame of a late model Cadillac Escalade.

Ray got into the Audi and started it up. The radio blared mariachi music and he shut it off, happy with the silence inside the car.

The doors of the garage closed behind him and he swung the Audi down Adams toward the entrance to the highway. Ray Cobb hadn't left Los Angeles since he'd arrived there almost a decade before. It was time to put a couple of old demons to rest.

He hit the gas and matched the speed of traffic. The rain had stopped, but the slick black of the highway sputtered the last remnants of the storm up onto the windshield. The wind pushed the droplets up and over the hood of the car and the drying water left nothing but small outlines of dust on the newly waxed paint.

The black Audi melted into the sea of cars and was soon an anonymous spec in a caravan of sparse commuters, all heading toward the corona of the sun cresting the horizon.

44

"It was nice of her to come."

"Yeah, she's good like that."

Nick's friend, Hank, stood with him in the grass of Holy Cross Cemetery. The rain had been gone for a week and in true Los Angeles fashion, it was eighty degrees the first week of February. The former partners watched Willie Grant slink away in her conservative black dress, still sexy on crutches, her left leg in a full brace. She got into her car without turning back.

"She might've been the only one in the department besides me who could stand to spend every day with you," Hank said.

"Yep. I fucked up," Nick said.

"And you realize she'll never go out with me now."

"She wouldn't have anyway," Nick smiled.

While Nick dealt with all of the funeral arrangements, Willie took care of clean-up in the Lowell Seward case.

The investigation of Shadow Dance was handed over to Marconi and Narco. From what Nick could get out of Willie in their brief chat after the memorial service, the Pasadena cook wasn't talking about his distribution network and there was no obvious connection between him and Bernard. The florist felon didn't know how Seward got the recipe either, whether someone in the organization gave it to him, or if he'd had another chemist reverse engineer it.

On a normal day, all the unanswered questions in the motivation of the murder of Lowell Seward would've driven Nick insane. But he'd already lost plenty because of his obsession with an unimportant detail. Willie had put in for a transfer, citing personal disagreements. She never assigned blame to Nick for the split or resorted to malice. Like Nick said, she was good like that. As soon as all the paperwork was filed, he would have a new partner.

How many hours had he lost in the past few years? Scrutinizing case after case, determined to dig into every aspect, making sure he got even the smallest piece of information perfect in his reports. All his time spent poring over cold case files, dissecting seemingly unimportant details, looking for the invisible cracks—perhaps he'd pushed too far in the other direction. Good police work depended on delving into minutiae, but at what point does the dredging become trivial?

The funeral was a good opportunity for him to reexamine his priorities. The case was closed. Didn't matter how they got there. Marconi would figure out the rest.

Or he wouldn't. It wasn't Nick's problem anymore.

"The teeth look good. You have to soak those suckers in Efferdent nightly?"

"Nope. In there permanently," Nick said, snapping his new front teeth, "If I'd have known how nice they'd be, would've had them knocked out a long time ago."

Hank smiled, but didn't add to the joke. He put his hand on Nick's shoulder and squeezed.

"Gonna miss her."

"All she did was yell at you to watch my back."

"Sure, but there was love there. Plus, she sent me cookies after my divorce."

"What?"

"Every week for two months," Hank said.

"Her cookies were terrible."

"I know. But they were comforting," Hank said, "They found Cobb yet?"

"The girl was the last one to see him. Jimenez still likes him for the Mochulyak murder."

"But you know better."

"Yep."

"You made the right call. You know that, right?" Hank said, knowing when Nick's brain was working overtime.

He didn't tell Willie that Katie had pulled the trigger. When they interviewed the girl, she had no memory of what had happened that night in the dirty Skid Row apartment. Bernard took that secret to the grave. Until Willie told her in the interview room, she didn't even know Low Seward was dead.

Nick knew she'd gotten caught up in something she had no control over. The girl had suffered enough. When he came to Hank wondering what to do, Hank didn't give him advice either way, he just told Nick sometimes being right wasn't the most important thing.

He stared at his mother's coffin. The buffed mahogany reflected the blue sky—a false showpiece destined to be scuffed and buried in the dirt. A cemetery crew smoked in the distance, waiting just beyond the ring of floral wreaths. Once the last mourners departed, they would lower Janice Archer into the ground.

"I'm going to stay for a bit," Nick said, "Could you head out, make sure everything is set for the reception?"

"Sure thing."

They hugged a brother's embrace and Hank wandered off across the lawn.

Nick kicked at the grass, took a deep breath, and turned his back to the coffin. He'd already said his goodbyes a dozen times over.

Over the crest of the hill, he meandered across the lawn. Coming to the grotto of volcanic rock, he gazed at the bright flowers and the statue of the Virgin Mary. A sad smile crossed his lips as he read the passage stamped in green copper below the statue of St. Joseph. He sat down on the bench in front of the looming stone sculpture, his hands pressed to his face, more out of weariness than grief.

"Mind if I sit?"

Nick saw her legs before anything else. Tan and slender, they ran up to a figure hugged by a form-fitting black cocktail dress. She wore Jackie-O sunglasses underneath a netted veil. Bright red hair cascaded over her shoulders.

"Please."

He tried not to stare as she pulled out a pack of cigarettes and offered him one. He was about to refuse on instinct when he saw the pack.

"That was my mother's brand."

"I caught the end of the eulogy. Sorry for your loss," she said.

Nick took a cigarette from her pack and twirled it between his fingers. He put it to his nose and sniffed the tobacco and menthol through the thin white paper, but refused her offer of a light. She lifted her veil and lit the cigarette between her kissable lips, enhanced in flawless scarlet.

"Don't remember seeing you at the Commons. Did you know her?" Nick asked.

"No. I'm mourning someone else."

"Who'd you lose?"

"Wouldn't say I lost him," she said, "Just misplaced."

"Interesting way of looking at it."

She took one long drag of her cigarette, dropped the remaining butt, and ground it beneath the sole of her black heel. She picked up the litter and placed it into her clutch.

"Take care," she said, standing.

"Wait. What's your name?" Nick asked, hoping to make something good come out of the day.

"Not important," she smiled.

As she walked away from him, he watched the crease of the perfect round peach bobbing under her dress. She turned the corner beyond the stone grotto and as quick as she had appeared, was gone from his life.

He put the unlit cigarette into his pocket and stood up. Turning around to brush any dirt off of his pants, he saw a small phone sitting on the bench.

It wasn't his.

"Excuse me, you left your—"

Running around the edge of the grotto, he stopped. The redhead was nowhere to be found. In the wide expanse of the cemetery lawn, there weren't many places she could go.

"What the—"

The phone rang in his hand.

Thinking of nothing else to do, he answered it.

"Hello?"

"Play the voicemail," the redhead's voice said on the other end.

"Who are you?"

"Like I said, not important."

And then, silence.

He tried calling her back, but the number was blocked. Scrolling through the menu of the phone, he brought up the voicemail and hit play. He walked at a brisk pace, his eyes scanning the cemetery for any sign of the mysterious woman, but stopped in his tracks when he heard Ray Cobb's voice.

A long time ago you asked me what I was doing out on the streets. I'm sure I gave you some clever answer or another. Something to avoid the question. But honestly, I wasn't ready to answer yet.

I don't suppose I am now.

I may be a lot of things, but I was never a murderer. All I wanted to do was prove that was true.

Not sure it is anymore.

I'm sick of being surrounded by death, it following me around, so I'm going to see about getting clean. Fixing my mistakes.

You can come after me if you'd like, I'm sure I deserve punishment for whatever hand I had in the last few days' events, but we both know I'd just be a scapegoat for the real problem.

I didn't kill the man in the car. I didn't kill Viktor Mochulyak.

I left the man responsible for all this at the Russian Banya on Pico. You'll recognize his tattoo.

If you find him, his death will be clean enough to wrap all this up for you.

If you don't... you never will.

I know this incriminates me in his "accidental" death. I'll leave that to you. Don't know that I belong in prison, but I've done enough to deserve to be there. You'll get your chance to put me away if you want to take it, I'll come back once I've done what I need to do. And you'll be the first phone call when I'm back in town.

Almost every friend I thought I had has betrayed me. But you never did. I returned that faithfulness by betraying you. And for that I'm sorry.

My only regret is I sacrificed another friend to stay alive. A decision I made pretending to be ignorant of the outcome.

And this is why I have to go. I've been too selfish for too long.

Take care of yourself, Detective Archer.

Do what you think is right.

Nick listened to the voicemail again. Then he pulled out his phone and dialed Central Division.

"Jimenez. Any more bodies turn up with a Bear tattoo?"

"Not that I know of. Aren't you supposed to be at a funeral?"

"Just curious."

"Heard from Cobb?"

"No body in a bathhouse?" Nick asked, avoiding the question.

"You got something to tell me or what? I gotta go deal with a DB on Wall. Old lady drank herself to death, passed out in the middle of the street. Still has a smile on her face. Not likely a homicide, but gotta go through the motions, you know. Wonder if we can get through one day in this city without a homeless getting dead."

"Yeah," Nick sighed, "Know what? Nevermind."

He put his phone into his suit coat pocket and looked down at the burner in his other hand.

"What the fuck are you into, Ray?" Nick whispered to himself.

The distraction would be welcome. A reason to bury himself in work. But he had a reception to get to. And after that, he had to give himself permission to grieve. Letting go was going to take time. Time he couldn't waste exhuming buried details that wouldn't affect Ray's ultimate fate.

Besides, it was Jimenez's case. No need to stick his RHD nose where it didn't belong.

He scrolled through the phone's menu. The cursor highlighted Ray Cobb's voicemail.

Detective Nick Archer paused, then hit "Delete."

Want to be the first to know what happens to Ray Cobb and Nick Archer next?

Join the Strange Scribe mailing list at strangescribe.com

I greatly appreciate you taking the time to read my work. Please consider leaving a review. There are so many amazing writers out there trying to get noticed, reviews are one of the only ways for writers to break free from the pack. It makes a **HUGE DIFFERENCE**. It doesn't have to be long, just honest. Three sentences are a big deal.

Also, tell your friends about **The Last Will and Testament of Ernie Politics** and **The Last Dance of Low Seward** to help spread the word.

Thank you!

For the conclusion of Ray Cobb and Nick Archer's story, read
The Last Days of Ray Cobb,
Here's a preview...

"Propinquity."

"Hmm?"

"Propinquity. It means an affinity or kinship," Detective Hsu said, his face glued to his phone.

"Great," Nick sighed.

He had only been partners with Hsu for a week. They weren't exactly bosom buddies. On paper, David Hsu was a good a cop. College grad. Detail-oriented. Loved the hell out of paperwork. But his social skills sucked. Like his need to read his "Word of the Day" out-loud every morning, no matter what sort of environment they were in. Under the on-ramp of jammed cars honking to squeeze onto the 101 freeway, Nick could've used a break from the vocabulary lesson.

"It can also mean nearness, either physically or psychologically," Hsu said. He put his phone away and looked both ways down Juanita Avenue. "You think anyone had *propinquity* with the victim at the time of death?"

"Pretty sure they all did," Nick said.

The short stretch of Juanita between Beverly Boulevard and the 101 had become a mini-version of Skid Row over the years. A small group of homeless people who the gentrified Arts District had pushed into the underside of Silverlake's hipster haven.

The tiny tent city was the homeless equivalent of upscale living. If there was an economic tier in street residency between a fifteen-dollar tent bought at Target and Section 8 housing provided by the city, the structures on Juanita fit the bill.

Tents tethered together with tarpaulin and cardboard boxes. Pressboard stolen from construction sites to set up a makeshift latrine. The sheer innovation of the homeless who had put the mini-subdivision hovel together was impressive. A few of them were feats of engineering and architectural genius. Each tent-house built on Juanita was going to be there for a while. Even if a bad El Niño came through, some of those makeshift houses would withstand the weather better than the mudslide-prone mansions in Nichols Canyon.

What the residents of Juanita Village had to worry about was the body. The victim was inside one of the smaller tents. The "owner" was in custody, but he swore up and down he had an alibi from the night before, complete with witnesses. He'd told the girl she could sleep there if she needed to. It seemed like a hollow gesture for a man who looked like he didn't give a fuck about anybody. The corner of Wilshire and Alvarado, where he claimed to have slept the night, had several security cameras. Nick and Hsu would know soon enough if his story checked out.

He must have been confident that the girl was too far along to give him any action. Some guys were grossed-out about that sort of thing. They're happy to pick through festering garbage for a stained baseball cap, but God forbid they have sex with a beautiful woman just because she's growing a life inside of her.

Scratch that. *Had been* growing a life inside of her.

Her life was gone. Whether the baby's heart still beat was anybody's guess.

"We may be looking at a Caesarian kidnapping," Hsu said. A search of the area hadn't come up with an aborted fetus.

"That sounds made up," Nick said. He knew Hsu would elaborate, no matter what his response had been. It was his way. If Hsu had read about it within the last five years, he would regurgitate it to anyone in the nearby area. Nick had made the mistake of going out for a beer with Hsu on the first day they were assigned together. *Jeopardy!* was playing on the TV above the bar. The guy had an explanation for every fucking answer. And yet, the only thing Nick had retained was that priapism was the medical term for an erection lasting over four hours. How that ended up in a discussion about a quiz show he couldn't remember. Though he had a vague recollection it had started with an answer about Grecian wine.

"It's rare, but becoming exceedingly common. Usually premeditated. In the old days, it was called a hysterical pregnancy. There was a lot of preparation that went into keeping up the illusion. Now, all a perpetrator needs is access to a social media profile and a sonogram. For months, a woman can post about how she's expecting. When the time comes to produce the child, they go into a panic, find a pregnant woman, and take the child by force."

"Sounds a little Manson Family to me," Nick said.

He regretted it as soon as he'd said it. One of these days, he might get Hsu to play along with his sarcasm.

And on that day, he'd buy a large cake.

With buttercream frosting.

And those little flowers on it.

Today wasn't that day.

"Oh, no. The murder of Sharon Tate and her unborn child was more of a ritualistic sacrifice than a crime of envy. In Caesarian kidnappings, the death of the mother is merely a by-product of her housing the unborn individual the kidnapper wishes to abscond with."

Abscond was the "Word of the Day" yesterday.

Nick wondered if there was going to be a day where Hsu didn't use one of his new vocabulary words.

"Have you had enough of a breather?" Nick asked.

"I'll be honest," Hsu let out a sigh, "for as detached as I try to be, this is hitting close to home. If you don't mind, I'll conduct more interviews."

The murder hitting too close to home was the extent to which Hsu talked about his life off-the-clock. There were pictures of his pretty Korean wife on his desk. All of them were of her alone, standing in front of some landmark — Stonehenge or Golden Gate — nothing of them together. It was as though she'd brought her husband along on her vacations to serve as her personal photographer. Either that or she had similar pictures sitting on her desk of him, alone, in the same poses.

Nick still wasn't sure if her name was Jin or Jen. Hsu only mentioned her in passing. Which Nick found strange because Hsu had once gone on for an hour about the migration patterns of the North American pronghorn antelope. Nick also knew Jin or Jen had been sick, causing Hsu to take an extended leave of absence from the force. When he came back, he was assigned to Nick Archer.

Willie Grant, Nick's former partner, had asked for a transfer after he'd accused her of leaking the details of a high-profile investigation to the press. This was only hours before she stopped a young entertainment assistant high on psychedelics from putting a bullet in Nick's brain.

Nick watched his new partner approach the homeless witnesses, each of them spooked by the yellow tape and uniforms. Street instinct was to disappear when the cops showed up, but they wanted to know who it was in the tent. By the time they'd realized it was an outsider and not a member of their little community, they were stuck being held for questioning.

There was bruising around the girl's neck where she had been strangled and held down. He didn't see any hair or skin under the fingernails. The victim hadn't gotten a hand on her attacker. If she had, the medical examiner was going to have to do some digging for it. There would be plenty of DNA evidence to collect, but the tent looked dirty enough that every piece pulled would come from someone with a record. Those who lived on the streets didn't do a great job of avoiding the law. A better bet would be to watch the hospitals for anyone coming in with a newborn in distress.

Nick emerged from the tent and made a beeline for Hsu. .

"Anyone report hearing a child crying?"

"Haven't asked."

"If our perp meant to keep the baby alive, it was making noise. And at that hour, a child's screams would wake up the block."

There was probably more he could learn from the body, but he didn't want to go back into the tent. Forensics would give him plenty to go through later. Then he could examine it without the mixing smells of shit, body odor, and rotting viscera.

Juanita looked like an ancient excavation site. Cordoned off with yellow tape, each of the tent structures stood empty, their residents held for questioning. Forensic techs in full blue pajama suits took detailed photographs of each, the most attention paid to the torn-apart woman by the freeway. Each of the structures would be cataloged and stripped, some of them taken apart and boxed up. These people's homes would be destroyed because they lacked permanent address-es. Rights pertaining to search, seizure, and private property were non-existent because they lived on the sidewalks. Nick hoped he could get enough of a story out of some of them before they realized what was happening.

No one thinks about how many rights they retain just from the ability to close their doors. In all the time Nick had spent trying to understand the street community and how they lived their lives, he would never really relate to them. He would always be one of the normal people. The "haves." A cop who can steal their property and mark it as evidence just because they slept on the wrong block.

Among those waiting to be questioned was a Hispanic man, about twenty-five years old. Dark clothes, faded, but coordinated. The emblem on his Yankee cap was grey from dirt, but the bill remained crisp and unbent. He kept getting on and off a BMX with scuffed paint, holding onto it to make sure it wasn't heaped into evidence with anything else. A uniform was watching him, scolding him from hopping onto the seat, afraid he would bolt from the scene. Nick could see the man trying to play it cool, but his eyes were darting toward the lean-to made from Rite Aid shopping carts. Colored bungee cords held the structure together. He jumped any time an officer or tech got too close. That house was his.

"What's your name?" Nick asked.

"You guys gonna be done here soon? I got to get my work uniform, man," Yankee Cap said, not answering the question.

"You're probably not going to get back in there today unless we find something definitive in the next half hour."

"I didn't have nothin' to do with this, all right. Weren't even here last night. Was at my mom's."

"Can she confirm that?"

"No. She wasn't there, otherwise, I wouldn'ta been."

"Doesn't make for a great alibi. You know whose tent that is?"

"Thought that guy said it was his, um... Yusuf... the Muslim-looking guy."

Yankee Cap nodded in the direction of the tent's confessed owner. Nick was glad Hsu wasn't with him at the moment.

He would've made an irrelevant comment about Muslim not being an ethnicity.

"That's not what I asked," Nick said.

"People come and go. I was only staying for a few days 'til I got a new place," Yankee Cap shrugged. "Can't I get my clothes and go? I'm gonna be late."

"A few days, huh? You got a driver's license?"

"All right, shit. I'm gonna reach for my wallet. Don't shoot me."

"You see my gun out?" Nick asked.

"I watch the news. You don't need no excuse."

Nick held his hands up in supplication, away from his service weapon. Yankee Cap pulled out his wallet and tossed it over. Nick flipped through the worn flaps. Not much in it but a bunch of club cards, a Costco employee I.D., and a California driver's license. He snapped a picture of the license with his phone.

"Forno Garcia," Nick read. "Forno? You get teased a lot as a kid?"

"What the fuck for?"

"No one clever enough to call you Porno?"

"What's the law say about grounds for police harassment?"

"Meant nothing by it, sorry. My mouth moves quicker than my brain sometimes."

"Okay, you saw it. Gimme it back."

Nick flipped to the back flap and noticed there were eight crisp hundred-dollar bills inside.

"Costco pays pretty well, huh?"

"Man, what the fuck?" Forno took a step forward, but the uniform was quick to block his way. "You looking for a bribe, dirty pig?"

Nick closed the wallet after replacing the I.D. and put it back into Forno's hand.

"Hsu," Nick called across the tape. His partner made some last notes with the haggard woman he was interviewing and trotted over.

"Yeah."

"This is Forno Garcia. My partner, Detective Hsu."

"You want a handout, too?" Forno asked Hsu.

"Forno, did I take any money from your wallet?"

Forno counted the bills. Twice.

"No. Don't mean you won't later."

"Is that the confirmation you needed?" Hsu asked, "I've got a few more I need to get to over there."

"Have the unis do it," Nick said. "I think we've spotted a person of interest."

Forno's eyes darted back and forth between the two cops. They could see he wanted to bail and wanted to bail hard.

"Okay, Forno, it's honesty time," Nick glanced back at Forno's tent. It was next in line for photographs and cataloging. Forno was huffing and sweating. "Whatever you got in that tent is now potential evidence in this case. We're going to pull down each of those tarps and canvases that you probably spent days stringing together, and we're going to find any dirty little secrets you might be hiding. Maybe even a murder weapon."

"I didn't kill nobody! I just—"

"Want to get to work. I know. You typically get your pay-checks in cash?"

"How much did he have on him?" Hsu asked.

"Eight Franklins. Foil strips."

"Legit money," Hsu said. "You don't believe in banks, huh?"

Every conversation Nick had ever had with Hsu had been strained and awkward. Hsu was in cop-mode now. He knew how to mirror his interviewee. Even his posture had changed. A by-product of years spent in Vice.

"Since when is it a crime to have money?"

"It's not, as far as I know," Hsu said, "Just a matter of how you got it. That's enough for a down payment on a small apartment. If I had that kind of walking around money, I'd upgrade my living arrangements."

"Obviously, you haven't looked for an apartment in L.A. lately. Probably live in Valencia or some shit."

"Chino Hills," Hsu said.

Forno watched the crime scene techs move one tent closer. "There's nothing in there. Don't take my tent apart, man," he whined, "That's all I got."

"That license expired two years ago and my guess is that permanent address expired with it," Nick said. "The way you were twitching at the officers milling around your tent made me think it was more than just a crash pad for you. So, you see how I might be suspicious with your handful of lies along with your lack of an alibi and wallet full of cash?"

"That sort of information might even make you a prime suspect," Hsu added.

"I just live on this block. I didn't do nothin'."

"Who else lives on this block that we don't know about?" Nick pointed over to where the girl was found. "Whose tent is that, really?"

Forno stared at the detectives with a pleading look in his eyes and took a deep breath.

"I dunno," he mumbled.

Nick turned to Hsu. "Rock Paper Scissors?"

"I grew up playing Odds and Evens," Hsu said. "I would prefer odds."

"Suit yourself."

In unison, the detectives held out their fists.

"One, two, three, shoot."

Nick held up two fingers, as did Hsu. Evens.

"Winner's choice," Hsu said.

Nick turned back to Forno, smiling.

"All right, Forno, you don't know anything. But somebody does. You want to point us in the right direction?"

Forno was watching them carefully. His brow scrunched up in confusion, wondering what the cops had decided with their little game of Odds and Evens.

"Under the overpass on Virgil. Zeke been there forever. Knows everybody who sets up down here. Everybody that comes and goes on the regular. Thinks he's king of the fuckin' mountain, but he ain't nothing but a troll under a bridge."

"What's Zeke look like?" Nick asked.

"Hunched back. Dreads. Muthafucka looks like some kinda Igor George Clinton," Forno said, "Can I go?"

"Well?" Hsu asked.

Nick looked at Forno, who was twitching to get back on his bike.

"I'll look for Zeke," Nick said.

"You sure?" Hsu asked.

"Yeah, I'd rather be out here."

Hsu nodded.

"Forno, we're going to head downtown and make sure you've got your story straight," Hsu said. "I can call your boss to tell him you'll be late."

"Am I under arrest?" Forno asked.

"Do you want to be?"

"No."

"Then get in the squad. I'll even buy you lunch. We'll put your bike in the trunk."

Forno hung his head, but did what he was told.

After the car had pulled away, Nick turned back to the scene and scanned the tents. He could interview every person living on that street until he was blue in the face and come up with nothing. With a murder this brutal, there was one guy he knew who would have his ear to the ground. A guy who would take an interest in a woman's uterus being torn open, her body left to rot in a dirty tent. But that guy was long gone. And Nick only had one connection to him left.

He dropped it into the inside pocket of his suit coat every morning and didn't touch it again until he emptied the contents at night. The last thing Nick needed his new partner to see was that he was carrying around a second phone. The type of phone that was notorious around Vice and Narco as hard to trace. It would raise a lot of questions Nick couldn't answer.

"Got a tip on a witness," Nick called to the closest uniform, "Heading over to Virgil for a bit."

He could feel the stares of the detained homeless as he passed. People who wanted nothing more than to be left alone. People like Ray. As Nick made his way up the street, he could feel the burner phone thumping against his chest with every step.

He should have snapped the SIM card, broken the thing in half, taken a ferry to Catalina, and dumped it over the side into the ocean. Instead, Nick kept it with him, waiting for it to ring. Waiting for the man at the other end to ask for his help.

But as far as Nick knew, Ray Cobb was already dead.

To buy
The Last Days of Ray Cobb
Visit Strangescribe.com/books

Thanks to my early readers of both Ernie Politics and Low Seward: Chuck Kreuser, Sean Gallagher, Michael Williams, Robert J. Peterson, Ward Roberts, Corrie Nahimi, and Mike Nelson. All of your insights and notes have helped make these books better. You saw all the things I chose to ignore. Jermaine Johnson at 3 Arts Entertainment is the best literary manager a guy could ask for, thanks J.J. for your faith. Thank you to my parents, Robert and Nadine Grusnick for their constant support in all of my crazy endeavors. And thanks to you, the reader. Without you, this is just a pile of paper.

Brad Grusnick graduated from Northwestern University with a Bachelor's Degree in Theatre. He also studied Comedy Writing at The Second City Chicago. He is originally from Wausau, WI and lives in Los Angeles. His first novel, The Last Will and Testament of Ernie Politics, is also gross.

The characters in this novel sometimes make light of their situation on the streets, but homelessness is a real problem in the world. For more information on how you can help in the fight against the homelessness epidemic in the United States and throughout the world, please visit:

Nationalhomeless.org

ighomelessness.org

Made in United States
Troutdale, OR
12/27/2024

27321244R00198